To CRM

"Stick with me, Kid, and I'll take you places."

And you always have...

ONE

PHIL PORTER HAD NEVER QUITE FIGURED out how to ask a grieving family for his money. He knew there was some sort of decorum to observe, a platitude he should give first, but he was bad at those types of things so he always went for the direct approach. Besides, he had a flight to catch, and he wouldn't be put off any longer.

He circled the block looking for a place to park his subcompact rental. The car didn't agree with his frame, and Porter was glad he'd be returning it soon. Cars choked both sides of the street. He found an empty handicapped spot, pulled in, and left the car running.

The hill to the Blanchard home was steep and Porter was embarrassed to realize the climb left him a bit out of breath. He tried to pretend he wasn't, instead focusing on the row of houses he was walking past. They were like something out of a movie or television show—tall, three stories, but narrow. They were nice, in a West Coast sort of way, but Porter balked at the prices he knew they'd fetch.

He soon saw a large group of people gathered outside number eight-two-eight. Discreetly taking deep breaths through his nose, he waited in the crowd until his way to the center was clear. He listened to everyone giving what sounded like mostly hollow condolences. How many different ways were there to convey one's sympathy?

Sure he could do better, Porter stepped up to the small woman in the middle of the group, gave his best concerned look, and tried his hand at offering a condolence. "Mrs. Blanchard?"

He towered over the woman, who might have been attractive during happier times. Porter hadn't been around for any of those. Her mousy hair hung limply around her face and her skin was sallow and drained of color. Still, she had a warmth that Porter couldn't help but admire.

"Hi, Porter."

"I wanted to tell you I'm sorry about how everything turned out. If I could have changed things, I would have." His condolence sounded worst of all.

Mrs. Blanchard hooked him by the elbow and pulled him to the side, away from the prying ears and eyes of the rest of the mourners. "I know you did your best. Things have been... crazy the last few days. I never got a chance to thank you."

"You don't need to—"

"Yes. Yes, I do. If you hadn't... well, you know. You were there. I'm saying that no matter what happened, you deserve to hear that. Thank you."

She slipped her hand into Porter's and clasped it tightly. He gave her a restrained squeeze back. She looked up at him, tears in her eyes, then buried her head in his chest.

Porter gently patted her on the back as she sobbed. After several moments, she pulled away, face wet, and dabbed at her eyes with her shirt sleeve. "I don't think Jimmy and I are going to make it."

Porter searched for words, not sure how to answer the broken woman.

"None of our friends would want to hear something like that. They think that somehow we'll bury Evanna and just move on, everything good as new. He's changed since she's been gone. He's different and I worry he'll never be the same. I don't expect you to say anything, I just needed to tell someone. I'm sure you'll be leaving soon, so it might as well be you." She dabbed her eyes again.

"I'm sorry to hear that," Porter said. He wasn't sure if it sounded more genuine this time.

"Me too, Porter. Me too. Go talk to him." She pushed him on the arm, directing him toward the house.

He was several feet away when she spoke again. "Porter?"

He looked over his shoulder.

"Be gentle. Please."

Porter nodded and walked across the sidewalk and up the wooden staircase with its perfect balusters. He stepped through the open door and into the foyer of the well-appointed home. Despite the weather and the crowd of people bustling around, the place felt cold. Three times he'd been there and three times he'd felt like it was someplace no one really lived, at least not since Evanna had gone missing.

Stepping past the kitchen, he saw a folding table full of casserole dishes and desserts. Friends and family pitching in, trying to make sure people had enough food, as if food would make everything better.

Porter wondered if anyone would be mad if he made a plate on the way out.

He walked through the first floor of the home, looking over everyone's head, searching for Jimmy Blanchard. He was nowhere to be seen, but Porter followed the smell of cigars and scotch, and the raised voices of a group of men, to a small doorway and a staircase that led to the basement.

Careful not to hit his head, he ambled down the stairs,

pushing through the haze of smoke until he was in the center of a partially-finished game room. The walls were cinderblock, but there was carpeting on the floor and a pool table halfway across the room. On the far end was a crudely constructed bar top.

Jimmy Blanchard was behind the bar, staring down at the plywood that held his rocks glass.

Porter passed several groups of men, glancing at the numerous plaques and awards hanging from screws drilled into the cinderblock. Firefighter of the year. A promotion to captain. Photos of different firehouses over the years.

"Mr. Blanchard?" Porter said to the top of the man's head.

His blond buzzcut was just starting to thin on top. Porter saw the pink skin on the man's head and neck was flushed red.

"Mr. Blanchard?"

The older man didn't move or register Porter's presence at all.

The men in the basement were loud, a raucous gathering to brighten their friend's spirits. Porter could overhear half a dozen conversations, most recounting some former glory: a savage fire extinguished, a game-winning touchdown scored, a bar brawl settled.

Porter raised his voice and reached across the bar to put his hand on Blanchard's shoulder. The man swatted Porter's hand away and stood tall. He was shorter than Porter, but most were.

"Don't touch me," he said in a voice only slightly slurred.

"Fair enough. I was wondering if you had a minute."

"Talk," Blanchard said, tilting back the rest of the brown liquor in his glass.

"Best we talk in private," Porter said.

"Why?" Blanchard raised his voice, loud enough that the other conversations in the basement stalled as they took note. "You don't want everyone to know what a piece of shit you are?"

Porter stared through the man. "I did my job. We had a deal."

"Your job was to find her. I even offered double if she was alive."

"She wasn't. I'll take our original amount," Porter said, coolly.

"What if I say no? Huh? We never had a contract or anything like that. What if I tell you no? These boys down here'll drag you upstairs and throw you out on your ass."

"You're too smart to do that," Porter said.

"Hey Jimmy, everything okay?" a voice said from the other side of the room.

Porter adjusted his position so that he was standing with his back toward the cinderblock wall, Blanchard on his left, the rest of the room in front of him.

"*Is* everything okay, Jimmy?" Porter said.

Blanchard rubbed his head, his nose bright red against the dark circles underneath his eyes.

The voice spoke again. "Hey, dickhead, why don't you take off?" Porter saw that it came from a burly man with a thick mustache, a shaved head, and a pool cue. "Whatever you came for, it ain't happening today."

"No?" Porter said.

"That's right."

"Hmmm," Porter said. "I think I'll hang around. Unless you have a problem with that?"

The burly man smiled and walked toward Porter. In a pitiful attempt, likely slowed by alcohol, he swung the pool cue at Porter's head.

Porter tilted his head and let the cue clang against the cinderblock wall behind him. He stepped in, hit the man with two elbows to the bridge of the nose, and pushed him, sending him sprawling to the carpet.

Another man was on Porter in an instant. The man swung a big right hand toward him, but Porter had the reach advantage. He stuck a stiff jab into the man's face, then grabbed him by his shirt collar and slammed him face-first into the makeshift bar Jimmy Blanchard was standing behind.

Porter held him up by the collar and stared down the rest of the room, then slammed the helpless man's face into the wooden bar again. He let go of the man's collar and let him slump unconscious to the floor.

Porter stepped back to the cinderblock wall and looked at the room. "Well? Which one of you assholes is next?"

A murmur rolled through the room, men smacking each other on the arm, bolstering their courage. There was no way he could take them all, could he? All they had to do was coordinate an attack.

Three men grouped together, slowly advancing around the pool table toward Porter. He reached down and picked up the pool cue that had fallen to the floor.

"All right, but remember—you guys had a chance to leave," Porter said, his voice dropping an octave. "Come on then, man up."

"Enough," a voice said, thin but loud enough to be heard over the dull roar in the basement. "I said *enough*."

Mrs. Blanchard came pushing her way through the crowd. "Mike. Rob. Go back to your drinks and leave this man alone."

The men turned, grumbling threats at Porter, but their faces betrayed that they were glad to be called off.

Mrs. Blanchard looked down at the man bleeding from the nose and the unconscious man in a pile at the base of the bar. "Jimmy? Jimmy, stop this."

Blanchard's eyes broke from Porter and he looked across the plywood bar top at his wife.

"Just pay him, Jimmy. Fair's fair."

Blanchard nodded and stepped around the bar, helping the bleeding man with the shaved head up, handing him a towel for his nose. "I'll go get my checkbook. I assume you'll take a check?"

"Not a chance," Porter said, returning the stares of the rest of the men in the room. "Cash only."

TWO

"'CASH ONLY?' Are you serious?"

Porter was sitting in the muggy Tampa backyard, recounting the events of the previous week. Ross wanted a thorough recounting and wouldn't stop pressing until he got it. They sat at a circular wooden table, polishing off a six-pack.

"I wasn't going to take the chance he'd put a stop payment on the check. Blanchard was pissed enough to do it, just to teach me a lesson. Then I'd have to go all the way back out there and put my foot in his old ass."

"His daughter's dead. You understand why he was pissed, right?"

"I understand it, but I don't give a shit. You know what I had to do to find that girl? I told you, I stabbed a guy with a fork. A fork. Let that sink in for a minute."

"I'm only saying sometimes you're allowed to have some compassion," Ross said.

"I have compassion, but I also have bills. If it wasn't for the reward, I'd rather be out here swatting mosquitos with you."

"How did the Blanchards even get their hands on twenty-five grand in cash? Who has that kind of money sitting around?" Ross said.

"All that money comes from donations. Church, friends, and family. Sometimes it's the Crime Stoppers; sometimes the police or FBI will offer the reward. I went with Blanchard to the bank—separate cars, of course—where all the reward money was in an account held by a trust. He made a withdrawal, then paid me. Easy stuff."

"So they're not rich?" Ross said.

"I don't think so. They had a couple of Hondas parked out front."

"Don't you think they could have used the money? Help them rebuild their lives or something like that?"

Porter took a long pull of his sweating Yuengling. He looked at the wooden fence as he swallowed. The Florida heat had split and cracked it in several places. The grass of the yard was short, but burned and dead in spots.

"That money isn't going to bring their daughter back."

"You don't say."

"Hell, it wasn't their money anymore. You can't advertise a reward for finding a missing person and then not pay it. What was I supposed to do? Tell 'em to keep it? Get real."

Ross shook his head. His red hair was curly, but cut low to mask the fact that he was fighting a losing battle with his hairline. "You might not be Bill Gates, but you aren't hurting. How many jobs have you taken in the last year and a half?"

Porter took another pull from his bottle and didn't answer.

"Seven. That's the seventh job you've had in the last eighteen months. And I know some of them paid you more than what the Blanchards did."

"So?"

"Your house is nice enough. You don't have kids—"

"I could have a kid somewhere, you never know."

Ross continued. "Your car's been paid off for years and you just keep piling up money. We both know you're set for a while."

Ross knew all the uncomfortable details about his finances. He was an accountant and was one of the few people that Porter trusted, which made him uniquely qualified to handle Porter's money. Ross did a good job and Porter had no complaints, but he didn't think he was doing all that well in the money department.

"You know how it is. Ever since I quit the Feds, life got expensive. Healthcare's a bitch when you pay it yourself. I have to save for retirement, pay Trish alimony. The little things add up," Porter said.

"Trish has never taken a dime from you." The accountant struck again.

"I've tried to give it to her, but she says she doesn't need it. I think there may have been a Beyoncé song playing when we were talking."

"It's because she's honest," Ross said.

"Are you saying I'm not?"

"Of course not, but she's still a better person than you are. That's why she doesn't take anything from you. So alimony is out." Ross picked at his beer's label.

"Fine, but I still need to look out for number one."

"I think number one is set for a while," Ross said.

"What's your point?"

"I'm saying you might want to think about doing something just because."

"Just because what?" Porter said.

"Because it's the right thing to do," Ross said.

"Is there a point coming? If so, would you mind getting to it?"

"Just listen to me for a minute." Ross paused, and Porter could tell he was choosing his words carefully.

"How can I when you can't even figure out what you're trying to say?"

"Shut up and listen. You know where my office is?" Ross said.

"I do come to your place of business, remember?" Porter said.

He knew the area well. It was a so-so part of town that was experiencing a resurgence. *Gentrification*, they called it. Still, the rent was cheap enough that Ross could have an office in a nice fifteen-story building. Not the top floor, of course, but somewhere near the middle.

"You know the billboard outside of my conference room window?"

"The one with the ambulance chaser on it? What a low-life," Porter said.

"That's the one. Except they changed it a couple weeks ago."

Now that Porter thought about it, it had been a while since he'd gone to Ross's office. He'd been busy in California and, before that, working a job in the Midwest. Even if he were in town, there was no need to go to Ross's work. He drafted money out of his account when necessary, and any meeting of the minds could be done at someone's house over beers.

"Good. No more scummy lawyer. What's the problem?"

"They put up one of those missing kid billboards. The first week or so, I didn't think much about it. But the more I saw it, the more the picture stuck in my mind. She's the cutest damn kid. I stopped eating in the conference room. I just can't look at her," Ross said.

Porter eyed his friend. "You on your period or something?

What's with all the emotion? I'm pretty sure the doctor can give you something to help you out."

"Don't," Ross said. "Just don't."

"Relax. There are dozens of those billboards up around town. I see them, everyone sees them. I'm sure the cops are doing their jobs," Porter said. "Sometimes this type of shit takes time."

"If you let the cops do their jobs, you'd never get paid," Ross said. "You can't trust those idiots to do anything right."

"You're dealing with this in a bizarre way. You don't even know this kid, Ross."

"I can't help it. Every day I pull up to the office and there she is, smiling," Ross said. "It's so damn sad."

"Apparently so."

Ross looked down, picking at his label again, avoiding eye contact with Porter. "You want to know the worst part about it?"

"It's not you getting in touch with your feelings? That's pretty bad from where I'm sitting."

"You're a dick, you know that?"

"Fine, Ross, what's the worst part?"

Ross didn't answer.

"Don't be a bitch, just tell me."

Ross finally ripped the label completely off. "It's the reward money."

Porter drank his beer. "That much?"

"That much? It's seven hundred fifty dollars. Seven hundred and fifty measly dollars, Porter. That's all. I've never seen a missing poster with a reward that low. You just made twenty-five grand. I'm talking about seven hundred and fifty dollars. That's all the money her family could pull together. They're sitting there, desperate to get their little girl back, and all they can come up with is seven hundred and fifty shitty dollars. Where's the police money? Where the hell is the FBI money? I thought about kicking in some myself, like maybe it would help somehow," Ross said.

"That's what this is about? You want me to throw in with you to bump the reward up? Hell, all you had to do was ask. I'll donate to the cause," Porter said.

"No, asshole. I want you to find her."

THREE

"FIND HER?" Porter said.

"Don't act like you don't speak English," Ross said.

"I thought you just wanted money or something."

"What are you, an idiot? I am telling *you*—the one guy I know who has ever found a missing kid—about a missing kid. You sit there and pretend like I'm asking you for money. My cousin's a dentist. When I call her and complain about my teeth, she knows good and damn well I'm asking for an appointment," Ross said.

"Touché, honkey," Porter said.

"I'm not joking," Ross said. "I never ask you for shit, but I am now. I need your help."

"You ask me for shit all the time."

"When?"

Porter was quiet for a few moments. "There was that time in sixth grade you wanted me to stop Pete Guyrich from taking your hat every day."

"If you have to go back twenty-five years to find something, then I think I'm due for a favor, don't you?"

Porter stood and walked over to the blue recycle bin by the

gate in the wooden fence, and tossed the empty bottle in. He liked the sound the bottles made when they clinked together more than any thoughts of saving the environment. He walked back to Ross at the table, stopping to stare at one of the citronella tiki torches burning on the patio.

"Will it help you stop being so weepy?" Porter said.

"Come on, man, this is serious."

"So is having low testosterone," Porter said.

"See? This is why I didn't want to tell you. This exact reason. I knew you'd screw with me."

Porter sighed. "Let me think about it."

"Thanks, Porter, I really—"

"I said I'll think about it. I know you have an unhealthy attachment to this girl, but this case isn't something I'd normally take. Working this close to home isn't a great idea and the money isn't exciting. There aren't a lot of reasons to stick my nose into this."

"Helping me isn't enough of a reason?"

"Definitely not," Porter said with a smirk. "I thought I'd remind you I'm not running a charity."

"Whatever you say, you greedy bastard," Ross said.

"Greedy? C'mon, you can do better than that."

Porter and Ross spent the rest of the night getting more and more drunk, and eventually broke into a terrible bottle of Scotch whisky Porter had forgotten he had. Things devolved into shots and the type of insults reserved for only the best of friends. Porter got the best of the jabs but, bolstered by the brown liquor, Ross held his own.

Ross hadn't mentioned another word about the girl. He was smart enough to know not to press the issue. Once Porter decided to decide, there was no rushing him.

THE NEXT DAY began with a massive headache. Porter dragged himself into the builder-basic kitchen and drank two bottles of water, then made his way across the cool tile floors to the bathroom.

The shower did little to help his head, so he finished up, dried off, and got dressed. He stopped by the kitchen again on his way out, to collect another bottle of water and three folded packs of Goody's powder. He had never found anything better for headaches than that disgusting powder. He emptied all the packets into a shot glass then turned it up into his mouth. The bitter taste was unpleasant, and he chased it away with another bottle of water.

He grabbed his keys and sunglasses, and slipped his holster and pistol into his waistband. He covered them with his untucked shirt and then stepped out into the daylight.

Tampa was a busy town, but the mid-morning drive from Carrollwood to Westshore wouldn't take long. Porter passed several landmarks that he knew by heart: the Bucs stadium, Mons Venus, Westshore Mall. He had lived in Tampa for over twenty years and had grown up driving these streets. It was easy enough to get around. It didn't hurt that the people who'd laid out the city had been intelligent enough to use basic north-south and east-west for the main thoroughfares. It baffled Porter when he went to a new city and nothing made any sense.

Pulling up in front of Ross's office, he saw the billboard that was causing Ross so much heartburn. A palm tree obscured the picture and Porter couldn't make it out from his angle, so he walked into the building's lobby and up to the security guy at the front desk.

"Smitty, just the guy I was looking for."

"If you're looking for me, I must be in trouble," the old man said with a laugh.

Porter was unaware of the man's full name; 'Smitty' had

always sufficed. He worked the day shift at the office building, diligently controlling access to the upstairs offices. The old man had worked there for as long as Porter had been going to the building.

His large, graying afro looked strange on top of such a slim body, but it suited him. Smitty's 'USMC' tattoo looked more faded than ever, bleeding into his charcoal skin. Rumor was that Smitty had been some sort of high-speed guy in Vietnam and had retired to Florida once his career in the Marines was over.

"I ain't seen you in a while. How's life treating you?"

"Like stir-fried shit. Ross and I tied one on last night and I'm paying for it big time."

"I think Mr. Gianullo is a bad influence on you. I'll bet if it wasn't for him, you'd have read your Bible and turned in early last night," Smitty said.

"Finally, someone understands me. I don't go looking for trouble, it finds me."

"I know that's right. Mr. Gianullo told me you were coming by; go on up."

"Call him Ross, Smitty. He has such an ugly last name. Maybe if he ever gets married he can take hers. Anything would be better."

Smitty laughed and Porter walked to the elevator. He pushed the button for the eighth floor and ran his hands over his face, trying to wake himself up. His beard was getting long.

As a teenager, Porter had once quit a job because his manager had said even one day of stubble was too much, and told him to go home, "scrape his face," and come back once it was done. Porter never went back. Something about shaving made him feel emasculated. And that didn't even take into account the razor bumps he'd get on his neck if he wasn't meticulous with the prep work and finish of a shave. It was easier to have a beard.

Getting off the elevator on the eighth floor, Porter turned left and came to a large glass double door. It had been an IRS office, and was left empty when the agency outgrew the space and moved. If you looked hard enough, you could see the remnants of the IRS seal on the glass.

Communist-gray cubicles ran the length of the back wall, ending at a wooden office door with a small vertical window in it. The cubes reminded Porter of his old workplace. It seemed like every government office had the same terrible furniture. He turned right towards the office and stopped at the first cube on the left, knowing he would find Tessa.

"Tess," Porter said.

"Hey, sweetie. What did you do to him last night? He looks awful," Tessa said.

She was a brunette, and attractive in an odd way. Porter always thought her mouth was too large. Big lips and teeth. Still, she wasn't a bad-looking girl, and was an even better person. Porter not-too-secretly hoped Ross would find the guts to make something happen with her. He knew they'd be good together.

"Your boss is a lightweight; I can't be held responsible for that. Ross isn't working you too hard, is he?"

"Please. He couldn't work me too hard if he tried."

"I agree. I think you're too much woman for him."

"That's not what I meant. I mean... It's just... Get out of here," Tessa said, looking flustered.

"I'm just saying..."

Porter kept walking, down to the office with the window. He pounded on the door several times and let himself in. Ross sat with the shades drawn, ceiling fan on full speed. He had a large wooden desk, one that hadn't come with the office. Fancy furniture one would find in a lawyer's or judge's office. Ross tilted his head down from the headrest.

"You gotta bang on the door like that? How about a little courtesy, huh? This is a place of business."

"Business, huh? You doing someone's taxes on your eyelids?"

"Shut up. I blame you for this."

"Maybe when your balls drop you'll be able to keep up," Porter said. "Until then, stay on the JV team."

"You don't feel bad at all?" Ross asked.

"Nope," Porter lied. "I feel like a champ."

"Okay. You win. I know my place in the world."

"Good. That's all I've ever wanted."

Ross moaned and rubbed his head.

Porter sat in the guest chair across the desk. "I gave what you said some thought. I'll look into things."

"Just look?"

"That's all I can give you. The reward is shit and you know I don't like working this close to home. There's always blowback. So, I'll take a look and see what I can see. If I think I have something, I'll pass it on to the detectives working the case. I still know a few guys at the sheriff's office that'll listen to me. That's the best I can do."

Ross stared at Porter, his bloodshot eyes focusing on Porter's nose. He started to say something and stopped. Then he took his feet off the desk, stood up, and walked around the big desk and to his office door. "Come on."

Ross led and Porter followed down the line of empty cubes. Past Tessa who was diligently working away, past the copy machine, into the conference room. Ross opened the door and stepped to the far side of the room. Porter followed him in, shut the door, and took a seat at the long, rectangular, glass-topped conference table. Ross found the cord for the metal blinds and gave them a tug. The blinds opened and Porter was face to face with Ross's missing girl.

MISSING: $750.00 REWARD
Danisha Hill
Black / Female / 45 Pounds
IF YOU HAVE ANY INFORMATION PLEASE CALL
813-555-2150

PORTER READ THE BILLBOARD, then looked at the face framed by the words. She was a dark-skinned girl, missing one of her front teeth. Her hair was braided into multiple thick braids, finished on the ends by hair ties with large, colorful, plastic balls. Her eyes were dark brown and her teeth a contrasting white. She was smiling and happy. Porter could see why the billboard could stick under someone's skin. He looked over at Ross, who had tears in his eyes.

FOUR

"ARE YOU STILL DRUNK? What are you crying about?"

"See? This is why I didn't tell you. I can't be upset without you shitting on me."

"I'm not shitting on you, but don't you think this is extreme?"

"No, Porter, I don't. She's a beautiful kid and she just disappeared. Poof, gone. That's tragic, man, don't you get it?"

"I get it, but it's everywhere. God knows how many kids poof and disappear every year. It sucks and I get it, but it's just life."

"But it doesn't have to be. Not this time. Not for this kid. You can find her, Porter, I know you can. I've seen you do it. She deserves a chance."

Porter looked at the picture for a few moments, the girl's smiling face burning itself into his memory. "She was a beautiful girl."

"She *is* a beautiful girl. *Is*."

"You know what I'm saying. Usually, after this long it means—"

"I know what it means," Ross snapped. He had taken a seat

across the table from Porter. His eyes were clear now, and a look of tenacity swept across his face.

"Okay. It's not over till there's a fat lady and all that shit," Porter said. "That number there, who does it go to?"

"It's Danny's grandmother."

"Danny? That's what we're calling her?"

"That's what Miss Leona calls her."

"Who's Miss Leona? Why do I feel like I'm playing twenty questions?" Porter said.

"That's her grandmother. She lives over by Ybor in some of the Section 8 housing. I have the address somewhere," Ross said, patting his pockets.

"Good enough. Give me the address and I'll swing by and talk to the grandma. Missing kid one-oh-one."

"Sounds good," Ross said. "I'll grab my keys."

"Negative, Ghost Rider. You keep your ass here. You have figures to calculate or a receptionist to harass or something. Let me work on this."

"I kind of want to help," Ross said. "It's important to me."

"I appreciate that, and if I need any accounting done, I'll let you know." Porter wasn't going to let Ross anywhere near this. First, he was too emotional about this situation and he wasn't thinking straight. Second, Porter wasn't sure Ross would appreciate his methods. There was no way he would understand the nuances.

Ross searched Porter's face, then exhaled and slumped back down in his chair. "Fine, but let me know if you find anything out."

Porter nodded, took a photo of the billboard with his phone, and walked out of the conference room. He stopped at Tessa's cube on the way out.

"He looks like shit," Porter said.

"I hate to see him like that. Think I should get him some Pepto or something?"

"Actually, I think you should give him a little kiss. He told me that's what he wanted," Porter said, a small smile creeping over his lips.

"Don't you start with me." Tessa chewed her lip. "You gonna help him out? With the kid, I mean."

"I'm gonna see if I can," Porter said.

"Then you be safe. Ross kept me in the loop when you were in California. Triads? That's scary stuff, Porter. If something happened to you, who would he use as a wingman?"

"Hopefully he never has to find out." Porter feigned a look of innocence, then walked out the glass doors to the still-waiting elevator.

With a wave to Smitty as he walked across the lobby, Porter slipped on his sunglasses and stepped out into the bright noonday sun. He trudged over to his Yukon, hangover pounding with every step.

The truck was a holdover from his previous life, when he'd made a good salary and his then-wife was a nurse. Plenty of money and no kids will lead to some indulgences. The Yukon was ten years old now, but had low mileage considering its age. It was a dark blue four-door model with a sunroof. Porter loved it because it was a comfortable ride, despite his large frame.

Stepping to the back of the Yukon, Porter popped the back hatch. He had installed a large lockbox in the spacious rear area of the truck, a lockbox he kept his firearms in.

There were stacks of folded laundry on top of it; Porter never knew when a situation would call for a change in clothing. He moved the pile to one side so he could access the lockbox.

Porter wasn't exactly a gun nut, but took advantage of his Second Amendment right daily. When he was a federal agent, he had been exposed to a culture that had imprinted on him the benefits of being prepared at all times. During his tenure on the job, he'd bought numerous firearms. Manufacturers almost universally had programs where law enforcement officers, military personnel, and other qualified people received deep discounts.

His usual carry gun was a Glock 17. It was a bit large for the average person, but for a big guy, it was great. Porter checked his shirt to make sure it sufficiently covered the holstered pistol. No stranger to the side of town he was heading toward, he needed to be prepared, but didn't want to advertise the fact that he had a weapon. Satisfied, he slipped an extra magazine into his pocket and slammed the hatch.

Driving across town gave Porter some time to think. Danny's point of contact was her grandmother, and he wondered where her parents were. Often when a child was missing, the culprit was a parent. He assumed the local detectives would have explored that. Barring that, he would try to ask around the neighborhood and see if anyone had seen anything. He often got better results than the police did.

The place Porter was headed had been hit by the 'stop snitching' epidemic a few years back. Several ignorant rappers had managed to convince most of the youth that cooperating with the police was a violation of the 'street code.' As a result, no one under fifty wanted to talk to the cops, even when it was about something serious.

Porter let his GPS guide him the short drive across town. Turning onto the final street, he saw a shabby, graffitied sign that read *Palmetto Acres*. The neighborhood was sprawling, with buildings as far as Porter could see. Each building was two stories, with apartments on the front and back. There were rusty metal staircases with a landing on the side of each building, leading to a walkway that ran the length of the second floor. The buildings sat in clusters of three, with some green space in an impromptu courtyard in between. Porter lost count of the number of clusters he passed.

That's a shitload of people, he thought.

The units were a faded salmon color. Maybe they had been burgundy at one point, but the sun had taken its toll. The grass was worn down to dirt in most places from all the foot traffic. There was graffiti on all sides of the buildings, some gang tags that Porter recognized and others that he didn't.

Porter rode down the main thoroughfare, Palmetto Avenue, until the GPS told him his destination was on the left. Somewhere in the sea of buildings was the apartment he was looking for. There were no smaller roads to get into the building clusters, just the roads on the perimeter of Palmetto Acres, and Palmetto Avenue, which bisected the neighborhood. Porter drove halfway in, pulled to the shoulder on the right and parked.

He pulled up the text Ross had sent him with the apartment number and got out of the car. As he hit the lock on the remote, two locals approached him. Young men, shaved heads. Their khaki pants were too big and too low, barely held up by their belts. One wore a wife-beater; the other, some type of yellow and black basketball jersey. Jersey spoke to him.

"What's good, my nigga?"

"Gents. What's the good word?"

"Ain't no good word, the only word is my word. Don't look like you from around here. I would know. I know everyone."

"Since you know everyone, you mind helping me out? I'm here to see Leona White. Which one is her building?" Porter said.

Wife-beater didn't say a word. He was standing several feet behind and to the right of Jersey. Jersey wasn't a big guy and stood average height, but Wife-beater was substantially larger and probably would have made a great lineman.

"Why would I show you where Miss Leona live? You look like some corny-ass bill collectin' nigga," Jersey said.

Porter was slightly offended at being called corny. He was wearing black and white Chuck Taylor All-Stars, blue jeans, and the white t-shirt he'd left untucked. Over that, he wore an unbuttoned shirt which hung loosely past his waist. He found his outfit comfortable and practical. Chucks were the quietest shoes you could wear, and when your feet were a size 13 wide, you needed all the quiet you could get. The outer shirt concealed his weapon and, if need be, could be buttoned up to be more presentable.

"Not a bill collector, but I need to ask her a couple questions," Porter said.

"What is you, a cop? We don't like five-oh around here," Jersey said.

"Do I look like a cop?"

"Nah. You too big and brown to be a cop. Plus, I never seen no cop in no old Yukon before."

"Very true. So how about it?"

Jersey looked at Porter for a little while longer, then put his hand to his mouth and whistled. A boy poked his head around the corner and ran up to the trio. Wife-beater whispered something to him and the boy took off running through the mass of buildings.

Porter eyed the two men. "Nice pants."

"Shut yo ass up."

Porter smiled.

A short time later, the boy reappeared, streaking around the side of the building, back toward Wife-beater. He whispered to Wife-beater, who nodded at Jersey. "Little Man'll take you over there."

"Appreciate it."

"I don't know what you want, but don't be messin' with Miss Leona. That's my word. Feel me?"

"I wouldn't dream of it."

The kid looked expectantly at Porter, shifting back and forth as Porter walked over to him. Porter got a better look at Wife-beater when he passed. He was about the same height as Porter, but probably had fifty pounds on Porter and was well past the three-hundred-pound mark. Porter didn't think he would be much trouble if it came to it. Probably.

Little Man wore dirty flip flops and cutoff jeans. He walked fast and stayed ahead of Porter most of the time. Porter tried to make conversation. He often found it was easier to pry some choice nuggets of info from children than from adults. "Is Jersey the shot-caller around here?"

"Jersey?" The kid looked over his shoulder, back to the two men they had left. "Jamal? Yeah, he's the man."

"Wife-beater his muscle?"

"His name's Terrell and you too nosy. That can get you in trouble. I'm only talking to you 'cuz I know you ain't no cop. That's the only reason Jamal even let you in."

"Fair enough. How about your name? I can't just call you Little Man."

"Everybody else does."

"What's your daddy call you?" Porter said.

"I don't got a daddy."

"What about your mama?"

"She don't call me nothin'. She ain't around."

Porter took the hint. As they rounded the corner, Porter found himself in one of the courtyards in the middle of the building clusters. There were clotheslines strung everywhere. At a graffitied picnic table sat a tied-up pit bull. Several paper bags with glass bottles were strewn about.

The doors facing him were all barred, as were the windows

of each unit. *Cheap protection,* Porter thought, *until there's a fire.* Per building code, there was supposed to be a quick-release latch, so people could get out in an emergency. Porter doubted these units had that feature.

Little Man walked Porter up to a building in the cluster straight ahead. It looked like all the others, and the front door was propped open with a large rock. Little Man knocked on the door. "Miss Leona?"

From deep in the front room, Porter heard the soft clapping of flip-flops a few moments before a short, slight woman appeared. Her coffee-colored skin went perfectly with her salt-and-pepper hair. She was wearing a see-through hairnet and an old blue dress with flowers on it.

"Miss Leona, this here's the man that's looking for you," Little Man said. He looked down at his feet when talking to the old woman.

"Thanks, baby. You know my hip wasn't going to let me walk all the way out there. I appreciate you very much."

"No problem, Miss Leona. If you need anything else, yell for me."

"Sure will, baby. And Keith?"

"Yes, Miss Leona?"

"Don't let them boys get you in any trouble. I tell you every day, you one of the special ones. Hear me?"

"Yes, Miss Leona."

Keith scurried off the way they had come.

Shit, he's really fast, Porter thought. *No wonder they use him as a messenger.*

"Miss Leona? My name is Porter. I'm here to—"

"I know who you are. Mr. Gianullo called a little while back and told me you were stopping by. I told Keith I was expecting you and to tell those other boys to send you back. If I didn't, you would have never gotten in here to see me."

"Never is a long time."

"That it is, baby, that it is," Miss Leona laughed.

"Are those guys out there a problem?"

"Problem? Jamal and Terrell? Oh no. It looks that way, don't it? Those boys and their friends look out for the neighborhood. This isn't the safest place anymore and the police don't like to come down here. We need someone to keep an eye on things. Sure, they should all get some real jobs, but they don't mean no harm," Miss Leona said. "I've known them all since they were born. Good boys."

"They're selling drugs, aren't they?"

"Sure they do. It's only weed, though. Mr. Porter, do you know weed is now legal in a bunch of places? You just got back from California, correct?"

Porter was confused.

"Mr. Gianullo told me. I'm not psychic, although I hear there are a bunch of them in California."

Porter laughed and shook his head. Ross had a big mouth sometimes. "It's just Porter, ma'am. California is a different kind of place."

"I imagine it is. Myself, I never left Florida. Never found no need. You went out there for business, is that right?"

Ross again. "Well, 'business' makes it sound a little misleading, but I was working out there for a few days. Once I wrapped everything up, I got back here as soon as I could. It was too hot out there for me."

Miss Leona laughed at that. She seemed sweet, with an easy smile and quick laugh. Something about her reminded Porter of his own grandmother.

"Well, it's hot here too, baby. Let's get off this stoop and into the A/C."

She motioned for Porter to follow her into the house. In the front room, much too large for the space, an old china cabinet sat crowded in the corner, displaying what looked to be rarely-used dinner sets. Wedged next to the china cabinet was a flowery sofa with a thick layer of protective plastic on it. Better to keep it protected than let a bunch of asses destroy it.

On the left past the front room was a bathroom, and beyond that, the kitchen. As Porter passed, a savory smell reached his nose, and he saw pots bubbling on the stovetop. The narrow hallway emptied into a small living room, with a large couch, a recliner that looked well worn, and a large floor model TV on the wall opposite. Porter looked around, sure this was how Gulliver felt on Lilliput. A small hallway led to what must have been the bedrooms.

"Have a seat, Mr. Porter, have a seat." Miss Leona gestured to the couch.

Porter sat down, conscious of his knees by the small wooden coffee table. "Thanks for the seat. And the A/C."

"Gotta beat this heat somehow," she said with a chuckle. Her smile slowly faded. "Mr. Gianullo tells me you have questions about my girl."

"I wanted to see if I could find out a little bit more about her."

"Well, if it helps you any, I can tell you who took her. I been trying to tell everyone, but nobody wants to listen."

The matter-of-fact manner in which she'd made the statement confused Porter. After a few moments, he spoke. "Miss Leona, you know who took Danny?"

"Sure, baby. It's always the devil you know."

FIVE

PORTER WASN'T sure what she meant and he didn't want to say something foolish, so he remained quiet.

"It was the neighborhood boys." The old woman reached over to the coffee table and picked up a tumbler sweating with condensation.

"The neighborhood boys? Jamal and Terrell?" Porter said.

"No, baby, not them," she said as if Porter had said something foolish. "You need to understand the Acres. Palmetto Avenue is the dividing line and right now you on the west side, where I stay. Like I told you, Jamal and Terrell and the rest of them on this side are good boys. The east side of the neighborhood, now, that's a whole different story. Those are different boys over there. They have different rules."

Porter thought back to his drive into the neighborhood. He had recognized some of the graffiti and gang signs. The stuff he didn't know was on the east side of the street. He hadn't thought much of it, but it made sense now: There were two different gangs in the same neighborhood.

"A few years back, the Acres was all one group. This is a big neighborhood, you understand. Jamal was in charge and things were the way they were. Nobody's proud of a gang, but they helped around here more than they hurt, and kept most problems from everywhere else from spilling over into the Acres."

Porter listened.

"Things changed when a new boy moved in. He was from up north somewhere. Came down here to be with his family, something like that. Lived on the east side of the Acres. He joined up with the boys and all went well for a while."

"And then?"

"Well, what do you think? He decided he wanted more."

"More of what?" Porter said.

"Everything. More control, more money. He said Jamal wasn't making as much as he should have been. The new boy, he wanted to branch out into other things—real drugs and robbing and selling women. Jamal wouldn't have that. He may be a little lost, but he has his own code."

"Can I ask how you found out about all this?"

"I hear things from lots of places. Sometimes from the other women in the neighborhood. Sometimes from Keith and the other kids when I watch them. Sometimes from the boys themselves. They know I'm a free ear if they need it. I try to help them if I can. Give them advice that'll keep 'em out of trouble."

Porter nodded. "So this new guy...?"

"Hector. He wanted to expand things. I guess he still had some contacts from his old life up north. He told Jamal they could step things up. Make more money. Jamal told him no. It's never been about the money for that boy. Hector didn't like that. So he got together anybody who'd go along with him and tried to make a move on Jamal. It didn't work."

"A move? What does that mean?" Porter said.

"Mr. Porter, I think you know exactly what I mean. They tried to sneak into Jamal's house and shoot him. But Jamal had been staying with his baby mama so he wasn't there. You know

Jamal was mad—whew, that boy was pissed. Things got pretty messy for a while. Lots of shootings. I even had a bullet come into my house." She pointed to a small, off-color patch in her rear wall. "Came in the front and went through the kitchen, through the opening to the living room and stuck in the wall. I was asleep."

"Good thing."

"I'm still good at something," Miss Leona laughed. "Eventually, Jamal realized the beef with Hector was tearing up the neighborhood. I think Hector was okay with that, but Jamal wasn't. He called a meeting and made a truce. No more shooting. Jamal would have the west side of Palmetto Avenue and Hector would have the east. They don't cross over, not ever."

"When you say 'it's always the devil you know,' you're talking about Hector?"

"That's right," she said drawing out the 'i' in dramatic fashion.

"How do you know Hector took Danny?" Porter said.

"She was going to an early start preschool, my smart baby. The last time anyone saw her, she was getting onto her school bus in the afternoon. The bus stop is at the front of the neighborhood. It won't come all the way into the Acres, so they let everyone off up there and the kids have to walk back. Thing is, there aren't any other kids who go to her preschool. I put her into a lottery for a special charter school. She's the only baby who gets off that bus."

Porter shifted his leg, careful not to bump the table.

"I always met her there, so she didn't have to walk alone. That day I had a terrible headache; it must have been my sinuses. I took a head pill and sat down for a bit. And I..." Her voice caught in her throat. She began to shake, first in her hands, then torso, and finally her head. She let out a wail of anguish.

Porter watched her. He was used to being played by

people, and he often watched them when they showed a large swing in demeanor. The best time to tell whether someone was genuine or not was when they got emotional. Porter hated fake criers, especially when they were doing it to cover up something. He was good at reading people, a skill born of years of practice.

Miss Leona wasn't faking.

She sobbed loudly at first, then fell silent for several minutes. She didn't look at Porter, as though he didn't exist and she was alone with her pain. After a time, she composed herself. She pulled tissues from the pocket of her dress, dabbed at her eyes, then blew her nose. Then she chuckled and shook her head, as if she were trying to shake it off.

"Whew. I'm sorry, baby. You didn't come over here to see all that. I was saying?"

"You took a head pill," Porter said.

"Right. I just hurt so bad. I usually take them early so they have plenty of time to wear off. This time I wasn't thinking and took it after lunch. I was knocked out in my chair when Danny got off the bus."

"What happened?" Porter said.

"I don't know. Nobody does. The bus driver was the last person who saw Danny. All I know is when my stupid self woke up, there was no Danny. My baby was gone."

"Then how do you know it was Hector and his boys?"

"No one else in this neighborhood would have messed with Danny. If Jamal and his guys saw her walking, they would have walked her home. That's how they are. No other people come into this neighborhood. It has to be Hector."

"What did the police say?"

"Not much. They came down and took a report. Kept asking where her parents are," Miss Leona said.

"They asked you that because when a child goes missing, it's usually a parent. Detectives like things that are easy and make sense. If you don't mind me asking, where *are* Danny's parents?"

"I've always been more momma than granny. I'm all Danny's ever had. Her father was a deadbeat. Never around, in and out of prison. My daughter got caught up with him, caught up with a certain kind of life. She's been gone for several years."

Porter didn't press to find out what that meant. "What did the detectives say when you told them about Hector?"

"They looked at me like I was simple. Wanted to know what proof I had that Hector took Danny. I told them I just knew."

"I'm sure they weren't too convinced by that," Porter said.

She laughed. "No, baby, they weren't. They sure weren't. Kept telling me I needed proof."

"Yeah, proof is a big thing."

"I guess so. They didn't help," she said.

"What else did you do to try to find her?" Porter said.

"What didn't I do? I walked around looking for her for hours, you know, after I talked to the police. I didn't even put my real shoes on, I was still in my slippers. I looked for her all night long, had me a flashlight and everything. My feet were bleeding the next morning. I didn't know what else to do. I asked Jamal and his boys if they had seen anything. They hadn't, but they helped me look for a while."

"Nice of them."

"They felt bad. A little girl from their side was gone. I told you, deep down, they really are good boys."

"Apparently."

"I tried everything. I put up flyers, I took out an ad in the classifieds of the newspaper. A friend helped me put something on the face-thing that all you kids use. Nobody knew nothing."

Porter nodded. "Tell me about the billboard."

"It was the last thing I could think to do. The company donated the space for me to use. I didn't get my medicine for two months to save up that reward money. I hoped someone would come forward."

Porter didn't have the heart to tell her it was a pittance. The world wouldn't care that she was a broken-hearted woman who'd sacrificed her health to scrape the money together. No one would care that it was the most valuable thing she had to give. Seven hundred and fifty dollars wouldn't be enough to get anyone to take her seriously.

"Thanks for talking with me. I think I have a better understanding of everything. Just a couple more questions before I leave?"

"Anything, baby."

"What's the name of the detective you're working with?"

"Detective Turnbull. I call him every week. He barely answers, and when he does, he doesn't have any information he wants to give an old woman. I haven't even been able to get a hold of him for a few weeks. I have his card on the refrigerator, just one second." She got up from the couch and flip-flopped her way into the kitchen. She reappeared a moment later holding a worn business card, and handed it to Porter.

"Thanks," he said. He took out his phone and snapped a picture of the card. "Last question."

"Sure."

"What's the name of the preschool Danny went to? I want to have a talk with the bus driver."

SIX

THE PRESCHOOL WAS 'Precious Adventures in Learning,' and Miss Leona took a few minutes to brag on her granddaughter. "Four years old and already reading. She loves books about princesses and knights. Loves 'em. She'll dress right up and pretend to be a princess right along with them little cartoon girls."

The police had already spoken to the bus driver, and had told Miss Leona he didn't know anything. Porter assured her he got better results when he asked people questions.

She was silent as she walked him to the front door. Porter was used to people asking questions about the process, or what he planned to do. Sometimes they would flat-out ask, "Are you going to find my so-and-so?" Miss Leona did none of that. When they got to the doorway, she pulled him down to hug him. She gave him a kiss on the cheek and said, "I'll see you when you come back."

That was it.

Porter nodded and stepped out of the house.

He'd only gotten a few steps off her stoop when he saw

Keith walking towards him. It made sense that Jamal wanted someone to keep an eye on him as he was leaving. Jamal couldn't know for sure that Porter was on the up-and-up. He could still be a "corny-ass bill collectin' nigga."

"Keith, huh?"

"You still call me Little Man."

"Nope. Keith's a good name. I think I'll use it."

"Whatever."

They turned the corner of the last cluster of buildings and Porter saw Jamal, Terrell, and his Yukon. New to the group, and leaning on his truck, were two guys he hadn't seen before. The newcomers were dressed like Jamal and Terrell, with khaki pants sagging low on their backsides. The larger of the two was black as night, with dreadlocks down to the middle of his back. He had no shirt on, displaying a powerful torso. The shorter man had lighter skin and struck Porter as Hispanic, maybe Puerto Rican. He had a green bandana tied tight around his head and tattoos showed on any skin that wasn't covered by his comically large white t-shirt. Porter had never understood the fashion, and figured it must be a hindrance to move around in. He walked up to Jamal and Terrell.

"Friends of yours?" he asked.

"Not me. They roll with the other side. And you on their side of the street," Jamal said. Terrell was as silent as before, with his arms crossed in front of him and his eyes on Porter's Yukon.

"Fair enough. I'll go say hello."

Porter walked the few yards to Palmetto Avenue, looked both ways, and then approached the two guys lounging on his truck. "Hey, guys, I'm taking off. Mind getting off my truck?"

Dreadlocks stood up straight and spoke first. "This your shit? I was wondering who it belonged to. I asked my man Jamal why his people was parking on my side of the street. He said you ain't with him. So if you ain't with him, and you ain't with us, then you don't belong, homey."

"I couldn't agree more. Feel free to move so I can get the hell out of here."

"You can leave. Follow the Avenue all the way out this bitch. Car's mine now," Dreadlocks said.

Porter saw Tattoo get off the truck and move to the right of Dreadlocks. The two new guys were close to each other, with Porter a few feet in front of them, his momentum carrying him closer. He felt the familiar weight of the Glock in his waistband, but was sure he wouldn't need it.

"See, douchebag, here's the thing," Porter said, with his hands open and up near his face. "That's mine." Porter closed the last step quickly and grabbed Deadlocks by the throat. He found that people often made a mistake when they tried to grab a person's throat. Your hand can't get good leverage on the entire neck; it's just too large. The front half, where all the soft areas are? Much better.

Dreadlocks was strong, but Porter was stronger. He squeezed just enough to keep him under control. Dreadlocks grabbed and pried at Porter's hands, but it was no use—he wasn't going anywhere. Out of the corner of his eye, Porter saw Tattoo pulling up the front of his giant t-shirt.

Only one reason for that.

Porter had been shot before, and he didn't plan on letting it happen again. With one final squeeze, he released Dreadlocks, who fell to the ground fighting for air.

Porter took a quick step sideways and smacked Tattoo's hands. He was still fumbling in his waistband. When Porter slapped at his hands, Tattoo's eyes went from the front of his shirt up to Porter. Porter rewarded him by opening his hands wide and boxing Tattoo's ears with a thunderous clap alongside his head. Tattoo shrieked in pain and brought his hands up to grab Porter's, which were still alongside Tattoo's head. Porter squeezed Tattoo's head like a basketball to secure the man, then slammed a half-dozen knees to Tattoo's face. When Porter released Tattoo's head he collapsed like wet paper, his face freshly altered.

Porter pivoted back to Dreadlocks, who by this time had managed to roll over onto his hands and knees, though he was still having trouble breathing. Porter took two steps and punted Dreadlock's face like a football. It was a solid kick that lifted Dreadlocks off of his hands and flipped him over onto his back, unconscious. Porter stole a glance back at Tattoo, then took several steps away from the pair.

"Man, I did not see that shit coming," Jamal crowed.

"I did," Porter said over his shoulder. "They should have, too."

"That shit was good, man. Shit made my whole day. Them fools needed that. I would do it, you know, but we supposed to be getting along."

"As long as you're having fun. Glad I could help."

"Don't get me wrong, you still corny, but at least I know you ain't no bill collector," Jamal said.

Porter turned back and stepped over to Tattoo's unconscious body, digging under the huge white t-shirt to reach into his waistband. He pulled out a small revolver and checked the cylinder.

It was loaded.

He stepped over the still-sleeping Dreadlocks and popped the trunk to his Yukon. He opened his lockbox and tossed the revolver in, then locked the box and slammed the tailgate.

He hopped into his front seat and turned the car on. It was thick with the midday Florida heat. He rolled the windows down to vent the muggy car and maxed out the A/C. As he shifted into drive, he looked over at the men who were still conscious. Jamal was on the phone, making big gestures with his hands, punching at the air. Terrell was looking straight at Porter with a small grin on his face, and he gave Porter a slight head nod as the Yukon accelerated away.

SEVEN

PORTER TOOK A LEFT out of Palmetto Acres and steered the Yukon along a perimeter street until he hit Nebraska Avenue. That would take him as far north as he wanted to go. He merged into the right-hand lane and held the speed limit. He hooked his phone up to the aux cable that hung from the display and dialed a familiar number.

"Ruas."

"It's me," Porter said.

"Me? Who's me? The only 'me' that calls my phone is my old lady and I'm certain you and I aren't sleeping together."

"That's because I keep turning you down. You're so desperate all the time, it's embarrassing. Where's your dignity?"

"Well, if you weren't so sexy, I might be able to contain myself. You know I'm a sucker for bald guys," Ruas said.

"I cut my hair low on purpose, but I get your point," Porter said. "I'll wear a hat next time I see you."

"That's all I ask," Ruas laughed. "Long time no talk, brother. How's everything? Trish?"

"She's doing good, I think."

"You think?" Ruas said.

"We split up a while back."

"I'm sorry to hear that."

"It is what it is," Porter said.

"She wanted it or you wanted it?"

Porter didn't answer.

Ruas changed the subject. "What the hell do you want? I'm sure you didn't find my number just to talk dirty to me."

"I'm just trying to stay out of trouble."

"Is it working?"

"Does it ever? Had a little dust-up with a couple fine citizens today, nothing noteworthy, but I wanted to get your take. What can you tell me about Palmetto Acres?"

"Complete shithole," Ruas said.

"I gathered that, Marco, I have eyes. You're the gang investigator; tell me about the gangs."

"What is there to tell? There was one and now there are two. We can't get much intel. I haven't been able to find a reliable snitch down there. It's slow going."

"I figured as much. I might be able to fill in some of the blanks for you guys," Porter said.

"Shit, I'll take all the help I can get. What are you doing in the Acres?"

"Just talking to a friend. Speaking of which, I need to ask you something," Porter said.

"Shoot."

"Tell me who's working a missing kid case."

"Why?" Ruas said.

"Just looking at it for a friend. Wondered which one of you guys was on it. I have a name, but I know how work gets passed off and shuffled around. Figured it was best to touch base with someone, even if it is an idiot like you."

"I resemble that remark," Ruas said with a laugh. "Hit me with the name and I'll look it up."

"Last name Hill, first name Danisha," Porter said.

"Danisha? The common spelling, I'm assuming?"

"Delta, Alpha, November, India, Sierra, Hotel, Alpha."

"Got it. Wait one," Ruas said.

Ruas's voice went silent for a couple of minutes; through the speakers in his car, Porter heard the soft sound of fingers tapping the keyboard. He was a fan of talking on the phone using his car's speakers. He felt it helped him hear better and he got to keep both hands on the wheel.

With no particular destination in mind, Porter took a left on Bearss Avenue. He heard a mumbling, like Ruas was reading to himself.

"Got it. Looks like Kevin Turnbull had the case, but now that it's been over a year it was moved to the Long Term Missing Unit. Some new kid has it, name of Rivera. I'll text you the number."

"Thanks, man. I appreciate it. Say hi to Kelly and the kids for me," Porter said.

"Of course. She's gonna want to have you over for dinner sometime. I hope you don't, because you eat too damn much."

"I'm a finely tuned machine, I can't miss meals," Porter said. The men shared a laugh.

"It was good to talk to you; it's been way too long. I know you're gonna make me regret saying this, but I miss you, buddy."

"See? I always knew you had a thing for me." Porter laughed and pushed the end button on his phone.

Porter soon passed over Dale Mabry Highway, the main north-south thoroughfare in Tampa. He pulled into a fast food drive-through, then sat in the parking lot of a closed grocery store to eat. A Johnny Cash album was playing on his phone and he took a few minutes to enjoy the meal and organize his thoughts.

Danny had been missing over a year and, despite his assurances to Ross, the odds of finding her were slim. Ruas said the case had been transferred to the Long Term Missing Unit. Moving the case to the LTMU meant that it wasn't much of a priority for the Hillsborough County Sheriff's Office. There would be no active investigation on the case; the file was just sitting in a filing cabinet or old box somewhere. Every day, the detective assigned would grab the oldest case, make a couple of phone calls if necessary, and update the computer saying they'd found no new information. That gave Miss Leona no chance of closure for Danny. While that was unfortunate, Porter could live with it. Plenty of people went missing every year, and not all of them were ever found. Some families just had to deal with it.

Still, Porter had some nagging thoughts about the case. He wondered where Danny's parents were. He wondered if the detectives had actually spoken with the school bus driver. The curious, investigative side of his brain wouldn't stop peppering him with questions. As a favor to Ross, he should at least speak to this Rivera person. It might help him connect the dots. Once he knew everyone had done their jobs, he'd feel better about telling Ross the bad news: There wasn't any easy way to find this kid.

EIGHT

THE CLOCK on the dashboard read nearly four. Porter thought about calling it a day and going back to his house, maybe see if he could finally kill off the remnants of his hangover. Instead, he decided to go to see Rivera, so he could talk to the detective in person and get a feel for where the case stood. A large chunk of the employees of the sheriff's office worked in or near the jail on Orient Road. Those building spaces weren't big enough to house everyone, Porter remembered, and they had to place some people at an ancillary office off of Kennedy Avenue, close to downtown. Porter figured Rivera would be with the other detectives there. He decided to take a gamble and pointed his truck south.

Traffic was light at that time of day. It wasn't rush hour yet and even then, most people would be heading away from downtown when they got off work. Porter made steady progress through the streets. He passed the Buccaneers Stadium and remembered the games he had gone to when he was a teenager. His dad was a sports nut. Porter didn't follow any team that much, but he'd liked to spend time with his dad.

After a half hour, he hung a left on Kennedy Ave and drove

a couple of miles to a free-standing building on his left, and pulled into the lot. The building looked like normal rental office space. In fact, other than a small stencil of the sheriff's office badge on the glass front door, there were no giveaways that the building housed law enforcement personnel. It looked like the headquarters of a telemarketing company.

Porter parked as far away from the front door as possible. He hopped out and dug through the trunk, locking his pistol, spare magazine, and pocketknife away. He shut the tailgate and walked toward the building.

Pulling the double door open, Porter was greeted by a rush of cool air.

He took a small step in and let the door close behind him. Porter looked around the rectangular room. There were two uniformed HCSO deputies, one next to the metal detector and one behind the small table. A door with a kickplate waited on the far wall.

"Gents," Porter said.

"Good afternoon, sir." The deputy behind the table wore a shiny badge which read *Raymond*. "Is there something we can help you with?"

"I hope so, Deputy Raymond." Porter liked to use a person's name if he knew it. It sometimes startled people who didn't know him, but he found it helped him seem more personable. He needed all the help he could get in that area. "I'm here to speak with Detective Rivera."

"Rivera? What time is your appointment?"

"I don't have one. I was in the neighborhood and thought I'd swing by."

"If you don't have an appointment, we can't let you in here," Raymond said. "It's against policy."

"Who just swings by a sheriff's office?" asked the other deputy, whose badge read *Fischer*. "If you need to speak with someone about a court date, you'll need to go to the courthouse."

"Interesting you would assume I have a court date," Porter said, "but that's not why I'm here. I have information about a case Rivera's working. Why don't you call and see if I can go back?"

Raymond looked at Fischer, who shrugged.

At least I'm in the right place, Porter thought.

Raymond picked up a landline and consulted a small piece of paper, its laminate peeling off, that was taped to the table. The deputy held the receiver to his ear. "Rivera. Got some guy here that says he needs to give you some info. Not sure, hold on... What did you say your name was?"

"I didn't, but it's Porter. It's about the Danisha Hill case."

"He says Porter. Yeah, he's a big guy. How the hell am I supposed to know? Okay, sounds good." Raymond hung up the receiver. "Rivera's coming out."

He wasn't an agent anymore, and they wouldn't let some random guy walk into their offices unescorted.

Fischer gestured to the table in front of him. "Sir, I need you to take everything metal out of your pockets and place it on the table, then walk through my metal detector."

Porter emptied out his pockets, which at this point only contained his wallet and phone. He looked at Fischer who waved him through the metal detector. There was a loud beeping noise.

"Are you wearing a belt? I didn't think that was the style," Fischer said with a smirk.

"It's the style if I don't want my pants to fall off my ass," Porter said as he moved backward through the metal detector. He unlatched his belt and set it on the table in front of Raymond, then stared blankly at Fischer.

"Try again, sir," Fischer said as he motioned his hand forward. There was no beep this time.

"Happy?" Porter asked.

"Generally, but I don't really care for your attitude," Fischer said.

"That's too damn bad." Porter threaded his belt through his jeans.

"You got quite the mouth on you, don't you?"

"Not generally, but I don't really care for your attitude," Porter said. "You guys wonder why people don't like you. I come here to see someone and I get to listen to your passive-aggressive bullshit. Just get Rivera out here already."

Fischer glowered at Porter. He opened his mouth to speak but Porter cut him off.

"Rivera."

Fischer looked to Raymond, who had a smirk on his face like he'd heard a joke everyone else had missed. He looked back to Porter and said nothing. About that time, the kick-plated door in the back of the entryway swung open, and Rivera walked in.

She had thick, curly hair and dark brown eyes, and was built like a gymnast or dancer—short and slight, but with a surprising amount of leg muscle showing through her dress slacks. She must have been a full foot shorter than Porter. Hanging on a lanyard around her neck was a laminated identification badge showing both her name and face.

"Rivera." Porter used her name without skipping a beat, disguising the fact that he was caught off guard that Rivera was a she. He silently chided himself about making assumptions.

"It's pretty close to quitting time. Thanks for making me stay late," she said. "I got him from here." She motioned to Porter and held the door with one hand to allow him to walk by first.

"Thanks, Rivera," Raymond said. Fischer just stood at his walkthrough, suddenly looking uninterested.

"Follow me," she said to Porter.

Porter stepped into the dark room. It took a few moments for his eyes to adjust and then he looked around to get his bearings. It was one big square room, with cubicles on the inside, ringed by perimeter offices. Cheap gray furniture dominated the space. This convinced him that no one who purchased furniture for a law enforcement agency had taste.

Rivera walked straight down the left side of the big square, heading towards the back wall. Along the way, Porter saw several bulletin boards covered with papers. Some were work-related: A most-wanted poster, some directive signed by the sheriff, a flyer to the annual department BBQ.

The rest were silly. A fake wanted poster with a candid shot of an officer, for the crime of buggery. There was picture of a broken-in trailer door, with the caption "11/05 - two hits." Pictures of the department Christmas party, all the officers wearing terrible sweaters. A Photoshopped head on the body of that cop from that TV zombie show.

Porter recognized these things. He'd been part of teams that did the same type of needling. When you work a dangerous job with a group of people, you become close. You often spend more time with them than you do your own family. These messages, pictures, and inside jokes were lessons in bonding. In a job like Rivera's you didn't care about people unless you laughed at and with them. The best units understood this.

For the first time in a long time, Porter felt a twinge of longing for his former career.

They passed a cubicle which, according to the nameplate, was her office. Porter paused in the entryway for a moment to get a look at everything else. The desk was immaculate, a nearly clean workspace. Prominently featured were three pictures of a young boy, but none of a man. A beat later, he'd caught back up with Rivera as she led the way into a room on the far wall. Porter guessed it was used to interview and debrief snitches. He walked through the door and sat down in a heavy metal chair.

No chance of assaulting your interviewer with this, he thought.

Rivera turned the blinds so they were open to the rest of the workspace, then shut the door. She took a seat opposite Porter and looked at him, as if uncertain what to ask first.

Porter saved her the trouble. "Real winners you guys have working the front door."

"You know what they say, good help's hard to find," Rivera said.

"You agree with me?"

"Mostly. Raymond isn't so bad, just unsure of himself. Fischer's an asshole."

"I gathered as much. Give you many problems?" Porter said.

"Not really. Probably a little racist, and I know he hates women. Always with 'darlin' this or 'spicy' that. He wants to sleep with me, but he's so mad about me being a woman who outranks him, he probably couldn't get it up," she said.

"That's more than I needed to know."

"Probably so. Regardless, enjoy that little nugget, the first one's free. Now it's your turn."

"For?" Porter said.

"Knowledge. Drop some. Why are you here?"

"I assume Ruas called you," Porter said.

"Obviously. I'd never have met with you if he hadn't given me a heads up."

"Never's a long time."

Rivera looked at Porter and scrunched up her face. "What

does that mean? Do you have something to tell me about the case or not?"

"What did Ruas tell you?"

"Not much. That you two are buddies and you have some info for me. How do you know him?"

"He used to be my Task Force Officer."

"Ruas worked for you? He probably should have led with the fact that you're a cop. Who do you work for?"

"I'm not in law enforcement anymore."

"Quit? Retire?"

"It's complicated," Porter said.

"Can it be that hard to explain?"

"Here's the problem. I need some information from you, but you're asking me about my background. If I tell you it's none of your damn business, I don't think you'll be feeling charitable with your information. So, I don't want to say it's none of your damn business," Porter said. "But it's really none of your damn business. See my dilemma?"

"No sweat. You came here for my help, but if you want to be a dick, that's your call. Ruas said to help you out if I could. But he said you'd call me to ask questions about a case. He didn't say you were going to stop by. Unannounced."

"Ruas didn't know I was coming. I figured I'd come down here and meet you in person. A little harder to blow me off in person than over the phone. Not that you'd do that..."

"You know how it is. I have other priorities, but you're right. You're here, what do you need? I'd appreciate if you spit it out, it's almost closing time," Rivera said.

"You have a cold case on Danisha Hill. Any way you could get me a couple statements out of the file? Maybe let me look at the record of investigation?" Porter said.

"Why would I do that? What's your relationship to this case?"

"I'm just a friend of the family. Call me a concerned citizen. I'm looking into it as a favor."

"Well, hell, since you put it like that, why not? Just give me a few minutes, Mr. Not-A-Cop-Anymore. I'm sure I can get you my whole computer. I could scrounge up the keys to a spare ride if you want? Some of the guys have extra uniforms in their locker room. Need a pistol too?" Rivera said.

"I would never fit in any of those guys' uniforms," Porter said.

"Good point. Seriously, why would I give you this stuff? It's HCSO property."

"How about as a favor to Ruas?" Porter said.

"I like Ruas; he's a stand-up guy. That's not enough of a reason."

"How long have you been a detective?"

"I just got off of ninety-day probation," Rivera said.

"In that time, have you ever closed a case?"

"Of course not. This is the LTMU. No one wants to get assigned here as a new detective. The evidence is cold and picked through by the time a case winds up here. This is where careers go to die," Rivera said.

"Then why are you here?"

"It's none of your damn business," Rivera said.

"Touché. What would closing a case do for you?"

"Get me out of here. Probably a transfer to Vice. I'm sure they'd dress me like a hooker and use me for john bait, but at least Vice is more exposure than this."

"I'm sure it is," Porter said.

"I mean it would be better for my career, asshole. What's your point? This case ain't getting solved. I looked through everything on my docket when I came to this unit. It's all colder than a popsicle."

"If you give me the info I'm asking for, I'll solve this case.

You can take the credit. You'll be wearing hot pants on Seventh Avenue in no time," Porter said.

Rivera was quiet for a few moments. Porter could see the pro and con discussion she was having with herself. "Solve the case just like that, huh?"

"It's a talent."

"And if you don't solve the case?" Rivera said.

"No harm, no foul. I'll burn any info you give me and no one will ever know you were involved. Let's be honest: We both know I could get most of the info I want by filing a Freedom of Information Act request through the sheriff. LEO or not, he'd cough it all up to avoid a lawsuit."

"But..."

"That takes too long. I promised a friend I'd look into it now," Porter said.

Rivera leaned back in her chair, exhaled, and looked at the ceiling for a few moments. She fixed her dark eyes on Porter. "Okay. Fine. I'll give you the info. Ruas says you're good to go, and at some point if you were a Fed, someone trusted you enough to give you a top-secret clearance. I guess that means I'll trust you. Wait here." She got up and walked out of the room, closing the door behind her.

After Rivera left, Porter reached over and checked the door handle. It was locked. He smiled to himself.

NINE

RIVERA RETURNED ten minutes later carrying a green paper file with a few hundred sheets of paper in it. She sat down, dropped the brick of paper on the table in front of her, and looked at Porter.

"This is most of the file. Some of the items were from internal databases, which I couldn't give you even if you were still a fed. I copied everything I could. I need you to promise me that this will not come back to bite me."

"It won't," Porter said. "No one who matters will ever know you gave me this."

Rivera pushed the file across the table. "Then I guess we're done. If you need anything else, feel free to let me know. Over the phone." She scrawled her number on the top page of the copied papers. "I assume you know the way out?"

"I think I can manage. Thanks for the help, Tina."

"Christina. How did you know my name?"

"You look like a Tina," Porter said as he stood up and collected the file.

"Asshole."

Porter smiled as he walked out of the room and back down

the hallway to the front door. He hit the exit bar and was let out behind Raymond and Fischer in the small front room.

Fischer gestured to the file. "What you got there?"

"It's an application for an online dating site. You interested?" Porter said.

Fischer scoffed. "Did our little Rivera put you up to that? She's such a peach sometimes."

"Yeah, she was a big help. We're going for drinks later. She told me to ask you if you wanted to go," Porter said. "She said something about you being the only real man in the building."

"You're just screwing with me, aren't you?" Fisher's eyebrows narrowed in suspicion.

"Of course I am. Go home to your wife, asshole," Porter said as he stepped out the tinted door and into the sunlight.

It was nearly five thirty and the sun was as hot as ever. Porter walked to his truck and retrieved the Glock he'd stashed, as well as his pocket knife. He leaned in to start the engine and rolled all the windows down while he stood outside.

Porter thumbed absentmindedly through the file Rivera had given him. It looked like so many he had seen before—full of junk. Things that weren't relevant to the case, just stuffed and stacked in the way of the real meat of the investigation. Something in that file would tell Porter what happened to Danny. All he had to do was look with the right eyes.

Problem was, he didn't want to spend the night doing homework for a case he wasn't very interested in. Still, he had promised Ross he would look into it. And Miss Leona. And now Rivera. It seemed he'd let too many people get invested in the outcome of this case. There was also that small tickle he felt in the back of his head—the one that told him he could figure things out. It was the tickle that played to his ego and said that the other people who had worked this case before were morons.

They probably were, he conceded. He left the parking lot,

pointed the truck west, and fought the traffic back to his side of town.

He stopped at the store on the way home and grabbed a pizza. Porter took his dinner and subsequent vodkas at his kitchen table, papers from Rivera's file in many neat piles around him. That night, tired and well lubricated, he went to sleep.

He woke up the next morning feeling like a champion. Vodka never gave him a hangover, and now he remembered why he stuck with it and avoided beer. He showered and made himself breakfast, but instead of dressing for the day, he put bum-around clothes on. Then he went back to the kitchen table and continued looking through the file, making notes to himself.

Porter stayed at the table all day, moving only to re-heat food and relieve himself. He relocated each page of the file as he read them and they were now facedown in one large stack. He had a page full of notes by early evening, and was about to make dinner when his doorbell rang. Porter grabbed his pistol from the kitchen bar where he'd left it and walked to the large, after-market front door.

"Who is it?"

"It's me. Open up, man."

Porter undid the double deadbolts and opened the door. Ross had big takeout bags of Chinese food. That looked better to Porter than a third serving of leftover pizza.

Ross looked at Porter and saw the pistol in his hands. "Expecting trouble?"

Porter shrugged.

Ross moved through the entryway and into the kitchen as Porter shut the door behind him and locked it. He put the takeout bags on the counter, glancing at the kitchen table as he did so. "What's all that shit?"

"Casefile for your girl." Porter grabbed a couple of plates from the cabinet.

"Wait, like the actual police file? How the hell did you manage that?"

"I just asked for it." Porter tore open the top of the takeout bag. "It's amazing what people will do for you if you're nice to them."

Ross laughed harder than he should have at that. "You being nice? Give me a break. Is this illegal? Are we committing a crime right now?"

"Relax, we aren't committing a crime; this was released by a representative of the sheriff's office. It's part of the Freedom of Information Act. Everything's on the up and up. Still, we may not want to go advertising that we have it."

"I knew it," Ross said as he ate an egg roll.

They were both silent for a few minutes as they ate. Porter located the General Tso's and paired it with some vegetable-free fried rice. He hated the way the onions and bean sprouts crunched with the rice. Weird texture, he always thought. Ross knew him well enough to get it special-made. That's what best friends were for.

Ross broke the silence. "So, in this extremely legal file," he said as he made air-quotes, "did you find anything interesting?"

"I've been looking at it all day. I have more questions than I started with, but I have more answers too. I wondered about Danny's parents. According to a police interview, the mother is dead. Died of an overdose a couple years back. She was Miss Leona's daughter."

"That's a shame."

"Cocaine's a hell of a drug."

"Not funny," Ross said at the reference.

"If you say so. I got no sympathy. It isn't like we haven't

been telling people for years that drugs are bad. If you keep using, big boy rules apply."

"Fair enough. It's just sad that Danny won't have her mom around."

"Is it? She's better off having a grandma who's on the level than an addict for a mom," Porter said.

"What about her dad?" Ross said, changing the subject.

"He was a real winner. Went to prison in Starke for a while, then he got out and overdosed in some fleabag motel."

Ross grabbed another egg roll. "What was he in prison for?"

"Primarily trafficking the stuff that killed Danny's mom. There was more shit too—pimping, theft, stuff like that. Classic scumbag."

"Okay, so mom's dead, dad's dead. What else?"

"The detectives interviewed the usual people. People from the neighborhood and from her preschool. No one knew anything. Or, no one wanted to talk."

"That's normal, right? Who wants to talk to the cops?" Ross said.

"Sure, it's normal. But two things stand out to me, and I'm not sure how important they are."

Ross was focused intently on Porter.

"You're just gonna look at me like that? It's kind of unnerving."

"Stop joking for a minute and tell me what stands out to you. Please."

"First is that there's no record of the police interviewing Hector. Strange, considering that's who Leona told them took her granddaughter. He's one of the first people they should have interviewed. But they never did. Paper says they tried to meet up with him a couple times and he never showed. So they gave up."

"Just like that? They just give up on the kid?"

"Not much they can do. The word of an old lady doesn't carry much weight unless she saw Hector take Danny. Since she didn't..."

"Nothing," Ross said as he slammed his fist on the table.

"Easy, Tonto," Porter said.

"What's the other thing?"

"Look, if this is bothering you we can—"

"What's the other thing, Porter?" Ross said, louder than he needed to.

Porter looked at his friend for a few moments, then picked up a piece of paper. "According to the notes, the bus driver was a douche about things."

"What do you mean?"

"He pulled the 'talk to my lawyer' act. The detective believed it was because he was scared to get blamed for anything. Bus driver has a clean record and there was no reason for them to suspect anything. Normal guy, wife and kids. Moved to town from New York a couple years ago. They didn't push it."

"Do you think they should have?"

"Maybe a bit," Porter said. "Cops don't care if a suspect lawyers up. If they're doing their jobs right, they have evidence or other witnesses and his statement doesn't really mean shit. It's not something that's generally going to make or break a good case. Sure, cops love a statement, but it's just the icing on a well-made cake."

"But the bus driver wasn't really a suspect, was he?"

"No, and cops hate it when someone who *isn't* a suspect lawyers up. They figure there's no reason to. The detectives aren't trying to bust them, just get some questions answered. It can be frustrating when the leasing manager at an apartment complex won't even tell you if a person lives there. Or if a bus driver won't tell you the last time he saw a missing kid. But it happens sometimes. Sometimes people are scared to talk to the cops."

"If they all looked like you, I'd be scared to talk to them, too," Ross said.

"Funny guy."

The pair fell into an easy silence as they ate, Porter shuffling through papers, occasionally stopping to look one over.

"What's rattling around in that big head of yours?" Ross said.

"I'm thinking it isn't looking too great. There's a severe lack of any intel to work with. I would have talked to the grandma, mom, and dad in that order. I always assume a parent took a kid because of a familial dispute. Then I'd work backward—talk to the people in the neighborhood and then the bus driver and staff at the preschool. That's where Danny's loop would lead: the neighborhood, then to school, then back to the neighborhood. With adults, it can be more difficult because they have cars and agendas and shit. That makes them more difficult to track down. Kids are usually easier."

"Then that's it? That's all you can do?"

"I've dug through everything. I'm not bullshitting you, there isn't much here."

"I know," Ross said, looking at all the papers. "I know you aren't."

"Still, I'm going to go speak with the bus driver. Unless I have a reason to press anyone in the neighborhood for more info, that's a dead end. Besides, I'm not too popular there now, I'd rather not go back for a while." Porter recounted the events at the Acres the previous day.

"You gotta be kidding me. Was the guy with the tattoos going to shoot you?"

"He thought he was," Porter said.

"I agree, you shouldn't go back there."

"Thanks, mom," Porter said.

"No, I'm serious. I didn't ask you to look into this for you to get hurt. I just thought... maybe... I don't know. I don't know what I thought."

"You're emotional, I get it. I have some of Trisha's old tampons in the bathroom if you need them."

Ross flung lo mein at Porter, who took it full in the chest, laughing. Ross looked satisfied with his retaliation.

"Don't worry about this anymore. I'll go talk to the driver in the next couple days and we'll go from there. Nothing we can do about it tonight."

"Think he'll tell you anything?"

"I can be persuasive." Porter walked over to the freezer and grabbed his bottle of vodka. He pulled two glasses from a cabinet and a bottle of orange juice from the fridge. He walked back over to the table, where Ross was looking at some loose papers, and sat a glass down in front of each of their places. "Tomorrow's Saturday, right?"

"Why do you ask?" Ross said.

"I don't want to send you to work all hung over again. Would you care for your usual reservation on the couch?" Porter said.

"Am I going to need it?"

Porter looked at the pile of papers on the kitchen table. "Yeah. Yeah, you're gonna need it."

And they drank.

TEN

MORNING MUST HAVE COME SOONER for Ross than for Porter because when he dragged himself out of bed, Ross's spot on the couch was empty. This wasn't a surprise. Porter wasn't a huge fan of waking early. He imagined Ross had headed home to nurse his hangover. Porter felt great: Vodka never failed.

He'd planned on taking the day off, a nice lazy Saturday, but changed his mind. The sooner he wrapped things up about Danny, the better for everyone. Ross would take it hard, but he had seen all the evidence last night and it wouldn't come as an unexpected revelation. Porter had given some thought to contacting the billboard company to see if they would move Danny's missing sign to another location, away from Ross's office. Somewhere out of Ross's line of sight. Porter would pay them if he had to.

Miss Leona had already steeled herself against the knowledge that they would not find Danny. Porter was sure he had given her some abstract glimmer of hope by showing up at her house, but he thought she was a practical old woman. She knew the deal.

Detective Rivera wouldn't care, much. Sure, she'd love to hit the strip with Vice, but having Porter look at things was a long shot for her. It wasn't as if she had an emotional attachment to Danny, Porter was sure she'd get over it.

Things could go back to the way they were before Porter had started poking around in a case he had no business looking into.

Porter slipped his gun into his waistband, and grabbed his sunglasses and a piece of paper with the address of the bus driver on it. He swung by the fridge to grab a bottle of water, and locked the door behind him when he left.

The bus driver lived in an older part of town, near Temple Terrace. The houses there were old, built when Tampa was much smaller, to accommodate the Baby Boomers' generation. Now it was a predominately Hispanic part of town. As Porter neared his destination, he saw corner stores turned into *tiendas*. The car dealerships signs stopped saying *Buy Here Now* and read *Comprar Aqui* instead. Porter didn't get over this way much, but his favorite Mexican place was on this side of town. He thought about stopping for the burrito Cancun, but decided he would wait until he had talked to the bus driver, Abel Quintana.

Pulling onto Quintana's street, Porter saw the familiar sight: rows of houses in pastel colors. He'd never quite understood the fascination. Most of the houses looked alike, with their stucco sides and asphalt shingle roofs. All had bars on the windows, and it seemed like every fourth or fifth house had a religious shrine in the front yard. Porter checked the address on the paper.

He was close.

The outside of Quintana's house was no different than the rest of the neighborhood. Parked in the driveway were an old minivan and a new sixteen-passenger van. Colorful graphics reading *Precious Adventures in Learning* wrapped the van. Porter imagined a take-home ride must have been the biggest perk of being a bus driver.

Porter nosed the Yukon in behind the new van, hopped out, and locked his door. He rang the doorbell.

The television was on and children were laughing. With two cars in the driveway, Porter reasoned the family should be home. He rang the doorbell again.

Still nothing.

He rang the bell a third time, and finally he saw a shadow appear behind the peephole and heard the door being unlocked. A short, thick man answered the door.

"Hey, my friend, whatever it is, we don't want any. Don't come back, okay?" Abel Quintana was mostly bald and had a thick mustache paired with the hairiest arms Porter had ever seen.

"I'm not in the selling mood today. My name's Porter and I'm wondering if I can ask you a couple questions."

"Questions about what?"

"Danisha Hill. Do you have a few minutes?" Porter said.

Quintana looked agitated and his head darted from left to right and back again. "Listen, Officer Porter, I already told you people I have nothing to say. If you have any questions for me, you're supposed to ask my lawyer. If you lost his number I'll be glad to give it to you again."

"Mr. Quintana, I'm not with the police."

"You're not with the police?"

"No, nothing like that. I'm just here as a friend of the family. I wanted to see if you could help me out."

Quintana's head darted back and forth again, surveying the street. "All right, then listen. If I wouldn't tell the *pinche* cops anything, why would I tell you? Piss off." The door slammed in Porter's face.

Porter stood for a moment looking at the door, then turned and walked back to the new passenger van. The driver's side door was unlocked. Porter reached his hand under the seat and found the lever to slide the seat back on its tracks. He hopped in and, after a brief moment to acclimate himself with the configuration, found the car horn. He pressed down and didn't let up.

Not ten seconds passed before Quintana's face peeked from the doorway to see what was happening. He had a look of panic on his face, but disappeared back into the house. Porter continued holding the horn down. The minutes crept by: one, five, ten. All the while, Porter kept the horn fully pressed. Somewhere around minute thirteen, the bus driver came charging out of his house and over to the driver's side window. Between the noise of the horn and the window being rolled up, Porter couldn't hear him, but it looked like Quintana was calling him everything but a child of God. Porter motioned to the passenger seat. Quintana stalked around the front of the van and climbed in. Porter let off the horn.

"Mr. Quintana, thanks for changing your mind and coming out to see me. I think we got off to a bad start."

"You're crazy, man, crazy. I have neighbors, man. What you think they gonna say? They gonna call the cops, man. They already call me and complain. What are you trying to do to me?"

"I'm not trying to do anything, but I do need your attention. Now that I have it, I'll ask you a couple questions. It's probably best if you answer. You were the last person to see Danisha before she disappeared, right? What do you remember about that day?"

"I already told you once, shithead, I'm not telling you anything. I'm not telling the cops, I'm not telling you, I'm not telling *anyone* what I know." His face was red and he was trembling.

"You know something you're not telling?"

"I didn't say that," Quintana said.

"Actually, you did just say that. Saying 'I'm not telling anyone what I know' implies that you know something, but aren't talking. That's a problem for me. Let's try it again. What do you remember about the day Danisha was taken?"

"Screw you, man. I'm gonna call the cops myself. This is harassment. This is a violation of my rights, man."

"It's not a violation of your rights. I'd explain, but I'm sure you wouldn't get it. Just tell me what you remember, and I'll be out of your hair."

"I'm calling the cops right now. They gonna arrest you for breaking into my van," Quintana said. He lunged out of the van and ran into his house.

Porter watched the man leave, then got out of the van and walked back to his truck. Having no desire to explain why he was there to the cops, and wanting no record of him having been at Quintana's house, he decided to leave. He backed the truck out and left the pastel neighborhood. That burrito Cancun seemed like a perfect idea, and he was sure he was going to need the energy.

ELEVEN

AS PORTER SHOVED bites of the chicken and shrimp burrito into his mouth, he considered the conversation with the bus driver. What was Quintana so worried about? Why not talk to the cops? Porter understood why people in the Acres were reluctant: Violence was very real there. Misguided or not, if you got labeled a snitch, you were in trouble.

But the old neighborhood Abel Quintana lived in wasn't nearly the same. It had seen better days, but the working-class residents wouldn't bother him for talking to the cops. He had to know that. What was making him so resistant? One would imagine a preschool bus driver having at least some soft spot for children. Didn't he want to help find Danny?

Porter shook his head and finished the last of his water. He hated that Abel Quintana had been so difficult to deal with, but he had to find out what the man knew, even if it was something small. The investigator in him wouldn't be satisfied until he knew. With no legal means to put pressure on him, there weren't too many other options. He paid the bill and headed out to his truck, dialing Rivera's number as he walked.

"Rivera."

"Tina? It's Porter."

"Christina, asshole. Christina. You know what, just stick with Rivera. What do you want?"

"I have a question about the Hill case."

"It's Saturday, Porter."

"And you answered your desk phone. What does that say about you?"

"How do you know this is my desk phone? Maybe I'm at home right now and you're interrupting my time off."

"Doubtful. Why would you give a random guy, Ruas's friend or not, your personal number? No cop gives out their personal cell if they can help it."

"You got me. I can't have some weird guy calling me at home, can I?"

"If you're into that sort of thing, I guess you could."

"What do you want?"

"I want to know why you're at the office on the weekend. I was planning on leaving you a message. They told me the LTMU cases weren't a priority. I can't imagine the sheriff pays a rookie overtime to sift through them."

"I use the office gym," Rivera said. "Saves me money. I check email before I leave, which I'm doing now, so unless you have something interesting to say, I'm going home."

"Before you do, was there anything about Abel Quintana that you didn't give me, because of the privacy policy?"

The phone disconnected. Porter looked down at the blank screen, which turned dark, then instantly lit up again, ringing and vibrating. He didn't recognize the number, but answered anyway. "Yeah?"

"Hey asshole, we're supposed to be keeping your involvement in this thing under wraps, remember? They record the phones at the office. Do you want me to lose my job?"

"I'm just asking," Porter said. "Something seems off and I wanted to know if I was missing anything."

"What else is there? Didn't you read the file?"

"I'm just grasping at straws. Anything you think you may have left out?"

"Nothing that could help you," Rivera said.

"Don't sweat it, I'll keep thinking. What're you doing tonight?"

"What, you going to ask me out for a drink? Fischer already had something to say about what you told him," Rivera said.

"He deserves it. I wanted him to feel like the pile of shit he is."

"Well, it worked. He asked me why I wouldn't get a drink with him sometime. Looked pretty hurt."

Porter had to stifle a laugh. "Too bad for Fischer. No drink for us, but I may need to give you a shout late tonight. Are you available?"

"Don't call me tonight, Porter. I'm grumpy when it's late."

"Perfect. Thanks, Tina." Porter hung up.

Porter drove to the nearest gas station and filled his tank. He headed inside, took a piss, and bought a pack of sunflower seeds and water. When he finished paying up he went back to his truck, got into the front seat, and headed back to Abel Quintana's.

It was dusk by the time he reached the mouth of the neighborhood. From his earlier internet recon, he knew the street Quintana lived on made a large loop, then led back out the way it went in. One way in and one way out. Porter moved his Yukon into an obscure corner of the pharmacy parking lot across from the neighborhood's entrance, and waited.

TWELVE

PORTER HAD NO CLUE WHEN, or if, Quintana would leave for the night, but he was hopeful. It was Saturday and people would be more likely to be out and about than on a weeknight. Regardless, Porter was prepared to keep an eye on the house until he saw movement. Luckily, that didn't take very long.

Forty-five minutes into his surveillance, a woman and two children left the Quintana home in the white minivan that was parked out front. The van pulled out of the driveway and headed towards the entrance of the neighborhood, where it went east towards 56th Street. Porter watched the van go by and refocused his attention on the house. He poured himself another mouthful of sunflower seeds and settled in.

Two hours later, Abel Quintana's front door opened. At this point, it was nearly nine o'clock and well dark outside. Fortunately, the porch light illuminated Quintana's face as he turned from closing the front door. He had a small bag in his left hand. Porter started the Yukon. He was thankful to be moving, because he had been contemplating pissing in one of his empty water bottles.

Quintana got into the driver's seat of his work van, with its happy wrap advertising, and started the engine. He didn't sit for long, and left the neighborhood heading in the opposite direction from his family.

Not going to meet up with the wife and kids, Porter thought.

He let Quintana get a block down the road and eased the Yukon out after him. It wouldn't be too tough to follow the big van, even in the dark, and Porter wanted to make sure Quintana didn't suspect he was being followed.

As a federal agent, Porter had followed hundreds of people. If there was one universal truth, it was that they rarely had any clue. There were times when he was sure his surveillance had been burned but when he later arrested the person, they hadn't seen him at all. People were oblivious creatures. In the moment, however, every turn or brake tap seemed like the beginning of a car chase.

Quintana made no such moves. He drove until he made a right turn north. Porter was two cars behind him most of the time. For a while he was right behind the big van, but there was no indication the bus driver knew.

The colorful van turned left into a brightly lit parking lot. Above, there was a large sign with faded letters surrounded by bright, racing bulbs that seemed to chase each other. The parking lot was almost full, and Abel Quintana parked in one of the outer rows, furthest from the building.

It was a bowling alley.

Porter took a right and pulled into the opposite parking lot. It looked like a thrift store that had gone out of business; there was a *For Rent* sign taped to the front window. Porter gave it a quick look and saw no external cameras. He backed into a spot in front of the vacant building and killed his lights.

Quintana must have needed time to find his bowling mojo, because he sat in the van for nearly twenty minutes. The clock on Porter's dash showed nine forty-five when the van's front door opened and Quintana slid out of the front seat, carrying his bag. He'd changed shirts in the car, and was now wearing an unfortunate bowling shirt.

Look at that gaudy thing, Porter thought. *Not enough money in the world.*

Abel Quintana held up his keys, made the van beep, and headed into the old building.

Porter sat for a few minutes taking stock. The blinking lights of the radiant sign gave him a good view of the parking lot. There were no cameras on any of the outer light poles. It looked like there was one above the front door, to catch people's faces as they entered. This wasn't the best neighborhood and it was possible the bowling alley had seen its share of robberies and bar fights.

Still, one camera wasn't a problem.

According to Rivera, Abel Quintana had a clean record. He was a family man who had never had so much as a speeding ticket, but this didn't matter too much to Porter. He had made a living listening to his intuition. Some people would call it their gut feeling or the little voice in the back of their head. Porter thought it was a subconscious collection of all available evidence a person could give him: body language, voice inflection, non-verbal clues. It was how he knew Miss Leona had been genuine in her grief when he'd visited her at the Acres. It was the reason he knew that Dreadlocks and Tattoo were an issue and Jamal and Terrell weren't.

It was also the reason he knew Quintana had much, much more to tell him.

Porter waited a few more minutes to make sure Quintana would be engrossed in whatever game he was playing, then got out of the car and went to his trunk. From the small pile of clothes, he grabbed a dark hooded sweatshirt. Opening the lockbox, he retrieved a dark pair of Mechanix gloves and a small spool of electrical tape. He stuffed the gloves in his back pocket and slipped his button-up off, replacing it with the sweatshirt. He locked up, pulled the hood of the sweatshirt up over his head, and walked toward the bowling alley.

THIRTEEN

PORTER STEPPED onto the gravel parking lot that separated him from Quintana and cursed under his breath. He would feel every little rock through his Chuck Taylors. As he got closer to the front door, he pulled out his cell phone and buried his chin in his chest as if on an important call. A quick peek up revealed that the front door camera was on the left side of the door.

Porter kept his head down on his pretend call, careful to avoid the camera and stepped through the front door of the bowling alley.

Once inside, a quick look revealed two things: First was that although the lanes were well lit, the rest of the establishment was dark; second was that there were no interior cameras. Porter had seen this often. A victimized business owner adds a camera to regain peace of mind. They don't think about all the proper angles they need to record. Half the time, the cameras aren't even running. Porter ended his fake conversation, but kept his hood up.

Inside, the place looked like every other bowling alley. A counter with a cashier and shoe rental up front. There was a small arcade and restrooms along the wall to the left of the cashier; a counter for food and beer pickup on the right, with some chairs and small tables. Porter looked around until he spotted Quintana's team near the middle of the alley.

All of them in those God-awful shirts, Porter thought.

He took a seat at one of the food tables so he could keep an eye on Quintana. He was a shit bowler. Porter watched as Quintana went frame after frame, failing to ever pick up a complete set of pins. Porter wasn't sure how you could come here enough to be on a team and have a shirt, but still be so bad at the game.

"Get you something, buddy?" A skinny girl with stringy hair was standing to Porter's left. The tag on her vest said her name was Adrestia. She tapped her notepad and chewed her gum.

"Busy night," Porter said. "Is it like this all the time?"

"Nope, just on the weekends. Extra busy on the first and third weekends of the month. Need anything?"

Porter didn't want to look out of place. "Water?"

"Tap or bottle?"

"How's the tap?" Porter said.

"Depends. Do you want dysentery?"

"Not a huge fan," Porter said.

"Bottle it is." The girl turned and headed through a set of swinging doors on the wall behind Porter. He watched her go, and turned his attention back to the bowling team. They looked like average guys, plumbers and electricians. Maybe a school-teacher or two. Men who needed some time away from their wives and a pretense to drink large amounts of shitty draft beer.

Adrestia materialized a few moments later with a bottle of water on her tray. "Three bucks."

Porter fished in his front pocket and peeled off a five from his money. He always kept his wallet in his back pocket, and his money in the front. Something he'd learned from his dad. "Son," he would say, "I've seen people get their wallets picked bumping into people in a crowd. It happens. But no one other than your mother should have their hand in my front pocket." Porter figured he was extra safe, since *no* one else should have their hand in his front pocket.

"Here you go," he said and handed the waitress the five. "No change, but I do have a question."

"The name, right? My family's Greek," the waitress said.

"You get asked a lot?"

"What do you think?" she said as she walked away.

Porter smiled and opened the water bottle. Before taking a drink, he pushed the hood off of his head. *There's only one camera in this place,* he thought, *and who knows if it's even recording. No sense in pretending anymore. Let him see me.*

Porter continued watching the shitshow, and Quintana didn't get any better. Multiple pitchers of beer went to his team's table.

It shouldn't be long now, Porter thought.

No one said anything to him for nearly an hour, not even the waitress. Porter imagined she knew he wasn't going to get drunk enough to tip her an incredible amount, so there was no reason to waste much time on him. Porter respected that. Finally, as he began to wonder if Quintana was Superman, it happened.

The last frame ended and the men were cueing up another game. Quintana stopped polishing his ball and set it down in the ball retriever. Speaking with his hands, he said something to the group and gestured backward, like he was hitching a ride in the opposite direction. They all nodded, and he stepped out of the lane and up to the worn-down carpet that ran the length of the hall. He turned right, away from Porter, and went through a small door next to the arcade.

About damn time.

Quintana entered the bathroom fifteen seconds before

Porter. Porter turned an about-face before opening the door, to make sure none of the other shitshow bowlers had the urge to evacuate their bladders at the same time. Seeing none, he pushed through the door.

The bathroom was a small affair, with a sink, two urinals and a stall opposite. The bathroom was empty save for Quintana, who was at one of the urinals.

Porter had been holding in a massive piss since his surveillance in the Yukon. *Might as well kill two birds with one stone.* He stepped to the urinal between Abel Quintana and the sink. It was the short one, for boys. He had a standard joke for that.

"Man, this water is cold. And deep," Porter said, as he unzipped his jeans and uncorked the waiting stream of urine.

Until that point, Quintana had literally been minding his own business. Most guys would lock a death stare onto their own unit while in proximity of another man peeing. No one wanted to let their eyes innocently roam around and get accused of meat gazing.

Quintana looked up and to his left. "What the fu—"

"Mr. Quintana, I gotta let you know that you are the shittiest bowler I've ever seen. You would be better off digging a hole in your backyard and burying the money you spend here."

"Are you... are you... following me? How... why..."

"I know it's tough to think while you have a hand full of hog. Real awkward; I get it. Don't worry, I'll talk, you keep aiming."

Quintana made no move to sheath his member, but anxiously looked around the bathroom.

"If I'm being honest with you, I wasn't too satisfied with the answers you gave me at your house. Deep down, I know you're full of shit."

Quintana looked at Porter. Porter could see him having a

quick internal debate with himself, and in a moment it was over. The bus driver had decided to continue his lie.

"I already told you, I don't know anything. That's the same thing I told the police," Quintana said.

"No, you said you wouldn't tell me what you know. That's different."

"I made a mistake. My English isn't so great. Just a translation accident."

"You were born in New York, you piece of shit," Porter said.

"Yes, yes, but I speak Spanish all the time. It's just a mistake. *Lo siento*." Quintana made an exaggerated shaking motion and zipped his pants. He moved back from the urinal, keeping his eyes on Porter.

"Listen," Porter said, "this can all be so simple. I just want to know what you know." He fixed himself and flushed the urinal. Noticing that Quintana hadn't flushed, he leaned over and gave his urinal a flush as well.

Abel Quintana was almost all the way out the door. "I tell you, I don't know who took the girl. Just leave me alone."

The bathroom door slammed shut behind him.

While Porter washed his hands, he looked at himself in the mirror. *There's no other way*, he reasoned. When he was finished washing his hands, he pulled his hood back up and reached into his back pocket and grabbed his Mechanix gloves. As he pulled on a glove, his gaze lingered on the plunger sitting in a bucket near the stall.

FOURTEEN

PORTER REACHED over and grabbed the plunger out of the bucket. He closed the rubber end in the stall door so it wouldn't move and rotated the handle until it was unscrewed. He let go of the stall door, and the rubber bottom fell down to the floor.

He stepped over to the sink and ran water over the wooden handle until it looked clean, then patted it down with paper towels. He stuck the plunger handle in his back pocket, covered it with his sweatshirt, then walked out of the bathroom and scanned left and right.

If Quintana had told his buddies Porter was there, things could get messy. It didn't look like that happened. The bus driver had returned to his group and was changing his shoes. He was going to make tracks. Porter moved toward the emergency exit on the left.

Approaching the exit, Porter had a brief thought that opening the door might sound an alarm. Deciding the alley was low-rent enough that the door wasn't actually hooked up to an alarm, he punched out of the exit door. No noise.

Good.

Porter was now outside the building, facing the street. He

couldn't see his Yukon from where he was, but he could see the top of that stupid van Quintana drove. He headed towards it.

When he got to the corner of the building, he took a quick peek towards the front door. No one was coming out. In front of him was the furthest right row of parked cars. There was just enough space between those cars and an old building they were lined up in front of for Porter to squeeze past. He used the space between the car's bumpers and the building as a walkway to approach Quintana's van unseen. He kept walking, the uncomfortable gravel digging into his shoes, until he got to the large Excursion next to the van. Standing in between the vehicles, no one could see him.

Porter took a knee and looked under the bumper, toward the front door. Quintana was standing still, looking around. He must have decided he was clear to go, because he hustled across the parking lot. Porter couldn't believe how quickly his stumpy legs could carry him.

Porter watched the stout man move, looking around and behind him. Quintana even jogged for a few feet—then he stopped. Porter thought he might go back the way he came, but after a few moments, he started walking again, this time at a normal pace.

Quintana was only two cars away, and Porter could no longer see his head from under the bumper. He stood up with his back towards the Excursion. He could hear Quintana walking on the gravel. Small crunches as he got closer. Porter reached into his back pocket and grabbed the plunger handle, holding it by his side. Porter heard the crunches get closer, then he saw Quintana's head clear the back of the Excursion. He was digging through his bag for his keys.

Porter had to take a shortened swing with the plunger handle since there wasn't much space between the two vehicles.

He took a small step that pivoted him left and smacked Abel Quintana on the mouth with the handle.

Damned short swing.

Regardless, Quintana dropped to his knees and gave Porter a look that said he was closer to sleep than wakefulness. Porter helped the transition.

He stepped out from between the cars. No longer boxed in by the vehicles, he was standing directly in front of his quarry. Porter brought the plunger handle in a big looping arc and struck him in the side of the head, near the temple.

Quintana departed from consciousness.

FIFTEEN

PORTER LET the plunger handle slide through his gloved fingers. He stepped over the bus driver and pulled him into a seated position, then locked his arms around Quintana's thick torso, bear-hugged the man, and dragged him between the two vehicles. Out of sight. Then Porter came back out again and looked around.

Nothing. No one had seen anything. This would be easier without witnesses.

He found Quintana's keys on the ground and opened the back doors. It turned out that while the van was manufactured to seat sixteen, the two back rows of seats had been removed to enlarge the trunk.

He threw Quintana's bag into the back of the van and then walked back to the unconscious man. There was blood pooling from his mouth and the beginnings of a serious black eye on his left eye. Porter didn't feel bad. He could have easily killed the man if he'd put any effort into his swings. As it was, he'd laid the plunger as evenly across Quintana's face as he could. He needed the bus driver asleep for a while, not dead.

Porter rolled Quintana onto his stomach and took his shoes

off, then threw them into the van. Reaching into his pocket, he found the electrical tape and bound the man's hands behind his back. Then, he grabbed Abel Quintana underneath the arms and pulled him to his feet. He was a heavy man, but Porter had the strength to cope. Porter lifted him off the ground and walked him back to the open van doors. Porter had to place Quintana in a fetal position to fit him in there. Before closing the back door, Porter grabbed a sock off the man's foot and stuffed it into his mouth.

The sock was dirty.

Porter gave the area a quick scan and, seeing that he'd left nothing behind, moved to the driver's door. Opening it, he slid the seat as far back as it would go, hopped in, and fired the van up.

He checked the gas gauge and found it was nearly full. Porter adjusted his mirrors and backed the van out of the gravel lot onto the main road, then pulled out onto Florida Avenue.

Florida Avenue ran north for several more miles until it became State Road 41. The state road would take you as far north as you wanted to go, merging with Nebraska Avenue and several ancillary roads. Porter knew just where he wanted to take Quintana.

Pasco County bordered Hillsborough County to the north. As a county, it was less populated and more rural. It had been experiencing a bit of a boom due to urban sprawl, but it was still quiet in most places. Porter stayed pointed north for nearly an hour until he found the place he was looking for.

When he was still a federal agent, Porter had worked a case that involved a methamphetamine cooking operation. The amateur chemists had bought a farm with thirty acres and used that as their base of operations. There were trailers and mobile homes everywhere on the land, and all were used as meth labs. The property was seized by the government as part of the investigation and would be auctioned off. Porter hadn't checked on the status of the sale in over eighteen months, but in his experience, the government system was so slow that it was likely the auction wouldn't be held for several more years.

Porter took a left at a closed and shuttered gas station and drove the van off 41 and onto the smaller surface streets. He idled down an unlit gravel road and came to a large gate made of round metal pipes. Posted to the front of the gate were several official-looking, laminated pieces of paper: seized property notices, no trespassing signs, the number for a twenty-four-hour law enforcement call center if anything happened on the property.

Chains barred the gate, but they were no match for the van. Pulling onto the property, Porter stopped the van, got out, and tried to set the gate as right as he could. He wasn't sure why he bothered; if he remembered right, there were no other farms down this gravel road, and the next neighbor was many acres away.

After pulling down the uneven driveway for several hundred feet, Porter found what he was looking for: the burned-out shell of a double-wide trailer. The meth lab that had previously inhabited it had caught fire and blown up, reducing the trailer to a charred husk. There were plenty of other trailers he could have chosen, but this one had the right ambiance.

Porter pointed the van at the trailer to take advantage of the lights, and left it running. He opened the double rear doors of the van and found Quintana fast asleep. He should have woken by now. The black eye was fully formed now—and worse, there was a raised welt the diameter of the plunger handle that ran the length of his head. Porter stifled a laugh.

Can't make him any uglier, he thought as he hauled Quintana's dead weight out of the van and hefted him to his shoulder.

Porter walked the man over to the front support pole of the trailer. Without letting the body fall all the way to the ground, he slid Quintana off his shoulder and stood him against the pole, holding him in place with one hand. With the other hand, he reached into his pocket and grabbed the electrical tape. Porter used his mouth to start the end of the tape unraveling and stuck it to Quintana's forehead. He fed it around and around the support pole several times until Quintana's head was immobile. The small roll of electrical tape didn't go very far, so Porter had to settle for only wrapping Quintana's chest to the pole as well. When he was finished, he gingerly took his hands off of Quintana and stepped away.

The tape held. The portly bus driver sagged, but was ultimately held in place, head and chest stuck to the pole, arms still tied behind him.

Porter was proud of his packing job. The bus driver looked like a caterpillar tied to a stick. Porter walked back to the van and sat for a couple of minutes.

Quintana wasn't going anywhere.

Porter was going to question Quintana, there was no doubt about that. There were two options for how to deal with this situation, and they both had pros and cons. Too much shock and awe and Quintana would tell him anything just to get him to stop. The information might be worthless

On the other hand, if he was too soft-handed, Quintana would lie his ass off and dodge questions all night. Porter would be in the humid field much longer than he wanted to be. There was a fine line. In this situation, Porter hoped the fear of what *might* happen would be Quintana's biggest motivator. He already knew Porter would hurt him—or at least, he would remember that when he woke up.

Porter wished he had bought another bottle of water from the Greek girl. This far from a city, it was pitch black out. The van's headlights illuminated the thick cloud of mosquitos that swarmed the area. Porter had rolled down his sleeves, but they still gnawed at his exposed face and neck.

I'm going to have to get this going, or I'm going to get eaten alive.

He took out his phone and started a voice memo, then slipped it into the front pocket of his outer shirt. Porter then walked over to the trussed Quintana and gently smacked his face. His eyes cracked open, then slammed shut. Porter smacked again and Quintana's eyes slowly opened.

Quintana was dazed and seemed to be having a hard time understanding where he was. He blinked hard a couple of times, then began softly crying.

Porter stood up, then leaned closer to the man. He wasn't interested in this side of the man, at least not so soon. He reasoned that Quintana's mind was still trying to process what had happened, and the crying was just a reflex, like when a baby wakes up in a strange place—which wasn't too far from the case right now.

"Hi. How's it going?"

There was no reply. Quintana just kept blinking the tears out of his eyes. Still, Porter saw a spark of understanding. Porter knew the man was coming around.

"You with me? Hey. Hey. You here?" Porter gave his face another smack. This time, Quintana focused on Porter. His lights were on again and someone was home.

"You're back. Good. Remember what happened?"

Quintana blinked his eyes again. "I remember... I remember seeing you in the bathroom and that's it. Why can't I... why can't I move? Did I get shot?"

"Nope, your legs work just fine. Does your face hurt? I imagine it does. Move your tongue around. I think you may be missing a tooth."

Quintana tracked his tongue in his mouth and checked his teeth. Porter saw the tongue linger on the left side of his mouth. "What happened?"

"I cracked you in your face with a plunger handle," Porter said.

Abel Quintana's eyes went wide. His face flushed with hundreds of questions, but he didn't speak.

"Yep, I cracked you right in your damn face. You know why?"

No words escaped Quintana's battered face.

"Because you tried to bullshit me," Porter said. "I don't like that, Abel. I tried to be so polite."

Quintana looked tentative. There was a lie on his lips, but he bit it off.

Good, Porter thought. *Maybe we can speed this up a little.*

"Did you break my neck?" Abel Quintana said.

"No, I didn't break your neck. You can't move because you're tied up."

"Where am I?"

"Do you feel these damn mosquitos? They're eating me alive." Porter walked over and unbuttoned his bowling shirt as best he could, tucking the flaps behind him. He unbuckled Quintana's shorts as well, letting them fall down to the ground.

"Sorry, but I'm not going to be the only one getting bitten all to shit out here. You get to share the love." Porter swatted his neck. "Where you are is a tough question to answer. You were asleep for quite a while. I drove you pretty far out of town."

"Why am I here?"

Porter walked over and smacked Abel Quintana in the mouth. "Abel, don't start that with me. I just told you why you were here. If I have to keep explaining this to you, we're gonna be out here all night. I don't want to be out here too much longer, on account of the bears."

Quintana's eyes shifted left and right. "Bears?"

"Shit, yeah. The bear population has boomed out of control these last few years." Porter was telling the truth.

"They had to open the first hunting season on bears in decades." Porter was still telling the truth.

"The Florida black bear is one of the most dangerous animals in the South. Every year they kill dozens of people." Porter was not telling the truth.

While the black bear population had boomed, they were of minimal risk to humans. Porter was guessing the New York City-bred Quintana had no clue about bears. But there was enough truth to the story that the bus driver could have read something in the paper or heard on the news about bear-hunting season.

"God, no. God, no. I don't want no bear."

"Yeah, well, I don't want no bullshit."

"But I can't. I can't, Mr..." Porter watched Quintana's face struggle to recall his name.

"Porter."

"Mr. Porter, I can't. Please. Don't make me tell you."

"Why not? What's the problem?" Porter said.

"He'll know. He'll know if I tell you." Abel Quintana began to cry again.

SIXTEEN

"WHO WILL KNOW? Who will know you told me?"

Quintana stopped crying and looked up. Porter saw a flash of stubbornness. "I don't have to tell you. You can't do this to me, the cops will get you for this."

"I doubt it," Porter said.

"You can't just hit people. You can't kidnap people, it's illegal."

"Oh, but you can just rape and kill little girls? That's what you're telling me?" Porter walked back over to the taped-up man and gave him an open-palm smack to his black eye. Quintana cried out in pain. "You're wasting my time, Abel."

"I didn't rape no kid. I didn't kill no kid. She was alive when I saw her."

"So you did see her?" Porter said. "I'm starting to get a little pissed at you."

Quintana looked frustrated.

"Look, I can stay out here all night. I didn't want to—shit, the mosquitos are killing me—but I don't have anything else to do. Maybe I need a hobby. Want to tell me about bowling?"

"Someone will come, someone will see."

Porter laughed. "You're so screwed and you can't even imagine. There's no one around for miles."

Porter moved behind the immobilized man. "You hear that?" Porter said, about nothing at all.

"What was that?"

"Bear. There's no telling if one will get you tonight or not. I figure we have time, since you're not going anywhere until you tell me what I want to know. You'll be out here for days in the Florida heat, with no food or water. What if you have to shit?" Porter feigned a shudder. "That would be the worst. Besides the bears, of course."

"I have kids. Please."

"So? Think they need a scumbag like you around?"

"I'm not a scumbag. I just... I didn't know what else to do." Quintana's head sagged against the electrical tape.

"Boo-hoo. You still aren't answering my question. What happened when Danny got off your bus?"

Quintana was quiet for several minutes. Porter let him be. Sometimes when people were at a tipping point, it was best to let them fall on their own. Finally, the balding man spoke. "You're not gonna kill me?"

"Sorry?"

"If I tell you, how do I know you won't kill me? You brought me all the way out here. I saw your face; I could tell the cops. How do I know you won't kill me to make sure you don't get into trouble?"

"I'm not too worried about it. If you tell the cops, they may talk to me. I'll deny I did anything, and there's no evidence to prove I was ever here," Porter said.

Quintana didn't look away. He wanted to be convinced. Convinced that telling whatever secret he was harboring could get him out of this situation alive.

"Look, if you tell the cops I will find you and kill you. Is that what you want to hear? Keep your mouth shut. Simple, really. You weren't hard to track down the first time; I imagine you can't run too far. If I kill you, your wife will probably start sending me a Christmas card to thank me. Who wants to be married to a kiddie murderer?"

"I'm not a murderer."

"Doesn't matter. What I'm telling you is this: I could easily kill you out here. And I would get away with it. I could find you and kill you later and I would still get away with it. It doesn't matter. The only hope you have of getting out of this alive is to speak up, unless you want your wife to be a widow."

Quintana looked at Porter and was silent again, but this time only for thirty seconds. Then he caught Porter's eye and spoke. "It was my brother. Damn it. My brother took her."

"Good. Now we're getting somewhere. Who's your brother? Give me a name."

"Hector. Hector Quintana."

Porter looked at him for a moment. "Hector? Hector from the Acres? That's your brother?"

"Yes."

"And the cops didn't realize the two of you were related?"

"He never talked to them. No one else would, all they knew about him was his first name."

Miss Leona was right, Porter thought; *it was the devil she knew*. "So, Hector took Danny. How did you figure into this?"

"All I did was let him onto the bus. He took her and he walked her to his car. There were no other kids around."

"I thought Miss Leona usually picked Danny up. How did you know she wouldn't be there?"

"I didn't. He called me, told me he was coming onto the bus and to shut up and do what he said. All I had to do was let him walk the girl off the van."

Porter sat down on the burned-out steps and thought for a

few moments. Things weren't making complete sense to him. He doubted he would be able to get the full story from Quintana, but he still didn't know enough. "How many times have you done something like this for Hector?"

"Just the once. Never any other times."

"Why? Why would you let him take the girl?" Porter said.

Abel looked embarrassed. "He's my little brother but... I know how he is. He could hurt me. Maybe kill me. If you knew what he did to our father..."

"I don't give a shit about your dad," Porter said.

"I know, I know..."

"So you *are* a scumbag. You let your brother take a girl. An innocent little girl."

Quintana was silent. Porter glared at him.

"Yes."

"Yes, what?" Porter said.

"I'm a scumbag."

"That's what I thought." Porter stood up and walked over to Abel Quintana. "Where did he take the girl?"

"I don't know. I don't know. All I did was let him take her."

"*All* you did?" Porter said.

Quintana didn't say anything. There wasn't anything else to say.

Porter stood in front of Quintana. He looked him over for a moment, then drew his pistol. He lifted it and pressed it into Quintana's nose. The man's breath grew short and ragged.

"I thought—I thought... you... said—"

"I changed my mind. Unless you have something else you can tell me, I don't see why we should keep dragging this out," Porter said.

"I don't—I don't ... know... anything... I don't know... I don't know..." repeated Abel Quintana, with his eyes closed. "I just... want... to see my... kids... my... kids... kids..."

Porter regarded him for a moment. He was telling the truth. Porter had wanted to take one last prod for any latent info, but Quintana had none.

"Tell you what, Abel. I think you've told me all you're going to." Porter slipped his Glock back in its holster. "I don't know what you're so scared for. I told you I wasn't going to kill you."

Quintana opened his eyes. He was still breathing fast, but no longer seemed to be on the verge of blacking out. "You aren't?"

"No."

"You're gonna let me go?"

"Shit, no. I never said that. You still have to pay for what you've done. I figure a little time out will do you good. In a couple days, I may call the cops and tip them off that you're out here."

"A couple days?"

"Yeah, more or less. I'll play it by ear."

"Please, Porter, just cut me loose now. Please. I want to see my kids. I won't do anything, just be with my kids and work every day a—"

"I didn't tell you? You have to quit your job. One of the terms of our deal. I just added it."

"If I quit, I won't be able to make a living."

"I don't give a good damn," Porter said. He placed his face inches from Abel Quintana's. "You never drive that bus again. Whenever I let you out of here, you go home, get your family, and move. Your Tampa privileges are revoked. *Entiende?*"

Quintana hesitated before answering.

"Listen to me. If I ever see you again, our deal is off. You know what that means?"

"I understand."

"Convince me," Porter said.

"If you ever see me, you'll kill me."

"Good." Porter walked away from Quintana and didn't look back. He hadn't brought anything with him, so he walked past the still-running van and kept going. He made his way to the metal gate and hopped over it. When he got to the street, he couldn't see Abel Quintana or the van's headlights in the dark. He looked left and right and walked left. He reached into his pocket for his phone, shut the voice recording off, and redialed the last number.

"Hello?" a groggy voice said.

"Tina. It's Porter. I need a ride. Bring a bottle of water, too."

SEVENTEEN

NINETY MINUTES PASSED before Rivera met Porter. He had walked back to the main road, to the dilapidated gas station he'd passed earlier. He was sitting on a large windowsill under the front window of the station when she pulled up. She wasn't in a county car, Porter could see by the license plate as he walked over and slid into the passenger seat.

"Spill it. You call me at one in the morning, you tell me you have info, you get me to drive all the way out here. Talk. Now."

"I told you I was going to call you later. You can't say I didn't give you a heads up. Got that water?"

"Come on, Porter," she said as she tossed him a bottle.

"Talked to Abel Quintana."

"Where?"

"He's in a field a couple miles from here."

"Are you kidding me? You call me out here because you killed a guy? Porter, I'm a cop, I can't—"

"Will you shut up a minute? He's not dead. He was very much alive when I left him."

"Left him where?"

"In a field, like I told you."

Rivera looked frustrated. "Okay, I'll bite. How did Quintana get into the field?"

"I kidnapped him."

Rivera looked like her head was going to explode. She screamed at Porter about being an accessory and losing her job, in colorful language.

Porter cut her off. "Listen, I'm already in your car. If what I tell you is bogus, you can just drive me to jail. Charge me with something. Waking up a detective on her day off or something. We have a long ride, so you might as well relax and listen."

Rivera took a few deep breaths. Once Porter knew she was listening to him, he told her the story, starting at Quintana's house and ending in the field. He left nothing out. When she seemed dubious, he played the recording from his phone.

"You know none of that confession is admissible in court, right? It's no good. I mean, you were a cop, I take it you know what the law is."

"I wasn't a cop. I was a federal agent. There's a difference."

"Fine, you were a fed. The evidence is still shit, no matter what you want to call yourself."

"Believe me, I know the confession is no good. That's fine, that's not why I got it," Porter said.

"It's not fine with me. The only reason I agreed to help you was because you told me you'd give me a case. This isn't breaking a case."

"You're thinking too small. Hector Quintana took the girl, do you doubt that?"

"How can I?" Rivera said. "His damn brother just said he did."

"So we agree. This is just the first step. I need to talk to Hector and find out what he did with her. Trust me, you'll get a better case, something much bigger than Abel Quintana."

Rivera was silent for a few minutes, her face illuminated by the dashboard display. Her hair, down and curly the first time Porter had seen her, was still wet and pulled into a bun. He noticed a dimple in her chin he'd missed during their first meeting.

"Let's say I agree with your bullshit logic. What's your next move?"

"I need a shower," Porter said.

"You're right about that. I hope I can get the smell out of my car."

"If you just got molested by a colony of mosquitos, you'd be in rough shape too."

"I'm not worried about your sensitive skin," Rivera said. "Man up a little. Tell me what your plan is."

"Shit, there is no plan. Not yet, at least. Let me talk to Hector, then I'll take it from there. I do need you to do something for me, though," Porter said.

"The ride isn't enough?"

"Can you get me everything else you can on the Acres? I mean everything. You had a little bit of info in Danny's file, but I need it all."

Rivera rolled her head back and forth for a few moments. "Yeah, I can do that. I'll call your boy Ruas back and ask him for whatever they can give me. I imagine he won't have a problem doing it if he knows it's for you." Rivera was quiet for a few minutes. "Do you think that girl's still alive?"

Porter was looking out the window and didn't answer.

"Porter?"

"I thought you were only worried about closing the case. What's it matter to you whether you find her alive or dead?"

"Because I'm not a heartless bitch."

Porter stared out the window. The landscape had grown less rural and there were large shopping centers with twenty-four-hour superstores. He never understood why people needed the option to get a kiwi at three a.m.

"You think I am? That's bullshit and you know it. I work the coldest cases in the world. Every day, I come to work and stare at pictures of people. Dozens of people, hell, hundreds. All of those people are gone. Here one day and disappeared the next. Their family can't find them. I can't find them. They're just gone."

Porter wasn't looking at her, but she had his attention.

"I shuffle papers around, make sure that their body hasn't turned up on a beach or in a shallow grave in the woods, then I put the case file back in my filing cabinet and move on to the next one. All day. That's all I can do. It's the worst job ever. I have to pretend like I don't care. I have to pretend—every time I see a little kid's smiling face, missing teeth or covered in ice cream—that they're just a file number."

"I understand," Porter said.

"How can you even begin to? Don't try to pacify me."

"When I was still on the job, I worked a bunch of child porn cases. Going after the distributors is one thing. But finding the manufacturers? Kicking in a door and recognizing a bed or a couch you saw in a video where a kid's being..." Porter turned from the window and looked at Rivera. "I get it."

"It's the worst. I can't even hope I'll find any of these kids, because they're all dead or tied up in a basement being used as a sex doll. The reality of that would break me. I have a son."

"I know."

"How did you... never mind."

The pair rode in silence for several minutes before Porter spoke up. "No."

"No, what?"

"I don't think Danisha Hill is still alive," Porter said.

EIGHTEEN

RIVERA DROPPED Porter off a few hundred yards away from the bowling alley. It was dark on the side of the road and the crickets were out in full effect.

"Just in case there are cameras. I can't have my license showing up."

"I get it. Let me know what you find out about the Acres as soon as you can."

"Until you sign my paycheck, I don't work for you. I'll get it done when I can. Until then, don't do anything stupid, you got me?"

"Define stupid."

Rivera let out an exasperated sigh and Porter shut the door. He watched her drive away, feeling like she might have made a good partner, in his former life. At the very least, she hadn't turned him in for kidnapping Quintana. Yet.

He walked up the main road until he came to the gravel lot of the bowling alley, then turned toward his Yukon across the street. He hit the door-unlock and hopped in, starting the truck to get the air conditioner going. He was drenched in sweat, mosquito-bitten, and hungry. Porter pulled out of the lot intending to head west and back to his house, but instead found himself driving north.

Staying on Florida Avenue, he followed a familiar path that took him to Lutz. Going west on Crenshaw Lake road, he was hit with a feeling of nostalgia. He had often taken this way as a teenager. Late for curfew and nervously checking the clock in his beat-up Plymouth, he'd take this twisted road at a higher rate of speed than was safe. Still, it was better than getting busted coming home late.

Crenshaw Lake spit Porter out on Van Dyke Road, which led him to a large subdivision. He hadn't planned on going, but now that he was here, there was no reason not to stop in. Following a familiar combination of turns led him to the front of his parents' house, and a parking spot he'd used as a teenager two decades ago.

Retrieving the spare key from its hiding spot, Porter slipped it into the door and felt the tumblers give way. He paused for a moment to prepare and then pushed the door open.

A shrill alarm went off as the burglar alarm snapped into action. Porter closed the door and took several long strides over to the keypad. Punching in the code, he was rewarded with silence. He stood still for a moment, hoping he'd killed the alarm in time.

There was no noise coming from the master bedroom. Pleased that he hadn't woken anyone, he took his shoes off at the front door and walked down a well-worn hallway to what used to be his room, now the guest room. Fortunately, his old dresser still had an accumulation of clothes from over the years.

Porter grabbed a towel from the hallway closet and headed to the bathroom. His family had owned the house for twenty years, and in all that time the bathroom hadn't changed. It wasn't dirty or run-down, just getting older.

Vintage, Porter thought.

He took his sweaty clothes off, made a neat pile on the floor, and set his gun on the bathroom counter. He turned the handle and waited a few minutes, then stepped in, letting the water wash away the grime of the evening. It was too bad it couldn't wash away his memory of Abel Quintana.

Finishing up, Porter grabbed the towel and stepped out of the tub. He regarded himself for a moment in the mirror, pulling at the dark circles under his eyes. He wrapped the towel around his waist, grabbed the fresh clothes, and stepped back down the hallway to the guest room. On his way, he detected the faint aroma of coffee.

Shit, he thought.

Porter shut the door and finished drying off. Putting on the clean clothes made him feel like a new man. Throwing the towel over his shoulder, he went back to the bathroom to grab his dirty clothes, but found only the Glock. Porter slipped the pistol into his back pocket and went to the kitchen.

Turning the corner, he saw a woman pouring two mugs of coffee. Behind her, the washing machine was running.

"Pretty efficient for four o'clock in the morning," Porter said. "Sorry I woke you up."

"I was already awake," she said.

"Sure you were."

"I'm an old woman. I don't need much sleep."

"You aren't old yet, knock it off."

"Shut up, kid. You'll be old one day. Just wait. Then when you tell people you're old and they don't believe you, you'll see how it feels."

They laughed.

"I noticed you have your... blaster? Do you kids say blaster? Is that the slang?"

"Sure, Mom, we say blaster sometimes."

"See, I'm old but I'm hip. I know things," she said.

"I bet you do."

There was silence for a few minutes as they doctored their respective coffees. Porter didn't like coffee. The taste wasn't too bad, but it always gave him the shits. Still, when you wake your mother up at four in the morning and she makes you coffee, you oblige.

"Anything you want to talk about?" she said.

"Worried because you saw the gun?"

"Not really," she said. "I know you always carry, despite how I feel about them."

"I've never understood how a retired federal agent could be scared of guns."

"Shut up, kid. I'm not scared of guns. I just don't need to have them around all the time. I used to tell your father the same thing, but he never listened. Remember when I found that revolver in his sock drawer?"

"Yeah, you were pretty hot about it," Porter said.

"He knew how I felt about them, so at least he tried to hide them from me. I didn't want you boys around all that stuff. A fat lot of good it did me."

"We didn't turn out that bad," Porter said.

"Maybe. How was California?"

"It was... unique."

"Any trouble?"

"Nothing I couldn't handle," Porter said.

"That's not an answer."

Porter swirled the coffee around in his cup. "Some trouble."

"Ross told me it was too late for that last girl. What was her name?"

"Evanna," Porter said.

"Well, Evanna's not your fault. You know that, right? Even though you tried, it isn't your fault. You did the best you could do."

"I know. I'm not ate up about it or anything, but it would have been nice to get her while she was still alive."

His mother didn't answer, instead putting some fabric softener in the machine before leaning on the counter. "So, what are you up to? What's got you up so late?"

"I kidnapped a guy tonight," Porter said.

NINETEEN

PORTER RECOUNTED the events of the evening and a general overview of what he was working on with Ross.

"What a low-life piece of trash," his mother said. "How could he just serve that poor girl up to them like that?"

"I'm not sure. He deserves worse than what he got. I'll bet he isn't even tied up anymore," Porter said.

"Rivera?"

"Yeah. I'm sure she called in an anonymous tip to the podunk sheriff out there," Porter said.

"The girl has her own conscience to worry about."

"I don't blame her. She's gotta worry about her job," Porter said. "If it were up to me, I'd have left him there."

"I bet you would have."

There was a comfortable silence as they cleaned up the coffee mugs.

"You know I don't question your judgment, right?" she said.

Porter nodded.

"Ever since you were a boy you always did what you thought was right. It never much mattered if it was actually the right thing to do or not. Those are two different concepts, you know? Two different things. Your dad was the same way."

Porter said nothing.

"You can't arrest people anymore. Maybe you need to let the police handle this. All you have to do is give them the info you have, and maybe they can get their heads out of the dirt and fix it," she said.

"Believe me, I'd rather do that. This job isn't paying me nearly enough for all this hassle. If I thought there was a chance they'd get to the bottom of things, I'd let them. We both know the cops would have never found out what Abel Quintana knew."

"Never is a long time, son."

Porter started to reply but bit his tongue.

His mother got up and walked across the kitchen to the table where he sat. She gave him a kiss on the forehead. "I want you to think about where you're going with this. I know you're willing to go all the way down the rabbit hole. Just be sure to have a way to get back out when you're done."

Porter nodded.

"What are you going to do now?"

"Thinking about using the guest bed. I'm beat," Porter said.

"I figured as much. Get some rest and we'll talk later."

With that she left him alone in the kitchen. Porter knew she was worried but wouldn't show it. He stood and made sure the doors were locked, walked into the guest room, and fell into a fitful sleep.

TWENTY

THE STREAMING SUN on his face woke Porter. He rolled over and groped for his phone. He'd been asleep long enough. He took a leak and went to the living room, where everything was still quiet. There was a note on the television.

I had errands to run. I know you'll be gone when I get back. Think about what I said last night. Be careful.

Love, Mom

p.s. - The laundry fairy was here. Next time, she expects a tip.

Porter laughed and put on his clothes from the night before. He got his wallet and phone, then slipped his Glock back into his waistband. He locked the front door behind him and stepped into the day.

Shit, Porter thought, it's *already a sauna out here.*

He started his truck, letting it idle and cool off while he debated what to do with the day. His phone interrupted his thoughts.

"How did things go?" Ross said.

"Wouldn't you like to know."

"Yes, as a matter of fact, I would. Did you find anything out?"

"Maybe."

"Don't dick around with me, I'm dying here."

"You buy me breakfast and I'll tell you everything. Sound good?"

"Deal," Ross said in an instant.

"I'll see you in a bit." Porter eased the Yukon onto the main streets and headed to Ross's house.

ROSS HAD BOUGHT his home when he was nineteen. He'd always been a saver: birthdays, Christmas, paychecks from the grocery store, odd jobs around town, he kept it all. During Ross's sophomore year in college he'd decided he wanted a house. This was during the days when Tampa had been awash with fore-closed homes. Every neighborhood had dozens of empty houses. The banks did all they could to sell them off at a deep discount and salvage capital.

Ross bought the worst house in the best neighborhood. It had belonged to a pair of formerly married lawyers. Their divorce was ugly, and between the wife destroying all the surfaces and the husband selling off all the appliances, the house was shot. The country club community had been skeptical of the young kid moving into their midst, but it didn't take long for them to realize that Ross not only had the best of intentions, but the capital and stubbornness to see a home renovation through. The first year he owned the house, he put all his free time into fixing it. Having no background in construction, he learned as he went.

Drywall was taken down to the studs; new flooring, cabinets, lights, plumbing, and even a new roof were added. Ross learned and did it all, and Porter helped every step of the way. Now the house was the best on the block, and everyone on the block had long since come to appreciate their fastidious neighbor.

Porter hit the call box at the gate of the community. There was no reply, just a high-pitched beep, and the gate pulled open on its automated track.

Pulling up in front, he found his friend looking fresh with a large coffee in his hand.

"You look like shit," Ross said.

"Me? You looked in a mirror lately? Where the hell did your hairline go?" Porter said.

"How can you be so savage, so early in the morning? Unless it's late for you. What did you do last night?"

"Did you order food?" Porter said. "I'm dying here."

"It's Sunday morning. No one delivers food now. People are at church and stuff. Maybe you should look into it."

"Dude, don't play games with me right now. I'll get back in the truck..."

"Relax, I have food in the fridge," Ross said.

Ross's cooking— bacon and eggs and toast—was just as good as ordering out, maybe better. Porter was stuffed and was feeling a little sleepy when he moved over to the couch.

"Coffee?"

"Nah, I'm good," Porter said.

"That's right, it gives you the shits."

"It does, and I already had some earlier. Didn't crap my brains out. It was nice."

"Where did you get coffee?"

Porter told Ross about going to his mother's house.

"Nice of you to go see her. I swear I talk to her more often than you do."

"That's not true," Porter said, wondering if it was or not.

"I like to check in on her, you know? I know the last few years have been rough."

"Things happen. People die," Porter said.

"I know, I know, but your dad wasn't very old."

"The men in my family don't live too long," Porter said. "It's kind of a thing with us."

"Maybe you'll buck the trend."

"Maybe so."

"Why you go over there so late?" Ross said.

Porter told Ross about Abel Quintana, the bowling alley, the field, and getting a ride from Rivera. He left nothing out.

When he was done, Ross was shaking.

"You just kidnapped him? Why didn't you call me? I would have come and gotten you. Probably shouldn't have called Rivera, she's a cop."

"I wish we could stop saying kidnapping. Quintana's a grown man; is kidnapping still the word to use? Why don't we have a better word for taking an adult against their wishes?"

"Don't dick around, I'm serious."

"Me too. Vocabulary sucks sometimes. How do you feel about man-napping?"

"Porter..."

He leaned forward on the couch. "See? This is why I didn't call you. You worry too much. You would have given yourself an ulcer by the time you got out there to pick me up. Besides, I wanted to get Rivera involved," Porter said.

"Why?"

"I think at some point I'm going to need her resources. I wanted to expose her a little to see how she would take it," Porter said.

"How did she take it?"

"Remarkably well," Porter said, "for being woken up in the middle of the night."

"How did you know she wouldn't arrest you?"

"I didn't, but I had a feeling. First, I had Quintana in a

county that was out of her jurisdiction. Granted, most cops can arrest in any county in their state if they identify a commonly-known law being broken—"

"Like kidnapping," Ross said.

"Let's call it man-napping. She could have arrested me, but that's so much paperwork. Then she'd have to tell people why she came out to see me in the first place. It makes her look complicit."

"You did that on purpose, didn't you? Were you going to blackmail her? Have her come out to a crime scene in the middle of the night so you can hang it over her head?" Ross said.

"No. She seems decent enough, I wouldn't do that to her. But she's not stupid, she knows the drill. Besides, Quintana's a scumbag. Even if Rivera did get her panties in a twist about it, how mad would someone be at me once they found out what he did to Danny? I'd get convicted of something, but by the time Steven Ajo fought it for me and we pleaded things down, I think the worst I'd be looking at would be an assault charge. That's not including what would happen if the media found out."

"And you thought about all that before you kidna—"

"Man-napped."

"Fine, before you man-napped Quintana?" Ross said.

"I thought enough about it to figure it was a good plan."

Ross sighed and stood up from the chair opposite the couch Porter was lounging on, and went back to the kitchen to refill his coffee mug. On his way back in, he stopped to lean on the large granite island. "So what do we do now?"

Porter didn't move. He was too stuffed with eggs. "We don't do anything."

Ross looked annoyed but didn't say anything.

"I wasn't kidding when I told you I wanted you to stay out of it. You're too emotional about it. You aren't thinking straight."

"I'm not thinking straight? You kidnapped a guy last night and there's a problem with my thinking?"

Porter didn't say anything, instead glancing to the television.

"I'm not emotional," Ross muttered.

"What's that?

"I said I'm not emotional."

"You seem pretty butt-hurt right now. What would you have done if I'd told you I was going to smack Quintana in the face with a plunger handle?" Porter said.

"That's a crazy thing to do, and I would have stopped you."

"Tried to stop me," Porter said.

"Yes, Porter, I would have *tried* to stop you."

"That's exactly my point. I needed to get that asshole to talk to me, he did, now we can move on. Stop all the hand-wringing. No one needs to cry for Abel Quintana."

"I'm not, I just can't understand what to do next. He told you about his brother, now what?"

"There isn't a big magic trick to it. I just need to keep asking people questions. Once I find out as much about Hector Quintana as I can, I'm sure I'll come up with something," Porter said.

"I'm not a cop," Ross said.

"I hope not. You're investing a substantial part of my portfolio," Porter said.

"Shut up, asshole. I'm trying to say I don't know what kind of stuff you want Rivera to get for you. I'm trying to follow along, despite the fact that you think I'm an emotional mess. Two heads have to be better than one, even if it is a head as big as yours. Fill me in."

"I'm looking for everything. Any tiny bit of information that helps us figure out who this guy is, what he does, and who he does it with. His criminal history, previous addresses, family history. How many kids does he have? Where do his baby mamas live? Where did he live in New York? What did he do there? Why did he come to Florida? What kind of warrants does he have? Where did he do time? Who did he do time with? What kind of car does he drive? Any shred of information we can find can only help."

"What's the point of all that? Suppose you get all this info, then what? Hector's not going to tell you anything. Why would he? He doesn't want to go to prison," Ross said.

"I think a conversation with him will be productive."

"Why?"

"I can be persuasive," Porter said.

TWENTY-ONE

ROSS AND PORTER cleaned up the dishes from breakfast and then watched football for the rest of the afternoon. Neither of them spoke about Danny, or Abel or Hector Quintana. The Tampa Bay Buccaneers were getting slaughtered and they spent most of their time arguing calls against the TV referees, as if the refs could hear them. Around six thirty, Porter got a call.

"Hello," Porter said.

"Porter, it's Rivera."

"Hey, Tina. What's going on?"

"It's Christina, asshole, how many times have I told you? Are you hard of hearing or just stupid?"

"Why? Christina is three syllables, Tina's only two. I like the economy of speech."

"Just don't," she said.

"You didn't call me to argue with me, did you?" Porter said.

"No, but I'll take the time to if you don't stop calling me that. I'm not playing, I'll kick your big ass."

"Excuse me, detective."

"Listen, I've got what I can on Hector Quintana, do you want it or not?"

"Yes, detective, I'd like that very much," Porter said.

"Now you're just being stupid. Where can I meet you to give you this shit?"

"I'm at a friend's place; do you want to come over here?"

"What are we, in college? I'm not coming to hang out," Rivera said.

"Your loss. We're going to order pizza," Porter said.

"Just meet me somewhere."

"Dinner," Porter said.

"Dinner?"

"Yeah, let's get dinner."

"Porter, I just want—" Rivera said.

"What, you don't eat?"

"Of course I eat," Rivera said.

"So let's kill two birds with one stone. I'm never going to be able to get the thought of pizza out of my head right now."

Rivera sighed into the phone. "You know, you can just come by the office on Monday, it doesn't matter to me."

"Yeah, but then I'll have to see those guys at the door again. You don't want to put me through that again, do you?"

"Fine, just make it quick."

"There's this great place in Ybor City, off Seventh Avenue. Shorty's?"

"I used to eat there when I worked side jobs. It's not too far," Rivera said.

"Great," Porter said. "Thirty minutes?"

"Fine. Don't make me wait." The phone disconnected.

"Was that Rivera?" Ross said.

"She's got some more info to give me. I'm gonna meet up with her and grab it. Maybe we can go through it later. Mind if I use your shower?"

"Shower? To talk to Rivera? Dude... are you trying to get laid?" Ross said.

Porter laughed. He showered and changed clothes. He was at Ross's place so often that he had a drawer full of personal items in a spare bedroom. Back when he was married, Trisha had not-so-jokingly told him that in fifty years, he and Ross were going to be the old married couple. He hadn't argued.

Porter walked out of the spare room and found Ross lying on the couch watching the evening football highlight show. "I'm out."

"Let me know if you come up with anything from Rivera. Like the clap." Ross had a smile on his face.

Porter laughed. "You feeling lonely? You could always call Tessa..."

Ross grumbled behind him as he shut the door and walked out the door into the humid evening.

It wasn't a long drive to Ybor City. Porter spent most of the ride trying to get in front of the questions he imagined Rivera might ask. He found it easier to have a conversation with someone if he had a cursory idea of where the talk might go. He figured Rivera would scold him about Abel Quintana, then admit to calling the local sheriff to set him free. Porter hoped there would be more info about Hector than admonishments about his methods.

There were some things he had no intention of changing.

Pulling off the highway, he turned onto Seventh Avenue, past the numerous nightclubs and bars of Ybor City. A bit like Tampa's homegrown version of Bourbon Street, Ybor was packed with places to have fun and get into trouble.

When he was younger, he had been a bouncer in most of these places. It was a great job for a college kid, especially a big guy with a temper. Porter had stopped when he went to work for Homeland Security. The pay as a federal agent was better than that of a knuckle-dragging bouncer, so there wasn't much of a competition.

Pulling into the familiar parking lot, he found Rivera's car already sitting there.

She must be anxious to get this over with, Porter thought.

He got out of the car, patted himself to make sure he had his wallet, phone, and gun, then headed into the pizza place.

Porter was greeted by a welcome smell. He wasn't sure if it was the dough or the sauce, but he loved it. His stomach lurched and he couldn't wait to eat. On the left side was a wall of stainless steel pizza ovens; on the right, booths, and in the middle several tables with their chairs pushed in around them. Porter made a detour to the counter adjacent to the ovens.

"Welcome to Shorty's. Help you?" said a thin, pretty blonde girl with tattoos.

"Yeah, I'm meeting the girl that's sitting over there. Did she order anything?"

"Nope. Just water."

"Okay, let me get a large pepperoni and Italian sausage."

"No problem," the blonde said.

Porter paid and got the little plastic number to put on the table for the pie delivery. He grabbed a cup for water and walked over to Rivera.

"You didn't think I'd come to Shorty's and not eat, did you?" Porter said.

"I don't care what you do, Porter. I've done my part. Here's the file, I have to go."

"Suit yourself, but I'm not looking at any of that until I eat pizza. It might as well be hieroglyphics."

"Porter—"

"Not doing it," he said.

"Fine," Rivera said. She gathered up her bag and pushed her chair away from the table.

"Come on, detective. Don't you want to at least explain this crap to me?"

"I'd be glad to, but you seem like you want to waste my time."

"I'm not wasting time, I need to eat. You don't want me to die, do you?"

"From the looks of you, you aren't in danger of starving to death," Rivera said.

"Ouch. That's how I get treated for making you wait?"

"And waking me up in the middle of the night. And getting me to work on my day off..."

"I get it. At least just keep me company until the food gets here. Then you can leave me. Come on, sit back down. I'll look like a weirdo all by myself."

Rivera looked toward the door, then back to her chair, and slid back into her seat. "You look like a weirdo regardless."

Porter looked at Rivera and Rivera looked around the restaurant. There were nostalgic posters from movies and television shows and comic books on the walls.

Rivera spoke first. "What's the deal with Power Man? Why is he rocking that terrible tiara?"

"First off, Power Man doesn't wear a tiara. It's a headband. It's just a little shiny. Second, Power Man is awesome. Who wouldn't want super strength and diamond-hard skin? I used to read his books when I was a kid," Porter said.

"Only when you were a kid?"

"I may still have a few of them somewhere."

"What did Power Man do?" Rivera said.

"He beat people up. He had a partner who was a karate expert. Maybe kung fu, I can't remember. They worked together, the 'Heroes for Hire.' People came to them with problems and paid them and they fixed the problems. Kind of like the Equalizer," Porter said.

"Is that a show? Never saw it."

Porter shook his head. "Did you have no childhood, woman?"

"Not really. Dad bailed and Mom worked three jobs so we could survive. I raised my brother and sister and didn't have time for movies."

Porter didn't say anything. He hadn't meant to open up a sore spot for Rivera. He enjoyed needling her, but didn't think she was at all bad. A little uptight, but he liked her.

After a much shorter silence, the blonde girl from the counter brought the pizza. It was enormous, easily two feet across. It was on a giant metal platform with legs so that it hovered above the tabletop and didn't take up any space. Porter grabbed a plate and handed one to Rivera.

"No thanks."

"Suit yourself," Porter said. "Your loss."

There was a brief pause, then Rivera reached for a plate. "Yeah, you have a point. It is Shorty's. Just don't get grease on the file."

There were another few minutes of silence as they ate. Rivera was much slower than Porter. He finished his piece, wiped his hands on a napkin, and reached over to her side and took the green file sitting there.

"So what did all your hard work at the office tell you about Hector Quintana that we didn't know yesterday?"

"He's bad news," Rivera said through a mouthful of pizza.

"I said something that we *didn't* know. We already knew that."

"That's what you think. Check his criminal history. It's all in there. He started out young—convictions for assault, conspiracy, strong-arm robbery, and involuntary manslaughter all before the age of eighteen."

"You got the juvenile records? How'd you manage that?"

"I know a guy who works in New York. We met at a cop

conference in Atlanta a couple years ago and kept in touch. I called him this morning; he was working a side job so he looked into things for me," Rivera said.

"Hector was a scumbag before he was even legal. I'm assuming he got out of whatever juvie home he was in when he turned eighteen?"

"Yep. Clean slate. He didn't waste any more time. More convictions for assault and petty drug stuff. Then his criminal history sort of trails off."

"Makes sense," Porter said.

"Sure, the older guys in the gang aren't going to get in trouble themselves and risk going to real, pound-me-in-the-ass prison when they can just let all the underage guys do the dirty work."

"Pound-me-in-the-ass prison?"

"Yeah, you know, grown-up prison?" Rivera said without missing a beat.

"I know what you meant. An old partner of mine used to say that. You just took me back a little bit, that's all." Porter smiled. "Where is Abel during all this?"

"Split town. He's older by about seven years. It looks like he left New York for Tampa as soon as he could, right when he was eighteen or so. He missed little brother's wild streak. Get this. You want to hear something even crazier?" Rivera said, leaning across the table.

Porter looked up from his slice.

"My guy in the NYPD said Hector was run out of New York for killing his own father."

TWENTY-TWO

"I GET IT," Porter said. "I can see it."

"You get it? How? Since when does killing your father make sense?"

"Cronus. Oedipus. Ramsay Snow," Porter said.

"What? Is that a joke or something?" Rivera said.

"Never mind. When I finally got to have a talk with Abel, one of the reasons he was scared of his brother had something to do with their father. Hector killing their dad might have left an impression."

"'Killing' might not accurately describe it. Apparently Hector had some of his guys abduct his father. They killed him, then chopped him up and put him in a barrel. No one found him until the spring when the ground thawed and some joggers saw a fifty-five-gallon drum sticking out of the ground."

"The ground's too hard to dig into during the winter. His guys must have gotten lazy," Porter said.

"I guess so. Dad was a criminal too, so it was an easy match on the DNA."

"What was his dad up to?"

"He was a mid-level guy in some organization or another.

His bosses weren't happy that Hector killed him. The cops couldn't pin it on Hector, but everyone heard what happened, since Hector couldn't keep his mouth shut," Rivera said.

"That explains the Florida move."

"How does that explain the Florida move?" Rivera said.

"Payback, right? I assume that Hector's father was part of the stronger gang: probably bigger, better, and more established. They'd just kill a guy for killing one of their members, like a show of power."

"Sure—don't mess with us," Rivera said.

"Exactly. In this case, it's a family business. No one wants to get in the middle of that; that's a messy situation. Combined with the thought that Hector's gang wouldn't want to war with the original gangsters, then it makes sense. Rather than kill Hector and make a bigger mess, they just exile him to Florida. Out of sight, out of mind, and both parties move on. It's gotta be better than open war," Porter said.

"Feels like you're reaching."

"Maybe, but think about it. Hector must have left New York with both gangs' blessings, or someone would have killed him before he left. Hell, someone would have got him down here if they really wanted to. He isn't exactly laying low," Porter said.

"At the end of the day, it doesn't matter why. He's here and he's a problem," Rivera said.

"He might not be for too much longer," Porter said. "I'm going to talk to him, see if he'll tell me what he did with Danny."

"Does it involve another kidnapping? No more kidnappings, Porter."

"I'm working on making man-napping happen," Porter said.

"What the hell are you talking about?"

"Man-nap? I think it fits better... never mind. Let me take a look at all this and see what I come up with," Porter said as he gestured to the file on the table.

Christina Rivera pushed the rest of the papers over to Porter, and he collected them in the file. She leaned against the chair back and looked at Porter as he shuffled through the papers. "I called Sheriff Rae's office anonymously and told them where to find Abel."

"I figured you would," Porter said. "I'm not mad."

"I don't care if you are. I just can't let someone die tied up in a field. That's not what cops do."

"I wouldn't know," Porter said. "I was never a cop."

"Well, I'm not sure it's in the handbook for federal agents, either." She picked at a piece of pizza. "You know this is pretty far out of my comfort zone, right?"

"What, dinner with a big brown guy? Mixed guys are people, too."

Rivera cracked a rare smile. "Shut up, stupid. You know exactly what I mean. The kidnap—"

Porter raised his eyebrows.

"— abduction. How about abduction? I'm not saying man-napping, that's so dumb."

"If it's the best I can get, I'll take it."

"The abduction is a bit much for me. It's all a little vigilante. Not really my speed."

"I don't blame you. I'm not going to ask you to do anything you don't want to do. That's why I'm not mad you told someone about Abel Quintana. You have to do whatever lets you sleep at night."

"How do you sleep?" Rivera said.

"It's not the best. I think I have sleep apnea. I may need one of those sleep studies."

Rivera gave Porter an exasperated look. "You know what I mean."

Porter knew what she meant and decided to be honest.

"I sleep like a baby. Better than a baby—I sleep like the

dead. I don't lose one minute of shut-eye over those people, or waste one second thinking about what I do to them. Abel Quintana isn't even on my mind."

"There's a 'them'?"

"Quite a few of 'them' if I'm being straight with you. Be honest with me, Rivera, we all know when someone is a shitbag. You feel it. You just know it."

Rivera nodded.

"A while back, I decided to make things hard on those types of people. If I run into one while I'm poking around at something, I don't mind making their life hard for them. Abel let a little girl be abducted. I don't feel the least bit bad for smacking him around and tying him up. He's lucky he talked when he did, or things would have gotten worse for him."

Rivera shifted in her chair and leaned across the table to Porter. "It's just... I'm a cop. As corny as it sounds, I'm supposed to help people. That didn't feel like helping people."

"Depends on how you look at it. Think you'll be helping Miss Leona when we let her put her baby to rest?" Porter said.

"Danny's grandmother?"

"I saw the old lady break down. I mean, all the way down. How do you think she's sleeping at night?" Porter said. "I care more about that than some asshole like Abel Quintana."

Rivera didn't say anything, just sat picking at a piece of pizza. Porter went back to looking through the file.

"It says here that one of the cars linked to Hector is an old Hyundai. Doesn't seem like the kind of car a shot-caller would drive."

"It's not his; it belongs to one of his baby mamas. He drives the Caprice with the big rims," Rivera said, pointing to a printout of vehicle descriptions.

"Could you imagine putting more money into a set of wheels than a car?"

"Priorities," Rivera said, checking her watch. "I'm gonna take off. You good?"

"Very. Thanks for all this," Porter said, tapping his finger on the file.

"Sure. I'll get with Ruas in the morning and see if he has anything else on the Acres."

"Just let me know."

Rivera stood up and got her purse together. "I will."

Porter glanced at the giant pie. Seventy-five percent of it was untouched. "You want to take this home? I'm not going to eat it."

"I won't either."

"You have a son, right? Don't young men eat a lot? I know I did."

"Actually, that's nice of you to think of him. Surprising," Rivera said.

"What? I'm not always an asshole."

"That remains to be seen. In any event, Kevin's only eight. He isn't a bottomless pit yet."

"It'll happen," Porter said with a knowing look.

Rivera nodded, shouldered her purse, and headed to the exit. Porter watched her go.

TWENTY-THREE

PORTER LOOKED over the information in the file Rivera had brought him. When he was a federal agent, the thing that made his life easiest was all the databases he had access to. He could find out almost anything, from when a person had left the country last to their parents' addresses.

Rivera's file wasn't as exhaustive, but it was damn close.

The tattooed blonde from behind the counter came out to take the pizza and box it up. Moments later, she was back, giving Porter his leftovers and wishing him a good night. Porter noticed a tone in her voice that hadn't been there when he ordered. Taped face-down to the top of his box was a piece of paper.

It looks like dinner with your girlfriend didn't go so good. If you want, give me a call sometime. I'm sure I like pizza more than she does. - Ashley

Her number was on the bottom of the slip. Porter smiled.

He pulled the file together and stood to leave, adjusting the pistol in his waistband. Grabbing the box, he headed to the front door, giving Ashley a little wave on the way out. She smiled.

Stepping into the humid night, Porter looked left and right

down the road. It paid to make sure there wasn't anything crazy going on. Porter remembered seeing enormous brawls on this street; it was best to not get sucked into one of those. Tonight everything was clear.

Porter fired up his truck and backed out, pulling onto Seventh Avenue and stopping in the middle of the road. A homeless man sat in the doorway of a closed head shop, a dirty-looking black dog with him. Porter waved him over and waited while the man slowly stood up and limped to the Yukon.

"You're really homeless," Porter said.

"What kind of question is that?"

"It wasn't a question, it was a statement," Porter said.

"What kind of statement is that?" the man said.

"I didn't mean anything by it," Porter said. "I just noticed that you seem like you're actually living on the streets."

"What makes you so sure?"

"Your beard is filthy. The thing that bothers me about the average panhandler that hangs out at intersections and asks for money: If life is so tough and you're on the streets, how is your shirt clean? How are you clean-shaven every time I drive past you? Once in a while I would understand a clean shave, but your beard should be in some state of growth."

"It looks like your beard is in some state of growth," the man said.

Porter smiled. "Got me there. You like pizza?"

"Of course I like pizza. What am I, an alien?"

Porter handed the man the box, making sure to grab the note taped to the top. "It's sausage and pepperoni."

The man took the box warily and opened it up. Satisfied that it was pizza and not a bomb, he looked up at Porter. "Thanks."

"Be safe tonight." Porter pulled away, following a familiar route back to his side of town.

Lost in thought, he arrived at his neighborhood in short order. As he pulled onto his street, an out-of-place car stood out to him. It was several houses down, on the opposite side of the street. His neighbors had all been the same since he'd moved in. He knew their cars, as well as the cars of their frequent visitors.

The Hyundai didn't belong.

Porter slowed as he drove past and took a quick look in the passenger seat. It was Tattoo from the Acres. Then everything clicked. The Hyundai was on the list of cars that Rivera had given him.

Hector's guys were coming for him.

TWENTY-FOUR

PORTER CONTINUED ROLLING to his house, his mind working furiously.

They must have taken my plate down the day I was in the Acres. Not too tough to get someone's address from their plate. Abel Quintana must have talked. They know he told me Hector took Danny. Now they want to shut me up.

There were at least three guys in the car, and Porter hadn't been able to see into the driver's side rear of the car. There had to be four guys.

Definitely four guys.

Porter was working through his options. He could call the cops. They'd take twenty minutes to show up, then walk up to the car and identify everyone. Someone in the car was bound to have a warrant. The cops would take that guy and send the rest on their way. Then at some other random and inopportune time, the rest of them would come after Porter again. Maybe with more people next time.

Not a good plan.

He could park the Yukon and go into his house. Grab a bigger gun, go out the back and circle behind the car.

Then what? Shoot them all?

He was sure a jury would agree that was cold-blooded murder. Going to prison didn't sound too appealing.

Not a good plan. I could just go into the house. And wait. Then it's their move. If they come in, it'll be self-defense.

Not a great plan, but the best plan, given the circumstances. It would have to do.

Porter pushed the garage door opener before he got all the way into the driveway. As the door rolled up, he slammed the Yukon's shifter into park. By the time he turned the truck off and grabbed the garage door opener from his visor, the door was all the way open. He hopped out, careful not to look at the men parked down the street, and pushed the door-close button as soon as he stepped into the garage. The big door roared to life. Porter waited near the back wall with the interior garage light turned off, pistol drawn and by his side. When the garage door fully closed, he twisted the handle of the big metal door, locking it from the inside.

Porter stepped into his house and locked the interior garage door behind him. The lights were off, and he was selective about which ones he turned on. There was no reason to give his assailants any more information than he had to.

He walked to the front door and checked the lock. The door was metal, with a reinforced door jamb. No way the Acres boys were getting in that way.

Porter checked the large sliding glass door that went to the backyard. It wasn't much different from an average sliding glass door, except for some minor upgrades Porter had given it. He had installed a pair of flip-down latches to the outermost door. When they were down, there was no way to get the door opened, whether it was locked or unlocked. Porter glanced over and ensured the latches were in place. Porter had also applied a protective film to the glass. The film wasn't bulletproof, but it did keep the glass together if it shattered. It would be tough to get through the window in the sliding glass door.

Porter's bathroom was the only door left.

Looking from the front yard, Porter's bedroom was on the right side of the house, nearest the street. Behind it was the bathroom, which had a door that led out to the backyard. Porter never used the door, preferring to come and go to the backyard through the big slider near the kitchen.

Porter hadn't fortified this door the way he had some of the others in his house. He'd added a deadbolt, but other than that it was stock. He planned to do more to reinforce it one day, but the task had slipped away from him. This door would be the easiest place for the Acres boys to make entry. And it was a choke point that would funnel them through the long bathroom and into Porter's bedroom.

This was the best thing for Porter. Their numbers were irrelevant if they were stacked in a single-file line. And when they came, he'd be ready.

Walking over to the gun safe in the corner of his room, Porter punched a familiar code. The door popped open and he reached in and grabbed his AR-15. Porter had a silencer attached to the barrel of the rifle. The technical name for it was a suppressor, as the device didn't silence anything. Shots weren't movie-quiet, but the silencer took the edge off of the rifle's loud report. Porter found this appealing if he had to shoot in the confines of his house. Hearing damage was not on his to-do list.

Porter considered his fields of fire. His rifle's round would penetrate through an intermediate barrier like drywall less than his pistol or shotgun; that was science. Still, if he took a shot and missed his target, his round would end up somewhere. Porter didn't want to be the one to put his neighbors in danger, so he'd be careful if he could.

Behind Porter's house was a conservation area, a swamp full

of cypress trees that couldn't be cut down. There was nothing back there for miles. Porter wanted to be sure that all his shots went out of the rear of his house.

He couldn't help where the Acres boys' rounds went.

He grabbed several extra magazines from a shelf in the safe. Overkill, to be sure. There wasn't much chance that he would need all these rounds, but with four thugs coming into his house, he wasn't taking any chances.

He closed his gun safe, then sat in a chair in the corner of his room. His back was to the wall, and he could see the door in his bathroom through the reflection in the bathroom mirror. When they came for him, he would know. He would be ready.

THE PROBLEM with waiting for trouble was the waiting. Porter sat in the chair for two hours and heard nothing. No furtive sounds of hood rats creeping around his house, no noise as one of them chambered a round into a shotgun. The house was silent as a tomb.

I hope it's not mine, Porter thought. His eyes were heavy.

In a tense situation like this, there was a tendency to get an adrenaline dump. The problem is, the body can only keep that level of preparedness going for so long. Porter's body wanted to relax.

Glancing at his phone, Porter saw that it was three a.m. *Okay, this is getting a little silly.*

He thought the guys would have made their move. Either they were extremely patient, or they'd left. Porter wanted to know which it was.

Exiting his bedroom in the darkness wasn't a problem. He was familiar with his home and there was no need to activate the flashlight on his rifle. When he got to the guest room on the far left of the house, he moved the blinds a bit and strained to see if he could still make out the car down the street. His view was blocked by a neighbor's palm tree.

Damn.

On his way back across the house, he stopped in the guest bathroom to relieve himself, but didn't flush the toilet. He wasn't an 'if it's yellow let it mellow' type of guy, but in this case if there was someone out there, he didn't want them to hear anything. He moved back to the kitchen and grabbed a bottle of water from the counter. As he passed the big sliding glass door, he saw a shadow in his backyard.

Then the shooting started.

TWENTY-FIVE

THE SLIDER SHATTERED as rounds came through the window. As expected, the protective film kept the window from shattering everywhere but did little to stop the incoming fire. Porter felt something bite into his left arm.

Shit.

He had his rifle but didn't return fire. He needed these guys to come through the choke point in his bathroom. If he shot back now, they would scatter, and he'd have gotten shot for nothing.

Running through the open space of the living room, he made it back to his room and his corner chair. His rifle had a sling on it, so he didn't have to worry about holding onto it as he moved. Getting back to his chair, he did a quick assessment of his arm.

Fingers can move. Arm can bend. Grip is good. Must not be that bad. Get your ass in gear.

He shouldered the rifle and moved the selector switch to semi. Every time he pulled the trigger, a round would come out, and Porter could pull a trigger like a track star on speed.

Pointing his rifle towards the bathroom, he placed the red dot of his optic in the doorway and waited. He heard the distinct sound of a shotgun shell being chambered, then the deadbolt of his bathroom door was blown off and the door swung wide open. There was a brief lull. Porter got to his feet. Through the mirror, he could see the first assailant enter his bathroom, armed with a shotgun. The next guy in was Tattoo, and the third was someone he hadn't seen before. The fourth was Dreadlocks.

Four killers in my bathroom. Wish I had a grenade.

Porter didn't have a grenade. What he had would have to be enough. He waited until all the guys were further into the bathroom, just before they would clear the doorway to his bedroom. He needed to be sure they were all in the bathroom at the same time.

Then he attacked.

Porter took a slight step to the right; just the smallest bit of his barrel was visible to the bathroom. Anyone who was observant enough would have seen part of the rifle's barrel and the red lens of the red dot optic, but nothing else. Porter used the bathroom wall for as much concealment as he could. He put the red dot on the first guy's chest and pulled the trigger several times.

The first guy in line realized he was being shot about the time the fifth round found his torso. He staggered and lost his footing, falling into the bathtub. He must have made a noise, but Porter couldn't hear it. Between the 'silenced' shots ringing in the bedroom and the blood pumping in his own ears, Porter couldn't hear anything.

Once the first guy went down, Porter took another step so he could shoot deeper into the bathroom. More of him was exposed now—his right leg, right arm, and half his face—but he figured it was a fair trade. Tattoo was next in line and Porter fired. From the looks of it, Tattoo was none too pleased about being shot. Backing up, Tattoo ran into the third guy as he tried to escape the fatal funnel of the bathroom. Running into the guy behind him held Tattoo up and gave Porter a stationary target. Porter continued firing.

Tattoo went down. Porter figured it was because the guy behind him had moved backward, no longer keeping him upright. When Porter stepped a little further to the right to see more of the bathroom, there were two shadowy figures running through the doorway into the backyard, beating a hasty retreat.

His first instinct was to follow, but he stifled that.

I'm not running into an ambush.

Porter stepped back into his corner and grabbed the extra thirty-round magazine from his back pocket. Dropping the magazine already in the rifle, he inserted the fresh one. He had no idea how many rounds he'd fired, but a full magazine always beat a not-full magazine.

Porter dropped to one knee and waited.

The air smelled like gunpowder, and there was a cloud hanging in his room.

Probably getting cancer right now.

It beat the alternative. He counted to sixty. Porter figured the Acres boys were long gone by now, but if they weren't, he wanted to give them time to make the mistake of coming back. No one did.

Porter moved the selector of his rifle to safe, reached into his top pocket, and grabbed his phone.

"911, what's the nature of your emergency?"

"I live at 18131 Peacock Road. People broke into my house and they had guns."

"Sir, are you safe right now?"

"I'm so scared, I thought I was gonna die. Please, I need help." Porter was not in fear for his life—not much, anyway. As someone who had spent plenty of time both with lawyers and in courtrooms, he understood what he needed to say to the operator to cover his ass. A recording that would get played in court. Being in fear for your life was one of the first elements of building a case for self-defense.

"We are dispatching units to your location. Can you tell me what you look like, so the officers will be able to identify you?"

"I'm a big guy with a beard. Tell them I'm armed, please—I don't want any trouble."

"I'll tell them. Secure the weapon when they arrive on the scene."

"I will; just tell them to hurry." Porter didn't want to get shot by some dumbass cop who thought *he* was the bad guy.

"They're on the way. Do we need to send medical attention?"

"Definitely."

TWENTY-SIX

PORTER HUNG UP WITH 911, then went through his contacts list and pressed the talk button. A groggy voice answered the phone.

"Hello?"

"Steven? It's Porter."

"Porter? What time is it?"

"It's time for you to earn some of that retainer money I have socked away with you."

"What did you do this time?"

"Some guys broke into my house. Some of their bodies are still in my house."

"Understood. I'll get on the horn. Don't say anything to the cops."

"I wouldn't dream of it." Porter thumbed the phone off.

Porter walked over to his front door and opened it wide. He stood inside the doorway and peeked his head outside. He wanted to be sure there were no surprises waiting for him before he stepped out.

Porter saw nothing, so he stepped out into his front yard,

and looked across the front of the yard. There was no one waiting, and the Hyundai was gone.

He activated the light on his rifle, swept it along the grass,
and saw several splashes of blood.

Maybe I hit one of the other two guys?

Sirens blared in the distance and Porter waited in his
driveway.

Two minutes later, patrol cars turned the corner of his
street. If the shotguns blasts hadn't woken the neighbors up
already, this certainly would.

Porter set his rifle on the ground, pulled his pistol from his
waistband, and placed it next to the rifle. He walked out to the
middle of the street and knelt down with his hands up in the air.
Despite having just been in a gunfight, what Porter felt the most
uneasy about was the upcoming interaction with the cops.

It wasn't that he thought cops liked to shoot people. On the
contrary, he had done the job and knew better. There were bad
eggs and Porter hoped they'd burn in hell, but he knew most cops
to be good people. Still, it was dark outside. The officers pulling
up to the house knew weapons had been fired. Porter was a large
and intimidating guy. It was only natural for the cops to be on
edge. They wanted to see their families at the end of their shift.

The patrol cars stopped one house away from Porter's. They
put their spotlights on him, and then one spoke through the PA
system in his car.

"Sir, please keep your hands up."

Porter complied.

"Are you the only one here?"

Porter nodded his head in a slow, exaggerated yes.

"Are you armed?"

Porter shook his head in a slow, exaggerated no.

"Lie on your stomach and put your arms out to your side."

Porter did, somehow resisting the urge to make an asphalt angel.

"Do not move."

Three officers had gotten out of the cars and taken up positions behind the various points of cover they could find. They had their weapons drawn, but none of them had aimed at Porter.

Good training, Porter thought.

Two of the officers approached Porter. The one behind him slid a cuff on Porter's wrist, then pulled his arms together to cuff the other hand. Once Porter was handcuffed, the officers holstered their pistols.

The officers walked Porter back to the sergeant, whose nametag read *Orvis*.

"Sir, are you the homeowner?" Sgt. Orvis said.

Porter nodded. "If you check my wallet, you'll find my license and my concealed carry permit."

Sgt. Orvis reached into Porter's back pocket and pulled out his wallet. Flipping through it, he confirmed Porter was telling the truth, then took the handcuffs off.

"Sorry for the precautions, Mr. Porter. That's for everybody's safety," Sgt. Orvis said.

Porter always loved this line; he'd used it many times. In reality, the handcuffing was to make sure you didn't do anything foolish and get yourself shot.

"I understand. Thanks for coming," Porter said.

"Your 911 call said assailants broke into your house. Are they still in there?"

"Here's the thing, sergeant: because of what happened here, I'm gonna need my lawyer present for any questioning."

Sgt. Orvis smiled. "You can never be too careful. Can you at least tell me if it's safe to send my men into your house? If not,

I'm going to wait on more people to show up and clear the house proper."

"I think your guys should be okay," Porter said.

"That's all I need to know." Sgt. Orvis gave the other officers the command, and they un-holstered their pistols and headed towards the house.

Better safe than sorry, Porter thought.

Sgt. Orvis keyed something into his walkie-talkie and then spoke to Porter. "Whose rifle on the ground?"

"Mine."

"Nice. Look better than the crap they issue us."

"It seems to work for me," Porter said.

Sgt. Orvis pointed to Porter's arm. The deep red of the blood had been masked by the darkness of his t-shirt, but was now leaking down Porter's forearm. "Did you get shot, Mr. Porter?"

For the first time, Porter remembered the bite of the shotgun blast. The rush of adrenaline he'd felt from the subsequent gunfight had dulled his sense of pain. Now it hurt pretty damn bad.

Rolling his left sleeve up, Porter saw three wounds in his biceps. One was directly in the middle of his arm, the other two were closer to the outside. All three looked angry.

"The paramedics should be here any minute. I radioed them and told them the scene was clear. We'll let them look at that," Sgt. Orvis said.

The officers Orvis sent to the house returned with their weapons holstered, shaking their heads. A dark-skinned man said, "The house is clear, Sarge, but it ain't empty. It looks like a slaughterhouse in there."

Orvis raised his eyebrows at Porter. "Really? What happened in there?"

Porter smiled. "I'm gonna need that lawyer, Sergeant."

Orvis nodded and got back on his radio. Porter recognized the 10-codes for things like the house is clear, the location they were at, and calling off further officers from coming to the scene. Then Orvis called their dispatch and asked for a crime scene investigations unit to come to the scene. The distinct wail of an ambulance rounded the corner. Orvis walked Porter to the ambulance.

The paramedics looked at Porter's arm and flushed it out with a saline solution. "Looks like there's something in there."

"Probably because I got shot," Porter said.

The paramedic looked at Porter, then to Orvis. "I'm not going to bother with this here, we need to get you to a hospital."

"You know what, just leave the buckshot. I'll take care of it. I could use a dressing so I don't bleed everywhere, though."

"Sir, I advise against that. This isn't going to fix itself. You're gonna need antibiotics, too."

"Thanks for the advice, champ, but I got it handled."

The paramedic just shook his head and produced a clipboard with what appeared to be a waiver. "Okay, buddy, suit yourself. I can't make you get treatment. If you'd just sign here for me, this is to—"

"Make sure I don't hold the city liable when I die of gangrene?" Porter said.

The paramedic laughed, and Porter signed the paper on the dotted line. Then the paramedic squirted a brown liquid on Porter's arm and wrapped gauze around it, taping the end so it would stay put.

Porter thanked him.

When the crime scene investigators arrived, so did the homicide detectives. Porter was glad they were here. Not that he particularly wanted to talk—or in this case remain silent—with them; he just knew he was one step closer to being able to leave.

A pair of detectives walked up to Porter and Sgt. Orvis. One was a white man, thin and reedy, and the other was a black female, her natural hair in a large round bun.

"Detectives Jacobs and Arrington, this is Mr. Porter. He's been very cooperative and he's waiting for his lawyer to answer any questions."

Porter liked the way Sgt. Orvis handled himself, and wished all cops were as knowledgeable.

"If that's everything, me and my guys will take off," Sgt. Orvis said. "Detectives, I'll give you my incident report by Tuesday morning. If you need anything further, please let me know." Sgt. Orvis turned to Porter. "Mr. Porter, I'm sorry we had to meet like this, but it looks like you have things well in hand."

"I do my best, Sarge." They shook hands, then Porter turned to the two new obstructions, hoping things would go as smoothly as they had with Orvis.

TWENTY-SEVEN

DETECTIVE ARRINGTON SPOKE FIRST. "What is your complete name, for the record?" She pulled a green notepad out of her pocket.

Porter gave her his name and date of birth.

"Okay, Mr. Porter. Is this your home?"

"Yes, it is." Basic biographical questions were not covered by Miranda, meaning the cops could ask those questions without reading a person their rights. Porter wanted to be helpful as long as he could.

"Are the guns we see on the ground over there yours? Do you legally own them?" Arrington asked.

Porter shook his head. "Detective Arrington, the sergeant told you. I really need my lawyer."

"Okay, Mr. Porter, if that's what you—"

Detective Jacobs waved his hands. His eyes were sunken in and he smelled of smoke. "Seems like an innocent man would answer our questions." He didn't seem interested in Porter's rights.

"Is that right?" Porter said.

"That's right," Jacobs said.

Arrington received a call on her cell phone and stepped away to answer.

"Is that how you made detective, with really stupid theories?" Porter said.

Jacobs bristled. "I'm not sure you know who you're talking to."

"I know I'm not talking to the brains of the team, that's for sure. That's unfortunate, since you're doing most of the talking."

"I guess you want to go to jail, don't you? I can take you to jail right now and leave you there for forty-eight hours. I don't have to charge you with shit. How about that, smartass?"

"You're gonna have a hell of a time getting me down to that jail," Porter said.

"Is that a threat?"

Porter didn't reply.

Arrington hung up her phone and walked back to the two men. "Jacobs. Can I speak to you over here?"

"Stay right there, sir." Somehow, Jacobs managed to make 'sir' sound like 'shithead.'

The two detectives stood several feet away and spoke quietly. Porter watched as Jacobs grew more animated as the conversation went on, and he was gesticulating wildly by the end. The detectives walked back to Porter.

"Mr. Porter, I just got off the phone with my captain. We have been instructed to let you go on your way tonight. Your attorney has agreed to make you available for questioning later in the week. We're finished. Have a good night."

"Thanks, Detective Arrington. You've been a pleasure," Porter said as he stared Jacobs in the eye. Jacobs stormed away, and Arrington followed.

When Porter was by himself, he took out his phone and hit redial.

"Porter. Did they talk to you?"

"Yeah, Steven, that was fast. I thought I was at least spending a few hours in processing."

"Not if I have anything to say in the matter," Steven said.

"I'm glad you do. How'd you pull that off?"

"I called Captain Jones. He was my old field training officer before I moved on to greener pastures."

"Being a fancy lawyer is a much greener pasture than being a cop," Porter said.

"Funny guy. Once I told Henry it was a self-defense thing, he agreed there was no reason to bring you in. I promised I'd bring you down for questioning, so don't make me a liar. Be available sometime this week, got it?"

"I promise."

"Before I let you go, is there anything you need to tell me? You can give me a full debrief when we meet up, but if there's anything that may go sideways about this, I'd rather hear it from you."

Porter could be honest; anything he told Steven Ajo was covered under attorney-client privilege. But in the interest of timeliness, he decided to hold off. He had somewhere to be.

"The basic facts are there. Four gang-bangers broke into my house, and I burned two of them down. The other two got away."

"Why are you so special to have people breaking into your house?"

"Super long story. I'll tell you later."

"Fine, Porter. Just make sure you do. And try not to shoot anyone else. You don't pay me that much," Steven said.

"I make no promises," Porter said as he hung up the phone.

He thought for a moment and headed back into his house. A crime scene technician looked at him funny. Porter ignored her and walked to his bedroom.

Jacobs saw him and moved to block his way. "You can't be

here. This is a crime scene. I don't care if it is your house, this is off limits."

"Relax. I just need some clean clothes," Porter said.

Jacobs shook his head. "Nope, don't care. It doesn't matter how good your attorney is, you can't pollute the crime scene. I'm telling you to leave and if you don't—"

Arrington stepped in between them. "Where are the clothes you need, Mr. Porter?"

Porter pointed to his dresser.

"You have two minutes, Mr. Porter. Please get your things and let us do our jobs," Arrington said.

"You're the boss," Porter said.

Jacobs stomped off back to the bathroom.

Porter pulled new clothes from the drawer and changed. Arrington watched him until he took his pants off, then she turned around. He slid his feet back into his Chuck Taylors, cursing under his breath at the blood on his shoes. It was hard to get blood out of Chuck Taylors.

Porter grabbed his phone and wallet and left the house, getting his car keys from the front table on the way out. Time to get his arm fixed.

He knew just the place.

TWENTY-EIGHT

THE SUN WASN'T EVEN over the horizon yet and it was already muggy outside. As Porter drove away from his house, he saw that the crime scene guys had removed his weapons from the driveway and were unrolling yellow tape around the perimeter.

He had to be careful not to hit anyone in the crowd of nosy neighbors that had gathered.

Porter pushed the car out Dale Mabry Highway and headed north. This time of the morning, the highway was still quiet and hadn't turned into a parking lot like it would during rush hour. He clicked through his phone, looking for the right song. Porter wasn't a huge fan of the new stuff they called rap, but he liked many of the older albums. He settled on Biggie Smalls's first album, *Ready to Die*.

Porter wondered if the Acres boys who had come into his house were ready to die. He wasn't.

In fact, he enjoyed living very much and, while he didn't *want* to kill people, in this instance he didn't feel bad. He knew the media and psychologists would expect him to be broken up right now. If his life were a television show, there would be a close-up shot of him, alone, and his hands would be shaking. Or better yet, looking at himself in the mirror and having some sort of crying jag. Porter thought he was ugly when he cried, so he wouldn't shed a tear for those assholes.

He wasn't heartless, just pragmatic.

Around the time "One More Chance" played, he took a right on Highway 54. That area had exploded in the last five years. Porter saw strip malls and movie theatres, chain Mexican and Italian restaurants that he didn't like. Before he bought his current place, he'd lived out this way for a few years. He preferred where he lived now. The older part of town was less frenetic, and the food at the mom-and-pop restaurants was better.

Porter turned into an enormous, pre-planned neighborhood in a town called Wesley Chapel. Some developer had realized he could make a neighborhood the size of a city. There were thousands of houses and several grocery stores; the developer had petitioned the county to build two elementary schools, as well as a middle and high school. The neighborhood even had its own post office.

Making his way through the cookie-cutter streets by memory, Porter soon approached his destination. The house was nothing special to look at; it was just one of many, but it was nice. It was down the street from one of the elementary schools, a five-minute walk for a parent and child. Behind the house was one of the community playgrounds. In the evenings and weekends, there were children playing everywhere while their parents chatted with friends.

Porter drove up in front of the house. The driveway was empty so he pulled in.

Must be parked in the garage.

Porter sat in the car for a minute, preparing himself. He felt a flutter of anticipation in his stomach. He hated that feeling, but he couldn't help it. He'd had that anticipation since the beginning, and the feeling had never gone away. He checked his face in the rearview mirror to make sure he was presentable, then stepped out of the car.

Moving up the walkway, he noticed the lawn was being kept well and that there was a new bed of flowers under the front window. He stepped up to the front door and stood for a moment. He took a deep breath, blew it out, and then rang the doorbell. There was no answer. Porter waited a few seconds and then hit the button again, but still nothing.

I guess I'll go to the ER after all.

Porter turned to go back to his Yukon. As he took a step away he heard the deadbolt unlock behind him. When he turned back around, there she was. Her hair was wrapped up in a towel and she was beautiful.

TWENTY-NINE

"TELLY?" she said. "What are you doing here?"

He winced. He hated that nickname. "Hey Trish. I thought you weren't home."

"You must have thought I was home if you came over."

"I mean you didn't answer, so I thought maybe you'd gone to work or something," Porter said.

"Just in the shower. Got held over for an overnight. You would have known that if you had called me first."

"Yeah, it's just... it's pretty early and if you were asleep I didn't want to wake you up."

"You just thought you would wake me up with the doorbell instead?" She smirked at him.

"I've never claimed to be the smartest guy," Porter said.

"So is there a point to... oh my God. Why are you bleeding?"

Porter looked down at his arm and noticed that the gauze the medic had given him was saturated and some of the excess blood had trickled down to his forearm.

"That's kind of why I came by. I got shot."

Trish looked at him with concern. "Telly, how did you get shot? Why aren't you at the hospital? You know what, never mind, just get in here." She grabbed him by his uninjured arm, pulled him through the doorway, and shut the door behind her.

He had once carried her over that threshold; funny that she was dragging him over it now.

They went into the kitchen and she pushed him toward a barstool under the island in the middle. He complied and pulled the stool out to sit down. She disappeared into the room he knew was the bedroom.

Looking around, Porter was pleased to see that things looked almost the same as they always had. To be fair, there was a more feminine flair to the place now, but that was to be expected. He had always been the Great Wall of China, holding back the rampaging hordes of shabby chic and thrift store finds. Porter imagined she decorated freely now.

There was the big island in the kitchen, with the quartz slab on it. Porter had wanted granite, but she'd said it was too *en vogue*. The cabinets were a roughed up white color. *French farmhouse*, Porter thought, *or was it French revival?* He couldn't remember. From his stool he could see the big leather couch he'd left behind. Her spot had a folded-up blanket on it. He heard footsteps from the bedroom and turned towards them.

"I grabbed my old kit in the bathroom. I upgraded to a new one, but all the stuff in here is still in date. It's a good back-up. You know, for whenever men who've been shot show up on my doorstep."

"This happens to you a lot?" Porter said. "I guess the neighborhood's not what it used to be."

"Oh yeah, all the time. Last weekend the living room was full of shot-up people. I should have charged a cover. Pull your sleeve up."

"Maybe I should just take my shirt off. It would be easier to get to it."

"No way, hot stuff. There isn't going to be any Chippendales action around here. Just the sleeve will do."

Porter complied, rolling his left sleeve up as far as he could. It got caught on the gauze and snagged, and he winced a little.

"It hurts that bad? I always thought you were tougher than that. How bad is this, Telly? What am I getting myself into?"

"The paramedic who looked at it said there were three shotgun pellets. It looked rough, but he cleaned it and—"

"You already saw a paramedic?"

"Yeah," Porter said.

"Then why are you here?"

"He didn't take the pellets out," Porter said.

"Why on earth not?"

Porter was quiet and looked down from his stool at her. When he didn't reply, she paused rummaging through her medical bag to see why. She looked up at him and knew. She softened her look.

Freckles, Porter thought, *always with those freckles.*

She held his gaze for a few moments and then went back to looking for supplies. After a few more seconds, she was ready.

"Okay, let's get these bandages off and see what we're working with." She peeled away the tape and gauze, and after a couple of moments had the wound exposed. It wasn't looking too great.

"Look how angry this is," she said. "You should have gone to the hospital. You need stitches, an antibiotic, and probably something for pain."

"It's just a flesh wound," Porter said.

She didn't laugh. She had always been a great nurse, caring and knowledgeable. Porter knew that after they had split up, Trish had dived back into her studies and gotten certified as a physician's assistant. PAs had more duties and autonomy at the hospitals and offices at which they worked. He knew he was in good hands.

"Okay, so how do you fix me?" Porter said. "Shouldn't be too hard, right?"

"Yes, it's going to be hard, Telly. This is why you need to go to a hospital. This isn't a surgery center. You need professional help."

"You're a professional, aren't you?" he said with a grin.

"This isn't fix-at-home stuff. You need an x-ray to see if there are any chips to your bone, or fragments that may have splintered off the pellets. Go to the hospital. I'm serious."

"Trish, I don't have time for the hospital right now. I have some important things I need to take care of. I promise to go as soon as I can, but I can't run around all day with my arm like this, can I?"

She gave him a noncommittal look.

"Come on, I'm serious. Patch me up and then I'll be able to handle some things. Help me out here, babe." It slipped out.

Trisha gave him a look that made him regret saying the word 'babe.'

"I'm sorry. I'm sorry. It's an old habit. I won't do it again, I promise."

"Telly, I can't do this. I mean, I can fix your arm. But I can't do... this," she said, gesturing back and forth between the two of them. "If it's going to be like that..."

"I know. I won't do it again."

She nodded.

"Thanks for fixing the arm. I appreciate it," Porter said.

"You're welcome," she said as she turned back to her bag.

"Besides," Porter said, "don't you want me to tell you how I got shot?"

"Actually, I really want to hear that."

For the next thirty minutes, Porter recounted the events of

the last few days. He started with Ross's billboard, ended with ringing her doorbell, and left nothing out except Ashley the pizza girl giving him her number. They might be divorced, but Porter wasn't stupid.

Trisha spent the time asking further questions while she went to work on his arm. Putting gloves on, she first cleaned his wounds. Then, with forceps, she dug into each channel and fished around for the pellets at the end. It hurt Porter badly, but he gritted his teeth.

"Don't be a wuss," she said.

Once the pellets were removed, Trisha cleaned the entire area again, then pulled out her large suture needle and stitched him up. The wounded area was irregular and it wouldn't be easy to stitch. Porter didn't care that he wasn't going to find work as a male biceps model. He was just glad that it was Trish working on him.

"You killed those two guys," Trish said.

"I kind of had to, don't you think?"

"Sure. Better them than you. But it seems so... serious."

"Killing someone usually is," Porter said.

"What I mean is, them coming to your house is serious. Why did they do it?"

"Because they know that I know what they did to Danny. That they kidnapped and killed her. They want to stop me from telling anyone. "

"I don't think that's it," Trish said.

"Really?"

"Yes, Telly, really. I don't think that's it. They already got past the cops, right? I mean, the cops couldn't find any evidence linking them to Danny's disappearance."

"No, but the cops suck at their jobs," Porter said.

"Yes, I get that. You are much better at these things than they are."

"Thanks."

"It's true," Trisha said. "I'm not trying to inflate your ego. But Hector still should believe that there's no evidence to link them. Why risk a shootout at your house in the middle of the night?"

"Maybe it was payback. I smacked a couple of their guys around a few days ago. I'm sure they didn't like that. Then I man-napped the boss's brother. Maybe they were fed up and wanted payback. Ego's a powerful thing."

"Man-nap?" Trisha said.

"It's a thing I'm trying on for size."

She shook her head and continued stitching. "I don't think that's it. It seems like they're trying to protect something. Something they don't want you to find out."

"Something beyond their criminal enterprises?"

"Exactly. It doesn't make sense for them to come after you the way they did. Will you quit moving?"

Porter was quiet for a few minutes and let her work. He thought about what she said. Would they have sent the goon squad just because he'd tied up Abel Quintana? They would have to assume he knew they had taken Danny by now, but so what? The cops couldn't find evidence, so there probably wasn't any readily available. And Hector Quintana would know that. He was starting to think Trisha was right.

She always was the smart one.

"What I never figured out was why they took Danny. Abel Quintana didn't know. He would have told me if he did. I didn't get a chance to ask the idiots that broke into my house. They aren't in a talking mood anymore," Porter said.

"Clearly."

"I can't figure it out." Porter closed his eyes as the suture needle bit into his skin again.

"Well, why do people usually kidnap kids?" Trisha said.

"Most of the time it's the parents, trying to hurt one another. Mom won't let Dad see the kid, so he steals her away," Porter said.

"If it's the parents, where are Danny's?"

"Both dead. Mom a few years ago, dad more recently. He got out of prison and they found him with a spike in his arm a few days later."

"Right," Trisha said, "they didn't take her. What are other reasons kids get taken?"

Porter thought for a few moments. "There's always the pervert angle, the weird guy in the van handing out candy looking for a victim."

"I would usually guess that's what happened, right? Some pedophile saw her walking home from school and was overcome by a creep-juice rush to the head and stole her. Maybe he saw her walking every day and got real lusty and couldn't help himself. That's terrible to think about, but that's not what happened here either."

"No, it isn't," Porter said. "This was premeditated; it wasn't a pervert taking her in the heat of the moment. Besides, I have to imagine that several of the Acres boys knew about the abduction. Pedophiles keep their activities on the down-low. I can't imagine Hector took her to rape her."

"Doesn't seem like it. So what other reason would a kid disappear off the streets?"

The question lingered as Trisha finished up her stitches. She smeared some white cream over the sutures and dressed the wound with some fresh bandages from her kit. "I have a wild theory."

"How many stitches did you put in there?" Porter said as he looked down at his arm.

"Thirty-four."

"Holy shit," Porter said.

"I wanted to make sure everything was closed up. Do you want to hear my idea or not?"

Damn, that's a lot of stitches, Porter thought. "Yeah, hit me with this theory."

"I watched a documentary a few months ago about human trafficking. How they steal kids in other countries and bring them into the United States. There's a big market for these kids."

Porter was aware of human trafficking from his time as a federal agent. He hadn't considered this, because those kids were usually getting moved by large crime organizations, which were based in other countries. Sometimes cartels, sometimes terrorist organizations, they sold kids to people who had various uses for them.

It was the sort of thing that made Porter glad he didn't have any children, although he regretted that he and Trisha hadn't become parents. He'd always known she'd have made a great mother.

"You think Hector took Danny and sold her to someone?" Porter said.

"It sounds stupid when you say it like that, but sure. Why not? There has to be a reason they did it."

"It doesn't sound stupid. It's just as good a theory as any. I'll tell you what I need to do."

"What's that?" Trisha said.

"Have a talk with Hector Quintana."

THIRTY

TRISHA FINISHED WRAPPING Porter's arm, then cleaned up the island top she'd been working on. She told Porter to hang on for a few minutes, then disappeared into the dark bedroom.

Porter stood up and stretched. He knew Trisha had done a good job on his arm. Even better, she had taken his mind in a different direction about Danny Hill. He wasn't sure if she was right or not, but it didn't matter. At the end of the day all roads led through the Acres and Hector. Trisha re-emerged a few minutes later, just as Porter settled on the couch.

She had taken the towel off her head and combed her hair. She was no longer a blonde, but a brunette. Her natural hair color was a light brown. Porter had always wanted her to let her hair be natural instead of dyed, but she had refused. She thought it made her look mousy. Porter disagreed.

"Nice hair," Porter said. "Quite a change."

"I hate it. I've been so busy the last few months that I haven't had time to color it."

"I think it looks nice," Porter said.

"You always wanted me to be brown-headed," she said as she sat on the couch. She took the cushion farthest away from

Porter. "What's the plan? How are you going to get to Hector and talk to him? I'd imagine he and his people aren't going to be too happy with you. They're never going to tell you anything."

"Never is a long time," Porter said. "I think I have a way to talk to Hector and maybe do a little good for the Acres at the same time."

"You were always good at coming up with a plan. Following through, not so much sometimes."

The comment stung, and Porter let it hang in the air for a few moments.

Trish continued. "So here's the thing about your arm: I wasn't joking. It will get infected. You need to do something about it."

"Can't you give me something for it? A course of antibiotics or something?" Porter said.

"The prescriptions I write have to be under the supervision of a doctor. I can't just give you something here; I'm not a pharmacy. You really aren't going to a doctor?"

"I don't have time right now, Trish, but I don't want to get gangrene either, so..." Porter said, and looked at her with mock expectancy.

"I figured as much. I'll call a doctor at the hospital and ask them to call you in a script for a good antibiotic. Then you go to the pharmacy and get it. Deal?"

"I think that's fair."

"Later, when you magically find a good time, go to the doctor."

"I will."

Trisha didn't push the issue any further. "I'll have the doctor send the prescription to the Walgreens by your house."

"I moved a while back. I'm not on Leafwood anymore."

"You moved?" Trisha said. "I... I didn't know. How long ago did that happen?"

"It's been a year," Porter said. "I'm in Town and Country. I bought a little house."

"That's really great, Telly. I'm glad you have something that's yours now. I guess it just surprised me that you moved."

"I wasn't going to call you to help me with my couch," Porter said.

"Maybe you should have. I'm very strong," Trisha said, flexing her biceps.

They both had a laugh and Porter got up from the couch, heading towards the front door. "Thanks for helping me out, Trish. I was going to have a bad day if I didn't get this arm taken care of."

"What else could I do? You're too dumb to get medical help."

"I did get medical help," Porter said with a smile.

"You know what I mean. Where are you going now?"

"Simple. I'm going to talk to Hector Quintana and then I'll go from there."

"That doesn't sound easy," Trisha said.

"I said it was simple, not easy. But I have a few ideas."

"You always do," Trisha said.

At the front door, Porter twisted the knob to leave, but before he stepped over the threshold he turned back to Trisha. "I'm not sure what we're supposed to do right now. Shake hands? A brisk wave?"

Trisha reached up to him and gave him a hug. Porter hugged back. It wasn't long or intimate, but it was enough. She smelled like Ralph Lauren perfume, the one that came in the blue bottle.

It had been worth getting shot.

"Don't get yourself killed," Trisha said. "My mother would be devastated. She still likes you."

"Just your mother?"

"Goodbye, Telly-Porter," Trisha said as she shut the door.

Porter looked at the door for a second and smiled. He turned and walked to his truck, hopped in, and fired it up. By now the sun was up and the temperature was rising. Porter let the truck run for a few minutes, then threw it in reverse and navigated the streets out. After a few minutes winding past houses and playgrounds, he found himself on the main drag that would take him back to the highway. He rolled the windows down in the Yukon to get some fresh air. Then he reached into his ashtray and grabbed the piece of paper with Ashley the pizza girl's phone number. Porter looked at it for a second, then crumpled it up and threw it out the window.

THIRTY-ONE

AS HE WAS ROLLING around what he'd talked about with Trish, Porter's phone rang. He plugged his phone into the auxiliary jack and let the call come through his speakers.

"Yeah."

"What's going on, you big bald stud of a man?"

"I told you, it's shaved. I'm not bald. There's a difference. A guy with your hairline should know that."

"It's called a widow's peak, asshole. I'm not losing my hair," Ruas said.

"Sure thing, brother. I'm sure there's nothing to worry about. Kelly told me a long time ago that she would love you no matter what. She meant if you got shot and ended up in a wheelchair or something, but I'm sure that applies to scenarios in which you start looking like a chubby Bruce Willis."

"I'm big-boned," Ruas said, laughing.

"Like a dinosaur bone. What's up?"

"Christina Rivera got with me this morning asking for as much info about the Acres as I had. She said it was for you. I'm gonna give her what I got, that work for you?"

"Sure. I'll meet up with her and take a look," Porter said.

"You two working together?"

"Just following up that cold case I called you about. I'm sure it's nothing," Porter lied. "I'm trying to tie up a few loose ends as a favor to a family friend."

"Good luck with that."

"Should I be expecting problems?" Porter said.

"With the guys from the Acres? Probably not; I know how you are. I'm not so sure about Rivera."

"*Dime lo*," Porter said.

"I didn't really remember who she was last time you called, so I asked around. My buddy that used to work with her says she's a snitch. She ratted out some guys for sexual harassment and there was a big lawsuit. That's how she got stuck on the shit job she has now. I don't know about her one way or the other, but I figured I'd let you know."

"Thanks for the heads up, brother," Porter said.

"Anytime. And Porter? If you need something else, you call me yourself next time. I'd rather hear from you than Rivera," Ruas said, and hung up the phone.

There was no reason for Porter to go home. It would be in shambles after the events of the last night and Rivera would be calling him soon to go over the new information. Ross's office was close to hers.

Porter got off the highway and zig-zagged his way through the surface streets to Westshore and Ross's building. He parked and walked across the lot and into the lobby of Ross's building. Smitty was at his usual place by the door.

"Morning, Smitty."

"Mr. Porter. How are you, young man?"

"I've been better, Smitty."

"Not sure why; you look pretty good to me. Mr. Gianullo didn't tell me you were coming by."

"It's a surprise."

"No problem, Mr. Porter. Let me call up there and make sure you can go up." Smitty picked up a generic black phone and dialed some numbers.

Porter had been coming to this building for years. Ross had never turned him away. Smitty knew Porter and Ross had been best friends since childhood—and still, Smitty did his job. Porter respected that.

"Just spoke with the nice young lady that runs Mr. Gianullo's office. She said he's with a client but that their meeting is over in about ten minutes. She said you can come on up."

"To be honest, I'd rather stay down here and wait with you."

Smitty smiled. "I can't help but notice you got that big bandage on your arm. Get in an accident?"

"I got shot last night." Porter wouldn't have told many people, but he liked Smitty, and knew he would understand because of his background. "I'm not a big fan of getting shot."

"Me either. I got hit a few times, but mine were always in a jungle. How'd you manage in the States?"

"It's a long story, Smitty, and I know I'm going to tell it all to Ross when I get upstairs. I'd rather hear about you in the jungle."

Smitty looked surprised that anyone wanted to hear a story of his. Porter knew most people treated a guy like Smitty like the help. That was a shame, because old school guys like Smitty had the best stories.

"I got a quick one for you. In Vietnam, back when things first kicked off for us over there, I was part of a small team of people that did reconnaissance."

"Recce work?"

"Yes, sir. That's even what they called us—Recon. We worked in small groups, sometimes by ourselves. Hell, who am I kidding, it was mostly by ourselves."

Porter leaned forward on the counter.

"I was out by myself for two weeks. I'd run across a few guys, but no big groups or anything."

Porter knew what Smitty meant by 'run across' a few guys.

"I was creepin' along and felt like someone hit my hip with a baseball bat. It hurt so bad I almost passed out. Thank God I didn't, because they would've found me."

"Viet Cong?"

"Yeah, Charlie. I ran into one of their patrols. They were shooting at something else and I was in the wrong place at the wrong time. So I'm all by myself with this shot-up leg and I pull myself down a river embankment to be as quiet as possible."

"Sounds scary as hell," Porter said.

"It damn sure was. I'm down there and I hear a few more shots, then this little guy comes diving down the same embankment I'm hiding under. I went for my knife, to make sure he didn't kill me, but when he saw me, he dropped his rifle and put his hands up."

"Why was he scared? He had a whole patrol with him."

"He wasn't with those other guys. Later, once I got him to a translator, we learned he was a defector. He was trying to get south so he could turn himself over to the US. The shots I'd heard earlier were the patrol shooting at this guy. He didn't know I was hiding; he was just trying to get away."

"That's crazy."

"You're telling me. I didn't know what he wanted or who he was. Once I knew he wasn't gonna kill me, I figured I had a better chance with him than without him, especially since he knew the area better than I did," Smitty said.

"So what happened?"

"We hid there for a little while. Then it was quiet, so we decided to get moving. We avoided the patrol for a few hours, but eventually they found us. And when they did, I was real glad I wasn't by myself. The little guy was a great shot with his rifle," Smitty said.

"Things worked out?"

"Only downside was I got shot again," Smitty said.

"It's like you're a bullet magnet. Or the unluckiest guy ever."

Smitty shook his head. "No, Mr. Porter, I'm plenty lucky. Some of my guys never made it back, and all I got was this little limp out of the deal. I think that's fair."

Porter nodded. "You both made it?"

"Sure did. Me and that little fella made our way back to our base. The other guys looked at me like I was crazy for bringing Charlie to our house, but I knew he was okay. I never saw him after that. I went to the medic and then they shipped me to a hospital in Germany for a few months. By the time I got back to the jungle, the little guy was long gone. They told me they debriefed him and then helped relocate him to a safe place. I'm just glad I ran into him when I did."

"No regrets?"

"Not a one," Smitty said. "I'm sure it's been ten minutes, Mr. Porter; you should head up. Thanks for letting an old-timer bore you for a while."

"You didn't bore me at all, Smitty. In fact, you gave me an idea."

Porter shook a confused Smitty's hand and headed to the elevator.

He stepped onto the elevator and rode it up to Ross's floor. He almost missed getting off, he was so lost in thought. Porter stuck his hand in the closing doors at the last second, and the sensor forced them back open and he got out. He walked into Ross's suite. "Hey, Tess."

"Ross's clients just left. You can go in if you—what happened to your arm?"

"A roving band of ninjas. Those ninja stars are nasty business."

Tessa giggled. "You're so stupid. Ross told me what you were doing about the little girl. I hope you find her."

"Me too, Tess," Porter said. He realized something when he said it: It was the first time he had allowed himself to hope that Danny wasn't dead and in a shallow grave somewhere. He didn't like that development, because he knew what hope got you in a situation like this. "Has he eaten yet?"

"I'm already on it. When Smitty called up a few minutes ago, I ordered you guys some food. It should be here in a little bit."

"I swear Ross doesn't deserve you. You know that, right? Is he paying you enough? When's the last time you got a raise?" Porter said, raising his eyebrows at her.

"He's too cheap for a raise, Porter. Don't even tease me."

"Well, he should pay you more. I'm gonna talk to him and get this straightened out."

"You do that," Tessa said. "Let me know how it goes."

Porter headed to the big door that marked Ross's office and walked right in.

"When are you going to marry that girl, Ross?"

Ross was sitting behind his large desk, flipping through some papers. "What the hell are you talking about? Are you drunk or something?"

"I'm talking about that girl out front. The one that makes this place run. The one that just ordered us lunch without being asked to. The one I know you grossly underpay. You know she isn't working here because of the ambiance. You should ask her out," Porter said.

"You want to reward her for her hard work by having me hit on her?"

"Good point," Porter said. "That's more like a punishment.

Could you imagine going out with you? Disregard, forget I said anything."

"I know you didn't come all the way over here to talk about my love life. What happened with Rivera yesterday? Why did Steven Ajo call me about a new payment to his firm? And what the hell is wrong with your arm?"

"That's way too many questions."

"Don't make me drag this out of you, Porter."

"I'll tell you everything. But I have to wait for something first," Porter said.

"What?"

He propped his foot up on a chair in front of Ross's desk.

"You could at least take your foot down. That's real leather."

Porter didn't say anything. Ross looked down at his desk and went back to his papers. Neither of them spoke for five minutes. Then there was a knock at the office door and Tessa came in with a big bag of Greek food.

"Thanks, T," Ross said as Tessa left the room and shut the door behind her. "You ready to talk yet?"

"Nope," Porter said. He reached across Ross's desk, grabbed the bag of food, and walked out of Ross's office, leaving the door open behind him. Ross looked exasperated, but dutifully got up and followed him.

Porter walked all the way down the main hallway, waving at an amused Tessa as he passed, and turned into the conference room. Setting the bag on the table, Porter moved around to the windows and twisted the blinds open, then pulled the cord that pulled them out of the way. Danny's picture was staring back at him.

THIRTY-TWO

ROSS STEPPED into the conference room and looked at Porter.

"I needed a little reminder of why I got shot last night," Porter said.

"You got shot last night?"

Porter told Ross everything.

Ross was silent the entire time. When Porter finished, the first question Ross asked was, "How was Trisha?"

"I tell you I almost died last night and the only thing you can say is 'How's Trisha?' Not 'Hey, Porter, sorry I dragged you into this' or 'I guess I know what you mean by blowback now'?"

"Getting shot is good for you, don't be a bitch," Ross said with a grim smile. "Seriously, though, how was Trisha?"

Porter held his gyro with one hand and searched for the right way to answer to Ross's question. "She's... good."

"Good? That's it? You haven't seen her in over a year and all you can say is 'good'? How did she look?"

"Great."

"Now you're just being obtuse." Ross stared at Porter.

Porter was quiet for a few moments. "She's a brunette now,

and I liked the way she looked. She was wearing some old perfume I used to buy her, and she smelled like the good times. I didn't know seeing her would be so weird, but it was. Like there's a puzzle I look at on my kitchen table every day, but today I noticed there's a piece missing from it. I'm not sure where the piece is or if I can get it back into the puzzle." Porter stopped talking and took a bite of his gyro.

Ross didn't say anything. He didn't want to disturb the moment.

"It's just... I don't understand it. We've been split up a long time and I didn't think it would make me feel like this to see her again."

"You went to her place on purpose," Ross said. "You could have gone to the hospital."

Porter didn't say anything.

"What were you expecting to happen?" Ross said.

"I wanted to see her, but I didn't want to miss her."

They said nothing as they finished their food. When he finished his gyro, Porter picked at the pastitsio, pulling chunks of feta out to eat.

"I have two questions. What are you going to do, and how can I help?" Ross said.

Porter looked over at him. "I've got plans for Hector and his buddies. It's not going to be pretty. You aren't going to help me. We talked about this."

"We talked about this, but I'm not going to listen to you this time. I don't want to swell your head up, but this is my fault. I'll admit it. I should have never dragged you into this. You told me you didn't want to work too close to home and I begged you to do it. Now, because you did me a favor, you got shot, your house is a crime scene, and you had to kill a couple of guys. I can't even imagine how that feels. I'm sorry for that, I truly am. I can own that."

Porter watched Ross as he delivered his speech, and knew he felt genuinely bad about the situation Porter was in.

"But I think the worst thing about it, and I mean the absolute worst thing, is that seeing Trisha turned you into a little bitch." Ross erupted with laughter.

Porter couldn't help but laugh. The genuine moment had passed.

"Think it's funny? Wait until I tell Tessa how you really feel. Should I get her now? Tessa. Tessa," Porter said, getting louder.

The two had a good laugh and then were silent for several minutes.

"What are you actually going to do?" Ross said.

"I've been thinking about that. Talking to Smitty gave me an idea."

"I love that guy," Ross said.

"He was telling me about a time he was in Vietnam. Long story short, he had to work with his enemy to combat a greater threat. I think something like that may work out for us."

"What do you mean? Isn't Hector the enemy? You can't work with that guy."

"Use your imagination a little bit. Remember when I talked to Miss Leona?"

"Sure."

"She told me the Acres was split in two and Hector's crew was the worst. The older guys, Jamal and Terrell, looked out for the neighborhood. The only reason there wasn't an all-out war was because they were holding to a truce. What if I gave them a reason to move against Hector? With Hector gone, those guys can take over the entire neighborhood again," Porter said.

"Your big plan is to turn two street gangs into one super gang? That doesn't make sense."

"That's because you aren't being pragmatic. Someone is

going to run the Acres, whether you like it or not. Would you rather have Hector—who'll snatch a little girl off the streets—in charge, or the other guys? Easy decision for me," Porter said.

"What are you going to use Jamal and his guys for? Are you planning to get a bunch of thugs to have a shootout?"

"Am I an idiot? Why would I get in a shootout?"

Ross gestured to his bandaged arm.

"That was different. That was a checkers game. I had no choice but to react. We're playing chess now," Porter said.

"All I'm saying is, if you don't want them to shoot it out with Hector's guys and you can't get them to go to the cops, what good are Jamal's people?" Ross said.

"I'm still working out the kinks."

"Fine. You let me know when your genius plan comes together. I can't sit here all day, I have a client in fifteen minutes." Ross pushed away from the conference table. "You crashing with me tonight?"

Porter nodded.

Ross balled up his trash and stuffed it into the empty take-out sack. Then he opened the conference room door, and looked at Porter before he left. "Well, whatever you come up with, I'm helping. I have to do something."

Ross shut the door behind him, and Porter was alone.

THIRTY-THREE

PORTER WADDED UP HIS GARBAGE. Before he got up, he took a good long look at Danny's billboard. He would never understand how anyone could hurt a kid. He'd sat in federal court for years and listened to perverts, killers, and child pornographers explain why they had done what they'd done.

No one ever told the truth.

Your honor, I'm a sick bastard. Please send me to the lethal injection table. I deserve it, none of them ever said.

Instead, there was talk about rough childhoods, unstable relationships, and years of prior abuse. None of that ever worked on Porter. He didn't feel the least bit bad when they threw the book at the child abusers. In fact, it was the opposite. He always wanted to have a party every time one of them went away.

Porter stepped out of the conference room and walked past Tessa's desk. She was on the phone and gave him a look that said, 'Don't do anything stupid.'

He left the office, caught the elevator down, and waved at Smitty on his way out. He had a feeling it was going to be another long day. Porter walked through the front door and there it was. The heat. Always the heat.

He hated the heat.

The truck idled as it cooled the cab off, and Porter looked down when his phone rang.

"Hey, it's me."

"You're a 'me' now? Seems like this relationship is moving fast, don't you think, detective?"

"Everyone's phone has caller ID. I might as well say 'me' because you know who I am. I talked to Ruas this morning. He got me the rest of that info on the Acres you were looking for."

"I can be there in ten minutes. That work for you?" Porter said.

"I was going to go to lunch, but sure, I'll wait and structure my whole day around you. Never mind any other actual work I need to get done," Rivera said.

"Give me a break. You work the coldest of cold cases, remember? The hottest thing going is the Danny Hill case. It's your gravy train. Trust me."

"I'll be here. Try not to piss off any of my guys this time," Rivera said.

"I'll be a perfect gentleman," Porter said.

"I won't believe that unless I see it," Rivera said as she hung up.

It didn't take long to get to her office. He opened the lockbox; he had no gun to stash away, but he dropped his pocketknife in. He fished around for a minute, moving the stolen gun he'd taken from Tattoo, then shut the box and slammed the tailgate.

Stepping into the lobby, he was again greeted by a powerful air conditioner, as well as Officers Fischer and Raymond. They looked like they hadn't done a thing all day.

"You two again? Don't they set you guys up on a rotation or something? You can't be permanently assigned here."

Officer Raymond spoke. "It's a two-week rotation and this is our second week. I'll be glad when it's over. I'm sorry, sir, what was your name again?"

"Porter."

"I'll let Rivera know you're here," Raymond said.

Officer Fischer was at the walk-through metal detector again. "Look, it's the asshole."

"You're learning new words," Porter said. "That's cute. Let's try another one. Do you know what 'philander' means? Because Rivera does. So maybe you should knock it off."

Fischer's face turned red and he stammered.

"What's that?" Porter said.

Rivera opened the door and motioned Porter back. He looked at Fischer and strode past him, right past the metal detector. Rivera shut the door behind them. Together they made the walk back to her desk, where she paused to grab a thick file. Then she led Porter to a large conference room. The gray table was empty, save for a large black speakerphone.

No holding room this time, Porter thought. *I've been upgraded.*

"What did you do to Fischer? Why is he stuttering like an idiot?"

"Eh, nothing. Just giving him the business."

"Whatever you said looked like you confused him," Rivera said.

"I'm not even sure how the sheriff could hire a guy like that."

"There's no telling how he got hired, but he's not alone. We have plenty of mouth breathers working here."

Porter looked around the empty office. "Speaking of which,

where is everybody?"

"They all got called to assist Narcotics with a huge seizure. Just admin stuff, bagging and tagging. Glad I'm not there," Rivera said.

Porter could tell she wasn't being honest. The paperwork in a law enforcement job was the worst part of the job. Everyone likes arresting bad guys, shooting guns, and driving fast. Nobody liked evidence collection or chain of custody vouchers. The fact that they would leave Rivera, the newest detective in the office, behind during a shit job meant they didn't like her. Or trust her.

"What happened to your arm?" Rivera said.

Porter was tired of telling the story. Trisha and Ross were one thing; they got the full accounting. Rivera could get the Cliffs Notes. "Some guys broke into my house. I got shot. I shot back. Boom, here we are."

"Wait, the home-invasion last night was you? I heard all about that this morning."

"Really?" Porter said.

"During muster, the captain was telling us about a home invasion in Town and Country, how it seemed very organized and premeditated. They said the homeowner was lucky to be alive," Rivera said.

Porter scowled. "Lucky my ass. I had a better plan and was better prepared, so I won."

Porter watched Rivera working things out in her head.

"These guys that broke into your house, they were from the Acres, right? Even you can't have that many people that want to kill you."

"You'd be surprised," Porter said.

"Is this all related to Danisha Hill?" Rivera said.

"What do you think?" Porter said. He was getting exasperated and the throbbing in his arm was getting worse and worse.

"Okay. Is there something else going on that I need to know

about?" Rivera said.

"Why are you asking me all these questions? You know what's going on. Why would I lie to you about this stuff?" Porter said.

"Porter, I have to be honest with you."

"Aren't you usually?"

"I looked into why you got out of law enforcement."

Porter suddenly understood Rivera's new trust issues. "You're a detective. I assumed eventually you would detect. Did you talk to Ruas about it?"

"I tried, this morning when I called him for information on the Acres boys. All he would say was that you were a great agent. So I called your old office. No one there wanted to talk about you, until I spoke with some guy named Ling."

Ling was Porter's old supervisor, a paper tiger if there ever was one. He'd done a few short years at headquarters in DC and kissed the right backsides. Once he got his own office to manage, he floundered. Ling's massive ego had prevented him from learning from his subordinates and the office had suffered. He and Porter had gotten off on the wrong foot, and had never come to terms.

"Ling's a tool."

"He sounded like it, but he was happy to drop the dime on you. He told me about the evidence you... planted," Rivera said.

Porter stared at the file on the table.

"Why would you risk your career? Hell, risk your *freedom*?"

Porter thought for a few moments. "The subject of the investigation was guilty and flat-out told me so. Just because we couldn't prove it didn't mean he shouldn't have gone to jail. Honestly, he should have fried. If you'd seen the victims, you wouldn't ask me why."

"Ling said they weren't going to fire you."

"Our internal affairs concluded that it could've been an

accident, and that evidence got mixed up due to my careless-ness. They recommended I be suspended, but not terminated," Porter said.

"Were you facing criminal charges?" Rivera said.

"Most of the prosecutors suspected what I had done. Refusing to prosecute me was their silent support," Porter said.

"Then why quit? Why not just take the suspension?"

"I was finished as an agent. The prosecutors weren't coming after me, sure, but they'd never take another one of my cases. They'd always wonder if I was being honest. I didn't want to go through that, so I left."

Rivera looked away. There was silence for a few moments before she spoke again. "Do you regret doing it?"

"I hate when people say they wouldn't change a thing. If you wouldn't change some of the bad times in your life then you're a fool. Everything that happened ruined some great parts of my life, maybe the best parts. I can't get that back. Still, I believed I was doing the right thing, and I still think so."

"Now that I know this, it changes things," Rivera said.

"Things don't look too different from where I'm sitting," Porter said.

"I have to wonder if what you're telling me is true."

"Why? You don't have to believe me, but you believe your own ears, right? You heard the recording. You heard Abel Quintana admit that it was his brother who took Danny Hill."

"I believe the recording."

"Then things haven't changed. You don't have to be on board with my methods or even trust me. I couldn't care less. As long as I can prove what I'm claiming, then you don't have to worry about it. You're on this ride for a big case stat. You may be a new detective, but you know there's something here that needs looking into. Who's gonna do it? You? Your team won't even let you tag evidence with them. They're not going to follow you on a 'hunch' about a girl that's been missing for so long. If you ever want to figure this out, you need me."

They sat there, Rivera staring at a rap sheet and Porter leaning back in the faux leather conference chair.

"Things are complicated with the other detectives. It's not fair for you to throw that in my face," Rivera said.

"Maybe not, but I'm just laying it out for you. If you want this case closed, if you want out of this shitty assignment, I'm your guy. That hasn't changed. So help me."

Porter knew Christina Rivera wasn't a dumb person. She knew he was right, and besides, she was already deep in this. "Fine, Porter, but don't make me doubt anything you say. I need to trust you."

"Then trust me," Porter said.

Rivera pulled some papers out of the file. "What do you want with this stuff? How does any of it help us?"

Porter sensed the trust issue was closed, at least for the time being. He shuffled through the papers until he found a particular mugshot. "What can you tell me about this guy?"

Rivera looked at the FBI number on the mugshot and then matched it up with a rap sheet. "Jamal Hughes. He has a history of possession with intent to distribute, assault, and illegal possession of a firearm. He hasn't been in trouble for a while."

"When was the last time?" Porter said as he fished for another mugshot.

"Three years ago. He was convicted of possession and got sentenced to time served. He has an outstanding warrant for driving with no license," Rivera said.

"What about this one?"

"Terrell White," Rivera said. "He has no convictions for anything. Looks like he has one arrest for battery, but the assistant district attorney dropped the charges. He's clean."

"Or he's good at hiding his dirt. Either way, I think they'll do just fine."

"Fine for what?"

"I'm going to help them take the Acres back from Hector, but first, you need to arrest Jamal Hughes," Porter said.

THIRTY-FOUR

"WHAT ARE YOU TALKING ABOUT, Porter? Arrest him for what? You saw his record, he's pretty clean."

"You said he had an outstanding warrant, didn't you? Pick him up on that."

"It's driving with no license. No one arrests people for that," Rivera said.

"You have to. I need to talk to him."

"So go talk to him. What's stopping you?"

"Did you forget what happened last time I went to the Acres? If you want me to go back, I will, but you should tell those dopey detectives from last night to be ready for more bodies. I'm sure Jacobs would love a chance to pin something else on me," Porter said.

"Jacobs is working your home invasion?"

"With his partner," Porter said.

"Arrington isn't too bad. Jacobs is a moron."

"Okay, so do you want me dealing with them again? This time I'll definitely be booked in and processed while they try to figure out why bodies keep stacking up around me. That'll take time. You want this case closed, don't you?" Porter said.

Rivera thought for a few moments. "What's the point of arresting Hughes?"

"You get him down here, then I let him listen to the Abel Quintana recording. Once he knows I'm legit, I think he'll listen. I have an idea that'll work for both of us," Porter said.

Rivera was quiet for a few more moments. Porter could see her weighing her options, probably a lengthy pro and con math problem going on in her head. He knew that at some point Rivera would decide none of this was worth it. Probably best to let the dead stay dead and just stick it out on the Long Term Missing Unit. She wanted to get promoted, but she didn't want to get herself any further on the radar by doing anything dumb. "Fine. I'll go arrest Jamal Hughes. But I swear to God, Porter you'd better be right about this. If you aren't, I'll be severely pissed off."

Something told Porter he didn't want to see that. "When are you going to sack him up? Who are you taking with you?" Sometimes Porter couldn't turn it off. Now that there was an arrest taking place, he felt a tingle of excitement and he couldn't help but try to game-plan it.

"No one from this unit. They don't like me much and I don't want to tip them off that I'm working on this."

"You could call Ruas. He and his guys could help you. They're the gang unit, it makes sense for them to be arresting gang members," Porter offered.

"No, I don't want him involved. He may talk. I better just do it myself. I'll drive over to the Acres and have a couple of patrol units in the area back me up. That way no detectives are wise to it. The patrol guys are always looking for a reason to do anything other than sit at accident sites and write paperwork," Rivera said.

"Smart plan. Safer with backup, plus the uniformed guys are always hard chargers. They want a promotion."

"That's what they think, until they come to the LTMU and rot."

"We're working on that. Don't forget, at the end of all this is a pot of gold. When are you going to the Acres?" Porter said.

"How about now? It's not too late in the day. Might as well get it over with."

Porter had assumed this would wait until tomorrow, but the idea of getting it done today was appealing. "That works. Where do you want me? I can stay here or I can ride along if you want."

"Get real. The captain would chew my ass if he found out I left you here with no escort. And there's no way in hell I can bring you with me like you're some kind of college kid on a ride-along. Imagine someone finding out a disgraced fed was riding shotgun with me. I'd be working at McDonald's by the week-end," Rivera said.

"I think 'disgraced' may be too strong of a word. I'd call me a freelance former federal employee."

Rivera smirked. "Call yourself what you want. All I know is I've done more dumb shit since I met you... and if it gets any worse even McDonald's won't take me."

"I get it, don't worry. I'll stay way out of the way," Porter said. "Tell you what, I'll just go hang out at the bookstore a few blocks down. The second you get back with Hughes let me know."

"Fine." Rivera gathered all the paperwork and put it into the file. When she finished, she stood up and walked out of the conference room, motioning for Porter to follow her. They walked over to her desk, where she opened the standing cabinet in her workspace and pulled out her body armor and duty belt.

Detectives didn't carry around all the same gear that patrol officers did. Hell, most didn't even wear their armor when they were making an arrest. At least Rivera was gearing up before she went.

"I'll call you when it's done. Don't be far."

"Count on it." Porter headed to the exit, through the front entryway.

Officer Fischer was arguing with someone on his phone. *Probably the wife he's trying to run around on,* Porter thought. Officer Raymond had a spaced-out look on his face when Porter walked by.

Porter walked over to his truck and fired it up.

That went better than I expected. Letting the A/C run to cool everything down, he went over the plan again in his head. He was sure it would work—if he could get Jamal to play his role.

A short drive later, he pulled into the parking lot of the plain two-story building that housed the mom-and-pop bookstore. He figured he had time until Rivera called back.

He entered the bookstore, the smell of musty paper and old ink wafting into his nose. He said hello to the wizened old couple sitting behind the counter, then headed upstairs to the graphic novels. It made him feel much more grown-up to say he was reading a graphic novel than to say he was thumbing through a comic book. Deep down, however, he knew the truth.

Porter hadn't been the most popular child. Sure, he'd had Ross, but that wasn't until junior high school, and that was about it. He had moved often due to his mother's job, so he never had a chance to put down roots until the family settled in Tampa. The fact that he was bigger than everyone else put the other children on edge. Couple that with the fact that he was the darkest person in most of his classes, and he was an oddity. There were a few other friends, but Porter was never the guy who had large numbers of kids around him. Whenever his siblings bothered him, he would retreat into his room and read the comics he had bought with the allowance money he'd managed to save up.

Porter lost track of time as he flipped through a few of his old favorites. Taking a few of the ones that interested him the most, he went to the front counter and paid for them. He figured it was the least he could do after browsing through their stock.

He thanked the couple and walked out of the store. Before he could get to his car, his phone rang. It was Rivera.

"Where are you?"

"I'm close. What's up?"

"Come back to the office. We got him."

THIRTY-FIVE

PORTER DROVE the short distance back to the sheriff's office. When he arrived, he noticed that the lights in the lobby were off. Further down the building, he saw Rivera standing outside a small emergency door. Her clothes were muddy.

She motioned him to come over.

"How did it go?" he said.

"I think you can tell. Look at my clothes. Hughes ran from us. We caught him around the corner and when we did he didn't fight, but I had to get down there and cuff him. In the mud. This is not how I wanted to spend my Monday, Porter. I swear whatever you are pulling better be good."

Porter tried to stifle a smile, but he couldn't.

"That's funny to you?" Rivera said. "I'm not laughing. I should add some charges onto his warrant. Resisting arrest. Fleeing to elude warrant service. I'm sure I could find some more."

"Come on, detective, don't do that. We need him to make this whole thing work. Besides, it's not like he fought you. He was just a decoy."

"What do you mean decoy?"

"I mean he was a decoy. It's pretty common to have someone run and draw all the attention from the cops if they roll up. That way all the guys holding have a chance to get away and drop their drugs. Usually it's a juvenile or someone who won't get in trouble. In this case, it makes sense it was Jamal. He hasn't been in trouble with the cops in years," Porter said.

Rivera groaned. "Of course he was the decoy. I should have known that; I'm just so mad about my new Nikes. The whites were so white..." She trailed off. "You could have told me he would run. I could have put something else on."

"I'm not psychic, Christina Marie Rivera. I can't tell you things that are going to happen, just why some things do," Porter said.

"How did you know my middle... you know what, never mind. Let's get in there and talk to this guy so I can go home."

Rivera led the way through the emergency exit and into the back of the office. The place was deserted.

"You here by yourself? Not a great idea to handle arrestees alone, even a muddy bulldog like you."

"I wasn't alone. The patrol officers that helped me arrest Jamal helped me get him into the interview room. He's cuffed up, and the door locks from the outside. I wasn't going to mess with him again until you came back. I figured if you're as tough as you act we shouldn't have any issues," Rivera said.

Porter kept pace with her as she wound her way through the maze of cubicles until she arrived at the interview room door. It was the same room Porter had been in a couple of days earlier.

"What do we do now?" Rivera said.

"Now it's time to talk. We have to see if we can get Jamal on our side."

"What are you going to tell him?"

"The truth," Porter said and opened the door to the interview room.

Jamal Hughes had his head on the desk, and complained loudly when he heard the door open. "Man, this is some bullshit. I didn't even do anything. Y'all know you didn't catch me holding."

He lifted his head up as he spoke and saw that it was Porter who had entered the room. A look of confusion washed across his face, followed by disgust.

"It's the corny nigga. What you doing here? Thought you weren't a cop. See, this is some entrapment bullshit."

"At least you don't think I'm a bill collector anymore," Porter said.

"Oh, I know you ain't no bill collector. I seen that with my own two eyes. I just can't believe you're a cop."

"Jamal, I'm not a cop and you know it. I do have a question for you, though," Porter said.

"I ain't answering shit without my lawyer," Jamal said.

Porter smiled. Jamal was smarter than he let on. "Actually, the detective and I were just talking about her letting you walk out of here tonight. No need to go to jail over a no operator's license warrant. Right, Detective Rivera?"

"I should take you to jail. You made me chase you and ruin my new shoes. I'm pissed about that," Rivera said.

"I'm sure Jamal is very sorry for doing that. Aren't you sorry, Jamal?" Porter said.

"Man, I'm not—"

"Do you want to get out of here tonight? If so, say 'I'm sorry,' Jamal," Porter said.

"Fine. I'm sorry, Jamal. There."

"Close enough. Right, detective?" Porter said.

"Whatever," Rivera said, and sat in the chair nearest to the exit.

"Good. Now that that's done, I still have a question to ask you, Jamal," Porter said.

"What question, man?"

"Do you want to take back full control of the Acres?"

THIRTY-SIX

"THE ACRES IS ALREADY MINE, fool, what you talkin' about? Huh? You bring me all the way down here to ask me this dumb shit?"

"We both know that's not true," Porter said. "It's just the three of us in here; you don't have to front."

Jamal didn't say anything. He just shrugged his shoulders and looked at Porter.

"Thought so," Porter said. "I'm being straight with you. I want you in charge of the Acres and I want Hector Quintana gone. I think it should be easy to do that."

"Why? What Hector ever do to you, huh? What, you want a piece of his business?" Jamal looked at Rivera in the corner. "I mean, alleged business. Alleged."

Rivera glared at Jamal, then went back to work. She was holding one of her Nikes in one hand, dabbing at it with a paper towel in the other hand.

"It's pretty simple, Jamal. The day I met you I was talking to Miss Leona about her little girl. You know that, right?"

"Of course I know. Shit, everybody knows Danisha's missing."

"I told her I'd find out what happened to Danny, and I intend to keep my word."

"It's messed up, that little girl gone. Me and my guys tried to help Miss Leona, but we couldn't find nothing," Jamal said.

"What if I told you that Hector Quintana kidnapped her?"

"I'd say prove it," Jamal said. "Talk is cheap."

Porter pulled out his phone and scrolled through the videos until he got to the one he was looking for. "The voice you're about to hear is Hector's brother, Abel. Just listen." Porter sat the phone down between them on the table and hit play.

Jamal didn't say a word as the recording told the story. He sat there and listened, face getting redder the longer the recording played, and when it finished, he launched into a diatribe about what he wanted to do to Hector. It took several minutes before Jamal had calmed down enough to talk to Porter.

"You don't seem too happy," Porter said.

"Hell naw, I ain't happy. Not even a little. Danny's one of us. She belongs in the neighborhood. We're supposed to look out for each other. Shit's messed up."

"I agree. You going to help me fix this?" Porter said.

"I want to, trust me. You don't even know how bad I want to. But we got a truce right now. The last time I took a shot at getting rid of Hector, a buncha good people got hurt. Hector don't care, he'll shoot anything up. I'm not worried about my soldiers, they're real gangstas. It's all the other people I gotta worry about," Jamal said.

"I have an idea about how to make sure no one gets hurt. You interested?"

"Hit me," Jamal said.

Porter spent the next ten minutes outlining his plan. He left out a couple of crucial details he figured Jamal didn't need to know. Porter thought it was a good plan, but he didn't want Jamal to leak something that could hurt Porter. As much as he wanted everything to go smoothly, he wanted to live even more. "So that's why I need you. I won't get a meeting with Hector on my own."

"I can get down with that. I think this shit might even work," Jamal said.

"Good. So here's the thing: I need you to make this happen tomorrow afternoon. Think you can do that?"

"No doubt. I'll send a messenger to Hector and tell him we have to meet. I say it and it's done."

"Where do you meet?" Porter said.

"The old clubhouse at the back end of the hood. It's off Wendell Street, you know, that road around back? It used to be for the leasing agents and birthday parties and shit. Nobody ever goes over there anymore, so we use it. No interruptions."

Porter thought back to the map he had seen of the Acres. There was a small side street on the back edge of the property. That could work.

"Tell me more about the meeting. Who comes, how many people, things like that," Porter said.

Jamal spent five minutes telling Porter the lineups: how many people each guy got to bring, lieutenants, soldiers, look-outs, the whole setup. Porter was satisfied.

"Once we get that meeting, everything should go off without a hitch. Detective Rivera? You good?"

The fact that Porter had left out a few parts for Jamal meant that Rivera wasn't fully informed either. Porter didn't think she would appreciate some of the more nuanced parts and when it was all said and done, he knew she needed deniability. Better to keep her out of the full loop.

"Yeah, I got it. As long as Jamal has the juice he says he does, it should be smooth sailing." She left her chair, went over to Jamal, and took his handcuffs off.

Jamal stood up and rubbed his wrists where the cuffs had

been. Porter stood, too. The two men exchanged phone numbers. "This shit better work. I got a lot on the line."

"Don't worry, it will," Porter said.

"Hey cop lady, you gonna give me a ride back to the crib? You drove me all the way over here," Jamal said.

"Nope, but I'll walk you out the back. Come on, let's go."

Jamal groused but followed Rivera out of the interview room.

Porter stood outside the interview room going over some of the finer points of his plan. It had to work. He just needed Jamal to play his part and everything would work out. But just to be sure, Porter had a little trick up his sleeve—and it was a doozy.

THIRTY-SEVEN

AFTER A FEW MINUTES, Rivera came back into the office. By then, Porter had moved to her desk and was leaning back in the beat-up office chair.

"Jamal's gone. He made a call and said some of his boys were coming to get him. He didn't want me to wait with him. Said people would get the wrong idea about him if he was hanging out at a cop station. He walked off down Kennedy."

"He can't let people think he's a snitch. It'd be bad for his health," Porter said.

"I guess so," Rivera said. "Porter... about this plan. It seems like a stretch. Why would Hector's guys flip to Jamal? Aren't they all scared of Hector?"

"Probably so, but that's what the tape is for. Maybe a little evidence will convince them he's not the guy they think he is. We'll figure it out."

"What do you mean 'we'? There is no 'we' in this. I can't be involved with trying to take down a gang leader. I'm sure that breaks at least a dozen rules. I did my part, bringing you two together. You're on your own with the rest of this," Rivera said.

"It was the royal *We*. Look, if you need to cover your ass, I dig it. It's probably better if you stay out of it. But you can't tell me that having Jamal in charge isn't better for everyone involved. There won't be as much violence; there won't be any real drug problems, just weed; and there damn sure won't be any little girls getting snatched off the streets. Sounds like a win in my book."

"What I'm missing is what I get out of this deal," Rivera said. "You promised you were closing this case; you didn't say anything about playing kingmaker."

"Your case is only going to get better. You think Hector was the one who did the dirty work? Doesn't seem likely. I'll bet we can get him to flip on the guy who... did whatever they did to Danny."

"And you just want to flip your way up the ladder and see where it takes you?" Rivera said. "Real seat-of-your-pants type stuff?"

"Why not? We'll apply pressure as we go along and see who will tell us what. You could arrest Hector if you want, but you said it, the confession won't hold up in court. Let me build you a better case. I told you I'll do it, and I will. You just have to trust me."

Porter watched as Rivera took in what he was saying. She seemed convinced to go along with Porter's plan. "Fine, but I'm still not going to be part of what happens tomorrow. I can't afford to get in trouble."

"Don't sweat it, I'll get some help. I'll call you tomorrow evening and let you know what Hector tells me," Porter said.

"That's if he tells you anything."

"Stick with me, kid, and I'll take you places," Porter said.

"What?"

"It's just something my dad used to say." Porter stood up and patted his pockets to locate his keys, then moved toward the emergency exit with Rivera in tow. "Just keep your phone on."

Rivera pushed open the exit door and Porter stepped out into the night. It was muggy, but at least the sun wasn't out. He pointed at Rivera. "Phone on, detective."

"It better not be another late call or I'll arrest you myself," Rivera said as she allowed the emergency door to close between them.

Porter fired up his truck and put it into drive, pulling through the empty spot in front of him. He didn't have anywhere to go. His house was a wreck and he needed some rest before tomorrow.

Only one place to go.

———

"AND SHE JUST WENT AND arrested him? Just like that?" Ross said between bites of pasta.

"Rivera's smart. She knows Hector is the key and she want to find out what happened just as bad as anyone."

"I guess so. I just figured she'd be worried about getting into trouble."

"She is, and I don't blame her. But I came up with a plan to get things rolling."

"What can I do? And before you try to shine me off, just shut your damn mouth. I'm already involved. My best friend got shot, so I think that means I'm in now. If you try to tell me no, I'll—"

"You can help," Porter said.

Food fell from Ross's open mouth. "Did you say I can help?"

"I need your help," Porter said.

"Okay. Great," Ross said, before narrowing his eyes. "Why do you need my help?"

"I can't be in two places at once, can I?"

"Well, no," Ross said.

"That's where you come into play. I'll shoot straight with you, it's not the safest thing. Still want in?"

"I'm not a pussy. Just tell me what to do."

Over the next ten minutes, Porter outlined the plan to Ross. The full plan, more than either Jamal or Rivera knew. He trusted Ross—in this case, with his life.

After he finished, Porter listened as Ross tried to find holes in the plan. After all, analytical thinking was his strong suit.

"What if Hector's guys don't care about the tape?" Ross said.

"Everyone has a sister or mother or daughter or wife. No one wants women and children harmed," Porter said.

"Then how did Hector snatch Danny in the first place? He had to have help."

"There are some real savages that don't care, but they're few and far between. Only one thing you can do about those guys."

"What can you do about..." Ross's voice trailed off. "Oh yeah. There's *one* thing you can do about those guys. But that isn't my thing, right?"

"No, Ross, that isn't your thing. If the situation calls for it, it'll be my thing," Porter said.

"So, what's my thing?"

"Driving," Porter said. "I need a ride over to the Acres."

"That's the dangerous part? You want me to be a taxi?"

"How do you think they'll take it when my truck rolls up? I already slapped a couple of them around, and put two more in the morgue. They'll be pissed. In fact, I'm counting on it. The more pissed they get, the better for us. Trust me."

"I do, but that's not always a good thing," Ross said.

"What the hell do you mean? When have I ever steered you wrong?"

"What about that time you told me Betsy Vrabel wanted me to kiss her?" Ross said.

"Are you kidding me? I'm literally talking about life and death and you're bringing up senior year?"

"It was junior year," Ross said, "and I still have the lump on my nose from where she punched me. Just thought I should remind you, you aren't always right."

Porter shook his head. "You're an idiot. Maybe next time don't take dating advice from me."

"Aren't you trying to give me dating advice about Tessa?" Ross said.

"That's different. That girl's the one for you. She knows it and you know it, but you're too chicken to talk to her about it. So she hangs around waiting, and you pretend she works for you for the benefits, knowing full well she could work anywhere else."

"Maybe if I get out of this alive, I'll ask her out."

"Get out of this alive? You've been watching too many movies."

They finished eating and then cleaned the kitchen, few words passing between them. Porter recognized the feeling. Before an operation, he and his team had often had a similar quiet tension. It was a good thing; it helped to focus the mind.

After they cleaned the kitchen Porter showered, then fell into the guest bed, out of commission for the rest of the day.

THIRTY-EIGHT

THERE WERE no alarms set the next morning. Ross had texted Tessa the night before and told her he was sick and that she needed to cancel his appointments for the day. She was genuinely concerned about his health. Porter took another opportunity to prod Ross into asking her out. Ross balked at the suggestion, but his eyes betrayed the fact that he was considering it.

They made a large breakfast, ate, and then rested until the middle of the afternoon, flipping through the television until they found *Roadhouse* on some obscure channel. Patrick Swayze was big in the Porter home when he and Trisha were married. She loved him for *Dirty Dancing*, and *Roadhouse* was one of Porter's favorite movies. Hard to beat Swayze kicking ass.

Porter's phone shattered the calm.

"How did it go? The meeting's set? Good. What time? Okay, I got it. You remember what to do? Okay, we're on our way. Later."

"Who was that?" Ross said.

"Jamal. He got everything set up with Hector. We have a couple hours."

"They meet in the middle of the day?" Ross said.

"If you're meeting with someone who wants to kill you, wouldn't you try to do it in the daylight?"

"I'm not sure. I can't say anyone's ever tried to kill me."

"Maybe you'll pop your cherry today," Porter said. He pulled open Ross's laptop and punched in an address. "See this grocery store? This is where we need to be. When you come back, try to park as close to the front as you can. Got it?"

"I got it." Ross took a deep breath. "Anything else you need me to bring?"

"Grab a flathead."

"Flathead? You know what, never mind, I'll go get it."

Porter moved around the house collecting his things, then went to the driveway and started his truck. He waited for Ross to lock things up and hop into his practical Honda sedan, and they headed across town together, one behind the other.

The traffic was thicker than normal and it took forty-five minutes to get to the grocery store. Calling it that was being generous. It was a jumped-up gas station in a rundown building in need of repair, with two non-working pumps outside and a bunch of terrible, overpriced, packaged food on the inside. They pulled into the parking lot within seconds of each other. Porter motioned for Ross to park next to him.

Ross did as he was told and sat for a minute while Porter fidgeted in his truck, then rolled his window down when Porter tapped on the glass.

"Got that screwdriver?"

Ross grabbed the screwdriver and handed it to Porter, who went to work. His first stop was the rear of Ross's Honda. He knelt down for a minute, then came back to Ross's window and handed him the Honda's license plate.

Then Porter walked a row over and, after a quick look around, disappeared behind a Toyota Camry with big rims. He was quicker this time. He walked back to Ross's car, stopped to put the new plate on the Honda, then hopped into the passenger seat beside Ross.

"What's that about?" Ross said.

"Hector's guys at the Acres must have run my license plate the first time I was there. I doubt they'll see you, but I'm not going to take any chances. You can't use your real plate."

Ross thought for a minute. "What if they see this plate? Won't they go after an innocent person instead?"

"Maybe. But there are two things to consider. First, hopefully Hector and his guys will be in no position to retaliate against anyone this time tomorrow. Second, I don't give a shit about the person who drives that Camry."

"That's cold, Porter."

"It is what it is. Ready to drive?"

Ross nodded.

"Good. Let's go. We have a meeting to catch."

THIRTY-NINE

JAMAL WAS on his side of Palmetto Avenue, standing alone. He'd done what Porter asked him, even though he wasn't convinced it would get him anywhere. Still it was worth a shot, and having a meeting wasn't out of the ordinary in the least. That's what people did when they were beefing; they set up meets and made truces.

Jamal was done with truces.

Each side was bringing four soldiers for security. No one could bring weapons or cell phones. Being recorded while openly discussing business could be a problem for everyone.

The old clubhouse was a two-story structure with a big open room on the bottom, for hosting birthday parties or neighborhood meetings. It had long since fallen to ruin, as no one had parties there and the neighborhood never had any legitimate meetings, only the illicit ones that the gangs orchestrated.

The second floor of the building had several private rooms that could be used for various purposes. A couple of years ago someone had knocked down a wall between two of the rooms to create one large one.

The room was a rectangle, with several windows to let the

light in, and a bathroom with a slatted door at the end. The entry doors were on the same wall near the hallway, but one of them had plywood nailed over it. There was no need for two entrances. In the open space in between the bathroom and the end of the room closest to the street, someone had set up one of the plastic, folding-leg tables that people brought out to seat guests on Thanksgiving. It served as an impromptu conference table.

Whenever the rival factions of the Acres had to meet, this was where it happened. It was neutral territory, a place where gang members were supposed to be safe from each other.

Jamal looked at his watch and saw that it was about time. He walked back into his apartment and gave Terrell a nod. The big man was already ready to go. Three other men joined up with Jamal and Terrell and jumped into a car. They drove two streets over to the community clubhouse and parked outside.

"Y'all niggas make sure you keep an eye on shit. We don't want Hector trying anything crazy," Jamal said.

Except for Terrell, the other members of Jamal's security detail had no idea that there was a plan in motion. They thought it was business as usual, and would treat the meeting as seriously as they always did.

From the opposite direction, a small SUV appeared—Hector Quintana and his security. They pulled into a parking spot several spaces away from Jamal and got out of their ride.

Hector hopped out first. He was average height with dark hair. He wore his beard in a thin chinstrap that framed his jaw. Jamal spotted a new tattoo on Hector's neck, something in Spanish. Jamal knew the rest of the guys with Hector. Three of them he was friendly with. They used to roll with him, and had only gone to Hector for the promise of easy money.

The other was Mike. Jamal never liked Mike very much; he had a strange personality and was always talking about horror movies. He smelled like the African oils he was constantly slathering on his long dreadlocks. He must have gotten hurt because his left arm was bandaged and in a sling.

"Hughes," Hector said.

"Hector. Let's get this meet going."

"*Despacio*, my friend. You know we have to sweep the building," Hector said.

It was Hector's preference to have a member of each team walk through the building. Maybe he had seen *Casino* one too many times and thought someone was going to try to blow him up. Either way, he'd never relent, and Jamal nodded at one of his guys, who walked into the building with one of Hector's. The rest of the group stayed outside.

"It was nice of you to reach out today, Jamal. I was just thinking we needed to get together. It's been far too long."

That was one of the things Jamal hated most about Hector. He was always acting, putting on a show for everyone. The way he walked and talked was so fake, it turned Jamal's stomach.

In the back of his mind, Jamal was replaying the recording Porter played for him. He clenched his fist and stared at Hector. After a few moments, he took a breath and unballed his hand. If he lost his temper and went after Hector, it would ruin the plan. "I'm trying to see what you got going on, Hector. Maybe we can talk business."

"See, that's how a boss thinks, Jamal. There's always room for a collab."

The two men sweeping the building finished up, and the entire group moved into the lobby. There they took turns patting each other down and the rules were followed—with one exception.

"Jamal has his celly." Mike held up a phone with his good hand.

"Jamal, *no bueno, hermano*."

"Check this shit out. The phone's off." Jamal showed everyone. Then he took the battery out. "I'm not recording nothing. I gotta keep the phone, I need it to show you something later."

Hector thought for a moment. "That works, but you need to keep it on the table so we all can see it, and tell us when you're turning it on. *Comprende?*"

"Man, you know I don't speak that Spanish shit. You gotta come at me in English. Stop with all that *bueno* and *comprende*," Jamal said.

Hector smiled and started up the stairs to the conference room. Everyone else followed him, except for the two sweepers, who stayed downstairs to watch the front door.

No one else could come in or out.

Hector walked like he was a dignitary. When they got to the room, he waited for one of his guys to open the door for him. Hector eyed the table, then took a seat at the head.

All the other guys filtered into the room, with Jamal coming in last. When they were all seated, Jamal walked over to the table and set his disassembled phone on it. Instead of taking his rightful seat opposite Hector, he moved to the window directly behind his empty chair, and looked outside.

"You just gonna stand like that?" Hector said.

"Don't feel much like sitting," Jamal said.

Hector pushed his metal folding chair out and stood as well.

"I know you called this meet, Hughes, but if you don't mind, I would like to say something first."

"Of course you do," Jamal muttered.

"As you all know, I haven't been here for very long. I came from New York and moved here to be closer to *mi familia*. Family is what I want to talk about. I know we've had our differences in the past. Sometimes when there are too many alpha wolves in a pack, things get confusing."

Jamal looked out the window again, barely listening to Hector's speech.

"'Misinterpreted' might be a better word. The beef we're having right now is all a big misunderstanding. We all need to be more like family. If we reunite the two sides of the Acres, we can be more powerful than ever. We can make more money than ever. We will have more respect than ever."

That line piqued Jamal's interest. *This fool shot my crib up, and he thinks we gonna be tight.*

"I was thinking the same shit," Jamal said. "One Acres. That's what I want to talk to—"

"I'm sorry, Hughes, I wasn't finished talking," Hector said.

It was a power move. Jamal knew Hector was trying to make him look weak by interrupting him. All the eyes at the table turned from Hector to Jamal. Jamal showed no outward appearances of anger, but was boiling inside.

"You talk so much, I thought you was done," Jamal said. He knew it wasn't time to act yet, but Porter needed to hurry up. Jamal only had so much patience.

"We need to be one Palmetto Acres. I believe I have the right connections to expand our businesses. I know that if we work together, I can put a bunch of money in everyone's pockets."

It finally hit Jamal what Hector wanted from the meeting. He hadn't agreed to this meeting to see what Jamal had to say, or to discuss a more substantial truce. He was trying to get Jamal's guys to turn on him.

Jamal began to say something, but he was drowned out by the loud blaring of a car horn from outside. The horn didn't let up. Jamal raised his voice and pointed out the window. "Hey, Mike."

The man with the dreadlocks looked up. "What?"

"Ain't that the nigga that beat your ass the other day?" Jamal pointed out the window.

Mike stood up and walked to the window. The blue Yukon was in the middle of the street. He shot a look at Hector, who joined him at the window. Cursing under his breath, Hector barked at his guys to get downstairs. All four, including Hector, ran out of the room, down the staircase, and out the front door. As they approached the Yukon, it pulled away, leaving them chasing behind it in the middle of the street.

Hector yelled at someone to grab their car. While the driver ran to their SUV, Hector told his man on the door to keep an eye on everything. The man ran back to the entrance as Hector and his remaining guys took off after the Yukon.

Where is Porter going? Jamal thought. *We're supposed to get him up here to talk to this fool. Why's he driving away?*

HECTOR SCREAMED at his driver to push the SUV faster. The Yukon was idling by the exit to the main street. As the SUV got closer, it stayed just out of reach, fast enough to stay ahead of its pursuers.

The chase was short-lived. The Yukon pulled off the road and into a small, run-down grocery store. In the parking lot were three police cruisers, lights flashing.

"Look at all those cops. This guy has a rabbit's foot up his ass," Hector said. "You sure that's him?"

"That's him," Mike said, cradling his injured arm. "That's Porter."

Hector took a deep breath to calm himself. "No matter. He can't hide forever. Let's go take care of this *pendejo* Hughes. Then, maybe we go looking for Porter. *Vamanos.*"

The driver turned the SUV around and sped back to the Acres.

"You guys remember what we talked about," Hector. "By the end of the day, Hughes will be out of the way. Just watch my back, I don't trust those sneaky *putos*."

JAMAL and his security were waiting for Hector to return. He'd watched Hector tear after Porter and, at this point, had no clue what the big corny clown was planning, but it didn't look like it involved coming upstairs to talk.

"Let's get back at this," Hector said as he stepped from the SUV.

"I'm waiting on you. You find what you were looking for?"

"Just a matter of time," Hector said. "We need to sweep the building again?"

Hector's door guy spoke up. "Nah, we straight. No one went in while you were gone. One way in, one way out. I been here the whole time."

"That's why I keep you around, Darrell," Hector said. "Always paying attention."

There was another pat down, this time cursory, and they all headed upstairs. The group entered the conference room and everyone sat again—except for Jamal. This time he took the lead. "Hector, you already ran your mouth. Then you interrupted the meet to take a little road trip. It's my turn now."

"Of course, Hughes. Please continue," Hector said, as if granting Jamal permission to speak.

So fake, Jamal thought.

Jamal took a minute and looked at the entire table. He knew his guys were with him. He thought some of Hector's would be as well. There was no way Mike would switch sides, but Jamal would cross that bridge when he got to it.

"All right, y'all know I don't talk slick. You know me for real, 'cause we all came up together. We balled at the park. We drank together. We're family. Not a bullshit family like this fool's talking about—a real family. Terrell's with my little sister. The first time I ever smoked out was with you, Calvin."

One of the guys on Hector's side nodded his head.

"I think we let this slick-talking, New York asshole divide us up. Keep us at each other's throats," Jamal said.

Hector shifted in his chair, glaring at Jamal.

"And that stops today."

FORTY

"Y'ALL REMEMBER Miss Leona's little girl?" Heads nodded around the room. "You know who took her? Your boy Hector, that's who."

There were glances exchanged and several faces turned to Hector.

"Come on, Hughes, that's bullshit. Why would I take some little girl? I think you all know me better than that. I may be a lot of things, but I'm not a kiddie rapist."

"I never said you raped her," Jamal said, "I said you took her. Pay attention. We both know you did it, so why not just admit it to your people? Show them what kind of moves you really makin'."

"*Escucha me*," Hector said as he stood from his seat. "I came here today to talk about coming together. I hoped that Jamal would finally listen. Turns out, all he wants to do is lie on me. It won't work, *mentiroso*, no one's gonna believe this fairy tale."

Jamal stared at Hector and moved to the middle of the conference table, grabbing his phone and battery. Without a word, he assembled the phone and pressed the power button.

Hector's eyes darted across the room. "No! No! We said no phones." He came around the table, headed straight for Jamal.

Terrell stepped in between them, grabbed Hector by the front of his shirt, and sent the man flying onto the folding table.

"Hey," Hector screamed. "You can't do that."

Men from both sides stood to their feet, ready for action. Terrell grabbed Mike by his hair before he could make it to his feet and pinned his head to the table. The injured man flailed underneath him, but was unable to move.

"Wait," Jamal said in a loud voice. "Just wait."

The men on both sides paused for a moment.

"Get him," Hector screamed as he clambered off the table.

Terrell still blocked the path to Jamal as he held Mike's head on the table. The rest of the men on both sides were in the way. Hector couldn't reach his rival.

"We said no phones. We said no phones."

Jamal stood silently for a moment, the powder keg around him simmering. He looked at the faces in front of him. "I never lie."

He pressed play on the recording Porter had given him. The entire conference room heard Abel Quintana ratting out his brother. The entire conference room heard that the big talker who was going to take their gang to the next level had kidnapped one of their kids.

A kid from the Acres.

As the recording played, Terrell let go of Mike with a shove and moved toward the door. He cut an imposing figure, barring the only way out of the room.

When the recording stopped, there was silence in the conference room. The men standing around the table looked around at each other. Just moments ago, they'd been ready to go to war, now they were stunned by the recording they'd just heard.

Hector Quintana had turned his back to the room while the recording played. Now, he turned around, a scowl on his face. He straightened his crumpled collar and addressed the group.

"Fine, I did it. The question is, why? I did it for the crew."

"You didn't do shit for us," Jamal said, feeling the momentum shift.

"You all remember that fool Charles, right? He was locked down for a minute?" Hector said.

"Of course we know Charles," Jamal said.

"He came to my boy while he was locked up. Charles said he stuck the Aryans for some product and needed protection," Hector said. "What was I supposed to say, huh? I'd do the same thing for any of you."

There was a murmured consensus around the table.

Danisha's father, Charles, hadn't really been a member of the Acres boys. But he was from the Acres and the gang had a sizeable contingent in the local prisons. It made sense that Charles would seek protection from guys he knew.

"What's that got to do with Danny?" Jamal said.

"My help comes with a price, *pendejo*. I don't do anything for free. When Charles got out, he was supposed to pay up. I went to see him in some ratty-ass motel, and he told me he didn't have it. He couldn't pay us back." Hector looked around at the men. "You know what that means. I was about to handle him when he offers his girl as payment. Says if we let him live, we can have her."

"We?" Calvin, one of Hector's lieutenants, said.

Mike was fidgeting with his dreadlocks, trying to smooth the hair Terrell had grabbed. He didn't look up.

"Charles says we can have her. I think he thought I would do some perverted shit or something. It got me thinking. The squad could always use the money. That's what I always told you boys, that I got ways to make more money. We have to think big picture," Hector said.

"Keep going," Jamal said.

"There's a guy who knows how to move kids. I knew people from my life up north and they put me in touch. I let him buy Danisha and I made us a bunch of money."

Jamal knew this was the time to press. "What you're saying is, you stole one of our little girls and flipped her?"

"To make money for the crew. To make us strong," Hector said. He took a step backward, away from the harsh glares of the room.

"Then where's the money?" Jamal wasn't the least bit interested in the money, but knew this would be the nail in Hector's coffin. "How much did you give your guys? Because my guys ain't seen shit."

"I still have it. I'm waiting for the right time to dish it out. I wanted the heat around Danisha to die down a little. The cops were sniffing around."

Calvin stood up. "I don't give a damn about that money. That shit is dirty. I won't be part of this anymore. Even Gs gotta have a code. I'm out." He walked over to Jamal. "You still got space for me?"

"Of course, my nigga. You always welcome back. In fact, any of you who want back in, you're free to make that move. No questions asked," Jamal said.

There was a murmur through the group and then the rest of Hector's men, save for Mike, followed Calvin's lead. Calvin looked at Jamal and said, "I know Darrell downstairs will want out. We ridin' with you now."

Calvin and the other man waited for Terrell to let them past and left.

"You fools are making a mistake," Hector called after the departing men. "I did this for us. Don't you want to get paid?"

Jamal spoke to his two soldiers standing in the room. "Y'all leave too. I want you to spread the word. Tell everybody what went down. Tell them what a fraud-ass bitch Hector is. We'll catch up with you soon." Jamal's boys left the room.

Only Jamal and Terrell, Mike and Hector remained.

"You're done. Finished. Your fake ass better get while you can, because once everybody hears what happened, you're a target. I can't keep you safe—hell, I don't even want to. You thought you could come up in my hood and take over? Shoot up my baby mama's house? You're lucky I don't smoke you right now. That's my word."

Jamal moved to leave the room, but Terrell didn't budge.

"Now's not the time. Neutral ground, remember? We keep our word," Jamal said. "He'll get his."

Terrell shrugged and moved aside, letting Jamal leave, then followed him out of the conference room.

Hector was standing, trembling with rage, his face bright red. "How can they just leave? Disloyal, disrespectful bitches. Don't they know who I am?" He pounded the conference table. "Don't they know who I am?" Hector stood, palms flat on the table, seething.

Mike rose and walked around the table. His dreadlocks hung loose around his face. He put his good hand on Hector's shoulder. "Don't sweat this shit. Jamal don't have vision. He's weak. The other guys will see it. We just need to lay low for a minute. When my arm heals, I'll do Jamal and Terrell myself."

Hector nodded. "Yeah. Yeah, that's right. Hughes never should have started. It's a war he can't finish. He pounded the table again, punctuating his words. "You hear me, Hughes? You're dead. You're dead."

"That's right," Mike said. "Keep your head up, we'll make moves."

Hector pounded the table again and began to pace the room.

Mike started toward the back of the room. "Let me take a piss and we'll ghost this bitch. I have a place for us to keep our heads down. Give us time to think."

"There's nothing he can do to stop me. No way anyone can stop me. I run the Acres. Me. Once I'm back, you're gonna be my right hand, Mike."

There was a loud pop and Mike's face disappeared into a pink mist. He slumped to the floor, legs trapped underneath him. Blood leaked out from the hole that used to be his eyes.

"*Dios mio!*" Hector said, turning toward the sound of the gunshot. His eyes went wide with fear.

FORTY-ONE

-BEFORE-

"You trying to get us pulled over? We don't want any attention," Porter said. "Slow down."

"I don't know, I just want to get there and get it over with. I hope this works."

"What's not to work? You've got the easy job. Just drop me off, then go back to the grocery store and get the Yukon," Porter said.

"Easy for you to say. You aren't going to have thugs trying to kill you."

"Just remember to call the cops before you leave."

"You sure you have to do it like this? There has to be another way," Ross said.

"Hector will never meet with me without trying to kill me. I'm a big loose end to tie up. Literally."

"You are a big loose end," Ross agreed.

"Just stick to the script," Porter said. "I'll handle the hard stuff."

"Don't worry, I'll take care of my end. I promise," Ross said.

Ross slowed down and took a right onto one of the boundary

streets of the Acres. He followed it to the far end of the neighborhood, where he was the only car on the road. Next to the road was a ten-foot-tall privacy wall made of cinderblock and stucco. Peeking over the top of the wall was a two-story building.

"Stop here," Porter said. "This is it. Just remember what we went over. If you get spooked or something doesn't feel right, drive away. Keep driving until you get somewhere safe. You getting out okay is more important than me talking to Hector Quintana."

"That's bullshit and you know it. If you talking to Hector lets us find out what happened to Danny, then it is the most important thing. Get out."

Porter liked that fire from Ross. He got out and quietly closed the door.

Ross sped away.

Porter took a minute to size up the wall in front of him. The way the cinder block was stacked and arranged, it gave him toeholds the entire way up the wall. He stood for a moment, straining his ears.

Silence.

Porter took a step and jumped, grabbing the top of the wall. A flash of pain seared through his injured arm, but he gritted his teeth and held strong. After adjusting his footing, his next movements took him up and over the wall. He landed in a crouch and didn't move.

He again heard nothing and looked around to get his bearings.

The yard behind the old clubhouse was nothing but overgrown grass and a cheap playground, rusty from years of neglect. He couldn't see the road in front of the clubhouse, but he was concerned about being seen through the large sliding door which led from the bottom level of the clubhouse to the backyard.

His concerns were quickly allayed. Someone had boarded the slider up from the inside with sheets of plywood. Porter was alone in the rear of the clubhouse and no one could see him. He waited.

After ten minutes, his phone vibrated. Fishing it out of his pocket, he answered.

"Yeah," Porter whispered.

"I dropped the Honda off. Just called the cops and told them there was a guy with a gun in the grocery store. That should bring them out," Ross said.

"Definitely. When you drive out with the Yukon, make sure you head back to the grocery. You'll be safe no matter who follows you there."

"I will. You okay back there?"

"It's nice. Thinking of buying a timeshare here," Porter said.

"I'll bet. Give me a few minutes, then you're on."

"I'm ready," Porter said as he hung up the phone.

Staying low, he moved through the tall grass and came to stop behind the playground's slide. He looked to the left and right and still saw no one, although he heard voices from the front of the building.

Stay up there.

Porter was counting the time in his head. He got to six and a half minutes before he heard his Yukon's horn blaring from the street. Ross was a little slow, but he'd made it. The sound was coming from the front right of the building, so Porter went to the left side of the clubhouse. He moved quickly along the clubhouse's stucco wall, glad he'd picked a good spot. The way the building was tucked into the corner of the street made it impossible for him to be seen until he passed by the wall he was leaning against.

Porter made it to the front corner of the clubhouse and then poked half his face around it. Ross was driving the Yukon away from the building. There was a group of guys chasing him and everyone was looking that way. There was nobody by the front door.

This was his chance.

Sprinting, he covered the thirty feet from the edge of the clubhouse to its front door, then stepped in just as he heard a voice barking to get the cars. The lower level of the clubhouse was dark, and Porter's eyes didn't have a chance to adjust from the Florida sun. Temporarily blinded, he moved as far into the room as he could before running into the stairwell on the far wall. Feeling steps, he followed them to the right and found the landing. His eyes still hadn't adjusted as he took the steps, two at a time, to the second floor.

Stopping to catch his breath, Porter stayed close to the wall. He heard no voices on the second floor, so he took a minute. When he was able to see, he moved around upstairs. He checked two doors, finding them nailed shut, and then he saw an open door. He stepped into it and found a room containing a table, some chairs, and little else.

At the end of the room was a door with wooden slats hung awkwardly in the frame. Just what Porter was looking for. He stepped into it and pulled the door closed behind him. It caught roughly on the jamb, obviously a replacement door. It didn't take long for Porter to see why.

He'd stepped into a bathroom, with a toilet and sink. There were dozens of holes punched into the drywall, exposing the insulation. Porter could just make out how large the space was from the little bit of light streaming through the slats.

Not much privacy with this door, he thought.

He stood silent as a statue, trying to get his breathing under control.

Every breath sounded like thunder in his ears and he waited for a crew of Acres boys to follow the noise right to him.

There was silence for many minutes. Porter breathed deep and slow. His phone vibrated once, with a text:

They left the grocery. Headed back to you.

Porter slipped his phone back into his pocket and waited. After several more minutes, he heard people stomping up the stairs. A sizeable group of guys came into the big room and took seats around the table. Porter strained to try make out the figures. From his angle, he could see Jamal and Terrell, but didn't recognize anyone else. He could barely hear what was being said.

"It's my turn now."

Porter listened as Jamal told the group about Hector taking Danny. Then a guy with a small beard and a neck tattoo stood up and denied the accusations.

That must be Hector, Porter thought. *He looks different than I thought.* Then he realized he wasn't sure what he'd thought Hector would look like, but after hearing so much about the guy, he had expected a fire-breathing dragon. This was just a guy.

A brief fight broke out, as Terrell grabbed Hector and threw him across the table.

Moments later, Jamal played the recording for the entire group.

Hector stood back the entire time. His back was to Porter, but he was close enough to see him shaking. He started talking.

What did he say about Danny's father?

Jamal interrupted Hector with a couple of questions. By now, Porter could tell that Hector had lost the room. Some of the guys stood up and walked out. Jamal spoke again to the group and two more guys stood up and walked out. That only left Jamal, Terrell by the door, and Hector standing a few feet away from the table.

And Dreadlocks, Porter thought. *His arm looks pretty messed up. Good.*

Jamal said something to Hector and then turned to leave the room.

Porter watched as Hector slammed the table. For the first time, he could hear clearly what he was saying: ranting about wanting to kill Jamal. Dreadlocks stood up and put his hand on the smaller man's shoulder.

Hector was pacing now, cursing and yelling about the meeting. Dreadlocks was the voice of reason, trying to pacify his boss. He turned and walked toward the door Porter was behind.

Don't come this way. Not yet.

Dreadlocks kept walking, talking over his shoulder to Hector.

Dammit. Porter reached into his back pocket and pulled out the small revolver Tattoo had tried to pull on him several days ago. It was the only weapon Porter had, what with his Glock being confiscated and him not being able to get into his house to retrieve anything else. It didn't matter. Tattoo's revolver would do the trick. In fact, it was better that it wasn't his own gun.

"Let me take a piss and we'll ghost this bitch. I have a place for us to keep our heads down. Give us time to think," Dreadlocks said.

Although his view was obscured by the door, Porter aimed the revolver at the bridge of Mike's nose, holding it steady as the man drew closer.

"There's nothing he can do to stop me. No way anyone can stop me. I run the Acres. Me," Hector said, pounding his chest.

Porter held the front sight of the revolver steady.

"Once I'm back, you're gonna be my right hand, Mike."

Porter pressed the trigger straight to the rear of the pistol and Dreadlocks collapsed in a heap on the floor, blood squirting out of the front of what was once his face. The revolver was loud and crappy, but it did its job.

"*Dios mio*," Hector said as he whipped around, his eyes first going to his friend, dead on the floor. Then he looked up and saw Porter push the bathroom door open and point the pistol at him.

"Who the hell is Mike?" Porter said.

FORTY-TWO

HECTOR TOOK one look at Porter and bolted, passing the folding table and went tearing out of the meeting room, only to run headlong into Terrell's massive chest. Hector fell to the ground. He looked up at Terrell, then back to Porter, and stood, raising his hands.

Jamal was close behind Terrell and came into the room a split second later.

"Oh shit, Porter? What you doin' in here?"

"Sorry, Jamal, there was a change of plans. I thought this might work better."

Terrell had a large grin on his face. He wasn't bothered at seeing Dreadlocks with his face blown off on the floor.

"Damn, it's a good thing we didn't get far," Jamal said. "I was still trying to convince Big T that we should bounce. He wasn't going for it."

"Is anyone else from downstairs going to come back up?" Porter said. "I don't want to fight off any of Hector's boys if I don't have to."

"Hector don't got any more boys. Your recording took care

of that. Well, that and your heater. I told everyone else to bounce. It's just us," Jamal said.

"My man," Porter said. Terrell stood in the doorway again, a silent sentinel with a smirk on his face. Porter motioned for Hector to sit at the table. The man's eyes darted around the room, but he seemed to realize there was no way out. He lowered his hands and sat with a huff.

Porter pulled a seat and sat across from him. "You're Hector Quintana?"

Hector said nothing, instead glaring at Porter.

"You aren't what I expected," Porter said.

Hector still said nothing.

"Look, dummy, how long this conversation takes is up to you. It may be a while if you don't start talking."

Hector slowly nodded his head. "Well, what did you expect?"

"Sorry?" Porter said.

"What did you expect me to look like?"

"I'm not sure. The word on the streets is that you're a beast. A real monster. I'm not impressed," Porter said.

"It's not about the looks, it's about the presence. People know I'm serious, so they treat me that way."

"You're serious? I forgot, what with you sitting there like a little bitch. I should treat you like the serious man you are," Porter said.

He reached and grabbed the index and middle fingers on Hector's right hand, and jerked them ninety degrees. It was a quick, brutal motion. Hector howled in pain.

"If you're so serious, I probably need to make sure you can't shoot anyone. Do you pull triggers or do you just get the guys with the balls to do your dirty work? Were you at my house that night?"

Hector was clutching his hand, uttering a string of obscenities in Spanish. "I wish we would have killed your ass."

"Well, you tried. Fortunately for me, you guys really suck at the killing thing. Big time. A real crew might have gotten me, but you amateurs had no hope. You're lucky any of you got away."

"Maybe next time, I'll get it right," Hector said.

Terrell laughed from the doorway, his voice deep as thunder.

Jamal leaned on the wall next to him. "I doubt that, my nigga."

"You're probably gonna have to let that idea go," Porter said. "Let's switch gears. I'm here to talk about one thing. Do you know what that is?"

"Seems pretty obvious."

"Well? Are you going to talk about Danny, or am I going to spend more time putting my hands on you?"

Porter watched as Hector considered what he had said. "Why bother? I'm not stupid, I know how this movie ends."

"It doesn't have to," Porter said, resting the pistol in his lap. His arm hurt from jumping the wall in the backyard and it was beginning to throb. "If you tell me the truth, I promise I won't kill you," Porter said.

"You won't kill me?" Hector said.

"I'm a man of my word," Porter said.

"My brother mentioned something about that."

"How is Abel?"

"I don't know," Hector said. "He showed up at my house, told me he ratted to you about what happened, then took off. I went to his crib the next day and it was empty. Him, his old lady, his kids, all gone."

"See? I can be reasonable. Now, tell me what happened to Danisha Hill."

Hector hesitated a beat. He looked at Jamal and Terrell, then back at Porter. "I sold her."

"To who?" Porter said.

"A guy I know. That's what he does, he's like a broker or something."

"A guy. This is not the quality of info I was hoping to get." Porter reached over and grabbed Hector's pinky, dislocating it.

Hector gritted his teeth. "Oh, you... you son of a bitch. Stop touching me."

"If you want me to stop, all I need is some real information."

"Go get my phone, he's in there."

"No phones in here, remember?" Jamal said. "Where's yours?"

"In my ride, on the passenger seat." Hector swore under his breath.

Terrell moved and Jamal slid past him and disappeared from the room.

"Why Danisha?"

"I already told the guys," Hector said. "I don't owe you an explanation."

"Wanna bet?" Porter reached towards Hector, who recoiled.

"Okay, okay. Her deadbeat-ass daddy traded her for drugs and protection. He didn't care about that girl. When we showed up looking for our money, he offered her up *pronto*. No questions asked."

"Just like that?" Porter said.

"Exactly like that. He didn't want that baby; she was nothing to him. Life's cheap," Hector said.

"Don't remind me," Porter said, his hand tightening on the pistol's grip.

"If it makes you feel any better, we cooked the spike we gave him. That's why he overdosed."

"It doesn't make me feel any better," Porter said. "You were just trying to cover your tracks."

"Yeah, well, he's still dead."

"Lucky him," Porter said. "Tell me what happened after you snatched her."

"Tied her up, took her to a motel. Sat on her until my guy could come pick her up."

"Your guy makes house calls?" Porter said.

"Full service," Hector said with a smirk.

Porter grabbed the front of Hector's shirt and pulled him close. His arm protested in pain, but he blocked it away. He slammed the butt of his pistol into Hector's face twice. He raised the pistol a third time, but Jamal reentered the room with a phone in hand. He handed it to Porter, who lowered his hand and let go of Hector's shirt. "This yours?"

Hector didn't answer, his mouth full of blood and his hands holding his injured face.

"What's his name?" Porter said as he scrolled through the cheap burner phone.

Hector groaned, nothing understandable coming out of his mouth.

"I swear to God, I'll bash your skull in if you can't tell me." Porter raised the pistol.

"Candy Man," Hector said through a mouthful of blood. He spat a blob on the ground.

Porter scrolled through the contacts until he saw the name. For some reason, it churned his stomach. "What happens if you tell him you have another kid for him?"

"He'd be suspicious. I haven't talked to him in months."

"Will he meet with you or not?" Porter said

"I don't know if—"

Porter raised the pistol. "Yes or no?"

"Yes," Hector said, his hands reflexively going to his face.

"Do it," Porter said.

Hector fumbled the phone in his injured fingers, then placed it down flat on the table and typed with his thumbs.

Jamal had moved away from Hector, and was pacing the room behind Porter.

Porter watched as Hector texted the message and hit send. The thought of someone who dealt in children the way kids traded baseball cards unsettled him. The world was a screwed-up place.

"I texted him."

"Good. Now, what do I need to know about your texts? Special code words, or names for things or places?" Porter said.

"It's simple. Tell him you have something sweet and he knows you mean girl. Something sour means boy. He got back to me with an address. Just me and him, one-on-one, no boys or anything. We worked out all the rest of the deal in person."

"What does Candy Man do with the kids?" Porter said.

"I got no clue. I never bought one before."

"You just sell them, huh?" Porter said.

Hector sat quietly in the chair, holding his wounded hands in his lap, blood dripping from his face.

"How long does it take for him to get back to—"

Hector's phone made a small noise.

Didn't expect to hear from you again. Can't make this a regular thing. I'll let you know.

"See? That's it. He'll text back sometime later with an address."

"Almost like ordering a pizza. Tell me about Candy Man, what does he look like?"

"White dude. Glasses. Tall. Dresses like a professor or something."

"Good. Now I'll know him when I see him."

"What do you mean, see him? He doesn't know you, he

won't meet with you. You need me, you need me to do the talking."

Porter knew Hector was trying to make sure he was still useful. A gambit to stay alive.

"I don't need you, just your phone. I think I can handle it from here," Porter said.

"He'll never tell you anything," Hector said, eyes wide in fear.

"Never is a long time. I think I can be persuasive when I need to be. Don't you think?" Porter said.

"You don't need me anymore. I knew you were gonna kill me."

"I told you I won't kill you. I'm a man of my word," Porter said.

Hector had a small glimmer of hope in his eyes.

"I want your phone and your wallet. Got one of those?"

Hector motioned to his front pocket. "No wallet, but my knot is up there. It's yours. Take it all."

Hector Quintana adjusted as Porter reached into his pocket, pulling out a large stack of money, bound with two thick rubber bands. It was as tall as a Coke can.

"How much is this?" Porter said, tossing it in his hand, feeling the weight of it.

"Should be twenty stacks. Take it. Have it. I don't need it. Hell, I have more at my crib."

"Oh, really?" Porter said, turning to look at Jamal, still pacing behind him.

Porter stood up and stuffed the money into his pocket. He could feel the wad bouncing into his leg as he took a couple steps. He looked Hector in the eyes. "I wish I could say it's been a pleasure, but I won't lie to you. You're a shitty human being and I hope you rot in hell."

"But you aren't going to kill me?"

Porter picked up the gun he'd shot Mike with and put it in his shirt-cupped hand, wiping off any fingerprints that were on it. He offered it up to Jamal, who took it in his own t-shirt.

"Nope, I won't kill you. But those guys? I can't speak for them." Porter pointed at the other men in the room.

Terrell had a smirk on his face and Jamal nodded his head. "Don't worry, we're real good at speaking for ourselves. Porter, man, why don't you take off? We got this."

"My man," Porter said.

As Porter left the room, Terrell moved to let him by, holding a fist out as he did. Porter smashed it with his own and kept walking. He would never see Hector Quintana again. No one would.

FORTY-THREE

PORTER MADE his way down the stairs and through the lower level of the clubhouse. Pausing in the doorway, he looked left and right to see if anyone was waiting for him outside.

There was no one.

Hector had no more allies and Jamal's boys had long since cleared out. There was nothing outside but the SUV Hector Quintana had arrived in and the car that Jamal and Terrell had driven to the meeting. Porter hustled through the backyard and to the big cinderblock wall. This time he didn't stop and listen, instead taking several long strides and then hitting the wall, pulling himself up to the top and over in one fluid movement.

He landed, a stream of obscenities pouring from his mouth at the pain in his arm. He was starting to think he should have listened to Trisha and gone to the hospital.

As he shook his arm out, he looked up and saw Ross, waiting in the Honda.

"I thought you were gonna wait for me to call?"

"I thought maybe something would go wrong and you would need to get out of there quick. Like you might need a getaway car," Ross said.

"That's so sweet. You were worried about me."

"Shut up, Porter. I'm a nervous wreck. I've been sitting out here for a half hour. Every time a car drove by, I thought it was someone coming to get me. I kept ducking down and trying to stay low." Ross floored the sedan. "Tell me what happened."

"I have to make a call first." Porter pulled his phone out and called Rivera's cell. She answered after several rings.

"Porter?"

"No, I'm Porter. You're—"

"If you say it, I swear the next time I see you, I'll punch you in the throat. Is that what you want?"

"I was only going to say Detective Rivera, give me a little credit."

"Nice try. What do you want?"

"You at the office?" Porter said.

"Yes, and you can't come here, if that's what you're asking. There are too many people here right now."

"Meet me at the deli off Kennedy? Thirty minutes?" Porter said.

"This better be good." Rivera hung up the phone.

"I know where that is," Ross said, turning on his blinker. "I'll head that way."

"We have a stop to make first," Porter said, flexing his left arm. The jostling up and over the wall two times hadn't done the wound in his arm any favors. It hurt like hell, and it was feverish to the touch. "Go to that pharmacy by my house. Trisha was supposed to call me in a prescription."

Ross turned the car toward the new destination. Porter told Ross the entire story, leaving nothing out. By the time they got to the pharmacy he'd finished and he and Ross were sitting in the parking lot.

"Did you have to shoot Dreadlocks?"

"He was about to find me in the bathroom. What do you want me to do?"

"I don't know, something else."

"Like what? Tell the cops he was one of the guys who broke into my house? You're right, that's a great idea. Then I'd call the cops and turn over the pile of evidence that proves Mike and Hector took Danny while I'm at it," Porter said. "Slam dunk case."

"Okay, smartass. But now Jamal and Terrell know you killed him. Aren't you worried they could dime you out?"

"No. Why do you think I didn't shoot Hector myself?"

"Sudden development of conscience?" Ross said.

Porter laughed and got out of the car, heading to the pharmacy. He came back minutes later with a big bag. He opened the car door and got in.

"Conscience. That's a good one," Porter said with a mock laugh. He tore into the bag from the pharmacy. He looked over the two pill bottles, then decided on one and took two pills from it, washing them down with Ross's half-empty bottle of water.

"That's my water," Ross said.

"If you wait a couple hours I'll give it back," Porter said. He took a deep breath and turned to Ross. "I didn't kill Hector because if those two kill him, now they're involved. On top of that, they're disposing of the bodies, so they're in it as deep as I am. And their criminal records suggest they're fairly good at keeping hidden things hidden."

Porter rolled his shirt sleeve up, exposing the bandages on his arm. Blood had soaked through them. "They won't tell a soul. The other reason I'm not worried is because that no one can prove it was me. There's no evidence I was even there. I didn't use one of my own guns to shoot Dreadlocks. It was that crappy little throwaway I took off that Tattoo guy a few days ago."

"It's almost like you thought things out first," Ross muttered as he started the car.

Porter unwrapped his gauzed wounds and cleaned them out with a solution he had bought. Ross drove to the deli as Porter finished dressing his arm, sat back, and exhaled.

"What do you think's up with this guy Candy Man?" Ross said.

"I'm not sure how a guy like this operates. Is he a delivery service? Is he a collector? I couldn't tell you, but you can be sure of one thing."

"What?" Ross said.

"He's gonna tell me what he did with Danisha. I promise you that."

FORTY-FOUR

THE DELI WAS an old Tampa landmark. Porter wasn't a fan of the place. He never understood the appeal of a sandwich where the meat overtook everything else. A ten-inch stack of roast beef and then some cursory attempt at a bun. It was too much. He needed balance.

As the men pulled up, Porter saw an unmarked police sedan in the parking lot behind the building.

"Park up front. We don't want to be close to her car," Porter said.

The pair walked across the parking lot and into the deli. Ross turned to head to the dining room, but Porter stopped him.

"I'm starving."

Porter and Ross both ordered big sandwiches; Porter asked for extra bread. He figured if the deli couldn't be trusted to make a respectably sized sandwich, he could deconstruct his and reassemble it.

Porter peeled some of Hector's cash wad off to pay for the meal. The cashier's eyes went wide as Porter pulled the big lump out of his pocket.

The two walked through the dining room until they saw Rivera, sitting at a table in the back.

"You brought a friend," Rivera said.

"He's my valet," Porter said. "The term 'manservant' has fallen out of fashion lately."

"I'm Ross, the manservant." He extended his hand toward Rivera.

"Rivera, the detective," she said as she shook his hand.

"I feel like I've heard a lot about you," Ross said. "Seems like we're both caught up trying to keep this big dummy alive and out of trouble."

"Seems like it."

"I'm standing right here." Porter positioned his tray on the table and dropped both his and Hector's phones next to it. "I feel like I should be offended at being called a dummy, but if that's the consensus then I'll take it."

Porter sat across from Rivera, while Ross sat next to her. It was no move by Ross to be close to the attractive woman, but one born of necessity. He couldn't sit next to Porter at a table and expect to have any elbow room.

"How did things go at the Acres?" Rivera said.

"Before I get into that, you want some of this? These people can't make a sandwich. I got extra bread."

"This is supposed to be the best in the city. You saying they don't know what they're doing?" Rivera said.

"That's exactly what I'm saying," Porter said.

"He's always been this way here. I couldn't tell you why," Ross said.

Rivera accepted one of Porter's re-manufactured sandwiches.

"Hector told me what he did with Danny."

Rivera stopped chewing and looked at Porter expectantly.

"He said he sold her," Porter said.

"What? Where? To who?" Rivera said, setting her sandwich down.

"Some guy Hector called Candy Man."

"Who the hell is that?" Rivera said.

"I don't know, but I'm going to find out," Porter said.

"Really? Mind filling me in on your magic plan?" Rivera said.

"I have Hector's cell phone," Porter said. "I already told Candy Man I have another kid for him. I'm just waiting on him to get back to me with a location and time for the meeting."

Rivera's eyes lit up. "You're going to meet this guy? This is big. Like, really big. This is a huge break."

"It's a huge break in a bunch of cases, not just Danny's. This is what I've been trying to tell you. Hector was small potatoes. If you can get a hold of the Candy Man, you'll have a much richer stream to pull information from," Porter said. "Who knows how far that can go?"

"How am I going to do that? I can't do any of this illegal shit you've been doing. I can lose my job—or worse, taint the evidence so Candy Man gets off. Honestly, we shouldn't even be talking about how you got this info." Rivera motioned to Ross. "Especially in front of your friend here. No offense."

"None taken," Ross said. "Listen, I am a steel vault of secrets. I'd never tell anybody anything. Besides, I can't talk even if I wanted to. Porter and I have attorney-client privilege."

"Aren't you an accountant?"

"Yes."

"Attorney-client privilege doesn't work like that," Rivera said.

"How about best friend privilege?"

Porter's phone rang. "It's Steve, I need to take this. You two be nice to each other." Porter stepped out a side door into the parking lot.

"Best friends, huh? How long have you known that guy?"

"Too long," Ross said.

"He said he's doing all of this because you asked him to. Is that true?"

"Pretty much. The only reason he stuck his nose into this was because of me. Usually it's all about the money," Ross said.

"That's kind of heartless, isn't it? Finding little kids for money?"

"If you have a skill, no reason you shouldn't be paid for it. That just good business. Besides, every time he does one of these cases, it tears him up. He'd never admit it and you'd never tell, but I know him. Who wants to keep finding dead kids? I know I wouldn't."

"Then I suppose I should thank you for getting him involved. If this goes the way he says, I may get a promotion," Rivera said.

"Now who's being heartless?"

Rivera picked her sandwich back up. "That's not fair."

"I'm teasing you," Ross said.

Porter stepped back into the dining room.

"What did Steven say?" Ross asked.

"Set me up for an interview on Friday afternoon with those douchey homicide detectives. He also said I'm clear to go back to my house."

"Good. Now maybe you'll get off my couch," Ross said.

"You'll miss me." Porter bit into his sandwich. Just the right amount of meat. "Let's game plan this Candy Man situation."

"Good, I need a game plan," Ross said.

"I was talking to Rivera," Porter said. Before Ross could argue, he added, "We need to figure out how she fits in from the police angle. I know you're in, Ross."

"What do you mean 'the police angle'? What do you have in mind?" Rivera said.

"Let's assume Candy Man texts me back with the address of a place to meet. Hector said Candy Man met him in public. We can't set up a trap for him, since we don't know where he's gonna be."

"It would be helpful if I could talk to Hector. Get what info I can from him and maybe use it to get a warrant for Candy Man's arrest," Rivera said.

Porter tried to think of a tactful answer. "He said something about taking a trip. I think he didn't want to be around while the situation was playing out. Besides, no judge is going to give you an arrest warrant based on the alleged story I got off a criminal."

Rivera nodded her head. "Be nice if they did, wouldn't it?"

"Then what can you do?" Ross asked.

"I think the best we can do is go to the meeting. Just the three of us. When he sees I'm not Hector Quintana, he may rabbit. If he does, we need to follow him."

"Find out where he goes," Rivera said. "It's better than nothing, but it's pretty thin."

"I know," Porter said, "but it's something. If he's at a hotel, we can see what name he's staying under. Maybe we get lucky."

Rivera looked at Porter. "We're going to have to do better than that."

Porter knew Rivera was right. He had promised her he could help grow her case and that's what she expected. It wasn't unreasonable, but there was a big difference between the way he normally did things, and the way things needed to be done to hold up in court. "Whoever Candy Man hips us to will have more info about this operation."

"Maybe not," Ross said with a shrug.

"Whose side are you on here?" Porter said, punching Ross in the arm. "The most important thing is that we know where Candy Man is after we meet with him. We can't afford to let him rabbit; we might not have a chance to find him again."

"For once, I agree," Rivera said. "I'll stay in my car when you go meet him. Let me know if he moves and I'll follow."

"Good. We have to play this out. Once we get to the meeti—"

The Hector-phone made a small noise. Everyone at the table looked at it. Porter pulled it to him and read it to Rivera and Ross.

8p bookstore Bruce B

Porter glanced at his watch. It was almost seven fifteen. "How many bookstores are on Bruce B Downs?"

"It has to be the one by campus. The big two-story job with the coffee shop in the bottom," Rivera said. "No other one on that side of town is worth going to."

Two bookstores in two days, Porter thought. *It's like the universe is telling me I need to read more.* "That's forty-five minutes from now. Can we make that?"

"Of course we can," Ross said.

"Detective?"

Rivera already had her things and was moving toward the door. She stopped long enough to say, "I'm waiting on you."

FORTY-FIVE

THE GROUP LEFT THEIR MESS; Porter threw a twenty on the table to make it worth it for whoever had to bus that table. On the way to the parking lot, Porter put his hand on Ross's shoulder.

"I'm gonna ride over with Rivera. Just follow and I'll call you."

"Got it. You guys need to talk about cop stuff."

"You sure? Won't it be better to split us up?" Rivera said.

"It's okay, I'll need your help trying to spot him as he walks in."

"Fine. Get in," she said.

Rivera started the car and stomped the gas. She tore down Kennedy and then hooked a hard right onto Dale Mabry, heading north.

Weaving through the early evening traffic, Rivera took the requisite turns and made it to the bookstore in what must have been record time. They had long since lost Ross to a red light during the drive. Rivera paid no attention.

Porter gave Ross a quick call and told him to hang back in

the parking lot of the bookstore, keep his eyes open, and wait for a call.

When they got near the bookstore, Porter told Rivera to park in the lot of the tire shop across the street. The lot was full with spillover parking for a nearby Mexican restaurant. No one would see them over there.

There were big, floor-to-ceiling windows which allowed them an unobstructed view into the bookstore. They could see the front door, as well as most of the lobby of the coffee place which dominated the first floor.

When Porter checked his watch again it was seven forty-one. Early. Now they had a chance to spot Candy Man before he realized he wasn't going to be meeting with Hector.

"Can I ask you something?"

"You might as well. If I say no you're just going to anyway."

"Why do you say that? If you don't want me to ask you a question, I won't ask you a question," Porter said.

"Why would you start listening to what I say now?"

"I listen to you," Porter said.

"Since when? How many times have I asked you not to call me Tina?"

Porter laughed. "I just do it because it gets under your skin. True story? I called my friend Dave 'Dickface' for almost two years. No real reason, it just embarrassed him when we were in public."

"How did that end up for you?"

"I was one of his groomsmen," Porter said with a shrug.

"Well, I'm not Dickface Dave."

"Fair enough. What's the deal with that anyway? It's just an abbreviated version of your name. Own it."

Rivera reached across Porter's lap to her glove box, pulling out a small pair of binoculars. She scanned the front of the building. "The deal is, I don't like it, and I asked you not to call me that. Haven't you ever had someone call you something you don't like?"

Porter thought back to Trish calling him Telly-Porter. He hated it, because of why she did it. "Okay, detective, I'll knock it off. But don't leave me hanging. There has to be a story."

"You aren't going to let this go, are you?"

"Sure, I'll let it go. But think of how cathartic it will be to get it off your chest."

Rivera exhaled in frustration but kept her eyes focused on the binoculars. "I started to have a problem with being called Tina when I was fourteen. Before that, it didn't matter; it was just a name."

"What happened when you were fourteen?" Porter said.

"Do you remember that movie, *Napoleon Dynamite*?"

"Of course."

"Do you remember the llama?" Rivera said.

"Napoleon would feed it table food, right?"

"He would throw food at it and say, 'Eat your dinner, you fat lard.' So stupid," Rivera said.

Porter laughed. "That's right. Wait, the llama's name was Tina, wasn't it?"

Rivera pulled the binoculars down from her face. "Yes, the damn llama was named Tina. Who gives a llama a human name? All the kids at my school thought it was hilarious. They would walk by me and yell, 'Tina, eat your dinner, you fat lard.' It was so humiliating."

"Were you fat?"

"What difference does that make?"

"It would be like if someone called me short. People can say what they want; if it's not true, who cares?" Porter said.

"I cared. I was a teenage girl, Porter. We have hormones and periods and anxiety. We have crushes and when they walk by calling you a fat lard, it upsets you. You feel like everyone is ganging up on you, just to make fun of you."

Porter stole a glimpse at Rivera, the dashboard lighting illuminating her enough that he could see she was red-faced.

"To make matters worse, everyone at my school started calling me and leaving me voicemails. Then they gave my number to kids at other high schools in town and they called me, too. Hundreds of voicemails. My phone was ringing non-stop. I had to change my number. Now every time I hear the name Tina, it makes me so mad."

Porter couldn't stifle his laugh. "It's been fifteen years, right? You don't think it's a little funny?"

"No, I don't."

"Your call. When I was still in the feds, the shit talk was brutal. But I think that's how we bonded, clowning on each other. I guess I miss it a little."

"Well, I don't have to worry about bonding with the other detectives," Rivera said with a serious look on her face.

Porter let the comment hang in the air. He pointed to a man walking into the lobby of the bookstore. "Think that's him?"

Rivera was already looking through the binoculars. "I don't think so. Unless Hector thinks professors wear mullets."

"Have you seen academia style lately?" Porter said with a laugh.

The location of the bookstore gave it a diverse mix of customers. It was in an older, not-so-great part of town. Half the people who walked in were blue-collar types: a guy with a high-visibility road crew vest, two young women in their fast-food uniforms, a man who hopped out of a plumbing truck. The bookstore was also close to campus, so there was a steady stream of young people easily identified as students, since they all carried bookbags and never looked up from their cell phones.

No one in the store could pass for a professor, even by

Hector Quintana's loose standards. Porter looked at the dash; the time was seven fifty-five.

"You never answered my question," Porter said.

"What question?"

"The one I was going to ask before you hijacked it with your llama tale of woe."

Rivera smiled in spite of herself. "You can ask, but I can't promise I'll answer."

"That's fair. How did you get stuck in the Long Term Missing Unit? Seems like it'll kill your career," Porter said.

"You don't think I know that? Everyone who comes here is retired on duty. They're a group of misfits from other departments who couldn't get along. So they stick them here and no one expects them to ever make a case. Ever."

"But how? You seem like a good investigator. If you worked for me, I'd have you doing real work. How'd you get stuck on the throwaway squad?"

Rivera sat her binoculars down. "You want another tale of woe? Fine. I got pregnant my sophomore year of college. Despite that, I graduated on time and on the dean's list."

"Much higher than I did. Where's daddy?"

"Don't know, don't care. We are much better off, trust me."

Porter didn't say anything.

"Fresh out of college, I joined the sheriff's office. I'm amazed they even hired me, the way the guy who interviewed me for the job was hitting on me. He wouldn't take me seriously."

"Maybe that's why they hired you," Porter said.

"I thought that at first, so I made it a point to prove I belonged. I went to the academy and was my class president. I finished with top honors and even made the fitness wall of fame. Then I get to the real world. The three years I was on patrol, I was doing a damn good job. In the top ten percent of arrests made and tickets written. I was on my way to detective, no problem."

"Rocketship to the top," Porter said.

"That's what I thought. Then the asshole who interviewed me became my sergeant. In the beginning, he tried to do favors for me. Better shifts, newer patrol cars, cushy duties for overtime."

Porter knew local officers and sheriff's deputies relied on overtime to get by. The job didn't pay great, so most of them jumped at any chance for extra money. Things like working the local high school football games or sitting on the roadside during construction with the cruiser's lights on.

"I wouldn't let him give me special treatment. I'm not like that, it's not fair to everyone else. Then he asked me out and when I told him no, everything changed. I couldn't get an overtime assignment. I always got assigned to the shitty patrol car. You know, there's always that one that just won't run right."

Porter nodded his head.

"I didn't want to be treated better or worse than anyone else. I wanted my work to speak for itself. So I sucked it up. Drove the crappy car, dealt with no overtime. The whole while, he was saying grossly inappropriate things to me on a daily basis. I mean, everyone's taken the sexual harassment training, people know what they can and can't do. This guy acted like he was in an episode of *Mad Men*. I sucked that up too. I didn't want to make waves. Then he started blocking my promotion to detective."

"Doesn't a board vote on that? How could he stop it?" Porter said.

"A board votes on it, but they won't even vote if your last performance appraisal isn't satisfactory or better. This guy gave me two bad appraisals in a row, so the board wouldn't even look at my promotion packet. I decided enough was enough. I'd been keeping track of all the incidents, so I bundled all my evidence together and reported him to Internal Affairs and filed an EEOC complaint. Let me tell you, the Equal Opportunity Commission didn't see things his way."

"I imagine so. I think sometimes they invent problems in a workplace, just to have something to do. When someone has a real case, they're frothing at the mouth," Porter said.

"They sure were. After they reviewed all the evidence, EEOC found I'd been severely harassed and an administrative judge awarded me a settlement. The sheriff office's own internal investigation agreed with me and demoted my sergeant. They moved him out somewhere where he couldn't bother anyone else. As part of my settlement, they agreed to give me the promotion and award me back pay from the date I was first passed over for a detective job," Rivera said.

"Good for you. All's well that ends well?" Porter said.

"Hardly. I'm a pariah in the sheriff's office. They complied with the EEOC settlement and gave me a promotion, but you see where they stuck me. The problem squad. They have no intention of doing anything that may actually help my career. The other detectives in my unit don't want to talk to me because they all think I'm a snitch. People worry that if they work with me, I'll keep tabs on them and drop a dime. Never mind that two investigations proved I was telling the truth." Rivera kept searching the area through her binoculars.

"You know what they say; sometimes doing the right thing isn't doing the right thing," Porter said.

"Tell me about it. I swear, I've about had enough of this place. Screw these people. If I had someplace better lined up, I'd quit. But I don't, so I stay."

"That's why Candy Man's so important to you?"

"That's right. We catch him, maybe they'll move me to a

real unit. They have to if I make a good enough case," Rivera said.

Porter looked at the time and noticed they were no longer early. If Candy Man wasn't already hiding somewhere in the bookstore, he should be walking in any second. There still appeared to be no sign of a professor. Porter's Hector-phone made a noise. Porter fished it out of his pocket and checked the screen.

Waiting for you. Where are you?

Porter hadn't seen a professor-type walk into the bookstore. He showed Rivera.

"Shit. What are you going to say?"

"Bluff. Gotta buy us time to find him."

Here. Where are you? Porter tapped out on the phone.

Rivera redoubled her efforts to locate their targets. She still saw nothing.

Porter was deciding what to do. If Candy Man was inside, he would see that Hector wasn't walking in. That might spook him. Porter's real phone rang.

"Yeah."

"Hey man, I think I found Candy Man's car."

"Why do you say that?"

"I've been driving around since I got here. Nervous energy," Ross said. "There aren't that many cars in this parking lot and I think this one is the only rental. It has one of those weird barcode stickers on the front of the windshield. Plus, it has an Arizona tag. Who drives here from Arizona?"

The phone buzzed again.

Get in here or I leave.

Porter said to Ross, "Is there a guy in the car you're talking about?"

"Yeah. He's in there texting on his phone," Ross said.

"That's him," Porter said. "He's so careful, he won't even go in until he sees Hector. I'm not going to get him out of that car."

"What's he driving?" Rivera said.

Porter relayed the question to Ross.

"A black Cadillac. One of the new fast ones," Ross said.

"Look for a black Cadillac," Porter said to Rivera.

"I already see the Cadillac," Ross said.

"Not talking to you."

"I see it," Rivera said. "West side of the building, tucked behind that old truck."

Porter strained his eyes until he saw it too. It was time to act before they lost Candy Man.

"Keep an eye on him, Ross," Porter said. "Just don't get too close."

"Okay," Ross said, and hung up.

Porter got the Hector-phone and typed out his message.

Give me a min.

"I need to get over to that Caddy."

"Then what? What if he bails?" Rivera said.

"If he takes off, follow him. Remember, the most important thing is that we know where he is for as long as we can. We can work things out from there."

"What are you going to do when you get over to the car?"

"Not sure yet, but at this point we don't have any other options. If this guy ghosts, we're back at square one."

FORTY-SIX

PORTER GOT out of the unmarked unit and looked around. They'd been well-hidden where they were sitting. To get to the Cadillac, he would have to cross the busy road to the parking lot of the bookstore. Porter figured he had a good chance of making it without being seen. He stood at the edge of the road, waiting for his opportunity to cross.

When a break in the cars came, Porter moved. He sprinted to the median, then hurried the rest of the way at the next break in traffic. Arriving behind the row of cars where Candy Man was parked, Porter made his way from bumper to bumper until he was next to a rusty F-150 with a topper over the bed. He leaned close to the tailgate. Candy Man's Cadillac was in the next parking place.

Porter knew this was his best chance to find out what had happened to Danisha Hill. To help Ross get some peace at night. To help Miss Leona find closure for herself and her baby. To help Rivera have the type of career she deserved. It was time for Porter to make it happen. He stepped around the bumper of the Cadillac to the passenger side.

He slammed his elbow into the safety glass on the window, smashing it into tiny pebbles that rained down inside the car.

Porter leaned down and looked in the car. "You Candy Man?"

He looked at Porter as if he'd interrupted something important. "You are not Hector."

He didn't look like Porter had expected. The word 'professor' had conjured an image of a scholarly type, walking across campus with a briefcase and a tweed coat with elbow patches. Candy Man's hawkish features gave him a predatory air, and he was as much a professor as Porter was a bill collector.

"You got me. I'm not Hector."

"May I ask why you are destroying my car?"

"That's a terrific question. Let me ask you something first."

"It is rude to answer a question with a question," Candy Man said.

"That's what they tell me. I'm going to break decorum. When you meet women, *if* you meet women, do you introduce yourself as Candy Man?" Porter watched his hands, still on his cell phone. He couldn't be sure Candy Man wouldn't pull a weapon and if he did, Porter's face was front and center.

Candy Man stared at Porter, as if trying to gauge his intentions. He had a perturbed air about him as he answered. "That is a silly name. I did not give it to myself; it was invented by some associates. However, it is important for one to have a calling card. Brand recognition, if you will."

Porter wasn't sure if he wanted to strangle this guy or laugh at him. The fact of the matter was, he'd found him and he wanted to use this opportunity to its fullest. But before Porter could say anything, Candy Man spoke again.

"I was looking forward to a cup of tea. Shall we continue this conversation in the coffee house?"

The request caught Porter off guard. He was used to people begging. *Please don't arrest me, please don't hurt me, please don't kill me.* He was used to defiance. People who would fight and cuss and lie. Anything to get out of the situation Porter had put them in. He wasn't used to this.

He decided there could be no harm in getting Candy Man into the open.

"Sure. Let's do tea."

Candy Man pulled the door latch and swung his body to get out of the car. There was no subterfuge. He didn't run or try to grab some hidden weapon. He just got out of the car. Porter walked around the hood to meet him. Candy Man chirped the key fob and locked the Cadillac. Together, they walked towards the front door.

Candy Man was almost Porter's height, but that was where the similarity ended. Brown corduroy pants hung off his rail-thin frame and his button-down was neatly tucked in. Porter stayed to the right and rear of Candy Man, ready for an attack that never came. They walked into the bookstore and turned into the coffee shop.

Porter imagined Ross and Rivera were confused. The last thing they would have expected was Porter and Candy Man walking into the building together.

When they arrived at the counter, Candy Man ordered a large hot tea.

"Would you care for anything?" Candy Man asked.

"No thanks. Coffee gives me the shits." Porter looked at the barista. "I'm sure you understand."

Candy Man gave Porter an annoyed look and turned to finish his transaction. When the order was ready, the pair turned and walked to a small table flanked by two tall wing-backed chairs.

Candy Man looked at Porter, who gestured to the table.

"Looks good to me."

There was silence for a few moments. Candy Man had the lid of his tea off and was stirring milk into it. Porter watched him the entire time. He had a peculiar way about him. A strange affect, as if he were unburdened by the current reality he was facing.

"You mind if I ask you a personal question?"

"Something other than the vaguely insulting one you asked me in the car?"

"That was a bit of fun, Candy Man. Don't take offense."

"Oh, I will not."

"Good. My real question is, where exactly are you from?" Porter said.

"What do you mean?"

"Your accent is... off. There's something strange about it that I can't quite put my finger on."

"Very perceptive, Mr. ..."

"Smith," Porter said.

Candy Man turned his mouth into a frown. "I doubt very much that your name is Smith."

"I could say the same thing, Candy Man." Porter made air quotes as he said it.

"Fair enough. Very perceptive, Mr. Smith. I am actually a transplant from the UK. I have been here a very long time and thought my accent was tamed sufficiently to pass for American."

"It's not bad. What brought you to America?" Porter wasn't sure where to take this conversation, so he resorted to his old law enforcement officer interview strategy. Open-ended questions, and lots of them. Let the person being interviewed take the conversation where they wanted. Inadvertently, they would give him answers.

"It is a long and sordid tale. The distilled version is, I came for school."

"Do you like it here?"

"I do. The States version of capitalism is an amazing thing. People will buy and sell anything," Candy Man said.

"Helps that practically everything's for sale."

Candy Man smiled. "Mr. Smith, as much as I'm enjoying our little chat, I feel the need to ask you some questions. I would like to determine your intentions."

Porter turned his index finger and middle finger into a mock pistol and pointed them at Candy Man. "Shoot."

"It is evident that you are not a police officer."

"What gave me away?"

"Several things, really. If you were an officer, there would be more of you here. You would have likely placed handcuffs on me from the outset. Additionally, you don't have the... look... of an officer of the law."

"Well, I gotta give you that one. I'm not a police officer."

"My next thought was that you were some sort of reporter. Trying to find a story about some of my more unscrupulous activities. But that does not appear to be the case, as they generally have some sort of cameraman for video documentation," Candy Man said.

"A 60 *Minutes* documentary or something like that?"

"Exactly," Candy Man said. "Which leads me to my third thought: You found out from Hector what type of work I do, and you want in. Maybe a piece of my pie, maybe all of my pie."

"I don't like sweets," Porter said. "I need to watch my figure."

"Barring those possibilities, I'm not sure who you are or why you are here."

"Let's just say I'm a concerned party. I need to ask you some questions. You need to answer those questions."

"A threat. I was wondering when that would come."

"Not a threat at all. I'm being on the up-and-up. You have to answer my questions."

"Or what? You will kill me? In public like this? Plenty of cameras saw the two of us walk in here together, Mr. Smith."

Porter smiled, acutely aware that he was on camera. "No, you need to answer my questions for your own satisfaction. I can tell the type of guy you are."

"And what 'type' is that?"

"The type that's too smart for your own good. You guys always want someone to know what you did and how you did it. If not, how can you revel in your own brilliance?"

Candy Man mulled over Porter's words, then nodded. "It is a bit of a burden, being the smartest person in the room all the time."

"You make my point for me," Porter said. "How does one get into the child-selling business?"

"I prefer to consider myself as a wish-fulfillment consultant."

"That's one way to look at it," Porter said.

"I merely provide a service. If people want to use it, that is their prerogative. But, to your point, it is the type of work that one falls into."

"How's that?"

"Oh, you know, it starts word of mouth. I helped some Russian and Italian friends of mine with some surplus inventory years back. Word gets around. Referrals. One eventually finds like-minded colleagues. I don't need to advertise," Candy Man said.

"So the mafia—sorry, Italian friends of yours had 'surplus inventory.' How do you fit into that? How do you find customers?"

"The internet, naturally."

"The internet?" Porter said.

"Of course. Have you spent much time on the dark web?"

Porter had heard of it. The dark, or deep, web was a place that could be accessed through the regular internet. A user had to download a special program on their computer to obtain access.

The dark web was enormous. If you imagined the online world as a house, the part that everyday people used—social media, video streaming sites, even pornography websites—accounted for the master bathroom. The dark web was the rest of the house.

Anything could be purchased on the dark web. There were websites where you could buy drugs and have them shipped to your home. You could communicate with arms dealers and purchase caches or weapons. The dark web ran primarily on Bitcoin, which was an untraceable virtual currency, and the criminals who used it were all but out of the reach of law enforcement. Porter was aware of a few cases that had been successfully run through the dark web, but not many.

It was the wild west.

"So people just roll up to your dark-web website and pick out which child they want? You're like Amazon for pedophiles."

"I would not say we are nearly that successful."

"We?"

Candy Man stopped for a moment and considered his next words. "I believe it is safe to say that I work for a… consortium. I think that's the best way to put it."

"You made it sound like you were a freelancer, making his bones in the dirty cyber world," Porter said.

"It is a bit more complicated than that. I could get into it all, but I fear you would not understand. Best we keep things less complicated," Candy Man said.

"Works for me. I'd love to talk to you about all this and get to understand your 'consortium,' but I've had a long day. How about I get to my original point?" A twinge of pain shot through Porter's arm.

"Splendid."

"I'm interested in the whereabouts of one child," Porter said.

"Am I to assume it is the little black girl for whom I transacted with Hector Quintana?"

"Correct."

"Interesting."

"What's that?" Porter said.

"I have never had anyone contact me after a deal was done, let alone ask about a child's whereabouts. Forgive me if I may be so bold—are you her father?"

"No."

"I was wondering. It is obvious you are some sort of... minority, but you are not quite dark-skinned enough to be her father."

"I'm pretty sure that's not how genetics works," Porter said.

"I suppose not. And what is your relationship to her?"

"A friend of the family."

"Quite the resourceful friend you are. Finding me is no easy task. Am I to understand that I will be doing no further business with Hector in the future?"

"That's a safe bet."

"I could say 'what a shame,' but I wouldn't mean it. I never liked Hector; he was just a small-time crook. A stooge. I don't like to work with people who are not professionals. However, he knew me through mutual acquaintances. When he called me and told me had a child, it would have been folly to turn down an opportunity at a generous payday."

"Understandable," Porter said.

"As to your young negress, what is it you would like to know about her? I fear I cannot tell you much."

"Why? You know where she went. You know what happened to her. All I need to find out is who did what to her.

Maybe where she's buried. The family would like to have a proper funeral."

"Why would you presume she is buried somewhere?"

"That's what you guys do with kids when you use them up. You get rid of the evidence. Nobody wants to go to prison," Porter said.

"In most cases, yes, they are disposed of. Eventually. Once the product has outlived its shelf life, it must be discarded."

Candy Man's detachment made Porter's teeth ache. Then he realized they ached because he was clenching his jaw. "So where was this girl 'discarded'?"

"To the best of my knowledge, she has not been discarded. That girl is still very much alive," Candy Man said.

FORTY-SEVEN

PORTER HAD BARELY LET himself contemplate a scenario in which Danisha Hill was still alive. He was sure part of that was a defense mechanism, to steel himself against the eventuality of finding her lifeless body. The other part of it was experience and common sense. Finding one of these kids alive was no small feat. It happened, but even for Porter it was rare.

"Mr. Smith?" Candy Man said. "Mr. Smith, are you still with me?"

Porter cleared his throat. "I'm here and I'm tracking. You say the girl isn't dead?"

"I certainly think not. The man to whom I sold her has very little capacity for violence. Once he is done with his purchase, he always calls me to arrange removal. He is more of a long-term renter, if you will. The children serve his purposes and when he tires of them, I facilitate the endgame."

"I'm sure I don't want to know the details," Porter said.

"Likely not."

"How about you tell me who you sold her to?"

"Why would I do that?"

"Call it a favor."

Candy Man laughed an ugly, haughty laugh. It must have been a fake, put on for show, as it went on for almost a full minute. Porter barely stopped himself from reaching across the table. As the ugly laughter died down, Candy Man turned to Porter. "I am sorry, Mr. Smith, but I do no favors. Besides, it would be poor business practice to divulge the identity of my customers."

"I'm sure you can make an exception," Porter said.

"Well, I *am* a capitalist. If you had something to offer me, perhaps I could be persuaded."

Porter was thinking of what he could offer the Candy Man. Nothing he had was valuable. Then he remembered the big knot he'd pulled off of Hector. He had hoped to keep that for himself, some compensation for his efforts in looking for Danny. A little payback to himself for being shot. Porter reached into his front pants pocket and pulled out the brick of money.

"Think this will persuade you?"

"Well, now, what is this?"

"Your lucky day. It's just the amount of money it'll take to buy the location of the girl, and keep me from ripping your head off," Porter said.

"Lest we forget, Mr. Smith, there are cameras everywhere. Surely, said head-ripping would be a bit messy?"

Porter dropped the wad onto the table in front of Candy Man. "Get on with it."

Candy Man peeled the rubber bands off the stack of cash. He made a show of it as he unfolded the wad, then faced and counted the bills. He had no regard for who might be looking at him.

Porter looked around; no one was paying attention to them. The café was mostly empty and the few patrons who were there were engrossed in their laptops or the books they were perusing.

Five minutes passed before Candy Man looked up from his

task. "A bit more than twenty-three thousand dollars. Not a bad sum. You just happened to have this on your person?"

"Lucky coincidence. So about the info I need?" Porter said.

Candy Man folded the stack in half, rubber banded it together, and slipped it into his inner jacket pocket. "I am sorry, Mr. Smith, but I still cannot provide you with information."

Porter leaned closer and lowered his voice. "What do you mean? I paid you, you son of a bitch, now out with it."

"Temper, Mr. Smith, temper. Frankly, it isn't enough money. I do not work so cheaply. I will, however, be retaining the money. Consider it payment for wasting my time this evening." He raised his cup and sipped his tea.

Porter's face flushed. He decided he'd drag Candy Man into the bathroom and make him talk. Make him spill his guts about everything. He didn't care about the consequences; he just wanted to wipe the arrogant smirk off the child broker's face.

Then he contained himself. He didn't think Candy Man would talk—not from a beating. And if Candy Man didn't talk, Rivera would never make a case. Not to mention the fact that the man was right that numerous cameras had no doubt seen the two of them walk in together, and were likely trained on him.

Porter sat still in his chair and weighed his options.

Candy Man wasn't sitting still: He was leaving. He picked up his phone from the table and pulled the wad of money out from his coat, slipped off a bill, and dropped it on the table. "I detest bussing my own table. I find that, even in a place like this, the staff doesn't mind doing it if you leave them something. In this case, *you* left them something." He smiled his obnoxious smile at Porter. "Mr. Smith, I believe this concludes our conversation. I must let you go now." He turned on his heel and walked away from Porter, out of the coffee shop and into the parking lot.

Porter watched him leave. He wanted to follow him out, and

call Ross and Rivera, but he didn't want to let Candy Man on to the fact that he had people with him. It would put him on edge. He had to give it space and trust that Rivera was up to the task of following him. Once Candy Man was no longer near any of the windows, he stood and hurried towards the exit, pulling his phone out as he went.

"Ross."

"Hey, man, what happened? What the hell was that? Who did you go in there with? Was that Candy Man?"

"Too many questions. Come to the front and pick me up. We have to see if we can catch up to Rivera."

Ross was in front of the bookstore in a matter of seconds. Porter hopped into the Honda and they took off.

"Which way did they go? Did you see her?"

"No, I was on the other side of the building. I saw Candy Man leave, but once he turned the corner he was gone. I didn't know if I should go after him or not, so I waited for your call," Ross said.

"You did the right thing," Porter said as he punched in Rivera's phone number. The phone rang but there was no answer. He didn't leave a message. "Just drive out to the front, maybe we'll get lucky and see them."

They didn't get lucky. Candy Man's rental was nowhere in sight; likewise Rivera's unmarked unit. Porter had Ross drive slowly and canvass the area, but there was no sign of either of the vehicles. It was as if they had vanished. Porter kept calling Rivera's phone, but she never answered.

"I bet she lost him," Ross said, "and now she's pissed. No wonder she won't answer the phone."

"There's nothing else we can do right now."

"What do you mean, 'nothing we can do'? We had him, now he's gone. You lost him," Ross said.

"Don't you think I know that?" Porter said, louder than he needed to. "Huh? I know that."

There was silence in the car as Ross made ever-expanding circles looking for a sign of either of the cars.

"Where are we going?" Ross said.

"Swing me by my place. I need to get some things."

"It's over? That fast?"

"Just drive the car. I'll tell you about that creep on the way."

Ross drove while Porter spoke, recounting the conversation with Candy Man. Ross chimed in and asked appropriate questions, but nothing extra. Porter was upset about the way he had handled the meeting and Ross didn't want to stir him up any further.

When they arrived at Porter's house, they found it in the same condition Porter had left it in. There was still crime scene tape on the inside and large pools of blood in his bathroom. It looked like someone had been kind enough to screw some plywood over the shot-out sliding glass door. Porter went to his gun safe, opened it, and grabbed the twin of the Glock that had been confiscated by the police. He'd felt naked without it.

Not that it would have done him any good against Candy Man.

"Just get what you need and let's go back to my place. I don't want to stay in here any longer than I have to. It's disgusting," Ross said.

"Next time a bunch of thugs break into my place to kill me, I'll ask them to wipe their feet first."

"I'll be in the car," Ross said.

Porter grabbed an old backpack from his closet and tossed in some essentials, as well as some extra ammunition and magazines. Slinging his backpack onto his shoulder, he turned his back on his house and its state of disarray.

FORTY-EIGHT

THE RIDE to Ross's house was silent, a rarity for the two of them. Porter and Ross always had plenty to say to, and often about, each other. This was different. A feeling of frustration hung in the air.

When they got to Ross's house, Porter dragged his backpack off to the guest bathroom, where he stayed for nearly a half hour. Ross didn't interrupt him, and took the time to clean himself up and order pizza. They'd both feel better with food in their stomachs.

Porter came out with fresh clothes on and a new bandage on his arm. He was flexing and rotating it around like it hurt him. He walked to the kitchen island and grabbed several slices of the pie, as well as both of his pill bottles, and sat down on the couch. Ross was watching a football highlight show.

They ate in silence for a few minutes. "Do you think he was telling the truth about Danny being alive?" Ross said.

Porter slammed his plate on the table. He leaned back on the couch and spoke slowly. "I don't know if he's telling the truth, Ross. I have no reason to believe he would lie about it. He knew he was walking out of there, and he wasn't the least bit scared of what would happen after our conversation. That usually makes a person bold. He was so cocky, too. Makes me sick. I should have done something about it."

"What could you do?"

"Something. Anything. I should have dragged Candy Man's ass out of there and beat it out of him."

"You said that wouldn't have worked," Ross said.

"Well, I'm a moron."

Ross said nothing, because there was nothing to say.

"The damn money, too," Porter said under his breath.

"Huh?"

"I said 'the damn money.' I gave Candy Man that money."

"What you took from Hector?"

"Twenty-three grand."

"I didn't know you gave him that. Why?"

"He made it seem like I could pay for info about Danny. I didn't see what other choice I had. Maybe he was lying, you know? Get me to pay up. Just more money in his pocket."

"Honestly? I'm impressed that you gave him the money. I know how excited you were to get it from Hector."

"It's way more important to find the kid. And I'm going to."

Ross didn't say anything.

"No matter what it takes. Candy Man talked about the deep web; maybe I can find him there. I'll go up to New York and beat the bushes if I have to. This isn't over."

Porter's phone rang. He pulled it from his pocket and checked the caller ID. "Nice of you to call me back."

"I've been busy. Ask me why."

"Why what?"

"Ask me why I've been busy," Rivera said.

"Rivera, I'm not—"

"Just ask me why I have been busy, Porter."

"Fine. Why have you been busy?"

"Because I got Candy Man. He's sitting in an interview room right now."

FORTY-NINE

PORTER AND ROSS arrived at Rivera's office in record time. She was outside waiting for them. "Let's talk out here."

"What happened? Where did you go?" Ross said.

"When Porter went into the coffee shop with Candy Man, I drove past the rental and took down the plates. I ran the information and called the rental company to find out who rented the car. The company told me it was rented to a man named Bartholomew James."

"So?" Porter said.

"I ran Mr. James through the NCIC and found no major crimes, and a minor history of DUI," Rivera said.

"DUI? You're killing me," Porter said.

"Shut up and let me finish. He had a minor criminal record, but that wasn't the interesting part."

"What's the interesting part?" Ross said.

"The interesting part was Mr. Bartholomew's date of birth. It was 1939."

"1939?" Porter said.

"Yeah, you know, after 1938, before 1940?"

"Are you saying Candy Man was born during the Great Depression?" Porter said.

"Don't be stupid, he obviously wasn't. You can tell by looking at him it's not even close. So I figure he must be using a stolen credit card or something for the rental. He wouldn't use his real name, right?"

"Right," Porter said, starting to see where Rivera was going.

Rivera paced the blacktop, shoes scuffing along. "I needed to figure out who Candy Man is, and this was my chance. All I had to do was stop his car and check his ID. If he gave me a different ID, then I'm busting him for not having the rental car in his name. If he gave the Bartholomew James ID, I know he's full of shit, because he isn't in his eighties. It didn't matter what he did, I'd have probable cause to arrest him. I just needed to stop him."

Porter broke out into a gigantic smile.

"Why did you stop his car?" Ross said.

"He had a taillight out."

"No shit?" Porter said.

"It can be a rough neighborhood. At some point between when he went into the coffee shop and when he came out, someone kicked his taillight out."

"Did you see it?" Ross said.

"Technically speaking, I may have 'watched' it happen," Rivera said using air quotes.

"Wait a minute, are you saying you—"

"Shut up, Ross," Porter said.

"Yeah, shut up, Ross."

"Shutting up now," Ross said with a sheepish look on his face, like he had just figured out what happened.

"What happened when you stopped him?" Porter said.

"I pulled him over and asked for his license. He gave me the Bartholomew James ID. It has Candy Man's picture and an appropriate date of birth, but I knew it was fake. I sat in the car pretending like I was running his information, but I was just waiting for backup. Backup shows up, and we arrest the guy. He was weird and calm about the whole thing. Now I have a reason to take him back to the office and put him on the glass."

'The glass' was slang for an electronic fingerprint machine. Before computers became common, a person's fingerprints were recorded with ink and paper, and the fingerprints were sent off to the FBI to classify. It could take weeks to come back and let you know if the prints matched someone in the FBI database.

Now, all you had to do was inklessly roll and capture images of someone's fingerprints into a computer program, then electronically submit them for review to the FBI's West Virginia NCIC server. A reply usually came back in minutes and then you knew exactly who you had in custody, if they had ever been encountered by law enforcement before.

"If he didn't come up in the NCIC query, you still wouldn't know who he was," Porter said.

"Worst case scenario, nothing came back when we ran his prints. I'd still hold him and charge him with giving a law enforcement officer fictitious information."

"That's a pretty weak charge," Porter said.

"It is, but when it went to court, there would have to be an initial appearance before a judge..."

"And either Candy Man or his lawyer would have to cough up a real name, or be held in contempt," Porter said. "Smart."

"I figured if we could get his real name, we could build a better case. A real case. But I didn't have to do that."

"Why?" Ross said

"Because when I sent his prints, I instantly got a hit back."

"What database?" Porter said.

"NCIC. Our man has a nice criminal history. Candy Man is actually Clive Michelson."

Ross and Porter looked at each other.

"Clive?" Ross said. "Much less spooky as a Clive."

"You sure? 'Cause that's a pretty creepy name," Rivera said.

"What did he get convicted of?" Porter said.

"Hacking. Can you believe that? He's a computer nerd."

Porter rubbed his face, absorbing everything Rivera told him.

"It gets better. Clive is still on federal probation. He isn't supposed to leave the state of New Jersey. You know what else he isn't supposed to do?"

"Access technology?" Porter said.

"That's right. He's violated that condition of his probation, since he has a smartphone."

"Is probation going to lock him up?" Porter said.

"I haven't been able to get a hold of anyone up there. I'm sure they will, though," Rivera said.

"As happy as I am about that, I'm not sure how this helps us right now," Porter said.

"What do you mean? This is our foot in the door. Who knows what this could lead to?"

Porter told Rivera about his conversation with Clive Michelson and the man's claim that Danisha Hill was still alive somewhere. She looked deflated. "I had no idea she was alive. We have to get him to tell us. Any ideas?"

"I have one, but it's out there." Everyone looked at Ross. "Let Porter talk to him."

"Why? Last time it didn't work so well, remember? I don't want to step on my dick again."

"Things were different last time. Michelson had all the power. He thought he was untouchable, but he knows he's in trouble now. Maybe he's willing to make something happen to save his own skin."

"I don't mind if you take a crack at him. The fact is, our case with him is non-existent. Other than the fictitious info to a cop, we aren't going to be able to charge him with much. The feds are going to go after him. They won't care if you talk to him, since you aren't a cop anymore."

"You like to rub that in, don't you?" Porter said.

"I mean, you aren't a cop anymore. It is what it is. I won't be able to make a case with anything you find out, but that's okay. If that little girl is alive, finding her is the most important thing," Rivera said.

Porter thought for a few moments. The scenario was different now. He needed leverage to get Michelson to talk, and he thought he might have some that would work.

"If you're okay with it, I can give it another shot."

"Give me a few minutes to get ditch the uniform and then you guys can come in."

Porter and Ross sat on the hood of Ross's car talking about the turn of events. They knew things had swung in their favor, and they wanted to make sure they capitalized on it this time. Several minutes later, a patrol officer came out of the side door and drove away in a marked unit. Rivera appeared behind him and waved them in.

"No one else here?" Porter said.

"Nope, just us. Everyone else is gone for the day. I told the patrol guy I'd need help transporting Michelson to jail, but that he could bail for a while and take a break. He'll be back in an hour or so."

"Great. Nobody else showing up?" Porter said.

Rivera shot him an exasperated look. "You know nobody else would show up to help me. Besides, once I write the report up, it'll look like we're holding him for minor charges. Nothing for anyone to get excited about."

"Good. Remember, keep the cameras in the interview room off. We don't need this recorded."

"They'll be off," Rivera said.

"Do you have his phone?"

"Michelson's?" Rivera said. "In his property bag. Why?"

"You'll see. Just grab it," Porter said.

Rivera went to a long table that spanned the length of the wall near the evidence room and grabbed a see-through plastic bag. She tore open the end of it, slid out a smartphone, and handed it to Porter. He thumbed it to see that it worked, but found it password protected. Porter nodded and stepped into the interview room alone. Ross and Rivera went into the adjacent room, to watch the interview through a two-way mirror.

Porter pulled a chair away from the table and sat across from Candy Man.

"This should be good," Ross said.

FIFTY

"MR. SMITH. It seems I was incorrect about your occupation."

"Clive Michelson? Really? I'd go by Candy Man, too."

"You cut me to the quick, Mr. Smith. It occurs to me, it does not seem fair that you know my real name but I am still in the dark as to yours."

"The name's still Smith. Sorry to disappoint."

"Fair enough."

"Clive, I want to let you know something. Everything we say in here is off the record. There is no recording software running at this moment."

"Likely story. Forgive me if I choose not to believe you."

Porter leaned over and slapped Michelson with an open hand. When he had righted himself in his chair, Porter delivered a backhand that stunned him. Michelson's cheeks both burned bright red.

"I don't want to hurt you, Clive, but I had to prove a point."

"That there are no recordings being made of this conversation? Point made. If we were being recorded, you would never do that. I would have your job and a sizeable sum from the city."

"Exactly. Hopefully you believe me now."

"I do," Michelson said, hand on his cheek.

"Moving on. Clive, are you aware how screwed you are?"

"I have a small inkling."

"I thought you might. You are going to get your federal probation revoked. That's bad for you. You'll get, what, twenty-four months?"

"A fair estimate," Michelson said.

"But twenty-four months isn't all that bad, is it?"

"It is not. You would be surprised at how comfortable federal prisons can be."

"They're much nicer than state prisons. A white-collar guy like you, it'll be a pretty easy piece of time," Porter said.

"We understand each other."

"See, here's the thing," Porter said. "I still need to find that little girl. I think you are going to find it in your heart to help me."

"I am not sure why I would do that. It is best if I don't involve any of my... other activities... into this. The only reason I will entertain this discussion is because I know this is off the record."

"Nice that you believe me now."

Michelson rubbed his face again with his uncuffed hand.

"Call me crazy, but I think you want to tell me where the girl is."

"Crazy."

Porter smiled. "What happens when the FBI finds out about all the kids you've trafficked?"

"How would they find out about that?" Michelson said.

"Before we get to that part, let's think of the logistics. The FBI will head up the investigation against you. Maybe ICE will run the investigation since they get involved in human trafficking cases, but let's face it, the FBI wants all the glory they can get. There'll be a large task force."

"Naturally."

"I'm sure your victims span many states. The state agencies will have to be involved. Once they start finding bodies, then the states will each want you to be tried in their state. No doubt some of the states have the death penalty."

"No doubt," Clive Michelson said. He looked uncomfortable, and it had nothing to do with his smarting cheeks.

"Some of these states come after you with the death penalty. Maybe they get it, maybe they don't. Hell, I'm no judge, I couldn't pretend to know."

"I very much doubt anyone would give me the death penalty. I have not killed anyone."

"I believe you, but the law doesn't work that way. It's pretty easy to rope you into a conspiracy to commit murder charge. Didn't you tell me you helped facilitate the removal of bodies from one of your clients? That you handled... how did you phrase it... 'disposal?' Smells like a conspiracy to me. Besides, the states all have their own laws. There's no telling what kind of shit you'll get charged with. It kind of makes me excited."

Clive Michelson was silent for several moments, then found his smug look again as he spoke to Porter. "This is a very nice yarn, but you are forgetting one key thing. There is no evidence I had anything to do with any children. What you know and what you can prove are two different things."

"You're right, Candy Man, I can't prove anything. I have no evidence. Except this." Porter reached into his pocket and pulled out Michelson's smartphone. "You and I both know there's plenty on this phone to lead investigators in the right direction."

Michelson laughed his ugly, haughty laugh again. "To think I was actually starting to be concerned. If all you have is my smartphone, you have nothing. You can't even open it with the encryption."

"Are you sure about that?"

"Mr. Smith, I went to an Ivy League school for computer science. When I was arrested I was one of the five best hackers on the planet. What do you think?"

"I think technology is never as good as people think it is. Remember when the FBI asked Apple to open a terrorist's phone for them? Apple told them to screw off, but it only took a couple weeks for the FBI to find some nerd in a basement who could figure out how to break into it."

Michelson looked around nervously.

"So you do remember that? I'm guessing they can figure out how to open just about anything nowadays. One of these law-and-order judges will be glad to sign a warrant to get this phone opened. Unless..."

"Unless what?" Michelson said.

Porter leaned in and lowered his voice. "Unless you tell me where Danisha Hill is. If you tell me, I see no reason I can't let you have your phone for a few minutes before it goes into evidence. What you do with it is up to you."

Clive Michelson took Porter's meaning. If he could have access to his phone for a few minutes, he could wipe it of everything. Like a fresh, new phone. Porter figured Michelson's employers would appreciate him killing any sort of trail into their enterprise.

"I have a strict policy about client confidentiality."

"I remember. Just think about how some of those powerful clients of yours are gonna like their names being dragged into the open. All over the news. I'd be surprised if you even last long enough to go to trial. Plenty of accidents happen in jail."

"I was just realizing that in this limited case, I believe I can make an exception."

"I thought you might see things my way," Porter said.

"All I have to do is tell you where the girl is, and my end of the bargain is upheld?"

"Yep."

"Then consider our deal struck," Michelson said.

"Start from the beginning."

"The beginning is a long way back. Let me make this quick. The client who purchased your girl is a businessman who lives in the state. He has more than enough money to afford my services and has used them often."

"He buys these girls, rapes them, and then gives them back to you?"

"Mr. Smith, this man doesn't rape young girls. He subjugates them. He likes to keep young, black girls as his slaves." Michelson smiled.

"Slaves?"

"He is a rancid racist. It offends my European sensibilities, but his money spends. He doesn't have the heart to kill them, so once they grow up he sells them back to me at a reduced rate."

"No one notices this?" Porter said.

"He lives in quite a compound and leaves very infrequently. The girls stay in his house and never come outside. Other than some hired security, no one else ever sees the inside of his compound. This collector's taste is so particular that when Hector Quintana texted me about his girl, I knew instantly he would be in the market. It also helped that he was somewhat local. I prefer to avoid moving children across state lines."

"Girls?"

"I'm sorry?" Michelson said.

"You said 'girls.' How many kids are we talking about?"

Michelson thought for a moment. "I believe he only has one right now. But there have been several over the years."

Porter just wanted to say something witty or insulting, but he had nothing. The thought of a little girl trapped in a compound made him ill. "Where is he? How do I find him?"

"His phone number and address are in my phone. If you would permit me to open it, I will be glad to give it to you." Candy Man held out his hand.

Porter smiled at him. "I'm not sure I'm ready to give you this yet. Our last deal gave me trust issues. Give me the code and I'll open it myself."

"That doesn't work for me. No one gets the code. People breaking the encryption is one thing. That will take time and I can implement contingencies. I cannot have you swimming through my phone at will."

"How about a compromise? Use your thumb to unlock it. Direct me to your client's contact info and I'll lock your phone. Once I verify the info, I'll give you your phone."

"This doesn't seem like it is the smartest plan for myself," Michaelson said.

Porter shrugged. "You said you used to work with the mob. I wonder how they're gonna feel when some don gets outed over this? What am I saying—I hear they're a forgiving bunch."

Michelson exhaled, long and slow, then stuck out the out the thumb of his free hand. Porter stood, walked around the table, and seized his thumb, holding it still on the home button. The phone unlocked.

"Go to contacts. Scroll to 147."

Porter looked. All the contacts were numbers. No names or letters at all. He scrolled to 147. "You remember all these numbers?"

"I have a very good memory. You'll see a phone number and a series of other numbers."

"Is that latitude and longitude?"

"Very perceptive, Mr. Smith. That is the location where I

drop off and pick up for this particular client."

"Understood. You don't mind if I check this out before I believe you?" Porter said.

"Naturally."

Porter read the number out loud, then the latitude and longitude. He waited a moment, then repeated the information. Then he leaned back and looked at Michaelson.

"You got to the bookstore awful quick tonight. Where were you coming from?"

"Driving distance."

"You were already close, huh? Brokering another deal somewhere?"

Michelson closed his mouth and looked down at the table. Porter just sat, looking at Michelson. After a few moments, he looked up, studying Porter's face, but as the silence lengthened he appeared to grow more uneasy.

"I thought you said you were going to verify my information."

"I am."

"You are just sitting there."

"Correct," Porter said.

"Why?"

"I'm trying to decide if you're telling me the truth before I go check for myself. You can't imagine how frustrated I'll be if I believe you're giving me good intel and it turns out you're lying," Porter said.

"I assure you, it is—"

Porter cut Michelson off. "Maybe I'm just sitting here deciding whether to kill you or not. I'm leaning towards the former. You're a shit human being. There are no cameras here. I could tell everyone you attacked me."

"Now wait a minute—this is not part of our arrangement,

Mr. Smith." Michelson had gone pale and began to sweat. "I don't think this is right at all. You must rethink your plans."

"I don't have to do anything but stay brown and die."

There was a knock at the interview room door. Porter answered, opening the door just wide enough that his head could fit out. Candy Man wouldn't be able to see who he was talking to or hear the conversation.

"The phone number and address check out. Property belongs to some rich guy. I'll tell you the rest when you come out."

"Thanks, Rivera," Porter said.

"Porter, you can't let him wipe that cell phone. We need it to try to—"

Porter closed the door, cutting her off.

Porter turned to look at Candy Man, who had grown more ashen and was trembling slightly. "Relax, I'm not going to kill you, stupid. My people were listening to the entire conversation. They checked your address out while I was sitting with you. Two-way mirror. I was just killing time."

"You appear to be a man of your word. I was not worried at all," Michelson said.

"Sure you weren't," Porter said. He sat back down opposite of Michelson, holding up the man's cell phone. "A deal's a deal. You gave me info about my girl, I let you wipe your phone. Here you go." Porter handed Candy Man's smartphone to him.

Candy Man reached his free hand out and grabbed the phone. There was a smug look on his face, as if he had always known he would get out of this situation. As if he had won. But when he went to pull it away from Porter, the phone wouldn't move. Porter had the phone in a vise grip and didn't release it.

"You know, on second thought, I don't think I am going to give you this back."

Panic washed over Clive Michelson's face. He pulled

harder, but it was no use. The phone was going nowhere.

"Mr. Smith, we had a deal. I must insist you honor it."

Porter smiled an easy smile. "Insist, huh? That's pretty good, Candy Man. It's not gonna happen."

Candy Man released the phone. "I suppose I should have never expected you to honor our deal. The most likely outcome would be for you to renege."

"I suppose that makes me a reneger, doesn't it?"

Candy Man didn't find the humor.

"You can blame it on the fact that I think you should be in prison for what you did to these kids. You could blame it on the fact that you took my money at the coffee shop. But honestly? I just don't like you."

Clive Michelson sat perfectly still, stewing in his anger.

Porter wasn't sitting still. He stood, gathered the phone, and looked down at Michelson. "Mr. Michelson, I have to let you go now. Good luck in prison." Porter stepped out of the interview room into the hallway.

FIFTY-ONE

MOMENTS LATER, Rivera and Ross burst out of the monitoring room.

"I thought you were going to give him that phone," Ross said.

"Me too," Rivera said with a frown. "I was about to kick your big ass."

"I'm not letting Michelson off the hook. He needs to fry for the things he's done, but I had to give him a little hope. I knew I couldn't get him to move if he didn't think there was something in it for him."

"Aren't you worried he'll tell his lawyer you conned him for information?" Ross said.

"Not especially," Porter said.

"Why not?" Ross said.

"Even if he tells his lawyer and they bring it up to a judge, it won't matter. Information relating to the Danny Hill case will be considered 'fruit of the poisonous tree.' Since the information was obtained illegally, anything we find out with that info isn't admissible in court," Rivera said. "Any charges for the Danny kidnapping will be a no-go."

"As long as whoever investigates the case gets a court order to open his phone, everything else in there will be fair game. If he even mentions it," Porter said.

"Why wouldn't he?" Ross said.

"I worked a case once involving a local sheriff's office. For years they had been arresting drug dealers and keeping part of the product for themselves," Porter said.

"The dealers never said anything?"

"Hell no. Could you imagine their lawyer in court? 'Actually, Your Honor, my client had ten kilograms of cocaine, not four. Please amend the indictment to reflect the change.' Of course they didn't say anything. No one will admit to doing any more than you can prove they did. The only reason anyone found out about the drugs is that one of the officers who wasn't in on the scheme found out and told us. If not, those cops would have been stealing people's drugs forever."

"It wouldn't make sense for Candy Man to say anything about Danny?" Ross said.

Porter shook his head. "Nah. He'll go down for everything on the phone, and he isn't even going to mention Danny. I'll bet he doesn't even tell his lawyer about it."

Rivera had several pieces of paper in her hands. "This is what I came up with for an address. Looks like it's over in Lakeland somewhere."

Porter took the papers and shuffled through them. "Otto Schmidt. Why does that name sound familiar?"

"Isn't he the Mattress King?" Ross said.

Ross was right. When they were kids, there was a series of poorly produced commercials on local television. A guy had a jingle about buying a better mattress from his store. Porter didn't want to get it stuck in his head.

"That's right," Porter said. "I wonder how he's involved?"

"There's no telling, but you guys have to get ready to go. That uniform I sent on break will be back soon."

"I know, I know. But before we leave, I want to apologize."

"What for?" Rivera said.

"I promised you a big case and it doesn't look like you're going to get one."

"It doesn't matter," Rivera said. "I want that girl found. By the time I get a warrant or bring in the FBI, who knows what could happen to Danny?"

"What do you mean?" Ross said.

"Porter stopped Michelson from wiping his phone, but what happens when he calls his lawyer? Michelson probably has some ethically devoid scumbag on retainer. I'm sure he'll tell his lawyer to warn the clients that their personal information is in jeopardy. Maybe even a code word to tell the lawyer to tell the clients to kill the children and get rid of their bodies. Like a fail-safe, so no one gets in trouble with the law. I can't get a warrant in time to stop that. You have to go." Rivera looked at Porter. "You have to bring back that little girl. At least save Danny."

Porter put his hand on Rivera's shoulder and squeezed it. "I'll bring her back," he said, as much to himself as Rivera.

FIFTY-TWO

PORTER AND ROSS left the police station and drove to Porter's Yukon, still parked at the small grocery store where they'd left it earlier in the day. The meeting with the Acres boys seemed like days ago.

"What are you going to do?" Ross said.

"It's simple. I'll go knock on this guy's door and tell him to give me the kid. I think he'll listen."

"That doesn't sound easy."

"I said it was simple, not easy. I have no idea what I'm walking into. What the layout of the house is, if he has dogs. Security. Hell, I don't even know if that's the place they're keeping Danny. Just because we got some info from Michelson doesn't mean it's legit. That could be the address of his favorite hot dog stand."

"I don't think so," Ross said. "I watched your entire conversation. He was telling the truth."

"I know, but I don't want to get my hopes up."

"I understand."

There was silence until they reached the parking lot and Porter got out of the car. "Okay, man, I'll let you know what I come up with." He shut Ross's car door and stepped over to the Yukon.

Porter heard Ross put the sedan into gear and turned to see his friend back up and block his exit route, trapping the Yukon in the parking spot.

Ross hopped out of the car, leaving his door open. "What do you mean you'll let me know? What kind of shit is that? You're trying to leave me behind?"

"Ross, this isn't for you. Trust me. It's going to be dangerous. I can't let you get hurt," Porter said.

"Let me get hurt? I'm a grown man. You don't *let me* do anything."

"Ross—"

"Don't shut me down. You know what this means to me," Ross said.

"No. You aren't coming."

"You can't tell me no, Porter. And you can't stop me. I'm going and I'm gonna help Danny."

"No, you aren't," Porter said, trying to take Ross's car keys from him. It was like trying to wrangle the keys from a drunk person. Ross wouldn't give them up.

"I'm not moving my car unless you let me go," Ross said.

Porter reached for the keys again. He could take them from him, for sure, but he didn't want to hurt his friend. That was the entire point of this argument and why Porter didn't want Ross going to Lakeland with him. He wasn't sure how this was going to play out, and he didn't want anything to happen to Ross. He grabbed Ross's left arm.

"Gotcha. Now give me the keys, Gianullo, you're pissing me off—"

Porter felt a dull thud hit the side of his face. Then another. Ross was punching him.

Porter let go of Ross's arm, moved, and blocked so the rest of the blows missed. To an observer, it would have looked like a father play fighting with his son. Porter stepped back again and, once he was out of the range of Ross's haymakers, began to laugh.

"You aren't getting these keys." Ross was furious.

"Do you remember that time you got into that fight at the bar I was working at?"

Ross scrunched up his face. "Of course I remember it. I'm not a savage like you, these things stick with me."

"You were sticking up for that girl, right, because that weird guy kept bothering her?" Porter said.

"Why?"

"I remember watching you swing on that big gorilla. A full-fledged overhand right to the jaw. I always wondered how he took that punch. I figured the guy had a cinderblock for a chin."

Ross looked at Porter, confused. He kept his fists balled but lowered them to his side.

"It turns out you hit like a bitch. It's like you have two marshmallows on the ends of your arms." Porter's laugh grew louder.

"Laugh it up, asshole," Ross said and raised his fists again.

"Do you remember what happened to that guy?" Porter said.

"Not really. I remember punching him and then everything got hazy."

"He hit you back, and you don't have a cinderblock chin. I saw what was happening and took care of him. I promise you, when he woke up in the morning he regretted messing with you and that girl," Porter said.

"Thank you for that."

"Look man, you might as well be family. Hell, I like you more than my real brother. I'm trying to keep you from getting in the way and getting hurt, that's all," Porter said.

"I realize that, but I'm a big boy. Hell, I'm older than you are. I want to help and I'm going to. Period."

Porter looked at Ross and knew there was no changing his mind. Ross was the single most stubborn person he knew. Besides, time was not on their side, and they needed to get on the road. "Fine. Move your car. You can come."

Ross looked at Porter gravely. "Thank you."

"Shut up and move your car already."

Ross ran off to move and park the sedan. Porter got into the Yukon and started it. While he was waiting for Ross, he tried to think of a plan to get Danny back, but nothing would come to him. It was too hard without seeing the location. He was going to have to wait until he got there.

Ross jumped into the passenger seat. "Thanks."

"Stop telling me thanks. If you're coming, at least make yourself useful. GPS this address for me. I have no idea where I'm going."

FIFTY-THREE

THEY DROVE into the night towards Lakeland, nearly the halfway point between Tampa and Orlando. Porter had gone there weekly as a child. There was a large church where his parents had liked to worship. He'd never understood why they couldn't have gone to a church that didn't require an hour-long drive, but it wasn't for him to decide.

As they drove, Ross compiled as much information as he could about Otto Schmidt. He even found the old 'Mattress King' ad on a streaming site and played it.

"I told you not to play that. I'll never get that shit out of my head now," Porter said.

"Sorry. Just trying to find out what I can. He kind of fell off the radar."

"The Mattress King?"

"It looks like he inherited the business from his father when he was a young man. According to this article, due to a series of good investments, he grew the mattress business twenty-fold. He used that and diversified into other things—real estate, hotels, things like that. His net worth is currently estimated at almost fifty million," Ross said.

"I guess I'm living wrong. I should have been selling mattresses."

"Weird thing is, he just disappeared. His shareholders say they haven't seen him in years. They know he's alive, because he'll call into the end of year meetings, but no one can get a face to face."

"I'll bet we do," Porter said.

"I checked Google and looked at the satellite view of his house."

"What are we working with?" Porter said.

"'House' is the wrong word for it. It looks more like a compound," Ross said.

"That's what Candy Man said. How bad is it?"

"The place is huge. It looks like it's an industrial area, with some kind of river behind it. There's a big fence around the whole thing."

"We can work with that. It's not ideal, but at least we know where he is. And if he's keeping a little kid tucked away, it would definitely be in a place like that. Big. Secure. He wouldn't want just anyone rolling up and ruining his fun, would he?" Porter said.

"I'm sure he wouldn't."

Silence loomed for several minutes until Ross spoke.

"Why can't we just call in an anonymous tip and get the cops to go there? Find Danny themselves?"

"Hold on, tough guy. An hour ago you were full of piss and vinegar. I seem to recall you sucker-punching me a couple times. Now you want to back out?" Porter said.

"It wasn't a sucker-punch. You were standing right in front of me—"

"That's true."

"—and you know I'm not losing my nerve. I just think it would be safer for the cops to go get Danny," Ross said.

"Safer for us, but not her."

"Why not?"

"Right now this Mattress King has no idea we're onto him. No clue. That's why we need to get there before Candy Man tips him off. Having the cops show up at his front door asking about kidnapped kids is a pretty good tip-off, don't you think?" Porter said.

"I didn't think of that."

"You're an accountant."

Ross smirked at Porter.

"All kidding aside, there is another practical reason it won't work."

"School me," Ross said.

"Because all the cops can do is knock on the front door and ask if they can come in and take a look around. Schmidt won't let them. They'd need probable cause to get a warrant to go into the house, or compound in this case. They won't have it, so they have no way in. That's not something we have to worry about," Porter said.

"Who needs probable cause when you have Porter cause, right?"

"That was terrible," Porter said, but gave a small chuckle. "You aren't even a father yet and you already have dad jokes."

The GPS said they were only a few minutes out, when Porter took an unexpected turn.

"Where are you going?" Ross said. "You missed the street back there."

"You said it was in an industrial area, right?"

"Yeah."

"Those places are always half-vacant. Buildings with busted-out windows, boarded-up doors. We need to find one and post up for a while, so we get a feel for the place," Porter said.

"Think we have time for that?"

"I think so. Rivera will stall things out as long as she can. I asked her to call before Candy Man makes a phone call. That'll be our cue that we're out of time. Besides, as much as I want to save Danny, I'm not rushing in there blind. I'm not bulletproof, remember? Speaking of which, can you grab my bag?"

Ross reached into the back seat and grabbed Porter's pharmacy bag. Porter grabbed one of the bottles and took two more pills.

"Don't you think you've taken enough of those?" Ross said.

"What are you, my mother? It's just antibiotics, man. I don't want to get my arm amputated," Porter said.

"You aren't taking the pain pills?"

"No. I need to be clear-headed."

"Does it hurt?"

"Shit yes," Porter said, and that was the end of it.

Lakeland wasn't a very large city and the industrial complex wasn't huge. It consisted of a self-storage complex and two large warehouses on the north side of a large, multi-acre parcel. The warehouses used to house a cigar manufacturing company, but the business had long since moved to a newer location. The brick buildings were three stories tall, lined with windows on every floor. Opposite them was a line of metal buildings with metal roofs. They were all single-story, but there were almost a dozen of them. They were strung out along the riverfront, which flowed behind them. The buildings were surrounded by a large chain-link fence topped with barbed wire. As industrial parks went, it wasn't very large, but it was private. The area wasn't too far from downtown, and after everyone left for the day, there would be no one around for miles.

Porter checked the map on Ross's phone and found a place to park the Yukon, about a quarter of a mile away from the industrial park. They parked off the road and out of the way.

Porter got into his lockbox and put on his darkest t-shirt. Then he grabbed two flashlights, a roll of electrical tape, and an extra magazine for his Glock.

The men walked through a grove of cypress trees until they ended up behind the storage unit facility. Following the back walls of the storage buildings, they continued parallel to the compound opposite the storage units until they reached the back of one of the tobacco warehouses. Long since abandoned, they knew it was currently for rent. The ad on the internet had said it was offered by Schmidt Realty.

"He must own this whole parcel," Ross said.

Behind the warehouse they were out of sight of anyone who would be looking from the compound, so Porter grabbed the plywood from a boarded-up door and wrenched it off. The plywood protested, but gave way. They walked in, and Porter leaned the plywood against the door.

"No one will know we're here. Let's get some elevation."

Flashlights off, they climbed two flights of stairs and reached the top level. There was a hallway running the length of the entire floor. The walls on the top level were made of brick, and much of it was crumbling onto the floor, having worked its way loose from rest of the wall.

Along the hallway were several doorways, none of which had doors anymore. Stepping through any of them would take a person into a large, almost entirely open space— the main working area. There had been rows upon rows of tables lined up to allow workers to roll the cigars. As it was now, it was completely empty, save for three walls which, along with the main wall, formed a small office immediately to the left when passing into the room from the first empty doorway.

"Supervisor's office?" Ross said.

"Probably," Porter said. He stepped past the supervisor's

office and took a few dozen steps until he reached the wall of windows, which faced the Mattress King's compound.

"Don't get too close. People could see you."

"No chance. We're standing in a dark room and looking out. We're good," Porter said.

Ross joined him by the windows. "What are we looking for?"

"Anything. Everything. We know nothing about what's happening over there, so whatever we can see will help us."

There was silence as the two men took in the aerial view. It was difficult to see in the darkness, and it looked like one huge compound behind the gated, barbed-wire fence. One enormous building where a tiny child was being held.

She could be anywhere, Porter thought.

"She could be anywhere," Ross said.

"That's not the worst part. See that little building near the street?"

"Yeah," Ross said.

"It's a guardhouse. See how there's a gate in front of it? It's to control access."

"You think he has security?"

"Candy Man said he did. It looks like if we go around the back, we can avoid them. That's the move," Porter said.

Ross looked around. "I have to take a piss."

"So piss."

"Where?"

"You're a man, right? Anywhere."

Ross looked around, then headed back to the supervisor's office and the privacy it would provide.

Porter shook his head and kept scanning the compound. He needed to find some sort of weakness, or at least make an educated decision about which section of the building Danny would be in.

It wasn't easy. It was the middle of the night in a dark area. The only lights were those in the compound. Some places had more lights than others. Porter focused his attention on a section near the middle.

Lost in concentration, Porter thought he heard Ross returning from his piss. He failed to notice a man in black pants and black shirt approaching him until the man was much too close. Porter heard a noise, turned, and was blasted in the face by a flashlight.

"What the hell are you doing in here?"

Porter raised his hands. "Easy, buddy, take it easy."

"I asked what you're doing here," the man said.

"I'm interested in the property. Just thought I'd look around."

"Bullshit," the man said. "We're always catching vandals in here. Thieves. Kids sneaking in to get laid. You got a girl with you somewhere?"

"Nope, it's the truth. I'm a Realtor looking for space for a client. If you get that light out of my eyes, I can show you my ID."

The man lowered his flashlight to Porter's hands. "Being a Realtor won't get you around a trespassing charge, but let's see the ID."

Porter moved his left hand to his rear pocket, but stepped a little closer to the man as he did. There was no time to deal with the cops. He was about to attack the man when he heard a wet thud, and the man went down in a heap. Standing over him was Ross, holding a brick.

"Did I just kill that guy?"

"Yes," Porter said.

FIFTY-FOUR

"ARE YOU SERIOUS? Oh shit. Shit, shit. I can't believe I killed a guy," Ross said.

"No, I'm not serious. He'll be fine. I think. The human skull is hard as hell."

Porter had the electrical tape in his pocket, but thought it best to save that for later. They looked around until they found some old twine, left over from bales of tobacco. Porter tied the man up and then sat him along the long interior brick wall.

They searched the man's pockets and found a wallet and ID showing he worked for a private security company called Parabellum.

"Pretty good name for a security company." Porter also found a radio, and in the man's holster was an old revolver.

"Help me check his arms and legs," Porter said.

"Why?"

"Just do it," Porter said.

The pair pulled up the guard's pants legs and saw nothing. It was harder to check his trussed arms, so Porter cut the man's long sleeves down the middle, pulled them open, and shone the flashlight on his pale skin.

Just what he didn't want to see: a large USMC tattoo on the man's forearm. Porter grunted and left the man sitting up in the corner.

"How did you know he had that tattoo?" Ross asked.

"I didn't, but I wanted to check a hunch."

Porter didn't say anything else. Ross looked at him. "What hunch?"

"There are lots of little rent-a-cop businesses. They pop up all over the place. Most of them aren't very good at what they do."

"I'm not following," Ross said.

"Companies pay more for experience. If you're a regular Joe, no military or police training, you get one rate. If you're a high-speed military guy, you get something else. When the military guys find a company willing to pay them well, they usually tell their buddies and other assholes they know."

"You think since this guy was military, the other guys on his team will be military?"

"Maybe. It's a decent assumption. It's a regular jarhead tattoo, so I don't think this Parabellum is hiring special-forces types, but any trained guy is tougher to handle than an untrained guy," Porter said.

"Think we can ask him some questions? Figure out the layout of the compound? How many other guards are on duty?"

"I said he'll be fine, not he's going to wake up sometime soon. Look at his head. You seen a knot like that before?"

"No."

"Trust me, he's asleep for a while." Porter walked over to the window and resumed scanning the area.

Ross took another glance at the guard, then he followed Porter over to the windows. He had no idea what to look for, but Porter was looking so he looked, too.

There were several minutes of silence as Porter continuously scanned the compound. Ross did so as well, but his focus darted to the unconscious guard in the corner at regular intervals.

The whole area was starting to lighten up as the day was breaking. Thankfully, the sun was an early riser this time of year. The effect was like someone slowly turning on the lights in a dark room. More of the compound began to take shape.

The part he believed Schmidt to be hiding in wasn't one large building, as Porter had thought, but four separate warehouse spaces connected by covered breezeways. Outside the building farthest to the left were several vehicles parked in a parking pad. There was a large, oval, metal container by the vehicles. Porter guessed it was gasoline to fill the fleet. There weren't any gas stations close.

On top of the left-most building was a large gray tank.

There must be a reason to have a propane tank top of that building, Porter thought. He turned his attention to the second building, then the third, then the fourth.

Porter took a longer look at the second.

While the roofs on buildings one, three, and four were metal, this second building had a flat, asphalt area. There were two large air handlers on the roof, as well as a water tank. There seemed to be some sort of access door in the roof.

Porter figured this was the living quarters. Metal buildings would be hot, so the air handlers were a must. The industrial park was out of town and would not have city water. The water tank fit. He still didn't know for sure where the kid would be, but he was starting to put together a guess.

The radio in Porter's pocket squawked. "Foxtrot 3, Foxtrot 1. 10-20."

Porter held the radio and said nothing.

"Foxtrot 3, Foxtrot 1. 10-20."

"Are you going to answer it?" Ross asked.

"Nope. 10-20 is the code for asking a person their location. This guy's team leader wants to know where he is."

"Is it bad if he doesn't answer? Won't they come looking for him?"

"Yeah, they'll be more alert than they should be. But there's nothing we can do about it. Hopefully, they'll assume he fell asleep somewhere. The sun is starting to come up but it's still early. Boring job like this, I'm sure the guys sneak off to get some shuteye all the time," Porter said.

"The radio called him Foxtrot 3. How many do you think there are?"

"At least four, maybe as many as six. There has to be one in the guard shack. I haven't been able to see him, but it doesn't make sense to have an empty guard shack. There has to be at least one in the building. No reason to leave it empty either. There was the guy we ran into, who must have been doing rounds. That leaves one more as a push man for the rotation through the positions. That's four guards right there. There could be another guy or two in the building. Maybe the team leader."

"Lot of guys," Ross said.

"It's not a small amount."

"So what are we going to do? Kamikaze this thing? Run in there like maniacs?"

"I have an idea. It's still early, but do you think the inside of that metal building gets hot?" Porter said.

"I'm sure it does. It's Florida, everything gets hot."

"Good. Here's what we do." Porter laid out his plan.

Ross was unenthused. "What makes you think they'll even come outside?"

"Probably not all of them, but at least some. We need to break up their numbers a little bit."

"Fine. When do we start?" Ross said.

"Now. Rivera hasn't said Candy Man made a phone call, so we still have time, but we need to get things rolling."

"I'm ready," Ross said.

"Let's go."

Checking the sleeping guard to ensure he was tied tightly, Porter led Ross out of the big room and down the stairs to the back of the warehouse. They stepped out and placed the plywood back over the door.

As they walked to the side of the building, Porter stopped and grabbed a heavy blue tarp covering a pile of used paint cans stacked against the side of the warehouse.

The day was dawning but it was still dark enough to have decent concealment. The pair followed the back of the warehouse until they reached the edge. They turned and took the side of the building until they were at the corner nearest the front. From that vantage point, the compound was directly across from them. They only needed to cross the dirt road that separated one side of the industrial park from the other.

After several moments of waiting and seeing no one coming, Porter sprinted across the divide. He reached the barbed wire fence, staying low, and looked around but saw no one. Porter took the heavy tarp and slung it over the fence. Then he motioned for Ross to cross.

Ross looked left and right and then ran to Porter. Porter made a cradle with his hands, and Ross put his foot into it. After a count of three, Ross stood up while Porter raised his arms. Ross grabbed the barbed wire, its sharpness tempered by the heavy tarp. Ross pulled himself the rest of the way up and tumbled over the fence. He landed awkwardly on his side. Porter looked through the chain link at him.

"Very graceful. You okay?"

"Fine," Ross coughed and sputtered.

Porter stood and took several steps backward. He sprinted

forward and put his foot halfway up the fence. He jumped hard, and barely reached the barbed wire. There was a sear of pain in his arm and he grunted. Using both hands to pull himself up and his feet to climb, he got his lower body over the fence. Then he let go and landed on his feet, momentum dropping him into a crouch.

"Your big ass made that look easy," Ross said.

"Don't let the size fool you," Porter said as he jumped and pulled the heavy tarp down.

No need to leave evidence that someone was in the compound.

Porter directed Ross to follow him to the side of the metal building. He sprinted towards the edge of the building, dragging the tarp with him. Ross followed as best he could, but Porter noticed he was limping.

When they got to the side of the building, Porter rolled up the tarp and left it on the ground, out of the sight of anyone who might be in the guard house. Ross stayed crouched, catching his breath.

"You okay?"

"I'm fine," Ross said. "I'm not going to hold you up."

Porter knew Ross was lying, but he didn't have time to argue about it. Besides, there was nowhere safe he could leave Ross down here. They had to make it to the top of the structure.

Porter moved to the back of the buildings and looked left and right. There was nothing back there but the river. The metal buildings didn't even have windows. It should be safe to move around back there.

Porter sprinted for his target, the center building with the air handlers and water tank. The men moved freely until they came to the section they were looking for. Porter looked around, and was disappointed to see there were no steps or ladders to allow them access to the top of the roof. Still, it was only a single story, so it wouldn't be too difficult to get up there.

He motioned Ross to step into his hand cradle again. Ross complied and was hoisted up to the roof. Porter jumped straight up and grabbed the edge of the roof, pulling himself up. Ross grabbed him under the arms and help pull him the rest of the way up. Porter rolled onto his back on the asphalt shingles and caught his breath.

Ross was up and looking at the air handlers. "I'm not sure how we break one of these things."

"Just rip stuff out. Flip switches and pull hoses. I'm no HVAC expert, but it shouldn't be too hard."

Ross looked around the handlers until he saw an on/off switch. He flipped that down. Then he found the plug which fed power to the units and unplugged that as well. The air handlers, which had been running furiously just a few moments ago, made a whining noise as they ground to a halt.

"I think I did it," Ross said.

Porter was still lying on his back. His injured arm hurt and, despite the tarp, he had managed to cut his hand on the barbed wire. He stood and walked over to the handlers to verify Ross's work.

"Good," Porter said. "Now we wait." The two took up a position behind the access door in the floor of the roof. Eventually, someone would come up to figure out why the air wasn't running anymore. Porter hoped the Mattress King was miserable in his metal cave.

FIFTY-FIVE

WATCHING the battle scene on his hundred-inch flat screen had left Otto Schmidt out of breath.

A man of excess, his life of privilege had led to him developing many appetites, of which buying children was but one. He'd grown large enough that getting around was not without its challenges. As such, he preferred to stay seated in his den, wedged into his favorite loveseat, taking up both cushions. It wasn't that he couldn't get up, but why bother when he could make his slave bring him anything he needed?

His den was the most plushly-appointed room in the entire compound. Every room was nice, befitting a man worth millions of dollars, but the den was his jewel.

There was the huge television screen against one wall, with a large leather sectional opposite. Another wall was lined with curio cabinets, which housed Otto Schmidt's other passion, Civil War memorabilia. There were swords from the both the Union and Confederacy, encased letters from the battlefield and large, complete uniforms hanging on mannequins. The other side of the room had large, framed maps of specific battles and an authentic cannon, which had been used during the battle of Gettysburg.

Otto Schmidt believed he'd been born in the wrong era. He fancied himself a southern plantation owner in a large antebellum home, with a bevy of slaves to attend to his every whim. Things being what they were, that wasn't a practical desire. Still, a remote location could afford the luxury of no prying eyes into one's affairs, and a deep pocketbook could buy silence from anyone who worked for him. Besides, the guards who kept him safe weren't allowed into his den and had no clue what he did in there.

As the battle of Antietam raged on his screen, Otto Schmidt clacked his dry tongue around in his mouth. Watching television was hard work. "Girl."

From a doorway appeared a young girl. A blue bandana pulled her hair out of her face. Her dark skin contrasted with the pastel dress that hung from her shoulders. A dirty apron, stained with food and drink, was tied around her waist. Despite this, her eyes were bright and clear. She made her way over to Otto Schmidt. "Master Schmidt?"

"I want a drink. Get me the sweet tea."

"Yes, Master Schmidt."

The girl went over to the bar and behind it, to the full-sized refrigerator. She poured a large glass of sweet tea and placed it on a silver tray, carefully walking it back to Schmidt.

"Can I get Master Schmidt anything else?"

"Go back to your place." The girl left the room and went back to her quarters, a small area off the den. There was a tiny bed, a nightstand, and nothing else in the room. There were no windows, and it was always dark.

Otto Schmidt continued watching his television for a while, but was growing more uncomfortable. The air in his den was thick and his greasy, balding head was sweating. Schmidt didn't like to sweat; it reminded him of exercise, which he liked even less. He waited for another episode of his show to end before he struggled to his feet. The backs of his meaty legs were drenched in sweat and stuck to the leather of his love seat. He went to the door that connected his den to the main area of his compound, and swiped the card he wore on a lanyard around his neck. There was a hiss of air and the door opened.

"Charles. Charles," he said, running out of breath by the second shout.

From an outer room, a thin man appeared. His smartly tailored suit, slicked back hair, and glasses stood in stark contrast to his shabby, flabby employer. "Yes, Mr. Schmidt? Is there anything I can do for you?"

"Yes, you idiot. Haven't you noticed it's hotter than a whore in church in here?"

"I noticed it growing warm, sir."

"Then what are you waiting for? Figure out what's wrong. Get a repairman in here." Schmidt pushed a large green button on the wall, and the door hissed and slid shut.

CHARLES COCHRAN HATED HIS JOB. Working for the fat slob angered him to no end. He was loud, he stank, and he always had a kid with him. Charles was the only one at the compound who knew the kid was trapped in that room. The guards had no clue.

Cochran rarely saw her, only when he dropped off food for her a couple of times a week. The job was strange, but the pay was exceptional. More than exceptional—it had made Cochran a millionaire. The kid thing bothered him, but at least he was sure Schmidt wasn't touching her. Schmidt couldn't molest anybody in his state.

Cochran opened a door and walked down a breezeway that connected Schmidt's den to the next large building. Excess memorabilia from Schmidt's inner sanctum was strewn everywhere, dozens of pictures and paintings nailed into the drywall. Cochran walked out of the building, through another breezeway, and into the next large building. This building was wide open inside, with a long rectangular table in the middle. On the rear wall was a refrigerator and on the opposite wall, a television. It was the break room for the guards.

Cochran walked up to the muscular man seated at the head of the table. "Fitz, Mr. Schmidt would like someone to take a look at the A/C. He thinks it's getting hot in here."

"His fat ass would be hot in an ice storm," Jason Fitzhenry said.

Cochran laughed. "Could you take care of it for me?"

"Sure. I'll have one of the guys go out and look at it. He can look for Prater while he's out there."

"Prater's gone?" Charles said.

"He hasn't come back from his rounds."

"Hmmm," Cochran said.

Fitz leaned back in his chair and looked toward the corner of the big room. That space was used as a gym, furnished with old weight machines, treadmills with fraying belts, and a couple of dumbbells and kettlebells. Nothing fancy or high tech, but it was enough for the guards to get a decent workout in.

"Scott," Fitz barked, "I need you to handle something for me."

"Why me? I'm in the middle of a set here."

"First, because you're the new guy and no one gives a damn about your sets. Second, because you were in the Air Force. That makes you a pussy. Third, because I said so. Do we have a problem?"

Cochran adjusted his glasses and moved out of the way. He'd never understood the mannerisms of type-A personalities.

Scott swallowed his pride. "What do you need?"

"Fat man says he's getting hot. Go out and see if something happened to the A/C. While you're out there, see if you can track down Prater. He's been quiet for a while. Find wherever he's napping and wake his ass up."

"10-4," Scott said and made a mocking salute.

"Keep it up, funny guy, and I'm going to check your chin for you. Just do what I say and get your ass moving."

"Thank you, Fitz. I'll let you know if anything else comes up."

"You do that, Cochran," Fitz said, emphasizing the first part of the man's name.

Cochran backed away from the table and the team leader, waiting for the day he'd socked away enough money that he could quit. Then he wouldn't have to put up with anyone's shit.

SCOTT GRABBED his towel and put his shirt back on, tucking it in before putting on his duty belt, which had his gun, handcuffs, Taser, and OC spray. He toweled his head off again and tossed the towel into the corner.

He stared at Fitz as he started toward the maintenance room. SEAL or not, at some point he was going to have to show that asshole who was boss.

Scott walked through the break room and into the memorabilia room. He continued down the big space until he found the small electrical room. He looked at the thermostat, but the digital readout showed no numbers.

"This thing busted?" Scott muttered.

He fiddled with the unit to see if it was accidentally turned off, but it was dead. He sighed and reached up, tugging on a heavy canvas strap that hung from the ceiling.

How the hell am I supposed to know what's wrong with this thing? Scott thought. Pulling the strap released a set of foldable, metal stairs. Scott unfolded the stairs, pushed them to lock them into place, and then ascended to the roof. Several rungs later, he was at the access door leading outside. Scott rotated the wheel on the bottom of the door until he heard a lock tumble and the door was free to move. He pushed it and it pivoted on a hinge, locking in place when it was vertical.

The sunlight was bright on Scott's face and he squinted while he climbed the rest of the way up the metal stairs and out onto the roof. He stood, hands shielding his eyes for a moment. Then Scott felt himself being elevated, and his world went black.

FIFTY-SIX

~BEFORE~

Porter and Ross had been waiting for someone to come and check the air handler for nearly an hour.

"How long do you think this will take?"

"No telling," Porter said.

"What are we going to do when someone comes out?"

"Knock him out, tie him up, push him off the roof," Porter said, listing options.

"Do you think Candy Man made a call yet? Think Schmidt is spooked?" Ross said.

"No."

"Why not?"

"Rivera would have called," Porter said.

"Is that blood?"

Porter looked at his hand. Blood from the gash the barbed wire had given him was dripping down his fingers. "Yes."

"Is it bad? Do you need a doctor?"

"Hold on one second, I'll just find one. Doctor? Doctor? Is anyone on this rooftop a doctor?" Porter said in a stage whisper.

"I'm sorry I'm talking so much, I'm just nervous," Ross said.

"Try to relax. We still have more moving parts. You can't get all geeked out on me now. You've done good so far," Porter said.

His hand did look bad, so he tore his sleeve off and wrapped it twice around the injured area. At least he could keep debris out of it.

"You think so? I think I killed that guy in the warehouse."

"You didn't kill that guy," Porter said. "Stop worrying about it. Besides, even if you did, is that a big loss?"

"I mean... yeah, it kind of is. I never killed anyone before," Ross said.

"These guys work for a scumbag who buys and sells little kids. Don't have sympathy for them."

Ross was quiet for a few moments. "I guess you're right, but it feels weird. I keep replaying it in my head."

"Put the movie on pause. Worry about it later. I need you here right now," Porter said.

Ross nodded and looked around. "Hey man, have you noticed any cameras?"

"No. I've been looking for them and there aren't any. Doesn't really matter though."

"Why not? I don't want my face on the news."

"It won't be," Porter said.

"You're sure?"

"Positive."

"I don't know how you can be so sure—" Ross said.

The door on the roof floor between them made a creaking noise.

"See? It worked. Just be ready," Porter said.

The creaking noise from the door continued. There was a click and the door swung open and stopped. Porter and Ross took a few steps backward so they would be behind the door and could use it as concealment.

A big white man came up the stairs, pausing halfway to rub

his eyes. His back was towards Porter and Ross and he couldn't see them crouched behind the floor-door. The big man stepped onto the asphalt roof and stood straight, blinking and still rubbing his eyes.

Porter stepped from behind the door and closed the distance between himself and the guard. While the guard was still facing away, Porter bent over and hugged both of the guy's legs tight. Porter then stood straight up with the man, inverting him a hundred and eighty degrees, and dropped him. He landed directly on his head, and went stiff as a board. Porter checked and confirmed that he was out cold.

"See? No problem," Porter said.

"Well, that's one way to do it. I prefer a brick myself," Ross said sarcastically.

"I said stop worrying about it."

The pair trussed the guard like a Thanksgiving turkey, arms and legs behind his back. Then, they untucked his guard uniform and stuffed the bottom of the shirt into his mouth so he couldn't yell for help. Porter went through the man's duty belt.

"He has much better stuff than the last guy. Here." He handed Ross the guard's Heckler and Koch pistol.

"You know I have no clue how to work one of these," Ross said.

"It's easy, just point and shoot. This H&K doesn't even have a safety." Porter dropped the magazine and made sure there were rounds. Then he pulled the gun's slide a small bit to the rear to make sure there was a round in the chamber. He handed it to Ross. "It's good to go."

Ross accepted it, careful to keep his finger off the trigger. Porter had at least taught him that much. "Fine, let's go."

"Listen, I know you won't like this, but I really need you to stay here this time."

"Porter—"

"Hear me out. I need you to watch this guy and make sure he doesn't wake up and cause a ruckus. Plus, they might send someone else up here to check things out. We can't have another guy find this one. Then everyone will know we're here."

Ross thought for a moment. "You're actually right. Someone has to stay here."

Porter grabbed the radio from the guard's duty belt and gave it to Ross. "Now we each have one. Keep your ears open in case you hear someone say something about the roof."

"What about you?"

"I'm going to drop in and take a look around. I'll be back," Porter said.

"What am I supposed to do if someone comes up here?"

Porter gestured to the pistol Ross was holding. "Unless you'd rather find another brick." Porter slipped through the hole in the roof without another word.

FIFTY-SEVEN

PORTER DESCENDED the folding metal staircase and found himself in a utility room, small and cramped. He thought about closing the roof access door and folding up the stairs. That would ensure no one could get to Ross. But then he thought better of it. He didn't want to trap Ross up there, in case they had to move quickly. There was also the possibility Ross could take one of them out. Under normal circumstances, that would have been a ridiculous thought, but Ross was ready and had the drop on anyone who would show up. Better to leave the stairs and access door as they were.

Porter got to the door of the utility room and tried the handle. It was unlocked and he slowly opened it, then looked left and right to orient himself. Porter stepped into the larger room and went all the way to the back wall. He'd hoped that the building with the A/C units would have been the living quarters. Nothing in here but a collection of junk and old memorabilia. He saw two doors, one on each side wall.

Which way would they keep a kid?

He headed left. If that wasn't the right way, he could sweep back across the remaining three buildings and know that nothing was behind him. Opening the door, he stepped into the breezeway.

It was covered but open on the sides. Looking up, Porter saw electrical wiring and silver air conditioning ducts on the underside of the covering.

They ran the A/C through all the buildings. No wonder it wasn't on top of the living quarters.

Porter pulled the handle of the door and stepped inside.

He was in a large open room, containing a table and several chairs. A television on the far wall was on mute. The smell of old coffee hung in the air. Porter waited for a few moments and heard nothing. He moved across the room and went out another door, through another breezeway, and into another building.

He was in a kitchen, large and modern like a restaurant's. There was the smell of bacon being fried and bread baking. Porter walked along with the wall at his back and passed a large stove. The man cooking at the stove wore a chef's coat, and was concentrating on his work. Porter kept walking; the man didn't notice.

Continuing on, Porter found himself in the prep area, with fruits and vegetables on stainless steel countertops, and then he moved toward the walk-in refrigerator and freezer. They were on the left-most wall, which made sense. There had to be a way for them to vent their exhaust outside. There was an interior wall that ran parallel to the outside wall, about eight feet pushed out. That wall created a hallway. Porter ducked into it and put the freezer and coolers to his back while peeking around the wall back into the kitchen.

No kids here.

He had decided to go back the way he came when he heard the handle on the walk-in cooler pop open, and a big guy with a shaved head emerged, eating an apple. He was dark-skinned and dressed in the Parabellum uniform of the two guards Porter had already encountered.

There was a frozen moment as both men looked at each other. Porter moved first. He stepped forward and launched an enormous right hand at the guard, but the guard was quick to react and raised his left arm, tucking his chin. The full effect of the blow caught the man on his biceps and forearm. The force pushed the guard back, but he was unharmed.

The man reached out and hit Porter with a quick uppercut. It was fast but lacked power. Porter's teeth slammed together, then he reached behind the man's head with his right hand and hit him with a pair of elbows, which split the guard's eyebrow open. The guard punched Porter with both hands in the chest, creating distance between the men.

Porter leaped at the guard again. This time the guard tried an overhand right, but Porter was ready. He slipped to the left and the guard's punch sailed past his head. As he was moving, he hit the man in the stomach, which doubled him over. Porter straightened up and brought his elbow down on the back of the bent-over guard's neck, near the base of his spine, and the man went down, convulsing. Porter stepped away to make sure there was no subterfuge. After several moments, he reached in and checked for the now motionless man's pulse. He found none.

Porter caught his breath.

He went back to the corner of the hallway to ensure that no one heard the ruckus. The chef was still cooking, and Porter saw no one else in the large kitchen. He checked the guard's duty belt. Except for a different model handgun, he had the same stuff as the guard Porter had taken out on the roof.

Porter took the gun and put it in his back pocket. He dragged the guard into the walk-in cooler and pulled him to the back, doing a decent job of hiding his body under several fifty-pound sacks of apples.

Porter shut the walk-in cooler and went back to the corner. The chef had moved to the other side of the room, so Porter hustled down the walkway with its rubber anti-slip mats, and went out the door he'd come in through.

Stepping into the breezeway, he fished the pistol out of his back pocket: a Sig Sauer P229. Porter was very familiar with this pistol. He'd had one as his duty weapon for several years when he was a fed, before he had wised up and bought his own Glock. Still, it was an accurate and reliable weapon.

Porter dropped the magazine out and saw that it was full. He checked the chamber, and found it loaded. Keeping the gun out, Porter decided he was done being sneaky. Besides, now he had another gun, one that couldn't be traced back to him.

One he wasn't worried about using.

He stepped into the next room and found it empty. Taking an immediate right, Porter traced the perimeter of the room. He found a small gym in the corner and a single-user restroom, but no people. His route had taken him to the door on the far side, which he opened, stepping into another breezeway. He wasted no time getting to the other building and opening the door.

Back to the museum. Porter realized this building was nicer than the other two. There was carpet on the floor and drywall covering the insulated metal walls the other buildings had. As Porter traced the perimeter of the room, he heard the door in front of him click open. In walked a small man with glasses, wearing a black suit. He didn't notice Porter leaning with his back against the wall, so Porter fell in behind him. He followed for a few feet, then tapped the man on the shoulder. The man turned, and seemed stunned to have a pistol in his face.

"Where is the girl?"

"She... she..."

"Spit it out."

"Are you going to hurt me?"

"Yes," Porter said.

"She's in the next building."

"Straight through the breezeway?" Porter said.

"Here, use this." The man took off his lanyard and gave it to Porter. Dangling at the bottom was a keycard.

"No loyalty to your boss, huh?"

"None. Please don't hurt me."

"How many people know about the girl?" Porter said.

"What?"

"How many people know about the girl you are keeping?"

"No one. No one. Just me and Schmidt. No one else. You can do anything with her, no one knows she's here," the small man stammered.

"That's good to know. Turn around."

"But..."

"Turn around," Porter said.

The small man turned around and Porter hit him on the side of the head. He fell as if someone had flipped a switch. He was snorting on the floor as Porter stepped over him and moved on to the next door.

He opened it and came face to muzzle with a pistol.

FIFTY-EIGHT

A MAN HAD his pistol in Porter's face, and Porter had his pistol pointed at the man's chest.

"You must be the reason I haven't heard from Prater for a while."

"Maybe. Is he the guy with the old revolver, or the big white guy you sent to check on the A/C unit? Or, wait, is he the brother that likes apples? I get confused."

"You took all my guys out?"

"I didn't get the guy in the gatehouse yet."

"That was Prater."

"Ahh. Must have caught him making rounds. I left the chef alone," Porter said.

"He's just a civilian."

"Then yeah, I took all your guys out."

"I gotta say, I'm pretty impressed," the man said. The name tag on his uniform read *Fitzhenry* and his arms were nestled snugly into the sleeves on his uniform. His skin had a leathery look, like he'd spent too much time in the sun.

"I'm not. They were shit. That's not their fault. I blame you; you're the boss."

"Good help is hard to find. That's not a cliché, it's the gospel. Sometimes you make do with what you got. If I still had my team of SEALS, you would never have gotten this far," Fitzhenry said.

"Never is a long time."

"That's right. And you're never getting to Mr. Schmidt."

"How did you know I was coming? Cameras?" Porter said. "I didn't notice any."

"Cameras? Hell, no. That fat bastard won't pay for any. He said good old-fashioned human power was what he wanted guarding him. Thought technology would make us complacent. I was coming in from having a smoke and saw you with Charles. Saw the little bitch give you the keycard. Knew it was a matter of time till you walked through that door."

"Well, you got me. Now what?" Porter took several slow, small steps backward, to create space between himself and Fitzhenry. This allowed him to raise his pistol until he had a clear shot at the team leader's neck.

"I'm not too sure. I figured I'd dust you when you came out here, but you pointing that pistol at me changed my plan. Now we're stuck."

"You could always see if action beats reaction. Try to get your shot off at me."

"I could," the team leader said, "but I'd rather not chance it. I'm not a huge fan of being shot."

"I understand your position. It doesn't blow my skirt up, either." Porter had taken several more small steps backward. The breezeway was several feet wide, but the lane was a hundred feet long, running from the back of one warehouse building to the front. True to its name, there was a breeze being funneled between the two buildings.

"There's no chance I let you walk. I don't really like this guy, Schmidt, but he's paying me. I have a reputation, you know? If word gets out I can't protect my clients, my work prospects are toast. This outfit I'm working for pays well; I'd hate to lose my job."

"We couldn't have that."

"Nope. Shoot straight with me; you got to Tommy?"

"Which one was he?" Porter said.

"Apple guy."

"No more Tommy," Porter said, focused on lining up the front sight of the Sig Sauer with the team leader's nose.

"He was good. You must be better."

"Count on it," Porter said.

"I have a crazy thought. Why don't we drop these pistols? Settle this like men."

"Not sure I catch your meaning, Navy."

"I haven't been in a real fight since I left the service. You must be pretty good to take out Tommy. I want to see how good you are," Fitzhenry said.

Porter looked at him.

"Come on. If you win, you can have Schmidt. When I win, I'll kill you. My reputation stays intact. Fair?"

"How do I know I can trust you?" Porter said. "That you aren't going to shoot me when I lower my gun?"

"My word is solid. See?" Fitzhenry broke the grip on his gun and raised his left hand, as his right lowered the pistol. "See? I'm an honest guy. Now let's say we get this thing going—"

Porter squeezed the trigger and shot the team leader through the face. Fitzhenry was dead before he hit the gravel.

"What are you, an idiot?" Porter said. The shot echoed between the two warehouses. Porter worked his jaw, trying to unplug his ears and stop the ringing. He worried that someone would hear the shot, but then realized no one was left to notice.

Fitzhenry said Porter had taken out all his guys. There weren't any other guards in the compound. Charles the assistant was asleep on the floor, the chef was three buildings away, taking care of breakfast. That meant Schmidt had to be behind the door of the last building. Collecting himself, Porter tried the door handle, found it to be unlocked, and stepped into the big building.

FIFTY-NINE

IT WAS AN ANTEROOM, running fifteen feet deep into the building and the entire length. The room was comfortably furnished, with a small television on the wall and a large, horse-shoe-shaped desk against the outer wall. Two monitors sat on the desk, as well as a picture of Charles the assistant and a woman.

In the wall separating the room from the rest of the ware-house space was a single, heavy looking door. Porter saw a place to use a key card. He pulled out Charles's and gave it a swipe. The door unlocked with a hiss, then popped and slid open. Porter looked through the threshold.

From the doorway he saw more junk. Glass cases sat lined up like soldiers, battle flags from the Civil War hanging inside. There were old flintlock pistols, muskets, and complete outfits displayed on mannequins. Old boots lined the baseboards, and there was even a cannon in the corner.

This space had drywall instead of metal walls and several large, fluorescent lights above. The lights gave the place a sterile feel, but it wasn't. It was dirty. Unkempt. The faint odors of sweat and urine burned at Porter's nose. Seeing no one from the doorway, he continued into the room.

As he moved in, Porter noted a large leather sectional in the middle of the room, opposite a wall with a bank of televisions. A quick scan of the room showed him that he was alone, save for the person sitting in the loveseat. The man was enormous, completely filling up a seat that was made for two people. His back was to Porter.

Porter walked up behind him.

"Charles, have you fixed this damn air conditioner yet? I'm stewing in my own juices over here. I just took a shower yesterday, I don't want to have to take one again today. Charles?"

Porter stepped around the side of the sectional. The big man saw him and started.

"Who the hell are you? How did you get in here? This place is only for me."

"Charles gave me the key card," Porter said.

"He wouldn't. Charles wouldn't do that. He's my assistant. I pay him well for his discretion."

"That's something you'll have to take up with him. Are you Otto Schmidt?"

"Of course I am. This is my house. Mine. You need to leave, I'm calling my guards." Schmidt picked up what looked like a garage door opener with a red button and pressed it.

"About those guards of yours." Porter shook his head no.

"What'd you do to my guards? Where are they?" Schmidt pushed the button again, then hit the unit with the palm of his hand.

"They're gone, Otto."

"Don't you call me that. It's Mr. Schmidt to everyone."

"I'm not everyone," Porter said.

"Lousy good-for-nothing guards. Can't believe they just left me like that. I think I pay pretty good." Schmidt tossed the remote aside. He fixed Porter with his sweaty glare. "I already asked you once, who are you? Don't make me ask again."

"I'm just a guy. What I want is more important."

"Fine. I'll play. What. Do. You. Want?" He enunciated every word and his jowls moved as he spoke. His face was red from the exertion of talking and there was a wet spot on his tent of a t-shirt.

Porter's stomach turned. "I want to know what you did with the girl."

"What girl?"

"Don't try to pretend you don't keep kids here. What did you do with the girl?" Porter said.

"I'm not pretending anything, you ignorant bastard. I can't keep track of them all," Schmidt said with a sneer. "What girl are you talking about?"

Porter's face flushed and he almost flew into a rage. Then from what looked like a closet, a little, dark face peeked around the corner at him. He composed himself. "Danny?"

The little girl nodded her head, then ducked back into the room when Schmidt shifted to look at her.

"Her? You want her? You can't have my slave. I paid good money for her."

"Slave?" Porter said.

"Yes, *slave*. I like to have one around. It makes me feel like I'm in the good old days, like things are the way they should be."

"Still waiting for the South to rise again, huh?" Porter said.

"God willing."

"I'm pretty sure God isn't on your side, but whatever helps you get through the night," Porter said. He looked toward the closet, again catching a glimpse of Danny.

"It's time for you to go," Schmidt said.

"Or what?" Porter said. "Unless one of those cannons over there works, you're fresh out of luck."

With that, Schmidt lurched in his couch. For a split second, Porter wondered if Schmidt was going for a weapon he'd concealed. He'd discounted the prospect, because the man thought he was protected. Porter raised his pistol.

The man struggled back and forth again. He wasn't reaching for a gun, he was getting up.

Finally on his feet, the behemoth kicked his stubby leg at the coffee table in front of him, sending it flying out of the way. "I said your black-ass needs to leave."

"Shit," Porter said, out of surprise rather than concern.

Schmidt leaned forward, getting his bulk moving, his momentum carrying him straight at Porter. Porter stood his ground, as the man barreled toward him. At the last moment, Porter took a small step to the right. As Schmidt lumbered past him, Porter pointed the pistol at the back of the man's knee and fired.

The report of the bullet was almost deafening. Although the room was large, it wasn't large enough to make the sound any easier on Porter's ears.

Schmidt fared far worse. The bullet had blown out the front of his kneecap. The man wriggled on the floor, too big to even reach down and grab his injured leg.

"You son of a bitch. You coon-lovin' son of a bitch."

"Coon-lovin'?" Porter said, baffled at the phrase. He'd never heard that one before. He wasted little time putting his knee in Schmidt's back, keeping him from even trying to roll over.

"Hurts, doesn't it?"

Schmidt roared obscenities, calling Porter even more names he'd never heard of.

"Say some off-color shit to me again, I'll screw my gun into your ear and turn your head into a canoe. You got that? Huh?"

Schmidt started to growl, until finally he was silent, if not quiet. His breathing was like a laboring elephant.

"I'm taking the girl, do you understand? Nod your head if you do." Porter kept one knee in the man's back and his hand gripped Schmidt's collar. His pistol was pointed at the base of the big man's skull.

Schmidt nodded.

"There is nothing you can do to stop it. Got me?"

Schmidt nodded again. "Don't kill me."

"Too late, that's happening," Porter said.

"Don't, you son of a bitch. I have money."

"That's not gonna do you any good right now," Porter said.

"I'll give it to you. All of it. Just don't kill me."

Porter glanced up at the corner. Danny was peeking around the corner with her hands covering her ears.

"How much?"

"How the hell should I know?"

"Wrong answer," Porter said, pressing the gun into the man's sweaty head, taking the slack out of the trigger.

"I don't know, go count it yourself. It's just a little bit. I pay my guards with it. And I want a damn refund," Schmidt bellowed, as if someone else could hear him.

Porter eased off the trigger and stood. From what he could see, Schmidt's leg looked like a chicken cutlet. "Where?"

"Behind the damn bar."

Porter looked at the bar near the wall. He looked down at Schmidt. "Don't go anywhere."

Porter stepped behind the bar and dug through the cubbies and drawers until he found a sizeable stack of cash, neatly banded as if it had recently come from the bank. Much neater and cleaner than the wad he'd taken from Hector, but a larger amount.

He looked around until he found a trash can. After dumping out all the candy wrappers, he put the bills in the bag and tied the top.

In the interim, Schmidt had begun trying to crawl toward the door. The effort had made his breath sound like it belonged in a lumber yard.

"I told you not to go anywhere," Porter said. He raised his pistol and shot Schmidt in the side of his good knee.

A roar pulsed through the room. Schmidt tilted, like a turtle on its back, and snarled. "You son of a bitch. You dirty, greedy, nigg—"

"Say it," Porter interrupted. "Go on."

"Dammit," Schmidt said, controlling himself. "Can't you just leave? You got what you want."

"Not yet," Porter said under his breath

He caught a glimpse of the tiny face looking around the corner again. He walked over to the closet, but discovered it wasn't that at all.

A tiny cot lay on the floor and a single, bare light bulb hung overhead. The girl obviously slept there. She didn't flinch or try to run as he approached.

"Danisha? Danny? Hi."

"Hello." Her face looked the same, but her hair was no longer in the braids Porter had seen on the billboard.

"Danny, I'm a friend of your grandmother. Her name is Miss Leona, right?"

"Yes."

"Okay, good. I promise I won't hurt you. Don't be afraid," Porter said.

"I'm not afraid."

Porter looked at her and knelt so he could be closer to her height. "Why not?"

"Because the knight saves the princess. He never hurts her. That's not the way stories work."

Porter smiled. "You think I'm a knight?"

"Yes. You don't have a sword, but you are big and tough.

And you're here to save me. That makes you a knight," Danny said.

Porter's next words caught in his throat and his eyes stung. He cleared his throat. "Are you okay, sweetheart? Did he hurt you?"

"No, he didn't hurt me. He was just mean. Mean like a dragon. See, he even sounds like a dragon."

Schmidt was roaring in pain, screaming a non-stop stream of profanity. He had used every slur Porter had ever heard, and some he hadn't even known existed.

"Don't worry about him. He won't hurt anyone else. I promise," Porter said.

"Good."

"Are you ready? If so, I need you to follow very close behind me. Grab my shirt and don't let go, okay? I have to be ready in case there are more dragons." He felt a small but strong hand grab his shirt tail. He led her out of her small space into the large room.

"You can't take her, she's mine," Schmidt said as Porter walked past him. "You can't."

Blood from Schmidt's injuries was pooled around him. His hands had gotten into it and as he clutched at his face in pain, the result was an amateur war-paint job, making him look even more unhinged.

Porter kept going, taking Danny to the entry door.

"Get back here, you son of a bitch. Girl. Girl, get over here. Girl! I own you. Get over here, now!" Porter felt Danny pull closer to his legs as he walked out of the room. They made it to the door and Porter swiped Charles's key card.

Porter waited for a moment. He wouldn't be careless now, not when he'd just found Danny. As the door shut behind them, Porter saw Otto Schmidt rolling like a beached whale. He would be going nowhere.

Once they were all the way into Charles's office, with the door shut behind them, Porter turned to look at Danny. "You're very brave, do you know that?"

The little girl nodded her head proudly.

"I need you to be brave for one more minute, can you do that?"

"One minute?" Danny said.

"Exactly. Count to a minute and I promise I'll be right back." Porter sat the bag of money down at her feet.

"Sixty?"

"Your grandma was right, you are very smart," Porter said.

He stepped back through the door to Schmidt's room, the sound of a sing-song voice counting up from one behind him.

Schmidt had managed to roll himself onto his back, but his legs hadn't made it the entire way and were tangled up underneath him.

Porter walked over to the man, looked down at him, and raised his pistol. Schmidt stopped grunting when he saw him.

Porter thought for something, anything to say to the man. He could think of nothing.

So he pulled the trigger.

SIXTY

"Okay, sweetheart, I'm back," Porter said, rushing back to the girl. "I'm sorry about all the stuff you had to see in there."

"Is the master dead?"

"Did he make you call him master?" Porter said.

"He told me to call him that."

Porter knelt again. "No one is your master, Danny. You never have to say that again, okay?"

"I know he isn't my master. I just called him that, so he wouldn't get mad. In my mind, I always called him something different."

"What did you call him?" Porter said.

Danny looked around, then she motioned Porter to come closer, so as not to reveal her secret to just anyone. She cupped both hands around his ear and whispered, "Fatty fat-fat." Her smile exposed her front tooth, which had grown in considerably since her billboard picture.

Porter stood and smiled. "Okay, sweetheart, stay close. This next little bit, I need you to close your eyes for me, okay?"

Danny nodded and slammed her eyes shut.

Porter led Danny through the next door, into the breezeway. Fitzhenry was still dead as a doornail, the inside of his skull painted along the gravel ground.

He hoped Danny kept her eyes closed.

He opened the next door and made sure nothing was waiting for him. Then he turned and looked at Danny, her eyes dutifully closed. "Okay, you can open."

"Is Charles asleep?" The girl pointed to the assistant's motionless body in the middle of the room.

"Yes. When he wakes up, we'll be gone," Porter said.

"I didn't like him either."

"Hold tight," Porter said, and continued through the building until he got to the utility room. He stepped through the cracked door, saw the lowered staircase, and shouted for Ross. The accountant's face appeared in the opening in the roof.

"You okay? I heard a gunshot a while back."

"Hey man, let's get out of here," Porter said.

"But what about the girl?"

Danny peeked around Porter's legs and looked up at Ross through the doorway in the roof.

Ross saw her and froze, his mouth agape. His chin fumbled as he tried to find words, but none came out. He ran down the metal stairs, stopped in front of Porter, and said, "Can I hug her?" He looked at Danny. "Can I hug you?"

Danny looked at Porter and nodded. Ross scooped the small girl up off the ground and squeezed her, weeping the entire time.

Nearly twenty seconds elapsed, then a small voice said, "Mister? Mister, you're squeezin' me."

SIXTY-ONE

PORTER GRABBED Ross by the shoulder and shook him until he set Danny down, his face wet with happiness. "I can't believe you did it. I can't believe you did it."

"Believe it. Now we have to go. There may be another shift of guards coming soon. Is that guy up there still out?"

"Yeah. He's breathing, I checked a couple times, but he hasn't moved." Ross wiped his cheeks with the back of his hand.

"Go cut him loose, then meet me back down here," Porter said.

"Cut him loose? Are you serious?"

"If he's out, he won't be able to do anything about us being here. He can't tell anyone. He hasn't seen our faces, so he couldn't dime us out regardless. Cut him loose. If he wakes up, so be it. If not, oh well," Porter said.

"What do you mean, 'if he wakes up?' Why wouldn't he wake up?"

"Some things have happened since I've been gone. I had to..." Porter looked at Danny, who was holding his leg and looking up at him. "...handle a couple things. You feel me?"

"I think so," Ross said.

"I think it's best if I cover our tracks. If the guys who are sleeping don't make it out, I'm not going to cry for them, but at least we can cut him loose and give him a sporting chance."

"Fair enough. What about the Mattress King?"

"He's not making it out," Porter said.

"Good."

Porter handed Ross his Spyderco knife. "Go cut him loose and get back here quick."

Ross took the knife and headed up the metal stairs. Porter knelt down to speak to Danny again. "Okay, sweetheart, I have to take care of a couple things. You can't be with me for this part."

"But I want to stay with you. It's safe when I'm with you," Danny said.

"Don't worry, you're safe. I need you to go with my friend, for just a couple of minutes. Can you do that?"

"The squeezer?" Danny said.

Porter smiled. "I'll tell him not to squeeze you too tight, okay?"

"You're coming back soon?"

"Super fast. Deal?" Porter stuck out his pinky finger. Danisha did the same, and they hooked them and shook them.

"Deal," Danisha said.

Ross made it down the stairs and stood next to the pair. "He's loose. Lucky for him, I guess."

"You ready? I need you to take Danny and go get in one of the cars out front."

"Which car? Where?" Ross said.

"There's several out front. Pick one that has the Parabellum logo on it, get in, and keep it running."

"I don't have the keys. How do I start it?"

"Those are company cars; the guys used them for rounds

and stuff like that. They'll leave the keys somewhere easy to find," Porter said.

"Okay," Ross said and turned to leave.

Porter grabbed his shoulder. "Wait, take Danny with you."

Ross looked nervously at Porter and at Danny. "What if something happens? I can't protect her. I don't want to lose her again."

"Nothing's going to happen. Just get out there, get a car running, and I'll meet you there in a minute. Danny, you ready?"

The girl looked at Porter with determination and grabbed Ross's shirt tail.

Porter led them through the building and out through the breezeway, into the guards' break building.

There were no guards. There was no one.

The television was on and the coffee pot was still warming burnt coffee, but all was quiet otherwise. The group arrived at the door.

"This is where we separate. You go left with Danny; I'm going into the kitchen," Porter said. He handed Ross the bag of money he'd taken from Schmidt.

"What's this?"

"Later. Ready?"

"I'm ready."

Porter opened the door and did a quick scan. There was no one waiting outside or in the breezeway. Ross had a fifty-yard walk through the breezeway and then a right turn, and he would be at the bank of cars Porter had seen from the tobacco warehouse earlier that night. With any luck, he could be ready by the time Porter caught up to him.

"Go," Porter said, and watched as Ross and Danny run down the breezeway. He stopped and pulled his t-shirt up over his nose, like an impromptu ski mask. Porter took a couple of steps and swung open the door to the kitchen building, gun brandished.

The chef was still there, starting some kind of soup or stew in a massive stainless steel pot. Porter walked quickly but quietly behind the man. He grabbed the man around the neck with his forearm. The chef was startled and jumped, but could go nowhere.

Porter said in a low voice, "Do you want to die?"

"No," the chef stammered.

"Good. Give me your phone."

The man reached into the top pocket of his white chef's jacket and produced a smartphone. He handed it over his shoulder to Porter.

"Just set it on the counter. What's the unlock code?"

"555555," the chef said with no hesitation.

"Good. You have a car here?"

"Yes."

"Get in it and drive. Don't stop for an hour. If you stop, I'll know." He let the chef go and the man sprinted for the exit, hit the door, and was gone. That suited Porter just fine. He did one final sweep of the kitchen and found no one other than Apple Tommy, still hidden under the fifty-pound sacks. Porter went back to the counter where the chef had been and unlocked his phone, dialing a phone number.

ROSS RAN DOWN THE BREEZEWAY, Danny in tow, until they reached the edge of the building. Ross stopped and peeked around, but no one was there. They stepped out onto the parking pad. There were eight cars parked. Two were white Jeep Cherokees with generic light bars on the top. Ross stepped over to one, but the door was locked. He stepped to the other; its door was also locked. He had a moment of panic.

What if I can't start the car?

He knelt down and checked the tops of all the tires. He had often left keys in that spot when trading off cars with another person. No keys on any of the tires. He felt a tug on his shirttail. In his panic he ignored it, until it became strong and persistent. He looked down.

"Try there," Danny said, motioning to the gas tank.

Ross thought for a second, then opened the Jeep's gas tank door. A singleton key attached to a fob from a car dealership fell out. "How did you know that?"

"I heard Charles's radio. Sometimes the guards would tell each other they were leaving the keys," she said.

Ross scooped her up and held her while he opened the door, tossing the bag of money onto the passenger floorboard. Once inside, Danny climbed into the back seat and Ross fired the car up. As they waited for Porter, a man in a chef's coat came barreling down the breezeway.

"Get down," Ross said to Danny, who slunk down to the floorboards.

It wasn't necessary. The chef started a Honda Civic that was parked on the end of the parking pad and sped out of the compound, breaking the small arm that was attempting to block the exit.

Ross looked at Danny, whose eyes were wide with amazement.

PORTER HUNG up the phone and locked the screen, not that it mattered in this case. He stepped over to the industrial cook-tops. They ran on gas, no doubt from the large gas tanker on top of the building. There were two stoves and each one had ten burners, all sporting a pilot light, save for the two that the chef had been using, which were fully lit.

Porter took the stock pot off the stove and left those two burners on high. He then went to the other burners and blew the pilot lights out, but turned their knobs to high so the maximum amount of gas could escape.

With the size of the reservoir on top of the building, there should be no problem filling the room and, eventually, igniting. Porter took the Sig Sauer out of his pocket and ejected the magazine and then the round in the chamber, which he caught in the air. He dropped the gun, magazine, and bullet into the stew the chef was making. Porter checked one last time that the two burners were aflame and walked towards the front door. Before he stepped out he took his own Glock from its holster and held it ready.

Porter opened the door and saw nothing. He hurried along the breezeway until he got to the small parking lot. Ross was sitting in one of Parabellum's Jeep Cherokees with the motor running. He raised one finger at Ross, telling him to hold on a minute. Porter walked over to the large steel oval that held the gasoline for the compound.

There were two spouts to retrieve gasoline from the big container. One was a large wheel with a big pipe with threading on the outside. The other looked the same, but had an attachment screwed onto it that mimicked the pump from a gas station. Porter walked to the pump.

He turned the wheel and flipped down a small lever next to the place where the pump attachment was connected to the pipe. Gasoline poured from the nozzle. Porter turned it towards the metal outside of the kitchen building and gave it a thorough soaking. He let it pour all along the base of the building, then sat the still pumping nozzle down on the ground. The incline carried the gasoline down the front of the kitchen toward the other buildings in the compound. Porter got into the passenger seat of the Jeep. "Did you see a chef take off?"

"Yeah, he came running down the breezeway into the lot. Danny and I ducked down, but he didn't even know we were here. He broke the little arm on the gate and he was gone. He wasn't stopping for anything. I didn't know if you wanted me to grab him."

"No, you did right. He was the only person in the compound who didn't know that Danny was being held or try to kill me. I didn't want to trap him in there. Let's go," Porter said.

"What about the guard at the gatehouse?"

"The guy you bricked. We're clear, let's get out of here. Quick, if you don't want things to heat up," Porter said.

Ross needed no further prodding. He slammed the car into reverse and drove out the now armless gate.

SIXTY-TWO

ROSS DROVE the borrowed Jeep back to where they had stashed Porter's Yukon the night before. Ross and Danny got out of the Jeep and into the Yukon, while Porter took a few minutes to wipe down the Jeep.

He figured they were good so far. No one had seen their faces—at least, no one who would be able to talk about it. Still, he thought it prudent not to leave any fingerprints around for the cops to dust. When they found the Parabellum vehicle, they would probably think it was a result of an employee out for a joy ride, but it wasn't worth taking any chances.

When Porter finished up, he grabbed the bag of money from the floorboard of the Jeep and got into the driver's seat of the Yukon. Ross and Danny were talking about her favorite Disney movies. Porter didn't know any of them, but Ross seemed to be an endless pool of knowledge about lions, princesses, and Greek gods. Porter pointed the Yukon back toward Tampa and began rolling. In the horizon behind them, a cloud of dark smoke was filling the sky, the beginnings of a major fire.

EVERYONE WAS STARVING, so they pulled into a fast food drive-through. Danny asked if she could have the meal with the toy.

"Of course," Porter said. "Isn't that what kids always eat?"

"Not always. Granny can't afford that very often, so me and her usually split a meal. Sometimes I'm still hungry."

Porter bought her four kids' meals, and made sure they included a different toy with each one. Danny looked like she was sitting down to a Christmas dinner.

There was silence as they rode back to Tampa—first, because everyone was eating, and later because Danny fell asleep in the backseat. Porter had given her his button-up shirt to use as a blanket.

Ross looked in the backseat and then at Porter. "What are you going to do with her? You can't just take her back to Miss Leona. That'll be suspicious."

"I'm going to take her to the police station closest to Miss Leona's place. They'll call her and that will be that. I was gonna to give her to Rivera, but there's no way that works. How can she explain a missing kid on her docket magically showing up at her doorstep? I want to help her career, not sink it."

Ross nodded.

"No one has to know where she came from. Danny won't be able to give them directions. In the end, all anyone will care about is that the girl is safe and goes back to her grandmother. It won't be connected to any of us. Better that way," Porter said.

Ross nodded again. He faced the window and looked out at the highway. "Porter, I just wanted to say—"

"Are you about to get all soft on me?"

"No. Yes. Maybe a little."

"Save it. You don't need to say anything," Porter said.

"You saved that little girl. Just thinking about her in there with that creep—"

"Don't think about it. It'll drive you crazy. Just focus on the important things."

"Like?" Ross said.

Porter looked at the blood-soaked sleeve on his hand and opened his fist a couple times. "Danny is safe, Miss Leona is getting her baby back, and now you know how to brain someone with a brick."

They both laughed. "I guess I do, huh? I can't imagine it'll be a useful skill going forward."

"You never know…" Porter said, his voice trailing off. He focused on the road.

SIXTY-THREE

PORTER DROVE to a small police substation two miles from the Acres. He parked on the same side of the street but was a hundred yards away. Danny would have a safe walk down the sidewalk that ran in front of all the buildings. Porter leaned back and gently shook the sleeping child.

"Danny. Danny. Gotta get up."

She sat up and rubbed her eyes, holding her toys with her other hand. "Is this home?"

"No, not yet. I need you to do something for me."

She looked at Porter.

"I need you to go to the police station, right there. You see it? The brick building with the blue roof?" Porter said.

Danny rubbed her eyes again and looked out the window. "It's close."

"Yes, sweetheart, it is. I need you to go to the police station and tell the officers who you are, where you live, and your phone number. Can you do that?"

"Why can't you take me?" Danny said.

"It's kind of hard to explain. I think it's better if the police don't know I helped you. They may want to ask me some questions I don't want to answer. But if you walk down there, they will get you back to your granny. You'll see her today, I promise. And I'll sit here the whole time, to make sure no dragons show up and try to hurt you."

"Promise?"

"I promise," Porter said.

Danny nodded her head and put a brave face on. "Can I take my toys?"

"Of course, sweetheart."

Danny nodded her head again and put her toys into the pockets of the outfit Schmidt had forced her to wear. She stood up and leaned into the front seat, hugging Ross. Ross hugged her back, this time with an appropriate level of force. Danny leaned over to Porter and hugged him tightly. He placed one large hand on her tiny back and gave it a squeeze.

Porter pushed the unlock button and Ross reached into the back seat and opened Danny's door. She slid out of the Yukon and walked away from the truck, down the sidewalk. She turned after a few steps and waved at the cab of the Yukon, then turned back and kept walking. Porter and Ross watched her walk down the sidewalk, turn right, and go towards the police substation's front door. She struggled a bit opening the heavy door, but an officer was exiting and noticed the small girl with the strange clothes on.

The officer bent down to talk to Danny. He stood, looked left and right, then put his hand on the girl's back and led her into the station. And just like that, she was gone.

SIXTY-FOUR

PORTER PULLED out of the parking lot. Ross was dozing against the window. Porter plugged his phone into the aux cord and called Rivera.

"Porter?"

"Why are you breathing so hard? Are you working out?"

"No. I'm running out of a federal courtroom. It's been crazy ever since you left last night."

"*Digame,*" Porter said.

"I was stalling Candy Man so he wouldn't get to make a call. I didn't want him to signal anyone and trigger them killing off the kids."

"Probably best that way," Porter said.

"While I was doing that, the FBI guy on duty got back to me. He said they were interested in the case. A convicted hacker in possession of a smartphone was too good to pass up. They even had the idea that he may have something on the phone he shouldn't. A few hours later, he showed up and interviewed Candy Man," Rivera said.

"What did he tell the FBI?"

"Nothing. Not about you or your conversation, not about his phone. He didn't talk about anything. He just asked for a lawyer. The FBI guy backed off the interview. We were going to let him finally make his call. I couldn't hold out anymore and the FBI had no clue I was stalling him for time. Then the craziest thing happened. I got a call from a nine-one-one dispatcher. She played me the tape of a conversation she'd had with an anonymous source. The source said Clive Michelson was in custody and knew the whereabouts of numerous missing children. He said also said that if Michelson called his lawyer, all the children would die," Rivera said.

"That's some tip," Porter said.

"Amazing, right? The source sounded very familiar, but his voice was kind of muffled, like he was talking through a rag or shirt or something," Rivera said with a dry bite to her voice. "Just no way for me to recognize it."

"The tipster sounds like a handsome fella," Porter said.

"Before Michelson gets to make his call, I play the recording for the FBI agent who's standing there with me. He calls his boss and they decide no call for Michelson. They just couldn't take the chance of getting kids killed, right?" Rivera said.

"And people say the FBI's full of idiots."

"The agent and I went to see the magistrate judge and federal prosecutor. This old magistrate came into his office early just to meet with us. We explained everything and played him the recording. The judge said the recording wasn't enough to bar Michelson from counsel."

Porter started to speak but Rivera cut him off.

"*But,* he said for the time being Michelson couldn't speak to *his* lawyer. The magistrate said that if there was the slightest chance that that conversation would mean someone got killed, he couldn't allow it. The magistrate appointed a public defender for Michelson. He said that eventually, he would have to let Michelson have his own lawyer, but providing him with a court-appointed one in the interim wouldn't violate his right to counsel in the slightest. Then the magistrate scheduled the initial appearance for forty-eight hours out. He also gave us a search warrant for Michelson's phone. Basically, we have forty-eight hours to get all the information we can before Michelson gets to get the word to his lawyer," Rivera said, talking a mile a minute.

"I notice you're saying we? You helping the FBI out on the case?" Porter said.

"It seems like I'm going to be. The agent I'm working with spoke to his supervisor, and they think since I got Michelson and I got the 'anonymous tip,' I should stay on and help."

"That's great. Once you guys get the phone open, you be the one to figure out that the string of numbers after the phone numbers are coordinates. The FBI will think you're a genius. If you play that right, you could be a TFO with them by the end of all this. They'll want you to work on the case with them," Porter said.

"You think so?"

"Definitely. It'll be way better than working the LTMU cases. Or shoving your ass into hot pants on Seventh Avenue."

"I imagine so. Porter?"

"I'm here."

"I've been afraid to ask you about Danny. I can't take bad news, not right now. Everything is going right."

"There is no bad news. You'll probably be getting a call about her sometime today. She's at a police station in town."

Rivera was silent for a few moments, choosing the right words. "Thank you."

"For?"

"The kid. The case. Everything."

"Don't mention it. Just know you owe me."

"Big time," Rivera said.

"I gotta go. Good luck with the crime-fighting, Christina Rivera. Tell Kevin I said hello."

"Thanks for finally getting my name right. Asshole."

SIXTY-FIVE

TEN DAYS HAD PASSED since Danisha Hill had walked into the police station. She'd become something of a minor celebrity. The news stations all reported on the missing girl who had miraculously turned up at a police station. The chief of police held a press conference to talk about the event—which was useless, as he knew nothing, but he couldn't resist an opportunity for some good press for both him and his department. There weren't any interviews with Danisha or Miss Leona. No news crew would go into the Acres for the story. They were all too scared.

PORTER DROVE his Yukon up the main dividing line of the Acres and parked in the same spot he'd parked the first time he'd rolled into the neighborhood. He didn't expect to have any trouble this time.

Jamal and Terrell were in their usual spot. Porter pulled a large box out of his trunk. It was from one of those online retailers, and it was heavy, even for him. He struggled to carry it over to the two men and set it down. They each gave Porter the kind of half-handshake, half-hug that tough guys do.

"Porter. What's good?" Jamal said.

"I'm not a corny-ass bill collector anymore?"

"I already told your ass you weren't no bill collector, we know that for a fact. But you still dress kinda corny." Jamal smiled at Porter.

"Things been quiet, I assume?"

"Yeah, ever since we... had a meeting with the other guys," Jamal said, looking around conspiratorially, "things have been quiet. Everybody's fallen in line. No beef."

"Good. And our friends?"

"I don't know what friends you mean. All I know is there were some gators down in Alligator Alley who ate real good a while back. Real good, you feel me?"

"I figured you guys had a way. I need to see Miss Leona. And Danny. Any issues with me going back?"

"Nah. You know the way," Jamal said. "Damn glad little Danny's back."

"Me too," Porter said, volunteering nothing. He heaved the large box into his arms again and walked the well-trod path, through the graffitied walls and clotheslines, back to Miss Leona's house. Hands full, he gently kicked at the door. Porter felt bad, but what else could he do? There was no chance he'd be able to pick the box up again once he put it down.

After a few moments, Miss Leona answered. When she opened the door, her face lit up. She hugged Porter as best she could around the box.

"Miss Leona. Think I could put this down and then we finish this hug?"

"Sure, baby, sure. Come on in." She held the door open while trying to stand as far out of the way as she could.

Porter took a few steps into the small apartment's sitting

room, not stopping until he'd passed the kitchen and made it to the living room. He set the box down, careful to avoid breaking the coffee table. Once it was safely out of his hands, Miss Leona attacked him. She was surprisingly strong for an old woman. The hug lasted nearly a minute; longer than a hug should have been, but Porter didn't mind. She pulled away and motioned to the box. "What's this?"

"Is Danny here?" Porter said.

"Yes, she's in her room. I kept her out of school again. She hasn't wanted to go back on the bus, even though it's a new bus driver. I don't blame her."

"I understand. Mind if she comes out here?"

Miss Leona called her granddaughter, and she came bounding around the corner. "Yes, Granny..." She stopped when she saw Porter.

Being with her grandmother had done her well. Her clothes were clean and contemporary, and her hair was shiny and pulled back into an intricate pattern of braids.

"Hi, Danny," Porter said.

"Sir," she said.

"If your grandmother doesn't mind, I have something for you," Porter said. He looked at Miss Leona, who nodded. Danny walked over to the coffee table and sat on top of it, nearest to the box. Porter pulled the box flaps open to reveal a treasure trove of DVDs. "I got you everything I could find with a princess or cartoon animal. I know you told my friend you liked them."

Danny's eyes lit up, and she started digging through the box's contents. Underneath the DVDs were a small television, a PlayStation, and boxes of Barbies, toy ponies, and princesses. The tiny girl bounced up and down, clutching a plush doll.

Porter looked at Miss Leona. "Take no offense to this, please?"

"Offense to what, baby?"

"I noticed your television is old. Older than old. It's ancient, really," Porter said.

Miss Leona laughed. "That it is, baby, but it usually gets the job done."

"If it's all the same to you, I'm having another one delivered. You gonna be around this afternoon?"

"Shoot, if I wasn't, I am now," she said.

Porter turned to Danny. "What are you going to watch first?"

"What are *we* going to watch, you mean."

"You want me to watch a movie with you?" Porter said.

"Don't you like princesses?"

Porter picked up a DVD box and turned it over. "I think maybe I can learn."

"Good. Plus, I don't know how to put any of this stuff together," Danny said waving at the television and PlayStation.

Porter smiled and began unboxing items. He could think of few better ways to spend an afternoon.

EPILOGUE

PORTER, exhausted from an afternoon of princesses and castles and Spongebob, was recovering in his backyard with Ross. Danny's appetite for movies had far outpaced his own, and eventually he'd begged off, but not before buying pizza for the household.

"What'd she say when you told her?"

"I thought the old lady was going to have a heart attack," Porter said.

"Good."

"Good that she almost had a heart attack?"

"No, dick, good that you did it. I wasn't so sure," Ross said.

"You thought I'd keep Schmidt's money? And you call yourself my best friend."

"I know how much you like money," Ross said.

Porter shrugged.

They were quiet for a few moments as they sipped their drinks. Porter had decided on a screwdriver. He wanted to take no chances with a hangover.

"You sure the accounts are set up? Non-traceable?" Porter said.

"Clean as a whistle. Listen, man, this is what I do. You worry about setting buildings on fire, I'll worry about the accounting. What'd you tell Miss Leona?"

"I told her there were a bunch of donations that had poured in after people heard Danny's story. That you were managing the money in a trust, but that for all intents and purposes, it was hers and Danny's. Then I strongly advised her to move and put Danny in a private school."

"Did she listen?" Ross said.

"I think so. She got out the phone book and started looking at apartments while I was there, but I think you may need to call her and point her in the right direction. Hire a moving company to help her. They don't have much, but the TV that showed up is a team-lift kind of situation."

Ross laughed and drank deeply from his glass.

"You sure that money'll last?"

"It'll last. With interest and if she's judicious with it, it'll probably get Danny through a couple years of college before it runs out," Ross said.

"Good. Miss Leona is frugal. She won't blow it."

"I know she won't. She's an honest person. You know what I didn't tell you?"

Porter looked at him and sipped his drink.

"Before you went over there to see them, during those ten days?"

"Yeah?" Porter said.

"Miss Leona called me several times. She wanted your phone number. She wanted to get a hold of you."

"I'm sure she wanted to say thank you. She hugged me pretty tight," Porter said.

"No. She wanted to give you the seven hundred and fifty dollar reward money. All of it. She said 'a deal's a deal,' and she's a woman of her word."

"She tried to give it to me when I was at her apartment today. It was all I could do to convince her I wouldn't take it," Porter said.

"You could have taken it, just to save a little face. Slip it to me and I'd put it in their trust fund. Sometimes old people get insulted if you don't take their money. They may not have a lot, but it's important to them."

"Nah. I can't take money from that old woman. Money isn't everything, Ross."

"I never thought I'd hear you say that."

"Never is a long time."

The End

WANT A FREE BOOK?

Sign up to my mailing list and you'll always be the first to know about my upcoming novels, as well as great deals on other books I find out about. As a bonus, you'll receive the Porter novella-Subtle Deceit- absolutely free. Interested? See below-

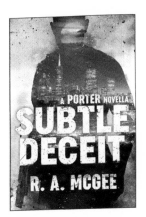

Tracking down a missing person takes a brilliant mind and bloody knuckles...

Porter has no match when it comes to tracking down a target. The former federal agent has built a business gathering leads from missing persons posters... if the reward is enough to line his pockets...

When Porter finds a potentially profitable case in the disappearance of a free-spirited co-ed, he never expects the father to offer a double reward if the girl is found in 24 hours. In a race against time, the former agent follows a twisted trail of frat boys, ex-lovers, and a vengeful crime boss. Porter vows to get to the truth before the day is through, no matter how much pain he needs to cause to get the job done...

Subtle Deceit is a gripping crime thriller novella that packs a psychological punch. If you like brutal action, a diverse cast of characters, and edge-of-your-seat suspense, then you'll love RA McGee's compelling tale.

Get *Subtle Deceit* to dive into a bloody thrill-ride today!

Sign Up At Ramcgee.com

MOVING TARGET

Maybe you have already read Subtle Deceit and you need more. You've come to the right place! The next in the Porter series is right here. Check out Moving Target :

A clan of drug pushers. A high-profile hostage. To track down his target, he'll cover the mountains in blood.

As a former federal agent, Porter does his best work outside the law. So when his friend from the FBI calls in a favor with a hefty reward, Porter heads straight for the heart of the Appalachians. Since by-the-books tactics failed to bring home an agent's abducted daughter, Porter gets free reign to crack skulls and take names while the agency looks the other way.

Deep in the heart of the mountains, Porter matches wits and muscle with rowdy bikers, money-hungry dealers, and a vicious Mexican cartel. As the chase for the kidnappers kicks into high gear, he'll need to strike fast to secure his payday... and save the hostage's life.

Moving Target is the second novel in an exhilarating series of crime thrillers. If you like unflinching action, gritty heroes, and white-knuckle suspense, then you'll love RA McGee's vicious rescue mission.

Buy Moving Target to follow the trail of broken bones to a brutal, psychological thriller today!

Available on Amazon now. Get your copy today!

ABOUT THE AUTHOR

I'm a lifelong fan of stories and reading. Because of this, I decided to channel that passion into storytelling. In the simplest terms, this is what motivated me to become a writer. I strive to write books that I think are fun to read, with action and violence and memorable characters.

I live with my patient wife, who happily reads the first draft of everything I come up with, and waits supportively when I bang my head against the wall hoping ideas fall out. Together, we corral our small tribe of children, who threaten to overrun us at any point and start a Lord of The Flies type society.

I love to talk with readers. Feel free to reach out if you'd like to chat about my books, someone else's books, comic books, Denzel Washington's movie *The Book of Eli*, Booker T. Washington, a book you wanted to write in fourth grade but never got around to, booking a flight, problems with your bookie, or any other book related topic. Except book reports. Screw book reports.

Best,

R.A.

ramcgee.com
info@ramcgee.com

 facebook.com/Ramcgeeauthor

 instagram.com/darewoodpress

twitter.com/ramcgeebooks

Made in the USA
Columbia, SC
06 June 2020